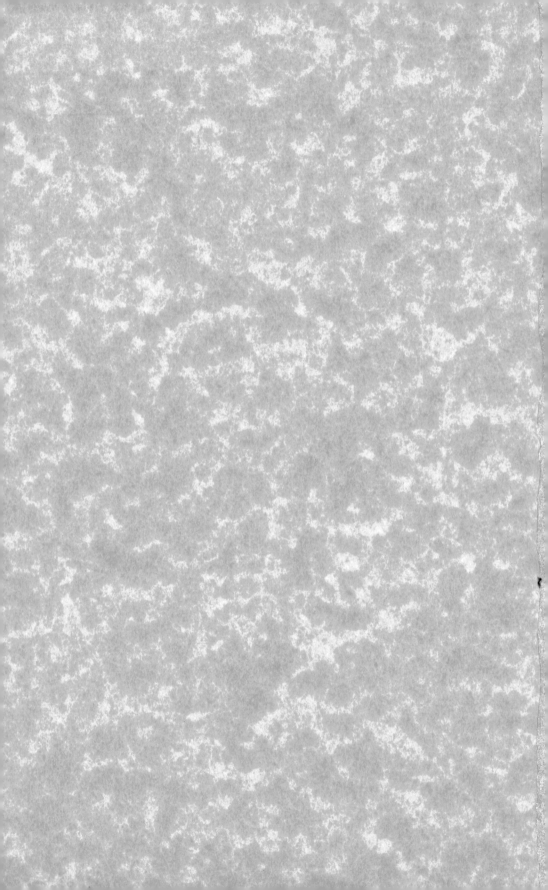

RECKONING

OF

FALLEN

GODS

TOR BOOKS BY R. A. SALVATORE

R. A. SALVATORE

RECKONING

OF

FALLEN

GODS

A TOM DOHERTY ASSOCIATES BOOK  *NEW YORK*

RECKONING OF FALLEN GODS

Copyright © 2019 by R. A. Salvatore

"The Education of Brother Thaddius" copyright © 2014 by R. A. Salvatore

All rights reserved.

Map by Rhys Davies

A Tor Book
Published by Tom Doherty Associates
175 Fifth Avenue
New York, NY 10010

www.tor-forge.com

Tor® is a registered trademark of Macmillan Publishing Group, LLC.

The Library of Congress Cataloging-in-Publication Data is available upon request.

ISBN 978-0-7653-9530-6 (hardcover)
ISBN 978-0-7653-9531-3 (ebook)

Our books may be purchased in bulk for promotional, educational, or business use. Please contact your local bookseller or the Macmillan Corporate and Premium Sales Department at 1-800-221-7945, extension 5442, or by email at MacmillanSpecialMarkets@macmillan.com.

First Edition: January 2019

Printed in the United States of America

0 9 8 7 6 5 4 3 2 1

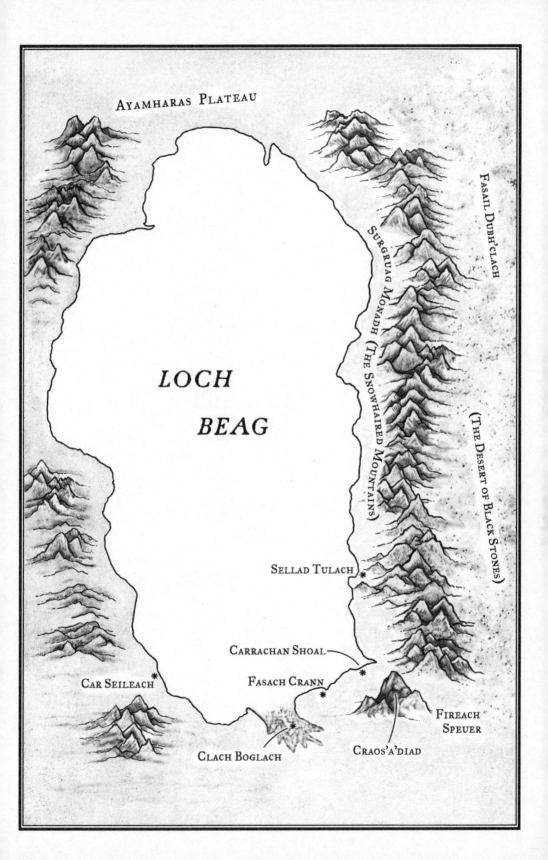

RECKONING

OF

FALLEN

GODS

PROLOGUE

Heavy one," Asba grunted. Young and strong, along with his two friends among the most celebrated young fishers and hunters in the village, the proud Asba could not deny the truth of his observation, could not even fake it enough to stand up straight under the weight of the laden pole. His shoulders ached, his arms strained, and his entire body felt compressed. The only thing stopping him from dropping the game pole altogether was a fear that his legs wouldn't grant him the strength to pick it back up.

Behind him, sharing the other end of the burden, his two companions laughed.

"Might even be a bear," his brother Asef replied. "Ever met a bear, then, brother? Big fat things, they are."

"Fat with meat," added the third of the group, a woman named Tamilee. "And sure, but 'twas the easiest hunt I e'er known."

"Aye, but this one's too big for the pole," Asba argued, convincingly, for they had dressed their treasure, a giant mountain bear somehow killed only hours before, quite thoroughly, removing anything and everything they could while still preserving the delicious meat. The season was late, with winter coming, and such a prize as this could not be ignored.

"Too big for us, you mean," said Tamilee.

Asef snorted derisively. "I still want the head," he complained, for Asba and Tamilee had insisted they cut it off and leave it. "And don't doubt that I'll be back for it."

"We're breaking the pole now," Asba reminded him. "It's for deer, not this. I'm still thinking that we should've left it and come back fast with a proper cart. I doubt scavengers will take much 'tween now and our return."

"Scavengers?" Asef replied doubtfully. The two were twins, though Asef was lighter and leaner than Asba. Still, they looked very much alike, with the same deep set but piercing blue eyes, their distinctive beards, a rarity in Carrachan Shoal, and singular, elongated humps extending from the backs of their skulls. Many in the village carried the more fashionable double humps, and the joke had long been that Imabab, the mother of the twins, had only had enough skull-wrapping prepared for one baby, so she had to split her work between the two. "No scavengers that I'm expecting, but deamhan magic killed this bear, to be sure, and I'm not thinking that the Usgar meant to be leaving it out to rot."

"Oh, aye, and when have the deamhan Usgar ever left a kill out for us folk to find?" asked Tamilee. She was the same height as her male companions, with a strong and sturdy frame and beautiful freckled dimples beneath eyes so blue they made those of the brothers pale in comparison. Like the brothers, Tamilee had an elongated skull, a simple stretch of the bone, backward and upward. Covering it, her hair was long and thick and orange. She usually kept it loose and wild, an apt reflection of her fighting spirit, except when she was hunting or fishing. For then, Tamilee was all business, and wouldn't let anything akin to vanity get in the way of her performance.

"We don't know that it was Usgar," Asba said, and he regretted it from the moment the words came out of his mouth, even before the snorts came back at him from Asef and from Tamilee, the woman he fancied would one day be his wife. Truly, it was hard to deny the logic behind their claim, for these villagers knew of no creature on the mountainside which could have inflicted such a wound on a giant mountain bear. Other than the great lake monster itself, these giants were considered the most powerful predators known on the entire Ayamharas plateau, even more powerful and deadly than the huge clo'dearche lizards—and they were too far from the water for those particular creatures to have been involved in the kill. The bear carcass had shown just one true wound, but such a wound! A hole had been bored right through the massive predator, belly to back, with everything in between—organs, backbone, guts—completely gone, as if a singular strike had simply blown a hole through the massive torso.

What could have inflicted such a terrific and terrible wound on a creature such as this, other than a huge spear tipped with powerful Usgar magic?

"The meat would have rotted," Asef said, speaking to Asba's earlier remark.

"The meat would have left," Tamilee corrected. "You do'no think they'd come back for their kill?"

Asba let out a sigh, ready to argue, wanting to argue as the pain in his shoulder became even more acute. But he deferred, knowing that his companions were right about both the killers and their likely intentions to return for the bounty. This bear had a lot of good meat on it, and with winter looming, the addition to Carrachan Shoal's food stores would prove invaluable.

The Usgar, who wintered at the top of the great mountain, Fireach Speuer, probably felt the same way.

That prompted another thought, and before he even mulled it over, Asba picked up his pace and blurted, "Be quicker then! We're not covering well our trail, and if they mean to return for the bear, they'll be glad to take a few slaves at the same time."

From behind, he felt a tug, and turned to find his brother staring hard at him.

"We're low on Fireach Speuer," Asef said, as if he felt compelled to deny even the thought of such pursuit.

"The Usgar track better than any man should," Asba countered. He hoisted the pole and ducked his head, flipping it to the other shoulder. He ignored the pain as the pole crushed down and picked up his pace once more, tugging the others along. Asef and Tamilee didn't argue, and soon were pushing him on even faster.

After all, it was getting dark.

And the Usgar often hunted after dark, their spear tips, aglow with magical fires, leading the way.

The old augur stared into the setting sun, though it hurt his close-set eyes. The red skin of his thick brow, his snout bridge, nose, and lips shone angrily in the light, in stark contrast to the bright blue coloring flanking the marking to either side. And all of that wash of rich color stood out distinctively against the xoconai's now-gray hair, which still remained thick and long, and the general golden-brown coloring of the rest of his exposed skin.

The augur weathered the sting of the fiery orb's brightness and would not look away. He curled his lips back into a smile that seemed more a snarl, his old teeth yellow now, his bottom fangs crooked and poking up over his large lips. These canines never stopped growing throughout the life of a xoconai, and having them protrude, as with the old augur, called for reverence among the people.

Or used to, the old augur mused, and grimaced.

The scowl didn't last. He erased it, reminding himself to stay focused and calm. He could not let either his impatience with the new ways or his giddiness at the coming event overtake him. Yes, this was a glorious moment for the old priest, but only if his words proved accurate.

He had to be certain, to the moment.

He retreated toward the small chamber atop the dome-capped pyramid, its sides, all four, stepped with ancient and weathered stones. Green with age, the copper sheets up near the pinnacle barely reflected the sun, and as he noted that, the augur couldn't help but grimace a bit, for he long had considered that patina symbolic of his own aging, and dulling. He lamented the symbolism and the larger loss, musing, and not for the first time, that the younger generations of xoconai did not understand the truth of their god.

The young ones grew soft with luxury.

They must never be satisfied!

He turned back to the mountains in the east, to see the bright reflections of the Teotl Tenamitl, or God's Parapet, the towering and seemingly endless line of mountains that shielded the lands of the xoconai nation of Tonoloya from the intrusions of the weak humans and the demon goblins. He knew the human name for the range, one that seemed soft, like human skin, and spoke of the mountains as "snow-haired." Such a pathetic disservice to this great divine barrier, he thought.

The old augur nodded as he considered the majestic mountain wall rising up east of his humble temple. He had followers, he reminded himself, and had dispatched scouts to the mountains in anticipation of the glorious event. He gave himself leave, then, to take in the magnificent view all around him.

From this one vantage point, and only this one plateau in the mountain foothills, when the light of the sun shone brightly, all six of the great xoconai cities could be viewed, two before the augur to the east in the mountains, two to the south on the wide coastal plain, and two behind him, near enough to the vast ocean to hear the breath of the waves. The augur slowly turned, basking in the majestic sight, the glorious glowing domes of polished gold and copper and brass of the great xoconai temples.

Yes, until very recently, the modest, faded nature of his little temple here in the foothills of Teotl Tenamitl had annoyed the augur. But no more. Not with the approach of the day the xoconai called Xelihui, the mid-point of the sun's journey from south to north. In the human lands east of the mountains, it was called the equinox, and there, too, the augur knew from ancient scrolls, it was, or had been, celebrated—but with feast and talk of bounty. So, too, had such lighthearted banter come to the xoconai, and most of the other augurs thought Xelihui a mostly inconsequential time; the omens were stronger at the Huitlat and Huihuiyac, the short day and the long day, at the end-points of the journey when the sun reached its southernmost or especially its northernmost points. On these days, the magic flowed strong, and the xoconai augurs made their predictions for the coming seasons.

But not this old augur, nor his father before him, or his father's father before him, nor his father's father's father! On this particular Xelihui, he believed, his great grandsire would at long last be proven right.

The sun would be eaten, and the augur's self-imposed exile would end.

That would be the day of Skath-mi-Zahn, and so, too, Cuowitay, the Day of the Xoconai.

Smiling his toothy grin, the augur moved through the small door into the entry tunnel of the temple. Inside the small chamber, a ray of sunshine pierced a hole in the domed ceiling. At the moment, it fell on the floor near the west wall. It would track through the room as the sun descended, and at its last light would reach the far eastern wall, tracking the prophetic mural painted there.

On Xelihui, this coming Xelihui, that ray, while it lasted, would align perfectly.

The old augur would go and tell them. He had foreseen it.

He would tell them, and then he would show them.

They would speak, but mostly, they would listen.

"Did ye hear that, then?" Tamilee asked, as she seemed to be asking every second, staggered, step.

"Heard not a thing," Asef started to reply, for the fifteenth time, and, as with the last few, prefacing the words with an increasingly annoyed sigh. This time, though, those words seemed quite out of place, as a sudden rustling of branches behind the three cut his answer short.

Up in front, Asba grimaced, but held quiet his groan as he eased the shoulder-pole off and down to the ground. He drew a thin, long skinning knife from the sheath on his left hip. He rolled his shoulders to try to loosen up as he stepped toward the sound, for he had been bearing the laden pole for far too long and the side of his neck was nearly locked in pain.

Following his lead, his companions, too, eased their burden to the ground. Tamilee came up beside him, holding a simple wooden club. Asba looked at it, and then at his own pathetic blade, and nearly laughed aloud at how ridiculously unprepared they were. They hadn't planned to be out this long, of course, for they had ventured from Carrachan Shoal merely to find some firewood and perhaps a few berries to enhance their dinner. But, as was typical with this band, they had traveled farther than they had intended, following the wind, following their fancy. Happening upon the dead bear, they couldn't rightly pass up a gift that would feed half the village in a grand feast.

Now it was growing late, though. The sun had dipped below the mountain to their west, leaving them in a deep and darkening shadow. They were nearly down the last expanse, nearly back to the village, but, given the dangers of Fireach Speuer, including one in particular that was on all of their minds, they were not nearly close enough.

The twilight deepened and quieted around them.

Asba went back to the front of the pole, bent low, and hoisted it up to his shoulder. "Come on, then," he said as he straightened.

Asef and Tamilee looked at each other doubtfully, then glanced back to the small pines and brush in the general direction of the rustling.

"If it is the deamhan Usgar, we'll not get back to the village in any case," Asba said to them. "The monsters run without tiring, over broken ground as if on a flat and grassy field. If it be the deamhan Usgar come to claim their kill, we are dead already."

"Says the fool who dropped the damned bear," Asef retorted, more anger than sarcasm in his voice. Anger wrought of fear, they all knew.

Glancing over their shoulders with every small step, Asef and Tamilee moved to the back of the pole. Asef hoisted it alone and set it in place, while Tamilee stood at the ready, her club in hand. She waved it about through some defensive spins and sudden thrusts, finding her fighting stance. Designed for finishing off sorely wounded animals, like a deer downed by a spear, the small club was hardly a weapon that might serve well against an armed opponent, let alone a deamhan Usgar, with his crystal-tipped magic spears!

"I know I heard something," Tamilee whispered as she moved back up toward the front of the shoulder pole.

"I heard it, too," Asba replied. "Probably a stoat or a giant toad. Not a deamhan."

"Are you saying that or hoping that?"

"Both," said Asba. "But mostly, I'm saying it."

"And how might you know?" asked Tamilee.

"Because we're alive and talking." Asba looked back at his brother. "All speed, it's getting dark."

The brothers picked up the pace, quick-stepping and grunting with every bounce of the heavy load. Tamilee moved about them, flank to flank, club in hand, peering into the gloom. She grabbed the bear suddenly, tugging back, halting the brothers.

"Here, now," Asef protested, and Asba was about to do the same, except he saw Tamilee's face. She tapped her finger over her pursed lips.

"A rustle," she whispered.

Asba looked past her, and it seemed to him that some pine branches were moving too violently for it to be just the evening breeze. He looked ahead on the descending trail. They were almost home. If they could make it just another two hundred strides, they'd be back to the cleared hill south of the village, close enough to shout out for help.

Asba thought of dropping the prize, that they could sprint to the safety of their home. But with this treasure, so much good meat, they'd be hailed as heroes in Carrachan Shoal. So he grunted and bent his back and doggedly put one foot in front of the other, verily pulling his brother along the descending trail.

There came another shake of branches, closer now, and the report of a stick cracked by an errant footfall. Asba picked up the pace, rushing with all speed. Tamilee grabbed the bear and hoisted with all her strength, shoving them all along.

They would be heroes, or they would be dead.

The xoconai augur approached the wall at the back, the eastern side, of his small temple, the images painted upon it so faded with age that many of the other xoconai, particularly the younger ones, who visited this temple didn't begin to understand the significance of the mural.

He paused at the small sacrificial altar before the eastern wall, the sunset, or *tyusk*, wall, and, still staring at the paintings, absently ran his hand across the flat stone, feeling the grooves for running blood. So many souls had been given here to Skath-mi-Zahn, the Glorious Gold, god of the xoconai. So many chests had been opened by the blade of the old augur.

Glorious sacrifices. Few of the chosen xoconai had even cried out in protest as the blade began to descend, as the augur pushed it slowly through their flesh, so glad were they to let their god drink of their blood.

Yes, the old augur had enjoyed many sacrifices at this, his altar, but still, it was the faded mural that held his attention rapt. It was fashioned in a mix of red-brown clay paint, oily black, and red blood, which, magically treated, had not turned brown or black with age. The only thing dulling the blood in the painting was the dust of time, and the augur hoped that he could revitalize the beautiful faces of the depicted xoconai with a good cleaning.

Not quite yet, though.

His eye roamed up from the bottom left corner, diagonally just above the center of the piece. He could make out the figures, so many figures, an army of xoconai, standing atop cliffs overlooking the sea with their toothed macana clubs raised in victory. Above them, high in the sky, loomed the Glorious Gold, Skath-mi-Zahn, astride his black dragon. And that beast, the mount of the god, devoured the sun itself.

Xoconai scholars believed that this mural, and others like it across Tonoloya, depicted the last great war, some sixteen centuries past, when Skath-mi-Zahn led his xoconai to victory over the peoples—the red-capped dwarves, the goblins, the trolls, the humans—of the western deserts. Indeed, the similar murals found in temples throughout the wide basin, from the western foothills of the Teotl Tenamitl to the very westernmost xoconai cities and settlements on the shores of Ilhuicaatl, the Great and One Ocean, were often labeled to that very point.

Perhaps those other murals did depict that long-ago battle, the old augur considered, and shrugged. For it didn't change anything regarding this particular mural, the one painted by his great grandsire.

The scholars had told him that this mural, too, akin to the others, depicted that ancient battlefield.

But the old augur knew better, knew the truth.

This mural had been created long before he was born, he knew, for he had spoken to the artist, whom he considered the greatest xoconai augur. Father of his father's father, the then young xoconai boy had heard the voice but once, beside the old one's deathbed. There his great grandsire had shared a vision revealed in a great spirit walk, after partaking of the small and round *prargaba*, the vision cactus. The ancient one's own blood had painted much of that mural.

The ancient one had a secret, whispered for the first time in his very last breaths, and into the ear of the child, who would become the temple augur, who was very young and had only been granted the audience at the request of the dying augur.

The mural did not depict the great xoconai victory of two thousand seasons ago.

It did not show the western waters of Ilhuicaatl.

It showed the other side of the Great and One Ocean, the eastern waters, far beyond Teotl Tenamitl.

The old one had seen and painted the future, not the past.

And this day, this augur, three generations removed, would read the signs of war, and the sovereigns and augurs of the xoconai would see his prophecy and would cower before Skath-mi-Zahn.

In what was likely his last, and was surely his greatest, vision, the old augur would be proven right.

Asba, Asef, and Tamilee sat with a half-dozen villagers around the bonfire in the center of Carrachan Shoal. The questions, which had begun as soon as the three had walked into camp, had not abated. How, the villagers wanted to know, had these three hunters slain a great brown mountain bear? The trio were not unskilled and were already gaining a reputation within the tribe, despite their youth. Often had their hunts yielded meat, but usually in the carcasses of the stoats and rabbits that lived in the nearby meadows, and on one occasion, of a deer that strayed too close to the forest's edge.

But a bear? There were legends of Carrachan Shoal hunters killing a bear, but none alive in the village had ever seen such a thing. So, of course, the questions began immediately when the hunters returned to the village, townsfolk gathering, faces full of excitement and awe. Without a word to each other, the three young friends had come to a common understanding, expressed initially by Asba when he gave Tamilee credit for the killing blow. The others played along, concocting a heroic battle story, building off the words of each other. Partly, it was to bask in the glory and adulation, but mostly, the three simply understood that it was best not to tell the villagers that they'd poached a kill, very probably from the dangerous Usgar.

Instead, they improvised and so fabricated a tale of a great struggle, each adding to the heroic battle story, one feat at a time. Asef had shot the beast with an arrow—no, four arrows!—in rapid succession, all centered on its belly! Asba had thrown his skinning knife, a perfect throw, right into the bear's eye as it charged! That had stopped it in its tracks, but had not killed it. No, the killing blow belonged to Tamilee, who struck with her club, hitting the hilt of Asba's knife, driving it deep into the bear's skull!

As each of them spoke in turn, they made sure to highlight their own skill and bravery in the feat. And, given that they'd hauled the huge beast back to camp—even dressed, it weighed as much as three grown men—none openly questioned their tale, despite some rather obvious inconsistencies. Asef, who also expected that Tamilee would marry Asba, particularly enjoyed that several of the villagers gathered around them were women— including some of the most beautiful young women in the town, not yet claimed in marriage. And they were hanging on his every word.

Soon after, the tribe's butchers returned with the first slabs of meat from the great kill. Most would be salted and placed in a natural ice cave not far away, but for such a feat as this, the most important members of Carrachan Shoal would feast this night, along with the three young heroes. The sun had nearly completely set, with stars twinkling up above the eastern edge of the plateau. The very last light of day glowed dimly atop Fireach Speuer.

Yes, Asba thought, this day could not have gone any better.

Reflexively, his grin leaving his face, he glanced over at his brother when he heard a sound like the scraping of wood against wood, one which had become familiar throughout Carrachan Shoal these past few years. He looked up and twisted about a bit to see through the gathering, and noted the approach of the one-legged woman atop her dolly, which was just a plank set with wheels. She worked her way through the crowd, her filthy and misshapen hands clawing at the ground and what was remaining of her one leg, which had been twisted and torn below the knee, scraping awkwardly to the side to propel her along.

"You didn't kill that," she said, pointing at the dead bear, half-skinned in the butcher's stall off to the side of the small clearing.

"Quiet, *deamhan*," Asef spat at her. Several other villagers turned to glower at the man, but he did not shrink back. Unlike most of the younger members of the tribe, his brother and Tamilee included, Asef often called this woman a deamhan, an Usgar, because her head had not been shaped to match the elongated skulls of the villagers. Her skin was darker, too, quite brown. Most of the tribe had fully accepted her, but even now, these years later, Asef could not look upon her with anything but scorn.

She ignored Asef and spoke directly to Asba. "You claim you killed it with arrow and knife and club, but there's a hole clean through the beast, and one too big for a spear, never mind an arrow."

"We cut that hole after," Asba stammered.

"You widened the hole to gut the thing, aye," said the woman. "After. Like you stabbed the eye. After."

Off to the side, Asef gasped, and many others followed.

"What do you know?" he demanded. "You are not of Carrachan Shoal! You are not . . ."

"I know bears," she retorted, not backing down even though many around her were shifting uncomfortably. "And I know the weapons you three carry. You could not have cut that hole, not all the way through. Not through the thick backbone of an animal that huge."

"We used fire, too," Asba began.

"No!" the woman cut him off.

"Why do you shame?" another villager scolded the woman.

"Not to shame!" the woman insisted loudly, drowning out the murmurs that were beginning to rumble through the gathering. "No, never, and we should all be grateful that Asba and Tamilee and Asef had the courage to carry such a burden back to us in this season when the winds turn cold. But we cannot ignore the truth of the bear's death, for all our sakes."

"What are you about?" another villager called at her.

"The flashes of lightning from last night," she said. "Usgar lightning! And not far from here, yes?"

All the judging eyes turned away from the woman to fall over Asba, and the crowd hushed as one.

"That was farther than these three went," one man protested. "The lightning flashed higher on the mountain than any today ventured."

"No," the woman on the cart argued, shaking her head so forcefully that her long dark hair flew side to side. "No, they went up there, where the Usgar had been, and they found a bear. A dead bear."

After a few heartbeats, an older woman asked Asba directly, "Is this true?"

Asba hesitated, then said, honestly, "I do . . . I do not know."

"But the bear was already dead when you found it?" the one-legged woman on the dolly pressed. She turned to the man who had doubted her. "Ask the butchers. They will know a fresh kill from a carrion find."

Asba swallowed hard, feeling the weight of those unrelenting stares. Finally, he nodded.

"To arms!" cried an older man. "We must set a double watch this night!"

"Triple the eyes!" another demanded, and all villagers were jostling then, trying to get to their families to make sure all preparations for a fast run to the boats were made. If the Usgar came, Carrachan Shoal would flee, all of them, to their boats and out upon the dark waters of Loch Beag.

Asba glanced over at his brother, to see Asef staring most hatefully at the crippled woman, this dark-skinned foreigner who had dared to shame him.

Tamilee came up beside Asba then, drawing his attention. Her crestfallen expression matched his own, for they realized then that they had greatly overplayed their hand. Just carrying the bear back would have brought them accolades, particularly when the cold winds blew and food grew scarce. But now, none of that mattered. Now, all that their fellow villagers would recall of this night was that these three young hunters had lied, and had put them all in danger.

The villagers of Carrachan Shoal quickly set into motion, setting sentries all about, readying racks of weapons (that would be of only minimal value against the power of the Usgar), and of paddles for the boats. Many went down to the water, preparing the boats, packing foodstuffs and blankets in case the tribe wound up out on the cold waters of Loch Beag throughout the night. The Usgar would not venture onto the lake. Never!

The sentry lines widened out all along the perimeter of the village, not to engage the deamhan Usgar, no, but to call back, then flee for the water.

The three young hunters didn't need to be prodded to the outermost guard post, a small watchtower nearer the low trees of the great mountain's foothills than it was to the nearest houses of Carrachan Shoal.

"Bah, but better to fatten the crows," Asef said, fuming, when the three were alone on their perch. "We should've left her to die, for her good and our own."

"Enough, Asef," Asba scolded. "'Tis our own fault, and you know it. We should'no've weaved a tale of false glory."

"Was enough that we brought the treasure of food," Tamilee agreed with a heavy and regretful sigh.

"But they'd still be scolding us for stealing the Usgar kill."

"Stole it or not, the Usgar are near, or were near," said Tamilee.

"Too near," Asba agreed.

But Asef grunted and punched the log rail of the watchtower. "She's a deamhan."

"Skin's too dark," Tamilee replied. "And less yelling, if you would, aye? With Usgar about."

Asef blew another snort, grabbed the rail so tightly that the blood was pressed from his strong hands, and stared out at the mountain night. The minutes stretched to hours, the sun long gone behind the western horizon behind them, across the long loch. The bonfire was no more, the embers glowing like a giant orange eye. The sky above cleared, clouds fast moving to the east, and the waning moon was just past full, giving the watchers a fine view of the surrounding area.

The quiet area.

But not too quiet, as if hushed before a predator's crouch. No, it seemed just another night on the banks of Loch Beag.

All about, the alarm had died with the fires, the villagers relaxing as one. Asba was the first to sit back. His arms were tired from hauling the bear. His shoulders ached from the press of that pole, and with the excitement ebbing, exhaustion flooded through him. So, he kicked off his muddy boots and settled into a crook in the wall of the watchtower. The midnight hour approached, and behind them, most of the village was asleep.

"No Usgar coming," he said quietly when his friends noticed him reclining. "May as well just sleep."

Tamilee started to protest, but Asef had already removed his own boots and plopped down beside his brother.

"Our own fault we're out here," Tamilee reminded them. "If we'd just spoken true, they would have sent others and sent us to our beds."

She shrugged and plopped down to sit cross-legged, her hands up on the rail, staring out at the tree line.

Asba wasn't sure if the woman meant to sleep or to keep watch like that, but he was sure he didn't care either way. His sighs had become yawns.

Just as he started drifting off, there came a sharp thud on the wooden watchtower beside him. Asba leapt up, ready to call an alarm, reaching for his bow. But he saw Tamilee shaking her head, and when he joined her at the rail and looked out, he saw not an Usgar raider, but a one-legged woman on a dolly, holding another large rock.

She threw a second one up at the tower, bouncing it off the wood, then snorted at the couple and began paddling away with those uncannily strong arms.

This second thud woke Asef from his slumber. He cursed loudly, rolled over, and nearly tumbled out of the watchtower before Asba could grab him.

"Damned woman," Asba said. "How might she be knowing that we weren't watching?"

"I was watching," Tamilee said, unconvincingly.

"My brother and me, then," said Asba. "How could she know?"

"She always knows, that one," said Tamilee.

"Because she's a deamhan," said Asef, and this time no one bothered correcting him. They just watched her paddle and scrape slowly back toward the village, then resumed their watch.

"Should've left her to die when she washed onto our beach," Asef grumbled again.

The beam of sunlight climbed along the eastern wall of the augur's temple, tracing across his great grandsire's mural. It was late in the day now, just a couple of hours left before sunset, and the beam of the westering sun approached the image of the sun on the wall, just below and to the right.

The old augur purred with satisfaction, running his tongue across what remained of his lower teeth.

The sunbeam would move more to the left in the next couple of days, to align perfectly with the image on the wall—the image where Skath-mi-Zahn's dragon was eating the day itself!

His fingers trembling, the old augur lit the censers at the four corners of his altar, then reached into his belt pouch and brought forth his shaped chips fashioned of the bones of the great condors that flew about the mountains to the east. He closed his eyes and chanted a prayer to Skath-mi-Zahn for guidance.

"Grant my vision true," he finished, and he opened his eyes for just an instant, to glance at the thrown bones.

In his mind's eye, through the power of Skath-mi-Zahn, the old augur drew mental lines between the bones, this way and that, discerning every shape they could form, drawing pictures from those lines in his mind.

Everything he saw confirmed his understanding and his private prediction.

Skath-mi-Zahn was with him, he knew. The Glorious Gold spoke to him now, and he understood.

The old augur breathed deep of the scented smoke filling his little temple. He opened his eyes and stared at the bones.

"Yes," he whispered softly, collecting them. He smiled his wide toothy grin, wondering how many other augurs would be casting bones this night. Not many, he figured, with Xelihui still a few days away, and itself not a common day of augury.

"Thank you, my ancestor," he said, looking to the mural with great appreciation. His great grandsire had left all of the clues right there, leading him to this momentous prediction, one that would restore honor to his family and his temple. For so many decades, centuries even, this temple, his family, had been mostly ignored, even ridiculed, even scorned. For the old augur's grandfather had misread the clues of his divinely inspired sire and had not heard the whisper of Skath-mi-Zahn clearly.

The old augur's grandfather had recklessly offered his prophecy anyway, and with confidence and demand, and the misreading of the signs had led to ruin for two entire tribes, and the burning of a fair-sized xoconai city.

The memories of the xoconai were long, generational even, and they had not forgotten, and so most had forsaken the old augur's bloodline and their temple. Only a group of young adults had come to follow him of late, men and women as frustrated as he with the softness of the xoconai world. The xoconai were the light, and thus the envy of all, and the light had to be protected, and protection came from strength.

"No more," the old augur, the last of his family, declared. While his grandsire had not passed along any of the information to the old augur's father before his execution, the oldest one, his great grandsire, had given him this gift. His family name would die with him, but not with shame, and this temple would become a shrine to the augur's family line.

He would go to the greatest city of Indondo, to the great temple, and he would tell them. They would spit at him. The peasants would laugh at him and jostle him in the crowded streets.

They would not believe him.

But the Xelihui would come, and Kithkukulikhan, the dragon of Skath-mi-Zahn, would eat the daylight, and they would be humbled.

The old augur closed his eyes and envisioned the march of the xoconai, hundreds of thousands, endless lines stretching from the splashing shores of Ilhuicaatl to the passes through the towering peaks of Teotl Tenamitl.

To the east, ever the east, so that the sun would both rise from and set into the waters surrounding the vast kingdom of the xoconai.

PART 1

WHEN THE DRAGON ATE THE SUN

They say and it's been told that god's dragon will eat the sun. And he will give it back, in golden light, to shine upon the Xoconai.

The short night passes, and the golden gift of the dragon so ends the long night. And each day in the golden light, will we know the glory of god shines upon us. And calls us to war, great war, the end war, and heralds then peace for a thousand years.

The time of the Xoconai. Glory be to Scathmizzane.

He who gave us Teotl Tenamitl, that on the sunset slopes, the lands of Tyuskixmal, we would find sanctuary against the darkness.

He who raised high the mountain parapet, the castle wall, to keep the foul men and goblins at bay.

They say and it's been told that the dragon will come when the wide-winged totot are few in the west, for the high lakes of Tyuskixmal have dried. But the great waters of Ayuskixmal, the sunrise slopes, remain, over the parapet of Teotl Tenamitl.

This time is now, and we are called to Ayuskixmal.

There in the lands of men, our half-kin are slaughtered. The bastard children of Scathmizzane, crushed now beneath the boots of men, will find vengeance and then peace. We are called to accept them and nurture them, and offer purity in their sacrifice that the blood of Cizinfozza be excised from them. And they will repay our mercy and lead us to the sea in the east.

They say and it's been told that in the west we will gather, and from the west we will march. The augurs will be the eyes, mundunugu the heart, anqui hunters the belly, macana the arms, cuetzpali the legs.

We will scale the parapets of Teotl Tenamitl and there beyond clear the Ayuskixmal, the eastern slopes, of canker's buds.

And from the mesa shoulders of the deep lake of the water dragon, we see the land before us, far and long to the east, and we look then upon the wide nation that will be ours once more.

There we welcome the bastard children of god. And we teach them and let them run before us to take their vengeance and mark our march.

The men will think their lands safe, but they will be wrong.
For then they will see the beautiful and terrible glory of the Xoconai.

They say and it's been told that the dragon sun will melt the gold, and the Xoconai will build their temples of it. The ugly gray stone of men will shine with brilliance when the Xoconai remake their castles to see the light, to shine like the dragon sun.

No more will those fortresses insult the eyes and weaken the heart. No more will they be thick and dark, for what need of wide walls when all the land is Xoconai? And in these thousand years of peace, the greatest weapon will be the dagger of sacrifice to the Glorious Gold, for under His light the enemies of Xoconai will hide in dark holes and there remain. Except a few, of course, to test our love, and these we will catch and give to Him.

They say and it's been told that Tonoloya, the empire of the Xoconai, will see the fiery orb of Tonalli awaken and climb from the sea, and then calm her fires and go back to her sleep beneath the wave, and all the lands in between will know peace and love.

And in the east, we will cheer the waking Tonalli.

And in the west, we will cheer the Tonalli before she settles to sleep.

And the children of the lands in between will salute the passage, and exalt in the prayers of the east and the west.

I am old now and I have said farewell. The riches of the world fly away one by one as I enter the shadow willingly. A shadow that darkens without, but brightens within. In my death, I see the freedom and the birth of that which will be.

And that is glorious.

—The Last Augur of Darkness

1

BLOODY WITCH

Work about the Usgar encampment increased that surprisingly warm late-summer day, as the tribe prepared to make the move to their winter sanctuary. While most of the creatures living on the huge mountain would sleep the winter in deep holes, or would migrate down further to the plateau, the Usgar tribe moved opposite, climbing to the mountain heights as winter neared. There, on the small meadow beyond the pine grove that housed their winter camp, they would be protected from the cold winds and deep snows by the warmth of Usgar, the Crystal God.

The winter was the time of peace for the tribe, when the hunters and warriors could rest, when all the world about them slept under a thick blanket of unrelenting snow.

But now of course was the time of preparation, filling stores and packing the tents to prepare for the great trek up Fireach Speuer's steep trails. Many years in this season, the tribe would launch a large raid upon the villages on the lakeshore below, but not this year, particularly not after the events of the previous night.

"It does not explain," said Mairen, the Usgar-righinn, or Crystal Maven, of the tribe, who led the Coven of witches and so was considered the most powerful woman among the Usgar.

"It is all the explanation you need," replied the warrior, Aghmor, mustering all the strength he could to show confidence in his impertinent reply. He had been summoned to Mairen's tent immediately upon his return to the encampment, taken by the arm by the witch Connebragh and tugged along unceremoniously before the eyes of many onlookers.

For all his anger at the indignity of being paraded about by a mere woman, though, Aghmor was well aware of the power of the one now standing before him. It didn't seem a wise thing to him to deceive, and to insult, the Usgar-righinn, after all, who was powerful in the ways of Usgar magic.

But it seemed more foolhardy still to cross Tay Aillig, the Usgar-laoch, the War Leader, and the cruel man's instructions had been clear.

"Elder Raibert is soon to arrive," Aghmor announced.

"You disturbed the Usgar-forfach?" Connebragh asked with a gasp.

Mairen held her hand up before the other woman to bid her to silence.

"What do you know of Ralid, who is not in the camp, and rumored to be wandering about the lower hills of Fireach Speuer?" Mairen asked.

Aghmor just shook his head.

"What do you know of Aoleyn, who is not in the camp this morning?" she asked more sharply.

Again, he shook his head, and this time he lifted his palms helplessly.

"Why were they out on the night of Iseabal's bloody face?" Mairen asked, referring to the goddess associated with the red moon, the Blood Moon.

"We do not know why," Aghmor replied.

"If you know so little, then why did you travel to the sacred plateau to speak with the Usgar-forfach?"

"I . . . I . . ."

When he had felt cornered earlier, Aghmor had thought himself quite clever in invoking the Usgar-forfach, the tribe's Elder who was once the Chieftain, who remained in the winter encampment all through the year. In truth and tradition, Mairen ranked below all the men of the tribe. In practice, however, only a handful of Usgar men dared cross her.

Aghmor had to hope that the fact that he had gone to fetch Raibert at the behest of Tay Aillig would be a warning to Mairen that she should take great care in scolding him. He was not acting on his own, but with the apparent blessings of the two most important and powerful men in Usgar.

"Where are they and why were they out of the camp?" Mairen asked evenly, her face a stern mask, unyielding and unbending and so unlike the other women of Usgar.

"We're not knowing that they're out of the camp at all," Aghmor lied, and stammered, feeling as if he was standing on muddy ground indeed.

Mairen nodded and put on a pensive face. She turned to Connebragh and asked, "Sister, how long would it take you, do you think, to get to the winter plateau?"

Aghmor began nodding, too, his mind immediately beginning to calculate the hours for such a journey up the mountainside. As soon as he had started that mental task, however, he caught on to Mairen's true question here, and he was sure that his subsequent gulp was heard quite clearly.

"Half the night," Connebragh replied, both she and Mairen looking to the warrior.

"Not quite as long to return, unless one took care in the dark, don't you think?" Mairen asked, and it was unclear as to whether she was speaking to Connebragh or Aghmor—not that it mattered, in any case, for the point of the question was certainly aimed at her knowing target.

"I am swift," Aghmor stuttered under the weight of those two gazes. "That is why Tay Aillig asked . . ."

"The sun is recently up above the wide shoulders of Fireach Speuer. The noon hour is only just passed," Mairen interrupted. "You went up the mountainside to speak with Elder Raibert as soon as we were done with Tay Aillig this morn."

"Yes."

"But how could he know then where Ralid might be?" Mairen asked, and when Aghmor didn't immediately respond, she went at him more forcefully. "You, too, were out last night, under Iseabal's bloody face. The night of the demon fossa. You were out—you were all out."

"I was with the Usgar-laoch," Aghmor stuttered, not wanting to admit anything, not sure where all of this was going. "He is War Leader. I cannot question . . ."

"Where?" Mairen said directly, and poor Aghmor swallowed hard.

Whispers sifted through the Usgar encampment that day, as news began to spread that members of the tribe were missing—although of the actual number being reported absent Usgar found a wide range indeed among the gossiping men and women, and particularly the children, who carried the news from one group to another, from the workers bundling supplies to the many guards posted this day, seemingly on every high rock jag and in the branches of all the tallest trees.

The warrior Aghmor had been rumored to be dead throughout most of the morning, and the whispers of his demise persisted even after he had returned. Ralid, too, was missing and rumored killed—some said it was a bear that had finished the poor young warrior, but those who believed they knew better insisted that it had to be the demon fossa. "For didn't you see the Blood Moon last night?" went the refrain whenever whispers of a more mundane death, like the notion of a bear, were spoken.

Whatever might be transpiring on the slopes of Fireach Speuer outside the camp, emotions were certainly running high within. The Usgar-laoch, Tay Aillig, was also missing, and although many had seen him leave earlier that very morning and he had apparently made no secret of his departure, the rumors were stubborn things. By early afternoon, most of the camp was certain that he'd been eaten by the fossa during the Blood Moon the previous night.

Gradually, though, the known truth had begun to win out, but that truth, too, did not inspire ease in the camp. The great Tay Aillig, the Usgar-laoch of the tribe, had been chased home after a losing battle with a great mountain bear, it was said, a defeat that had left a promising warrior, the missing Ralid, fending for himself on the lower slopes.

It was confirmed, too, that another of the tribe was missing as well: that headstrong young woman who had been named to enter the Coven, and who had been claimed as wife of Tay Aillig.

"Usgar-laoch is out searching for her," many claimed.

"He is desperate to find her!" others agreed.

"But he was out last night, too, I've heard," some chimed in, and with an edge of suspicion to the words. And the whispers grew, hinting that Tay Aillig had been angry with Aoleyn.

The gossip grew even more intense and suspicious-sounding when word came down that the great Usgar-forfach, Elder Raibert, was coming down from the high plateau this day, something that had not occurred in the memory of half the tribe.

Like most people in an environment as harsh as Fireach Speuer, the Usgar survived through ritual and tried tradition. So many anomalies in so short a time caused great stress among them, for the credo of life in a land unmerciful and with dangers unrelenting went along the lines of: "I did this yesterday and so I am alive today. If I do it again today, I will be alive tomorrow."

Adding to all of that tension, yet another very recent incident already had many people unsettled, for Aoleyn's expected ascent to the Coven had been facilitated by a tragic accident that had killed another witch, the poor woman fumbling with her magical crystals, her spell failing, leaving her to plummet to her death from a cliff. And of course, the previous night had seen the Blood Moon, the night of the demon fossa. The Usgar were the most powerful warriors in the region, feared by all.

But they, too, remained humbled by the demon fossa, and when the full moon shined red, when Iseabal showed her bloody face, they wisely cowered.

Not the previous night, however, not for all of the tribe, at least, and now they feared that they had suffered more losses. The Usgar were not numerous, less than three hundred strong, and every loss was painful.

The palpable nervousness wafting about the encampment showed itself in the fast-turned heads and gasps when a cry went out from a sentry on a high rocky jag further up the mountain. All the whispers began coalescing around that call, and all eyes moved to the indicated trail, winding down from higher up Fireach Speuer, beside some huge stones to the southeast of the camp.

A lone figure came into view soon after, far away, but a human figure, surely. From this point to the top of the great mountain was Usgar territory, where no lakemen ventured, and so the first murmurs spoke of Elder Raibert, the only tribesman known to be higher up the mountain at that time.

But no, it was a woman, walking not in the shaky gait of an elderly Usgar, but with confidence in her stride.

The calls and alerts and the cries for "arms!" died out quickly when the sentry who had first spotted the arrival called out that it was Aoleyn of the Usgar.

Nervous whispers became those of relief for many, of consternation against the young woman—how dare she go out on the night of the Blood Moon?—for many others. Aoleyn's reputation was already that of a free spirit, and that was no compliment. She was constantly battling against the leaders of the tribe, and against the dedication to order that had sustained Usgar as the dominant force on the plateau beyond the memories of any living man.

And still she had been chosen by Usgar-righinn Mairen to join the Coven, and more remarkably still, by Usgar-laoch Tay Aillig to be his wife!

The gossip flew on, growing in strength and salacious detail, when the distant figure dipped out of sight, below a bend in the trail.

The people in the camp could no longer see her, but a pair of sentries in a blind beside the trail east of the camp noted her clearly enough to see that Aoleyn was covered in blood, her hair matted with the stuff, her shirt torn ragged, her shoes crusted.

So much blood! And though her gait was determined and steady, she was leaning a bit to one side, where much of her clothing had been fully torn away.

"Go fetch Tay Aillig," one of the watchers said.

"He is not to be found," answered his partner. "He departed camp soon after speaking with the Usgar-righinn."

The other man nodded. "Then fetch Mairen," he decided. "The Crystal Maven can heal the girl, if there be great wounds beneath the shreds."

"Aye, and decide what's to be done with the lass, leaving like that," said the other. "She can'no enter the camp—none can, on Tay Aillig's word."

The other man nodded, and the sentry ran off to fetch Mairen.

The remaining man shifted uncomfortably. He didn't know this unusual young woman very well—unusual both in temperament, if the rumors were true, and in appearance, as he could see by his own eyes. She was curvy and quite short, the top of her raven-haired head barely touching the chin of most Usgar women. And while dark hair was not unheard of in the tribe, it was not typical, and Aoleyn's was as dark as a moonless midnight.

As were her eyes, black eyes, eyes that seemed to look through him, he thought, and would surely see through any lies or foolishness. And that crooked smile she so often wore—he had seen it many times from across the camp. Perhaps it was an honest smile, but to him it seemed one rooted in Aoleyn's belief that she knew things others did not.

"Loving the look of herself," he whispered, and aye, that was it. For to his thinking, this young Aoleyn wore upon her a confidence few warriors might match, and that no woman should even attempt.

If all of that wasn't imposing enough to the warrior, he reminded himself that this was Tay Aillig's wife, for some reason no one seemed to understand.

Now he was tasked with stopping this headstrong lass who had the ear and thrall of Tay Aillig.

"On word of the Usgar-laoch himself," he said to himself, but not as quietly as he had intended, when he dropped down from the blind to block the path.

"What word?" she asked, stopping short with obvious surprise.

"You can'no go in," the sentry explained. "None are to be entering the camp."

Aoleyn put her hand on her hip and gave him that crooked smile of hers, and the sentry hoped she didn't hear him gulp.

"Truly?" she asked.

"Aye," he said, and he looked up and down at the bloody woman, and thought he noticed something shiny through one of the tears in her shirt, near to her belly button, which remained tantalizingly out of sight. "Are you hurt, then? How can ye not be?"

"No," Aoleyn replied, and now she seemed suddenly uncomfortable, and she shifted a bit and brought an arm across her belly, covering up. "And should I tell my husband of your wandering eyes?"

The sentry swallowed hard again and looked up at her, shaking his head vigorously.

"I am returning from th'Way," Aoleyn explained. "I need to change my clothes and wash."

"Wash the blood, aye. And how, then, you can'no be hurt?"

The woman snorted and started past, but the sentry could not ignore the commands of the Usgar-laoch, orders which offered no compromise here. He held out his spear sidelong to block the trail.

"You can'no go any more."

Aoleyn stepped back and fixed him with a stare. "So are we to stand out here and stare at each other through the rest of this beautiful day? They're packing for the journey up the mountain. I've chores . . ."

"By word of Tay Aillig," the man said. "I'm not to go against those words. Are you?"

"I haven't yet decided," she replied.

"I can'no let you."

"You can'no stop . . ." she started to reply, but she paused, looking past him. Following that gaze, the sentry was truly relieved when he glanced back to see his partner returning, along with a pair of women.

"Where have you been, foolish child?" the Crystal Maven scolded, but the timbre in her voice changed and her eyes went wide when she took a good gander at Aoleyn. Connebragh spoke the surprise for both of them.

"What happened to you? By Usgar, are you hurt?"

Aoleyn flashed that smile of hers again, her dark eyes sparkling in the afternoon sun. "It's a long story," Aoleyn replied. "Might I change my clothes and wash before I tell it?"

"No," came Mairen's uncompromising reply.

Things had not been going well for him, but young Egard held faith that his uncle, the great Tay Aillig, would spin the disaster of the previous night into something worthwhile. Egard, Tay Aillig, and Aghmor had been down there, on the lower slopes of the mountain. They had tried to bait the demon fossa by tying a man they had captured to a tree.

They had gotten a bear instead, a great and huge mountain bear, full of rage. It had driven them away, three at least, after flinging poor Ralid aside.

Tay Aillig always had a plan, Egard reminded himself, but he shook his head at that notion, still trying to come to some understanding of why his powerful uncle, who could have any unwed woman in the tribe, and probably more than a few of the married ones, had settled upon Aoleyn.

Aoleyn! She was much nearer to Egard's age than to that of Tay Aillig. And she was an obstinate creature, disobedient and unaware of her place in Usgar hierarchy. Many times had younger Egard and Aoleyn locked horns, once even physically—and that had not ended well for the mighty young warrior. He had been but a boy, he reminded himself, but he winced at the mere thought. For no, he had been a young man, something driven home pointedly when Aoleyn's knee had risen forcefully into his groin.

Egard shook away the thoughts of that long-ago fight, and of Aoleyn altogether. He couldn't afford to be distracted here. Not now. Too much was at stake, though he wasn't even sure of what that might be.

He looked to the sun, beginning its descent over the huge, rectangular lake that marked the northwestern base of the great mountain of Fireach Speuer. Egard and his search party, seven other Usgar warriors, were low on the mountain now, much nearer at least two of the lakemen villages than they were to the Usgar camp, as they searched for Ralid.

There would be no Blood Moon this night, so the demon fossa was not a concern, he knew, but still, being this far down the mountain with so small a force could lead to great catastrophe.

That thought, too, he shook away. These were pitiful lakemen, and no threat to the great Usgar warriors, no matter the odds.

He cupped his hand beside his mouth and gave a series of yips, like a coyote's call, two short yelps and then three more. This was a universal call among the Usgar for occasions when parties got separated hiking the many jags and chasms of the mountain peaks, or to bring lost fellows back together in the white blindness of winter storms.

Others in the war party answered in the prescribed cadence, one yip from the first man, then two from the second, then one and two more from a third, and all done with perfect imitation of a coyote pack.

If the missing man heard the call, he would know to answer with a long howl.

Of course, Ralid wouldn't hear it, Egard knew painfully well, being fairly certain that Ralid was dead. The bear had hit him hard with its swatting paw, hurling him into the thick trunk of a tree. Egard could still hear the sickening crack of Ralid's shattering bones. The warrior grimaced as he pictured again his friend's body broken against the trunk, as he recalled the fight, where he, Aghmor, and mighty Tay Aillig himself had been chased away.

They had been forced to leave their prisoner behind, as well, the one Tay Aillig was using to bait the fossa.

That man—a lakeman, they supposed, though his skull was not misshapen, as was customary among the villagers who called Loch Beag their home—was also almost certainly dead, for they had left him tied up helplessly, and with a ferocious bear rampaging about the area.

Egard started another coyote call, for he had to keep up appearances. He saw another of his band coming over a low ridge to the side, and the man just shook his head. So Egard gave a sharp caw, the sound of a crow, the universal Usgar signal that a lost man was not yet found. The searcher near him similarly cawed.

Five other crow calls followed closely, and Egard snorted in frustration. They were in the area, and spread out wide enough that one of them should be very close to Ralid's body.

Then came a long howl from the eighth searcher, and Egard sucked in his breath. He steadied himself and headed for the caller, not really wanting to see Ralid's corpse. He was certain his friend was dead, but seeing it seemed as if it would somehow make it all too real. He had work to do here, he reminded himself. Tay Aillig had not sent him down here to fail. His hand went reflexively to his pocket, to some fabric he had stolen from a particular tent.

The eight men converged on a trail that Egard recognized, descending steeply to a clearing—to the clearing, he knew, where they had strung up the prisoner, where they had fought the mountain bear, where Ralid had been killed.

A heavy flap of wings greeted them when they came down onto the edge of that flatter and clearer area, as a host of buzzards flew off. Others remained, their wings out wide imposingly, crowing over their feast.

Usgar spears drove them off, revealing the gory meal: a huge pile of half-eaten guts.

"Ralid?" one of the searchers gasped, looking as if he was about to vomit.

"No Usgar," said another. "That's the belly of a beast, not a man, and most likely the guts of a bear."

"The buzzards eat fast," another remarked. "A bear ripped to . . . that?"

"Dressed," the man who had identified the pile clarified when he bent over the fly-covered remains. "Not eaten. The bear was dressed, skillfully so."

"Ralid!" Egard cried, trying to sound surprised and convincing, and when the others all looked at him, he pointed across the clearer area, to a large tree on the north side. It was hard to make out from this distance, and Egard would not have recognized it had he not known what to expect, but following his lead, the others, too, were able to make out the form of a leg, wrapped awkwardly around the bottom of the tree, bending in a way that a human leg should not.

Egard waved them by, and six fanned out and moved across the clearing to identify their friend, while the seventh continued his inspection of the gory pile of bear guts, noticing, too, to the side, the severed animal's head.

"Uamhas," one of the men approaching Ralid's body said, using the Usgar's derogatory name for the lakemen. He stopped and pointed to the ground. Two other Usgar joined him to help sort out the riddle of some tracks the man had noticed.

Egard wondered if those were his tracks, and those of his companions, but it seemed too far afield from where they had battled the mountain bear. No matter, though, for all the party was distracted then, so the man moved his hand into his pocket and looked for his opportunities.

"They leave deep tracks," the man inspecting the area remarked. "Burdened."

"With the prize of the dressed bear?" asked another at the scene.

Egard and two others arrived at Ralid's body. He was surprised that the uamhas hadn't taken the corpse, or desecrated it at least. Certainly, he would have pissed on the bodies of any uamhas he came across. He looked across the flat area to his friends inspecting the tracks, and figured that the uamhas hadn't even seen Ralid when they encountered, and apparently killed, the great bear.

No matter, he thought.

"Take him," he bade the others near him. "With all honor and care."

When the two lifted Ralid and began moving off, Egard began directing the others, sending three to follow the blood trail and see if the uamhas were still near, and moving the other two about the area to see if they could better discern all that had happened here.

He, too, went about that task, except instead of searching for clues, he planted some, then made sure that he directed the others properly so that they might find them.

"Who granted you passage out of the camp under the light of Iseabal's bloody face?" Mairen demanded when she and Connebragh got Aoleyn away from the sentry, far to the side and into the shallows of a rocky overhang where they would not be seen or heard.

Aoleyn stuttered for an answer.

"You're to join the Coven, girl," Mairen scolded. "Does that mean nothing to you?"

"Of course . . ." Aoleyn started to reply.

"Shut up," Mairen interrupted. "For once in your days, listen, girl, and do'no speak!"

The Usgar-righinn launched into a tirade then, scolding Aoleyn repeatedly, telling her of all the things she would need to change if she was truly to join the sacred Coven, warning her that her marriage to Tay Aillig would not protect her in this sacred endeavor, as the Coven was none of his concern. That he could not protect her even if he should one day ascend to become the Usgar-triath, the Chieftain of the entire tribe.

Aoleyn heard little of it, though she was wise enough to appear engaged. Instead, her thoughts were sorting out the fabrication she would tell of her ordeals of the previous night, and her great victory over that most awful demon fossa, one that would forever change the ways of the Usgar and their safety on Fireach Speuer.

Wouldn't Mairen feel foolish then?

"Usgar-righinn," she began respectfully, head bowed.

"Why do you believe you have anything to tell me?" Mairen snapped back.

Aoleyn lifted her head and stood strong against Mairen's withering gaze. "But I do," she insisted. "And when you've heard, aye, but you'll understa . . ."

"Shut up, girl," Mairen replied. "There's not a word you might be . . ."

"I killed the fossa!" Aoleyn blurted before she could be interrupted.

For a moment, nothing, then Connebragh gasped and Mairen's face screwed up strangely, the middle-aged woman falling back a step.

"Well, not killed," Aoleyn said before the others could recover. "But destroyed it, truly. It was a spirit thing, possessing a cloud leopard, rotting the poor creature . . ."

Mairen hit her, slapped her across the face, and it was no ordinary slap, but one enhanced by magic, by a burning, biting, shocking sting of lightning. Aoleyn flew backward, crashing against the rocky wall and cracking her head in the process, adding wet blood to the dried. She fell to the ground, hard, and rolled over onto her back, clutching her head, stunned.

"What is that?" she heard Mairen say, but it seemed like the woman was, far, far away.

Aoleyn felt hands on her, about her belly, and her eye focused just enough for her to realize that Connebragh was inspecting her. She felt a slight tug on her navel, and that brought her sensibilities flooding back to her.

Aoleyn gulped and tried to cover up. They had found her secret: her belly ring set with the magical gemstones she had extracted from the sacred crystals! She threw her arms across her abdomen, pushing Connebragh's hands away. She started to sit up, but Mairen was there, suddenly, kneeling heavily on her chest, pinning her back and pulling her arms aside.

"What is that?" Mairen asked her repeatedly, but all the desperate and dazed Aoleyn could answer was a frantic cry of "Leave me alone!"

The two women had her fully pinned, then, and Mairen drew out a crystal, one tinged with dark red flakes. Aoleyn knew the magic of this item, and she began struggling mightily as Mairen fell into the magical item and sent her vision through the crystal. Aoleyn had to beat her to the draw, but she could not, as Connebragh, recognizing her attempt at spellcasting, slapped her hard and repeatedly across the face, defeating her concentration.

Aoleyn knew she was doomed, for now the Usgar-righinn could see the emanations of magic, not just the items. Now Mairen understood the gems set in Aoleyn's belly ring, and the young woman's earrings, too, became quite clear to her, Aoleyn could tell by her gasp. Mairen tore them out viciously, then grabbed Aoleyn's wrist and pulled the pinned young woman's hand up before her eyes, shaking her head as she studied Aoleyn's ring, wound in magical wedstone wire and set with an enchanted ruby and serpentine stone. Mairen nearly broke Aoleyn's finger in wrenching that ring from her.

"Strip her!" the Usgar-righinn instructed Connebragh, and with the other woman's help she yanked and tugged and tore at Aoleyn's clothes, and punched Aoleyn hard whenever she resisted.

They found the anklet she had woven into her skin, one set with the blue stone of frost, and bars that could create lightning.

"What does it mean?" Aoleyn heard Connebragh say.

She felt Mairen's hand go to her belly, then a slight pulling sensation.

"It means," the Usgar-righinn replied, and she gave a sudden yank, tearing the belly ring from Aoleyn's flesh, "that our little Aoleyn has done a grave heresy here."

Aoleyn went limp. She just lay back helplessly and did not resist, barely whimpered, as Mairen pulled the anklet from her flesh. She thought, but only briefly, to try again to fall into the magic and jolt the woman away, but no, she was defeated. What point was there in even resisting now? For they knew.

They didn't even bother dressing her when they called the sentries over, instructing the men to take Aoleyn to her tent in the campground, and to empty it of everything but a simple blanket. "Bind her, hands and legs," Mairen ordered them. "And watch over her. She is not to leave, to have no visitors, and to have . . ." she looked right into Aoleyn's eyes as she finished, "nothing."

2

WITH HER HEAD CHOPPED OFF

A ray of sunshine awakened Talmadge, peering in through the hanging skin door on the village cottage. When the grogginess subsided, he remembered where he was, and so knew that it was late morning, at least. This was Fasach Crann, the lakeman village directly in the shadow of the huge mountain, Fireach Speuer, and it wouldn't know direct sunlight until long after the diffused dawn, particularly in this late season, when the arch of the sun moved further to the south, more directly behind the towering mountain.

The traveler wiped his eyes and tried to remember the previous night, one spent indulging in the fish wine made in the village, which tasted horrible but kicked like an angry centaur. He still had that awful tart flavor in his mouth, from green grapes so bitter they actually stung when chewed. Unfortunately, they weren't much better after being pressed into wine.

When he rolled over, more of the night's escapades came back to him, for his companion this night, a lovely young woman with two elongated humps on her skull, fashionable wheat-colored hair flowing thickly down both, sat across from him, wearing a forced smile and little else.

Talmadge tried to dissect that apparent discomfort. She certainly hadn't been uneasy with her nudity the previous night.

"Am I not pleasing to you, then?" she asked, and the man sucked in his breath uncomfortably, as he remembered more about the encounter, or more particularly, the lack of.

"It's nothing to do with you," he said. "I had a most difficult few days." He began to elaborate, but just sighed and let it go. How could he begin to explain the swirl of emotions that had filled his head since returning to Loch Beag and these lakeside villages? Once, this region, particularly this village of Fasach Crann, had been Talmadge's most cherished destination, where the intrigue and deceptions of the outside world could not catch him. But that was before the lake itself had risen up against him, in the form of the great sea monster that lurked in its depths. That creature had attacked him savagely in his flimsy little boat, had tossed it like a toy, and had taken from Talmadge the only woman he had ever loved.

That was years ago, and now, finally, he had dared to come back to this place, only to find himself captured by Usgar, beaten and stabbed, and tied up as bait for the demon fossa.

Another woman had saved him, an intriguing young Usgar who was not at all like the deamhan reputation associated with that warlike tribe.

He looked up toward the mountain, wondering what had become of that tough young Usgar, so deceptively small and pretty, yet so full of ferocity and surprising skill, the likes of which he had only once before encountered—in his lost, beloved Khotai.

That Usgar woman had left the cave of the demon creature battered and exhausted.

Should he have remained with her? Certainly, Talmadge hadn't been able to get her out of his thoughts since that night. She had saved his life, after all, and then he had dared to enter the cave of the monster to return the favor.

He looked back at the woman beside him, who had offered him her bed. He couldn't even remember her name. While most of the people from his land, from Honce-the-Bear to the east, wouldn't care much for the appearance of the lake folk, with their elongated skulls, Talmadge saw past that difference and thought they could be quite lovely.

This woman before him was quite lovely. He hadn't lied to her, though, and his problem had nothing to do with her. He wasn't sure he wanted to be with any woman who was not Khotai. Not even the unusual Usgar lass on the mountain, though she had intrigued him more than he had ever expected.

"Go on, then," the woman said, nodding, and she seemed calm and accepting. She looked to the door to a pile of clothes—where Talmadge's clothes had been, but these were not his. His were bloody and torn, with knife holes, but these were fresh and clean.

"You know . . ." He started to apologize once more, but the woman held up her hand to stop him, and this time flashed him a smile that seemed filled more with pity than anything else.

That struck him, and oddly. Because as he considered it, Talmadge realized that he didn't need any pity. Certainly not!

True, he wasn't much interested in having sex with a woman at that time, but that was more a matter of coming back here, of having Khotai so fresh in his thoughts. Aside from that, though, Talmadge felt truly well, even light. He had conquered his fears to come back to this place. He had faced near-certain death, and a surprising turn of fate—an Usgar woman, no less!—had intervened.

He shouldn't be alive, but he was. And the woman had destroyed the demon that haunted the mountain, burning it from the body of a possessed cloud leopard. That's what she had told him, at least, and he had witnessed the retreat of the leopard. After that, venturing into that high mountain cave, a dark place of murder, after feeling the coldness in there, supernatural, ghostly, demonic, Talmadge held no doubts about the Usgar woman's claims.

He went and gathered his clothes, and dressed quickly, then started away, but paused and returned to give a kiss to the wonderful lakewoman who had been so kind and generous to him.

"It had nothing to do with you," he whispered in her ear. "You are beautiful."

"I know to the first and thank you for the second," she said, and seemed at ease. "Next time you're visiting the town, then."

Talmadge looked at her and nodded, and felt as if that would be a distinct possibility.

Then he went out into the day, a spring in his step that he had not known for several years. He shouldn't be alive.

But he was.

"What did she do with these crystals?" Connebragh asked Mairen when they were alone in the shallow, the guards having departed with Aoleyn. Connebragh held up the items: ring, belly ring, ear cuff, earring, and anklet, and marveled at the smooth gemstones there. "Are you sure these were not simply taken in an uamhas raid?"

Mairen didn't respond, but it was certainly a possibility. Oftentimes, the Usgar war parties would return from the lakeshore villages with baubles such as these, though as to how unimportant little Aoleyn would ever have gotten her hands on them, Mairen could not know. Seonagh had shown her, perhaps. That one, who was Aoleyn's aunt and tutor, had often been troublesome. The Crystal Maven dismissed that thought almost as soon as it came to her, for Seonagh had been of the Coven and would have known that these gemstones from Aoleyn's jewelry possessed magical properties, for Mairen had seen them easily enough with her own red-flecked crystal.

Knowing that, Seonagh would have certainly destroyed them, cast them into Craos'a'diad, as was prescribed by the laws of Usgar. Any magic outside of the crystals was evil magic, by Usgar code.

No, Mairen was convinced that Aoleyn had fashioned these gems herself, particularly since the wire with which she had fastened them to her body was made of wedstone, the healing stone, the stone of the spirit that provided the fastest connection between a witch and the magic of Usgar.

Privately, Mairen thought Aoleyn quite resourceful and creative.

And dangerous.

So very dangerous, and it was the second issue that had her more rattled than the matter of her heresy with the sacred crystals. Aoleyn claimed to have killed the fossa. Was it possible?

How delicate and dangerous was this situation for Mairen! She had feared that Tay Aillig would somehow destroy the fossa—she was certain that was the explanation for the puzzles that had been presented to her this morning, with the missing warrior and the injuries she had seen on Aghmor and Egard. Why would any be out on the night of a Blood Moon, when the demonic creature was out and hunting?

That notion tied into Tay Aillig's promises to her on the cliff after the fall of Gavina. He had taken her, then and there, in a fit of shared passion, and had insisted that Aoleyn meant nothing to him, except as a tool for his ascension to become the Usgar-triath, the unquestioned Chieftain of Usgar. When Mairen had pointed out to him that such could not be for many years, since the order of ascension had already been put in place, Tay Aillig had confidently laughed at her.

Had he tried to kill the fossa?

Had he taken Aoleyn with him to do the deed?

He had promised Mairen a great role beside him when he became the leader of Usgar, and Mairen desperately wanted to believe him. But there was another matter here, one more troubling.

The Usgar-righinn, the voice of Usgar in the tribe, the leader of the Coven, did not want the demon fossa killed. The legend of the monster inspired fear, and that fear played into the power of the Coven. Of course, the witches were useful to the tribe in myriad ways, from enchanting the weapons of the raiding parties, to granting the hunters light feet that they could more easily transverse the dangerous mountain terrain, to healing wounds. The magical warmth of Usgar sustained the tribe in a place where they could not otherwise hope to survive, and so the Coven, and by extension, the Usgar-righinn, would always be valued.

But the fear of the fossa was paramount to Mairen's power. The witches alone could forecast the next Blood Moon and inform the tribe of its pending arrival. The witches alone would perform the ceremonies about the bonfires that would keep the demon fossa from invading the camp. The Usgar warriors feared little, but the fossa was at the top of that very short list. Removing it would steal much influence and prestige from the Coven, from the witches, and from Mairen.

"What a fool, that girl," Connebragh remarked, drawing Mairen from her thoughts. She looked up to see the other witch rolling the items over in her hands, eyeing them with intrigue—perhaps too much so. "Does she not know the beauty of Usgar? Why would she so destroy the blessed crystals?"

Mairen offered a weak little smile and a shrug in response, and, privately, was truly glad then that they had found the heresy upon the body of Aoleyn. To Mairen, Aoleyn's claims regarding the fossa were more troubling and more damning, but to Connebragh and all the others, these gemstones were the key, a sin visible to all. Whatever Tay Aillig might want for Aoleyn, the foolish young woman was now under Mairen's complete control.

She held out her hand and Connebragh handed over the five pieces of jewelry.

The damning evidence.

Now Mairen had to figure out if Aoleyn's claims about the fossa held any truth, and if so, to determine what she might do to mitigate the damage.

Certainly, it would have been better for Aoleyn if Tay Aillig had somehow killed the demon.

Perhaps he had, she reminded herself, fearing that he had used Aoleyn for just that purpose, and fearing more what that might mean for her.

Talmadge walked about Fasach Crann that late morning, taking in the sights and smells and noise of the place, wanting to burn it into his memory and use this warm familiarity to bury deeper the darker experiences he had known in this land.

Strangely, he thought, he didn't consider the events of the recent night on the mountain, when he had been captured, beaten, even stabbed, among those darkest moments. Talmadge was a frontiersman. He had known bloody fights and desperate situations. These were his expectations of the world, and so being brutalized by some deamhan Usgar tribesmen was not a shocking experience.

No, first there had been the incident with a man nicknamed Badger—Talmadge couldn't even remember his real name, and didn't care to try—where Talmadge had been nearly killed by a giant lizard and then had been forced to kill the man. That terrible day had stayed with Talmadge for a long time, and he vowed to never again take another person to this special and secret place called Loch Beag.

A stranger named Bryan Marrawee of Dundalis—at least, that's what the man had called himself—had helped Talmadge muster the nerve to return to these lands, and then a woman, the most special woman he had ever known, had convinced him to take her here with him.

And here, she had been killed.

That was the memory he now had to bury under the weight of normalcy. He loved Fasach Crann, and the smell of the autumn season in the foothills of Fireach Speuer.

The brutal events of his capture on the mountain, and his journey up the mountain with the strange woman, had intrigued him more than they had wounded him, not because of the capture, but because of the rescue, because of the Usgar lass who had shown such power, such compassion, such courage.

"Thank you," Talmadge whispered up the mountainside, to a woman he was sure he would never see again.

But now he had another problem. He had to get around the southern shores of the great lake, then up north a bit and past the village of Car Seileach before he would be on safer ground. The passes south of the lake were thick with Usgar, as he had learned the hard way the previous night, and the lake itself . . .

He didn't even want to look at Loch Beag, at the dark waters that hid a monster, a monster that had taken Khotai from him.

But then, how would he get back to the east, for the Matinee, the annual meet-up and celebration of all the men and women living in the frontier beyond the Wilderlands? How would he gather more skins and furs and jewels to trade, both in the Wilderlands to the east and then back here on the plateau around the lake? How would he live?

He pondered the notion of becoming a member of Fasach Crann. Would they have him, with his unaltered head, looking so much like a deamhan Usgar? And if he could never again muster the courage to go out on the water, what use might he be to the tribe, whose lifeblood was fishing?

No, it seemed an absurd proposition.

Talmadge meandered as he pondered and found himself by the dark waters of the huge lake. Yes, there was indeed a monster under those waters, one rarely seen, and whose only human victim in the last years, to anyone's knowledge, had been Khotai.

"There are more dangers from the bears and great cats and goblins back home," he told himself, and with a nod, he moved down the beach to an older villager who was tending a pair of smaller boats.

"Hail, Memmic," he said to the man, and put on a wide smile.

"And a fine day for yourself, Talmadge of the East," the man replied.

Talmadge smiled even wider at that reference, Talmadge of the East, a name tagged on him by an old gray-haired fellow and his balding friend, who used to sit by the lake and tease everyone who walked by with their long-practiced barbs. That was two decades ago, though, and both were gone now, but the nickname had stayed on, a fine reminder to Talmadge that these folks here in Fasach Crann considered him a friend. Again, he wondered if he might stay on here.

But not now.

"I seem to find myself without a boat," he said.

"Long walk, then," Memmic replied.

"I was hoping you might help me with that."

"Might. What have you to barter?"

Talmadge shifted on his feet a bit nervously. "Well, that's the problem, I fear. I brought little with me, had less after visiting Car Seileach, and lost even that along the way. I will be back next year, of course, and with jewelry and furs. First choice to Memmic, I offer."

The man snorted and went back to work on one of the craft. "You'll probably get killed and I'll be out the jewelry and my boat."

"I've been coming here for more than two decades," Talmadge protested.

"Not every year."

"True, but I will be back next . . ."

"And who's to say what dangers you might be finding, on the loch or about the loch, or in the east? If I'm giving you a boat on promise of a future payment, then I'm a fool."

"I . . ." Talmadge paused, really having little he could say in response to that.

"But," Memmic continued, "if I'm giving you a boat because you're Talmadge of the East, and a friend to me and the folk of Fasach Crann, then I'm no fool."

"But . . ." Talmadge paused in his counterpoint as he digested the response. "What?"

"I'm no fool," said Memmic. "Take that one." He pointed to a small boat, one very similar to the boat Talmadge and Khotai had been paddling when the loch monster rose up and attacked them.

Talmadge stared at the craft for a long while, mustering his nerve.

"I'll only take it as far as Car Seileach," he said, and Memmic nodded. "If it's still there when I return next year, I'll bring it back to you, and the added payment still holds."

"Were I worried about it, I'd tell you," said Memmic, and he went more diligently at his work, signaling Talmadge that there was no more that needed to be said.

Talmadge walked over and rolled the small boat, no more than a large canoe, really. He gathered up one of the two paddles and eased it down to the water's edge.

"Take the second one," Memmic told him. "Easy to lose a paddle, and hard to get to shore with just your hands."

Talmadge nodded and collected the second one, tossing it and his nearly empty pack into the boat. Again he paused, staring out at the huge and dark waters of Loch Beag, remembering all too vividly what lay beneath them.

The question loomed before him, like the dark waters of the lake. Was he going to allow his fear, that terrible memory, to dominate the rest of his days?

Which would win out here, his past or his future?

Talmadge blew a deep and steadying breath, and dragged the canoe out into the water. "I'll not forget your generosity, Memmic of Fasach Crann," he said, climbing in.

"Nor your friendship, Talmadge of the East," the middle-aged man called back to him.

Talmadge waved and put the paddle in the water, turning away from Fasach Crann, paddling due west.

He'd stay very close to the shore, he told himself, where he could see the bottom. It would be a longer journey than cutting a straight line to Car Seileach, which was more to the northwest.

Perhaps he'd dare that straight line on his return trip, he thought.

Or, more likely, not.

"She is secured?" Mairen asked when Connebragh joined her in her tent later that day.

"She is bound and naked on her floor, as you commanded," Connebragh replied. "There are no crystals in there."

Mairen glanced at her sidelong.

"No magic at all," Connebragh quickly assured her after the reminder that this strange young woman apparently didn't need the crystals.

Mairen looked over at a small table beside her bed, five pieces of magical jewelry resting upon it.

"Have you ever seen this before?" Connebragh asked.

"No."

"Perhaps there is some value . . ."

"No!" Mairen interrupted.

"How do we not know that Usgar didn't instruct Aoleyn in this new use?" the other witch argued. "You remember her test in the crystal caverns, when she not only survived, and not only kept her wits within that haunted place, but escaped up through Craos'a'diad, the very Mouth of Usgar! Why would the god have let her leave?"

Mairen didn't reply other than to simply stare at Connebragh.

"She claims that she destroyed the fossa," Connebragh said, lowering her voice and glancing around as she did as if she expected spies in every shadow.

"You gagged her?"

"As you ordered."

Mairen nodded. "You are to tell no one of that ridiculous tale."

"Aoleyn will . . ."

"Aoleyn will do as she is told, or she's to find a long fall in her very near future."

The threat spoke of Gavina, of course, but more directly, of the punishment for heretics: being thrown into Craos'a'diad.

"What will you do with those?" Connebragh asked, motioning with her chin toward the table and the jewelry.

"They go into the mouth of Usgar, the home of magic. They came from crystals, and so the god will make of them crystals once more." She paused and narrowed her eyes. "What will Usgar make of Aoleyn, I wonder?"

Connebragh's expression was not one of agreement, but more of surprise, horror, and even sadness.

"I did not say that we would throw her into the pit," Mairen said. "But she's made crimes against the god, and so she'll find punishment. She's not for the Coven, not ever. And ne'ermore will Aoleyn hold the blessed crystals in her hand. Such a waste, that. Her powers were undeniable, with few rivals. Threw it all aside, she did, for the love of her own image."

"She claims to have killed . . ."

Connebragh's voice faltered before a withering gaze.

"She did'no kill the demon fossa, and if you think other, then the next time Iseabal shows her bloody face, I'll invite you to wander Fireach Speuer and call to the beast."

Connebragh lowered her gaze.

"Has the Usgar-laoch returned?" Mairen asked, and Connebragh shook her head.

"What do you mean to do with the girl?" Connebragh dared inquire. "Are we to keep her bound and under the eyes of the warriors? I doubt Tay Aillig will be pleased by that."

"This is not about Tay Aillig!" Mairen scolded. "Aoleyn's crimes are against Usgar, and so against the Coven, and so against me."

"But she'll not face a throw into Craos'a'diad?"

Mairen thought it over and shook her head. "No," she said, thinking the young woman's crimes did not rise to that level. Surely, she wanted to throw Aoleyn into the pit, though. Aoleyn was Tay Aillig's wife, and so shared a bed that should be for Mairen alone. But Mairen understood the Usgar-laoch well enough to realize that he'd never forgive such an action. It was going to be hard enough to soothe the fiery man over Aoleyn's ban from entering the Coven—he was counting on the young woman's prowess with the magic of Usgar to carry him to great victories on the battlefield. He had watched her with Brayth, using the wedstone to establish a spiritual link with the man, then enacting powerful magics to lead him to great victories over the sidhe, and to nearly escape the demon fossa itself.

That was it, Mairen knew. On that field and through Brayth, Aoleyn had seen the fossa and had magically, intimately, battled the fossa. The Usgar-righinn had forgotten, but now that she considered it, Aoleyn's claim of defeating the demon carried more credibility.

"Go and free her," Mairen instructed. "But remain with her, wherever she goes. She is to touch no blessed crystals. Stop her with any means you can, should she try, even if you kill the fool."

Connebragh nodded.

"And keep the guards beside you both," Mairen went on. "Two strong warriors, but not with crystal-tipped spears." When Connebragh's eyebrows arched at that, the Crystal Maven explained, "Aoleyn might access that magic."

Connebragh sucked in her breath at the stark reminder.

"Do'no e'er think too little of that one," Mairen warned. "Else she'll melt the skin from your face."

She waved her hand then, and the younger woman turned and started to leave. Before Connebragh had even exited the tent, Mairen was moving toward a small chest she kept under her bed, one that held her private collection of magical crystals.

Yes, she thought, it was indeed possible that Aoleyn had destroyed the demon fossa, and had thus upset the order of things in dangerous ways.

Mairen found a crystal thick with gray. The wedstone, the most holy of Usgar's gifts, and one full of powerful tricks that could only be accessed by the greatest witches.

Clutching the crystal to her chest, Mairen let her thoughts and heart filter into the magic. She heard the music of Usgar, the magical vibrations within the item, and it made her warm. The powerful witch let her thoughts flow freely, let her spirit escape, and threw herself wholly into the magical item, filtering into it, becoming one with it, as if making love to it.

It beckoned her as she awakened its greatest power, pulling her spirit from her body and setting it free.

Unbound in the room, Mairen looked back upon herself, sitting and cradling the crystal, and saw there a bright light, calling her back to her physical form. But not now. Not yet.

Unseen, the ghost glided out of the tent and willed herself upon the winds of the spirit world through the encampment. She paused and turned, moving right through the side of the tent Aoleyn shared with Tay Aillig.

The troublesome young woman sat on her bed now, naked, but wrapped in a blanket, and rubbing her wrists where the bindings had been. Connebragh sat across from her, flanked by two warriors.

Aoleyn stretched out her shoulders and craned her neck, then suddenly turned to face the area where Mairen's ghost lingered, staring curiously.

Suddenly, the Crystal Maven felt more naked than her prisoner! Could Aoleyn somehow see her, or sense her presence?

No, it was impossible.

Despite her denial, the Crystal Maven backed out of the tent and was fast across the encampment and out onto the mountain. She wasn't held to the ground, so she floated up higher, looking down from above, soaring this way and that in her search for the Usgar-laoch. Free from her mortal coil, far and wide she flew, to all the haunts where Tay Aillig might be. She passed the cliff where Gavina had fallen to her death, the ledge where Tay Aillig had taken her so forcefully.

She lingered there, basking in the beauty of that memory, for she indeed loved the powerful man.

She went up to the winter encampment and saw Elder Raibert, the Usgar-forfach, preparing for a hike—down to the summer camp, she presumed. She passed over the pine grove and the sacred meadow known as Dail Usgar, the lea containing the great Crystal God, the physical manifestation of Usgar's magic, a shaft of godly power angled from the ground like a giant cock.

Flying up th'Way toward Craos'a'diad, Mairen spotted the uamhas slave at his work, his muscles thick and strong from the labor as he carved out step after step in this difficult stony incline. Mairen took great care to stay far away from him—the danger of spirit walking was the temptation of possession. Too near, and she might enter this uamhas's body and take command of it, but such was rarely a good thing, and always a dangerous ploy.

At the top of Fireach Speuer, even above Craos'a'diad, she found no sign of Tay Aillig, so down the side of the mountain she flew, soaring above the miles of stony vales and huddles of trees. She spotted some warriors, Usgar warriors, moving along a trail, and noted that they carried with them a body.

For a moment, Mairen despaired, but no, it was not Tay Aillig. It was Ralid, and these men, led by Egard, Tay Aillig's nephew, had been sent to find and retrieve him.

She moved past them down the mountain, again offering a wide berth.

In a clearing farther down the mountain, she found her lover. He walked about, bending low to study tracks, to sniff the blood, to watch a flock of buzzards attacking a pile of gore.

He carried a spear that Mairen knew well, one whose tip she had empowered before, one thick with green and gray flecks.

Her spirit went to him tentatively, calling to him silently, spiritually.

Aoleyn has returned, she imparted to him when she had joined. She could feel his revulsion, a natural reaction to the shock of having another will enter your body and mind.

"Mairen?" he asked aloud, and she heard his silent scream more profoundly: *Get out!*

You must hear me, she implored. *I will not stay! But Aoleyn has returned and she claims that she destroyed the demon fossa.*

Get out! his thoughts screamed, and she felt him fighting her, battling with all of his considerable willpower.

Mairen tried to silently converse with him, but he was too frantic, too desperate, and simply fighting too hard.

The Crystal Maven turned her power outward, surrendering control of the body for just a moment, just long enough for her to evoke the magic in Tay Aillig's spear tip.

A flash of lightning sent him flying. Mairen felt the jolt as well, since she was in the body, but unlike the host, she was prepared for it.

It may be true, she imparted stubbornly, and quickly, before Tay Aillig could regain his sensibilities and put up a wall of anger against her. *We can'no know with that girl. Foolish girl! Come back to camp with a trophy, Usgar-laoch. Take a creature, burn its head. If the fossa is destroyed . . .*

Something happened then, something Mairen could not have foreseen. Her connection was broken, shattered, and she was flung from the physical coil of Tay Aillig. Flung away, too, were her senses, and she floated on those spiritual winds helplessly for what seemed an eternity.

She didn't know where she was. She didn't know who she was!

As she regained her very identity, it seemed to her as if something had simply ended the magic that allowed her possession. She felt like a deer on the butcher's table, her head suddenly chopped off.

And she felt the magic fading from her, and understood then the grave danger.

Up the mountain she flew, with all speed and determination, but, as if in a dream, her journey seemed sluggish. She needed speed, but couldn't find any, as the magic withered, and when it died away altogether, she realized, she would be left out here, trapped as an unbound spirit and so . . . dead.

She saw the pinpoint of light ahead of her, far away, a brighter speck on a bright day, and she dove for it for all her life, needing to get back into her body before the magic faded altogether.

She came into her form and shuddered, stumbled, and fell to the floor.

"Mairen?" she heard, Connebragh's voice. She felt the woman's hands upon her, turning her over gently. "My Usgar-righinn, what is wrong?"

"It broke the magic," Mairen struggled to explain.

"Usgar-righinn?"

"It was like he chopped my head off."

Connebragh fell back a bit, staring at her, clearly at a loss.

Mairen wanted to explain it to her, but alas, Mairen didn't understand it either. She had been forcefully expelled from Tay Aillig's corporeal form, hurled out and away. But it hadn't been a battle of willpower that had defeated her possession—she had experienced such battles before.

This . . . this was different. The chords of magic itself had been cut, chopped off, expelling Mairen and nearly leaving her stranded outside of her body. She couldn't be certain of what that might have meant, but she suspected that her spiritual wandering would have been eternal, helplessly so.

She took Connebragh's hand and let the woman help her to her feet.

"Aoleyn is secure?" Mairen asked shakily.

Connebragh nodded. "She offers no resistance."

"Because she is broken," Mairen said, and hoped it was true.

Tay Aillig was still sitting on the ground, still trying to digest all that had happened. In his hand, he held a small stone, a sunstone, the gem of anti-magic.

Now that he had a moment to catch his breath, he wondered if he had been wise in waging this last battle. It was Mairen who had come to him, he realized then, though in the confusion and panic of possession, he had not even considered that possibility.

He rolled the small round sunstone over in his fingers.

He looked to his spear, lying on the ground to the side.

The Usgar-laoch gave a little laugh, silently congratulating Mairen on evoking the lightning magic of that spear tip. The jolt had defeated him.

Only then did Tay Aillig more clearly decipher the last message Mairen had imparted to him before he had used the sunstone to throw her out.

"What have you done?" he whispered to the empty clearing, though he aimed the question at Aoleyn.

A myriad of possibilities swirled before him as he replayed that last message in his mind over and over again. What gains might he find?

The days on the lake had not settled poor Talmadge as much as he had hoped. Still, he paddled right along the shoreline, which in some areas, like the swampy cove he had recently left behind, was actually more dangerous than the open waters of Loch Beag. Oh yes, the monster was out there in the deep, but monsters were in here, too! The clo'dearche lizards could kill him, certainly, and the swamp grasses teemed with venomous snakes and giant serpents that could enwrap a man, squeeze the life from him, then swallow him whole.

Talmadge could deal with those more normal creatures. The lake monster to him had become something more, something sinister, something beyond comprehension, almost godly.

He was glad when he at last came in sight of the groves of low willows that sheltered Car Seileach and gave the village its name. He could travel on land from this point forward, he knew, far from the hunting parties of Usgar.

He put in at the village beach and dragged his canoe onto the shore. The people here knew him, and greeted him warmly—and indeed, more came rushing to see him than Talmadge ever remembered before.

And they talked to him, or at him, many all at once.

"He is one of you," he heard.

"Of the east," another insisted.

Talmadge finally managed to calm them all enough to get a simple question in: "Who?"

"The man of the sun!" several said all at once, both excitedly and fearfully.

3

THE OBEDIENT BOY

U'at walked his cuetzpali, Huetwiliz, up the side of a boulder tumble, the lizard's padded feet securely sticking to the rocks at every angle. Often called collared dragons, these huge lizards served as mounts to the mundunugu, the elite cavalry of xoconai armies. Cuetzpali were docile creatures, as long as they were well fed, and easily controlled mounts, but when hungry, or when in battle, they were fearsome indeed, with claws on their forelegs that could rip an opponent apart and a mouth full of small teeth but with a bite strong enough to crush the thickest bones.

Cresting the top boulder in the high tumble took U'at's breath away.

He had summited the highest peak of Teotl Tenamitl, far east in the great range, and now the Ayuskixmal fell away before him, and the vast eastern lands beyond that. So different was this view from the one he had left behind, from the high peaks to the west and looking west. There before him down the western slopes lay the basin of Tonoloya, the nation of xoconai, their many cities shining gold in the lowering sun. There, he could see the great ocean far upon the horizon, but here there was no ocean, just land as far as he could see. Land far, far below him, as the slopes of the mountain range dove more steeply.

After taking in the view for many heartbeats, he walked his lizard a bit to the side and forward, to peer around one ridge, and once more U'at lost his breath. For there, far below, in the shadow of this mountain, lay a great rectangular lake, lined and hemmed by mountains all about.

"*Tzatzini*," he whispered reverently, wondering if he was truly standing atop that most sacred mountain. Could it be?

Tzatzini, or The Herald, was the mountain home of U'at's god, the Glorious Gold, and if this was truly that place, then the lake below . . .

"*Otontotomi*," U'at whispered with equal reverence. Was it possible that he was looking down at the ancient and most holy place in the long history of the xoconai? That he was even now walking the trails of the mountain home of his god?

Almost in a daze, so overwhelmed that his hands were shaking, he tried to turn Huetwiliz aside, toward a cave where he could leave the well-trained mount that he might more intimately explore this remarkable place. Finally, U'at gave up, dismounted, and walked the lizard into the shallow cave.

Overwhelmed still, U'at walked out of the cave and down the side of the mountain as if in a dream. Spear in hand, he set off on foot to see, to learn, to hunt.

He brought the makeshift hammer—just a stone wrapped to a stick with vines, and not one done with great care—down hard on the wedge, the one piece of metal the Usgar had given him. He was tired, though, and his angle was wrong. The stone head chipped when it clipped the edge of the wedge, then skipped down the side to hit him on the hand.

Bahdlahn cried out and dropped the tools, seeing that the hammer had come apart with the blow. He grabbed reflexively at his injured hand, only then realizing that the chipped stone had flown into his eye.

The strong young man, barely more than a boy, rolled to the side of the path, grimacing and growling, cursing the hammer, cursing the work, cursing the Usgar, and cursing life itself. Finally, he settled down and lay there on his back, staring up at the stars and the silvery moon coming up over the side of the mountain.

How long had he been working on this trail, the place the Usgar called th'Way? He had lost track of the days. A month? Two? How many stairs had he cut and carved in the stone and hard earth? How many logs had he shaped and placed to bolster the edges and keep the earth from washing away?

He imagined the trail behind him, leading all the way down to the hidey-hole he used when resting. The newer stairs were better than the first ones he had worked, as he perfected his technique.

"Or am I a fool?" he said, rolling up on one elbow to glance down the trail. "The deamhans will see the new steps and just make me go back and make the first ones better."

He gave a little laugh, so helpless. This was hard work, but was it worse than being down in the camp? At least up here, he didn't have to suffer the insults and taunts of the Usgar on a daily basis—in fact, he hardly saw the monsters.

He looked down at his bruised and bloody hand. It wasn't so bad, he thought, and noted, too, the clear definition in the tight muscles of his forearm. He was no more a boy, obviously, and had grown into a tall and strong man. The last weeks up here on the mountain, lifting stones and logs, wielding a heavy hammer incessantly, had tightened and thickened his muscles.

The Usgar thought him a stupid man, a true simpleton. That was the only reason he had been allowed to live into adulthood.

Bahdlahn sat up, clutching his hand and rubbing his eye with his bent wrist at the same time. He looked back down the mountain, back toward the Usgar summer encampment, though it was not in sight from this vantage point.

His mother was down there. His dear mother, Innevah, who had told him that he was stupid from his earliest days, and for his own good. Her cleverness was the only reason he was alive.

"All my love," he whispered to the mountain winds, and dared believe that the breezes would carry his words to Innevah's ears.

The pain in his hand hadn't brought tears to Bahdlahn's blue eyes. The stone chip had made one eye water, but no tears of pain or sorrow.

He could not say that of his reaction to thinking of his mother, down there on the mountain with the Usgar deamhans, suffering their crimes and injustices and humiliation.

He wanted to kill them. How he wanted to kill all of them!

But no, not all, the young man thought, and despite his pain and anger, and all the terrible things in his life, he smiled then and thought of her, that small woman with the black hair and black eyes who had grown up beside him and been so kind to him, who promised that she would not let Tay Aillig or the other Usgar kill him.

"Aoleyn," he whispered to the wind, and just speaking the word made him feel warm and comforted.

A while later, Bahdlahn sighed and turned his attention to his newest wound. It wasn't too bad, he believed. Perhaps a broken finger, and a painful gash where the hammer had removed a bit of his thumbnail. It would be okay soon enough, but was swollen now.

Bahdlahn gave another sigh. The day had been warm, so he had decided to spend most of it in his hidey-hole, figuring to work through the night. He certainly didn't want to fall behind now. The Usgar had been up here recently, and they had surely marked his progress. If they returned soon and noted that he had barely moved forward on their all-important stairway . . .

Another sigh escaped Bahdlahn. "I grow tired of your threats, Usgar," he whispered, and decided then to retreat to his den and sleep the rest of the night through.

Dark thoughts followed him down the path, one that he knew so well now that he skipped it easily, even in the moonlight, even when a cloud passed above, blocking the moonlight. By the time he arrived, the first glow of dawn had come to the northwestern slopes of Fireach Speuer, though the sun was still long from climbing the sky behind the mountain.

Bahdlahn had only seen eighteen winters, and doubted he'd see another five. The Usgar would not suffer him to live out his life, he was certain, and if they ever realized that he was not stupid, that he was not a simpleton, that he could plot to hurt them, or to run away, and might just do it, they would murder him.

"One day," he muttered, his litany against hopelessness. One day, he would collect his mother and escape, would carry her down the mountain to this lake town he did not know, Fasach Crann, which had been her home, from which she had been dragged by the deamhan Usgar with her belly fat with Bahdlahn.

"Bahdlahn," he whispered when he reached his natural shelter, and he smiled as he considered the name. He had been called "Thump." Just Thump, when he was young, a name aimed as an insult by the Usgar. They still called him that, all of them. Except for one, except for beautiful Aoleyn. To her, he was Bahdlahn, a word for the thundering hooves of a running deer, a graceful name meant not to insult, but to exalt.

The image of the woman filled his head as he crawled inside—he kept her with him as often as he could, in his thoughts and in his heart.

He moved through the tangled entry area to his sleeping hole.

He even started to crawl into it before he realized that it was not empty! He thought it a man, an Usgar, but suddenly then a fine spear set with an intricate and wide barbed tip reached out and stabbed at his face.

Flames ate the fur from the head of the dead creature.

Tay Aillig watched it carefully, turning it so that all the skin would turn a bright red, but not letting it burn too much so that it would obviously be the work of a fire. The bloat and carrion birds had done quite the mutilation on the bear's head already.

What good fortune that the uamhas scavengers had left the head behind.

Tay Aillig still wasn't sure what Mairen's spiritual intrusion into his thoughts was fully about. He wasn't even sure that he was following her instructions, or to what end. Mairen had told him to take a trophy, and to disfigure it, he believed.

She was going to try to claim his kill, this piece of carrion, as the dead demon fossa. To steal the glory of the act from Aoleyn?

He didn't know, and didn't believe for a moment that Aoleyn had actually defeated the great demon that had haunted Fireach Speuer from a time beyond the oldest memories of the oldest Usgar. But whatever madness he might find when he returned to the camp, he would trust that Mairen, ever the clever woman, would put things in the best light.

He had nothing to lose by following her instructions—if the situation became awkward, he could always claim the mutilated head to be that of an ordinary bear, after all.

He brought the water in the bark-lined hole he had dug to a boil, then eased part of the bear's severed head into it. He had made the right cuts in the skin and skull—were there any wrong cuts, after all? He wasn't trying to make it look like anything, for what Usgar alive could give a good description of the demon fossa?

He was just trying to make it look less like a bear, to instill some doubt, and shrinking this part of the snout, or warping it at least, should do that, as well as making its considerable teeth seem even larger.

The Usgar-laoch glanced up at the mountain, wholly in twilight gloom now, with the sun beyond the horizon past the waters of the lake. He would stay here this night, he decided, and he hoped that some uamhas would arrive to claim more of the prize, or perhaps return thinking that Ralid's body was still here.

Were that the case, he would enter the Usgar encampment with more trophies than the head of a dead bear.

Quick reactions alone saved Bahdlahn in that first moment of battle. He ducked his head and threw himself aside reflexively, and the thrusting spear did not catch him in the face, but got his right shoulder instead.

He felt the bite of the weapon, but the angle of the attacker was all wrong and it didn't sink in too deeply—he hoped. He clutched at the wound as he rolled back onto the path, th'Way, and felt the warmth his own blood on his hand.

He thought to come up to his feet and sprint away, but by the time he managed to stand, the man, or goblin, or creature—whatever it might be—was out of the hidey-hole and facing him, that bloody spear in hand.

It was taller than tall Bahdlahn, but much thinner, with tightly corded muscles showing under its strange clothing: fine fabric, black leather vest and strips about its bare arms, and what seemed to be a breastplate of wooden armor, a line of thin and small dark green branches or sapling trunks tied in a row down to its waist. Even in the dimness of the early-morning light, the golden color of its skin beneath the halo of thick gray hair was striking, but not nearly as much as the markings running down the center of the creature's face, where its flat and wide nose shone a brilliant red, abruptly shifting to flanks of pure blue, like the shallower waters of Loch Beag under an afternoon sun. Bahdlahn thought it a sidhe, a mountain goblin, one painted, perhaps. He had seen several of the monsters after a battle, when the Usgar warriors had carried some carcasses to the camp as trophies. This opponent did not look like them, though, other than its basically human form. The mountain goblins exuded crudity and brute force, but this creature moved with grace, and wore clothing superbly and intricately stitched—finer than the Usgar, even. Its nose was not long and crooked, but flat and wide, and its ears more resembled that of a human than a goblin.

"Lakeman?" he asked, for though it didn't seem human, it was much more so than the monsters the tribes called sidhe.

In response, the creature, or man, leaped at him, stabbing hard, and only good luck saved Bahdlahn from getting skewered by that surprisingly quick attack. For as he started to dodge, he rolled his ankle and pitched over sideways, tumbling down the decline of th'Way, which was steep enough at that point to put enough ground between him and the attacker for him to regain his footing.

Perhaps he should use the other language, the lakeman language his mother had taught him. He considered, but only briefly, for he had no time, as his opponent came on fiercely, stabbing repeatedly and driving him backward.

He started to turn and flee, but reconsidered immediately, having no idea of how fast this creature might be, or how well it might throw that spear, which was truly beautiful in design and would fly a long, long way. Would he take a few retreating steps, only to catch that deadly missile in the back?

Legs wide for balance, hands up beside his shoulders and wide, ready to strike, Bahdlahn danced around, side to side, trying to present no easy target.

The creature curled back its lips, revealing a set of shining white teeth, with fangs top and bottom. Not human teeth, surely, but they seemed too clean and straight and delicate for the mouths of the sidhe. No, these appeared more like those of the monkeys that the Usgar hunters sometimes brought back from their hunts.

"Don't get in close," Bahdlahn whispered to himself, not wanting to get bitten by that formidable maw.

But his own words rang hollow. Bahdlahn was no trained fighter, and he didn't know what to do!

His opponent stabbed straight for his gut. He threw his left arm across to slap the spear aside, at the same time throwing back his hips and sucking in his belly. He did manage to push the weapon off to his right, but his attacker stepped forward and bent low, surprisingly, turning with the blade. Before the unskilled Bahdlahn could understand the movement, the attacker came up fast, leading with its right elbow, which slammed Bahdlahn in the face, and sent him staggering back a step. Around and over went the creature, bringing its left hand, still holding the spear, in hard for a follow-up punch, and when Bahdlahn, hardly able to see and sort out the flurry of movement before him, tried to slap and punch to drive his opponent back, he hit nothing solidly. For his opponent was already falling back, leaping and straightening. It slipped its hands down to the base of the spear's shaft and swung it across down low like a cudgel, not a spear.

A cudgel with a sharp end, Bahdlahn realized as it strafed across his shins, cutting a long line across his trousers and his skin, both legs.

Stung, but not crippled, Bahdlahn fell back and straightened once more. His shoulder burned, as did both legs, and he tasted the blood flowing from his nose.

He didn't know what to do. He knew he couldn't fight this . . . whatever it was! He had often heard the Usgar warriors demeaning the mountain goblins, calling them weak and feeble, and unimpressive foes. Most of that was likely simple boasting, he understood, for if this warrior before him was indeed a sidhe, it was none of those things, its movements fluid and fast, and nothing weak about it.

Bahdlahn had to run. He knew the creature would cut him down with its spear, but he had to hope that it would miss that one throw, and that it couldn't catch him.

He started to turn, but found himself leaping instead, throwing himself into a dive to the other side of th'Way to avoid a sudden and ferocious charge and thrust, almost as if his opponent had read his mind and guessed his intent.

His eyes had tipped the creature off to his plan, he thought, but fleet-ingly, for he had no time to consider anything. He had to get up from his dive and roll. The creature was certainly pursuing and would have him easily if he lay on the ground!

He clawed at the ground as he tried to rise, his hand closing on a stone.

Bahdlahn was a very strong young man, but he didn't know how to fight. He had no knowledge at all of weapons, or of using footwork to gain lever-age on an opponent.

But there was one thing he could do, one thing he had learned quite keenly from his weeks up here clearing th'Way. One thing he had done a thousand times a day, every day.

Bahdlahn could throw.

He came around, falling back as fast as he could, managing to get one foot under him, to press him upright and further back.

His opponent smiled toothily, white teeth shining in the midst of that bright red central patch of skin. In no apparent hurry, and clearly with great confidence, it stalked in for the kill.

Bahdlahn pegged a stone into its chest.

It cracked loudly against the wooden armor and his opponent, as surprised as hurt, stumbled backward.

Bahdlahn was near his hidey-hole, near the place where he kept many small stones he had saved to use in propping and securing logs along th'Way.

He dropped low to grab at his cache, and came up throwing, firing missile after missile at the creature.

He clipped its skull with one, hit it about the chest and torso with others, cracked some against blocking arms, drawing gasps and "oofs" and shrieks of surprise and pain.

Bahdlahn nearly fell down to his knees and cried in relief when his obviously superior opponent turned and fled, leaping and sprinting up th'Way.

But Bahdlahn knew better than to let up, and he kept the barrage flying, even giving chase for a short way, until the creature broke off the path and leaped through some brush, which sent it on a long tumble down a grassy slope.

Bahdlahn threw one last stone and stood at the hedgerow, watching the creature regain its footing, far below, and disappear into the cover of some small trees and rocks.

"What do I do?" the young man asked himself, shaking his head, completely at a loss.

The question was answered for him, though, as the rush of battle faded and the wound in his shoulder, torn wider by his repeated throwing, sent him down to the ground in pain.

U'at was confident that he could have killed the human—it had to be a human, he believed. But he was mundunugu, riding at the command of an augur who served the old augur they had named the Last Augur of Darkness.

U'at and the other followers of that particular augur were not numerous—the old one was considered crazy and foolish in most xoconai circles. And his followers were often derided as fools for listening to his ranting about old traditions cast aside and the weak ways of the modern xoconai. Thus, this mission was critical. The day of the prophecy fast approached. If the old one was wrong, his interpretations erroneous, then U'at might find his path forward very different from that which he hoped.

His head had been filled with visions of great Tonoloya, an empire so vast that xoconai would see the sun climb out of the waters of Ilhuicaatl, the Great and One Ocean, each morning, and slip back beneath the waters in the west at day's end.

He loved the old augur. He so desperately wanted the prophecy to be correct, the vision fulfilled, the Glorious Gold returned.

If that was to be, then this place, if it was Tzatzini, would command the empire of the xoconai.

If this was Tzatzini, then U'at was the first xoconai to stand upon it in more than fifteen centuries, more than seventy generations—seventy-seven, if the old augur had correctly fashioned his prophecy.

With all of that at stake, U'at simply could not take the risk. He believed that he could have defeated the human, yes, but he took great faith that his spears and macana club would be stained with human blood soon enough.

4

UNCOVERED

She sat on the ground somewhere within the grove where the Usgar kept their slaves, her arms bound behind her to the trunk of a pine tree. Aoleyn was sure the uamhas, like Bahdlahn's mother Innevah, could hear her whimpering, and could hear the sharp questions her interrogators were hurling at her—but of course, since uamhas were considered no more than animals, Mairen and Connebragh didn't likely care.

The poor young woman could barely breathe through the cloth gag they had tied so tightly, let alone answer the questions. But those questions kept coming anyway, fast and sharp, and often followed by a slap or even a knee into her armpit.

"You stole crystals!" Mairen shouted in her face. "From where?"

"Where did you get those wounds?" Connebragh demanded before Mairen had even finished speaking—a tremendous breach in protocol that again reminded Aoleyn that this part of the interrogation wasn't really about gathering information.

They didn't want her to answer.

"Where did you get these?" Mairen demanded, holding up the three pieces of jewelry she had taken from Aoleyn. "How did you get these?"

"And where are the others?" Connebragh added. "The wedstone crystal?

You were wounded, but now are healed! Do not lie. The tender skin is clear to see."

She smacked Aoleyn across the face.

It went on and on—to Aoleyn, it seemed like half the day. They kept coming at her with questions and sneers and threats and slaps. Aoleyn had struggled against her bindings at first, and had tried to work her head and mouth to dislodge the suffocating gag, but to no avail—she had been bound by Usgar warriors, expert in handling slaves. She had even tried to reach out to the crystals and her gemstone jewelry which Mairen held— she could hear the vibrations of the magic, the song of Usgar.

But to no avail. She was battered and exhausted, and the Usgar-righinn held her own magic, too, and would allow no such connection.

It took the poor young woman some time to realize that only Connebragh was now battering her, both with questions and physically. She couldn't even see Mairen—had the Usgar-righinn left the natural chamber, its walls the drooping branches of the pine to which Aoleyn was tied?

If only she could speak! Connebragh was closer to her age, and she had never known the woman to be hateful. Seonagh had trained Connebragh not long before she had tutored Aoleyn, and had spoken highly of Connebragh's character. On the night of Aoleyn's testing in the crystal caverns, she was certain, Connebragh had been hoping for her to succeed. She was certain that the woman, as brutal as she was now being, would truly listen to her side of the tale.

But no, she could not speak, and could not interrupt the continuing verbal and physical barrage. On and on it went, and Aoleyn could hardly keep her head up, and forgot her earlier warnings to herself about why these two were treating her in this manner.

She had anticipated what might come when they exhausted her, but now, exhausted, she had all but forgotten, and so when Mairen was there, so suddenly, Aoleyn was caught completely off her guard.

Because Mairen wasn't beside her.

Mairen was inside her.

Connebragh's questions kept coming, and Aoleyn tried to ignore them. But she couldn't ignore them, not wholly, not in her thoughts, and so images swirled and memories lit up.

And Mairen was in there, exploring.

Aoleyn saw through the eyes of a bear, and sensed the confusion of the intruder. A paw swatted, breaking a man—Ralid—and throwing him. She turned from that thought as quickly as she could, and she was other animals, then, like a bird flying along the mountainside . . .

She felt Mairen's delighted disdain.

Aoleyn knew she was doomed.

The warriors who had ventured down the mountain walked back into the Usgar encampment that same night, faces grim, with Egard carrying the body of Ralid over his shoulder.

Gasps and wails and empty stares followed their every step, with many Usgar being swept up in their wake as Egard led them to the tent of the Usgar-laoch.

"Tay Aillig is not here," one man told Egard. "He left earlier this day."

"To gather Elder Raibert," another offered, though there seemed disagreement on that matter.

Egard didn't really care about the details at that point, as his entire action this day had been orchestrated wholly by Tay Aillig, and neither he nor the Usgar-laoch held any surprise as to the fate of Ralid.

"Where is Tay Aillig's wife?" Egard asked sharply, ending the budding debate.

The gathered Usgar turned their heads as one toward the pine grove off to the side of the encampment, where the uamhas were kept.

"With the Usgar-righinn," a man said.

"A prisoner of the Usgar-righinn," another added.

Egard nodded, then looked to his men and motioned for them to stay quiet. He wasn't sure how to proceed here, but he really didn't like the idea of showing his evidence against Aoleyn to the Usgar-righinn without Tay Aillig present. The Crystal Maven didn't particularly like him, he believed—but then again, as far as he could tell, Mairen didn't particularly like any man.

"We will wait," he decided, and he squatted down right there, in front of Tay Aillig's tent, laying Ralid on the ground. He motioned to some women to come and gather the fallen warrior, to prepare him for a proper farewell.

The Mouth of God, Craos'a'diad . . . high on the mountain, near the peak, looking down on the Usgar winter encampment.

Tents there. Tents? Surely, there could be no tents, with the wind and the cold . . .

Mairen's spirit fell back inside her own thoughts for a moment to sort it out. This was a mental construct, a structure of comfort. An odd choice for Aoleyn, she thought, truly so, given that this place was a sacrificial pit more than anything else. A place where heretics were thrown. She understood why Aoleyn might be imagining that place at this time, but as a source of comfort? A place with shelter?

No, not literal tents, of course, Mairen suddenly realized. These were containers, for memories, thoughts, emotions. The Usgar-righinn charged back into her victim, rushed for the tents, tore open a figurative flap.

A needle, dark gray, pressed against the belly of a young woman . . . blood, but healing immediately . . .

"How did you get the wedstone from the crystal?" Mairen asked aloud when she realized the composition of the needle itself.

Her verbal prod had her victim looking down at a crystal in her hands, in her memories.

But the tent flap swept shut, and Mairen growled in anger.

Another tent loomed before her . . . an owl flew silently over the Usgar encampment . . . a woman rushed out of a tent . . . uamhas . . .

A tent . . . an actual Usgar tent . . . a tent Mairen knew!

The owl again, watching . . . a witch, a friend, stumbling from the tent . . . a serpent . . . cries of pain . . . death!

"Caia!" Mairen cried aloud. "You knew!"

The enraged spirit of the Usgar-righinn no longer probed, nay, but attacked, tearing at the tent flaps, ripping and scrambling the pieces. She didn't want information now, she simply wanted to destroy, to kill.

Her victim fought back, terrifically, but it would not be enough, and Mairen was glad that they had exhausted and weakened this powerful young woman.

This young woman she would now utterly destroy.

Mairen flashed back into her own body, suddenly and violently, and so shockingly that her form went tumbling, losing its grip on Aoleyn and falling to the floor. At first, she thought her victim dead, then, when Aoleyn groaned, considered that the young woman had found the strength to expel her.

No, she realized, when she looked across the way to see Connebragh holding the gray-flecked crystal, the source of Mairen's spirit-walking and possession.

"You dare?" the Usgar-righinn roared.

Connebragh shrank back, but shook her head in defiance. "Look at her," she said, her voice barely a whisper. "You are killing her."

"I will kill her!" Mairen shouted.

"No, not like this," Connebragh argued, her tone uncharacteristically harsh and defiant. She shook her head vigorously and spun to the side, clutching the crystal defensively against her torso as Mairen slowly rose and began to approach. "This is not the will of Usgar. This is not our tradition. The tribe will not accept it. Aoleyn's husband, the Usgar-laoch, will never accept it."

That last sentence stopped Mairen in her tracks, for indeed, it rang with truth. Tay Aillig would never forgive her for destroying Aoleyn without his agreement, and privately, which was simply unprecedented and against Usgar tradition. They had a way to execute heretics, after all, and it was one that fed Usgar and so blessed the tribe.

She turned instead to Aoleyn and slapped her across the face, just once, releasing all of her anger with that single blow. Then she bent low and stared into the glazed eyes of the disoriented young woman.

"I know what you did," she said into Aoleyn's face. "And I know what the uamhas did to Caia, because you know, and knew, and said nothing."

Aoleyn seemed to focus on Mairen's face then, but whether she fully understood or not, the Usgar-righinn could not tell.

"Connebragh, gather the guards," Mairen ordered.

Mairen continued to stare, even when the two men entered a few moments later.

"Aoleyn's clothes?" one of the men asked, holding forth a dirty shift.

"None. Let her show herself in all her shame," Mairen replied. "But you and your partner can go ahead of us, and speckle the way from the trees to the center of the camp with splinters and sharp stones."

"Usgar-righinn?" the surprised man asked.

But Mairen was talking to Aoleyn then, and focused to the point where she didn't even hear the question. "You will crawl, dear," she promised. "All the way to the middle of the camp, naked for all to see. Nowhere to hide, girl. Nowhere to hide. Filthy and bloody, and they will spit on you, every bit of the way, and laugh at your tears of pain and shame. And I'll tell them to throw small stones, and throw shit, if they so please. Oh, but I will! You deserve every humiliation, and I'll see you get it."

To the side, Connebragh gasped at the severity of Mairen's judgment.

She had sent Connebragh ahead, Aoleyn knew, because she wanted the pleasure of this painful humiliation firsthand.

Mairen untied Aoleyn and pushed her to the ground. Hungry, weak, and beaten, both physically and mentally, the young woman offered no resistance. How could she?

"Crawl," the Usgar-righinn ordered.

Aoleyn turned her head to look up over her shoulder at the older woman, whose features seemed sharp in the low and harsh light from the diamond-flecked magical crystal. Aoleyn considered that for just a heartbeat—and got a kick in the ribs for her hesitance.

So, she crawled, with Mairen guiding her, prodding her. She pressed through the low-hanging pine branches and out into the open. Night had fallen, but the moon was still nearly full, though silver now and not covered by the bloody face of Iseabal.

A large bonfire roared in the encampment not far away to the west—Connebragh's doing, Aoleyn knew. Mairen had called for bright light in the camp, because Mairen wanted everyone to witness this.

Aoleyn crawled, now upon the path the sentries had made of sharp stones and splinters. They bit at her knees like angry little bugs, and her hand got especially pinched on one movement, and began to bleed.

But though she grunted a few times, the young woman refused to cry out in pain, and though she knew that all manner of ugliness would befall her, likely even an execution, she was determined that she would not cry, and stifled her sniffles and blinked back her tears.

As she drew closer, she realized that the whole of the tribe was out and about that bonfire, all taunting and cursing at her, and many holding objects. She crossed into the encampment and the rain of missiles began. Most were smelly and disgusting, like rotted mushrooms and wet bulbous weeds, designed to humiliate her. But some threw stones, and not all of those were pebbles.

Aoleyn kept crawling and shielded her face as much as she could, but not with her arms. She wouldn't give them the satisfaction of seeing her afraid.

A pair of legs appeared before her. The bare legs of a woman.

"Stop!" she heard Mairen command, and she was surprised that the Usgar-righinn had moved around her without her even knowing it.

She was right beside the blazing bonfire, the heat of it growing uncomfortable very quickly.

Aoleyn heard another voice that she thought she recognized. She started to look up, and did enough to see that it was Tay Aillig's awful nephew Egard speaking with Mairen. She only got a brief glance, though, as Mairen was quick to smack her in the face for daring to lift her gaze from the ground.

The two were whispering, and Aoleyn probably could have made out their words were it not for the continuing curses shouted around her, and the fact that she really wasn't sure she cared enough to listen.

It was over. All of it. Every hope, every dream. She had never known love, even physical love, for the one time she had been with a man, she had been raped. She would never know what it was to hold a child of her own, or to see the world beyond this one mountain, which the tribe thought huge, but which she found suffocating and small.

None of that would she know. It was over. Every dream. She took some comfort in that she had stayed true to herself, but in the end, she had lost to the traditions of Usgar.

Strangely, she didn't feel foolish, though her actions had condemned her, for she believed that she had done right in discerning a newer and better way to utilize the blessed crystals. Usgar could not be mad at her for that, she believed, if he was truly the source of such magic, for he had given it to her, after all.

How, then, could their god tolerate this?

But Mairen was the voice of Usgar in the tribe.

Some beads fell to the ground before Aoleyn. She looked at them curiously for a moment, then realized they were hers, though she hadn't worn them in a long time. They had been in her tent . . .

"We found these near the body of Ralid," Egard claimed, and gasps arose all around. "They're your own, Aoleyn, are they not? I've seen you with them."

"I do'no . . . I have not . . ." she stuttered, trying to sort out this puzzle. They were near Ralid? But how could that be?

"The bear," Mairen said then, and she laughed as if it had all come clear to her.

Aoleyn looked up, and Mairen did not stop her this time, as if she wanted the young woman to look into her eyes then.

"The bear," she said again, nodding. "You saw through the eyes of a bear. You possessed the bear."

"A bear attacked us . . . Ralid!" Egard cried, and Aoleyn caught the slip up, but if anyone else did, they didn't respond or show it. "You did it," he accused her, seeming as if he would leap upon her and throttle her then and there. "You murdered an Usgar warrior, who was my friend!"

The gasps arose again, and the shouts, and calls for Aoleyn to be killed. She had no allies here, she knew, although Connebragh, to the side, seemed more than a little uneasy with all of this.

"Admit it, child," Mairen demanded. "I was in your thoughts. I saw. You can'no lie here. Speak truly and so make this easier upon all of us."

Others called out at her, a hundred voices assailing her thoughts, jumbling them as she tried to find a place of calm and sort out some direction here.

The verbal goading continued unrelentingly, and finally, in sheer frustration, Aoleyn shouted out, "I did it!"

The tribe went silent around her, the only sound the hiss and crackle of the fire.

"You admit . . ." Mairen started.

"Aye," said Aoleyn. "They were torturing a man—all of them. Ralid, Egard . . ."

Egard kicked her in the side, blasting out her breath.

"Uamhas," he told the gathering. "We captured an uamhas. We . . ."

Mairen put her hand on his arm to silence him. "It does not matter," the Usgar-righinn told them all, her voice solemn and serious. "Aoleyn has admitted her crime, and it is not the only sin from this one. The Usgar-laoch will return soon and the Usgar-forfach is on his way to us. We know what must be done."

As she finished, she stared straight at Aoleyn, and the young woman noted the edges of Mairen's lips curling up in a perfectly wicked smile of grim satisfaction.

5

THE ELDER'S CLEAR EYES

Carrying his gory trophy, Tay Aillig climbed the trails of Fireach Speuer. At one point, he noted a snake skin off the side of the path, and thought to perhaps find the white-furred viper that had shed it.

If he could kill the snake and take its head, more specifically its fangs and poison sacs, perhaps he could plant them within his misshapen bear head, giving the trophy a more sinister, less typical appearance. A second set of fangs within the mouth, dripping with poison?

He dismissed the thought almost as soon as he had it. It was ridiculous to expect that he could get away with such a ruse, and if, or when, caught, his entire declaration would be shown as a fraud, and not as some simple misidentification of the creature he had slain.

He nodded as he considered again that he was carrying a mighty trophy all its own, even if no one believed that it was the fossa—and that was a claim that Tay Aillig would not openly make. No, he would let Mairen lead here, and meant to only describe his kill as something he had at first thought a bear, but then, after encountering it up close, became far less certain.

Let them draw their conclusions and voice their suspicions, he thought. That way, there would be no stench of a lie upon him.

Even if, in the end, it was decided that it was a mountain bear, that was no small trophy among the Usgar. Had any warrior in memory slain an adult bear single-handedly?

He came upon a rocky rise, still some miles below the camp, and he climbed to the top to gain a better vantage point.

His people were breaking camp, he believed, though it was hard to tell the specifics from this great distance, and the suspicion surprised him and made him more than a bit indignant. He was the Usgar-laoch, the War Leader! How dare they make such a decision without him, and while not even knowing where he was?

As he considered it, however, his surprise began to ebb. This was Mairen's doing, of course, and she knew where he was, and that he would soon be returning, or, now, that he would soon enough catch up to the migration. Given all of the strange events of the last few days, Tay Aillig soon enough found himself nodding in agreement with the witch's choice. There would be no more raids on the uamhas, they had long ago decided, and all the hunts had been completed, the stores ready for the long winter respite. Better to climb to the winter plateau early, for though the recent days had been warm enough, the weather this high up could change very quickly.

One year, Tay Aillig remembered, he had gone to bed, not even bothering to wear a shirt, for the air was so warm, only to wake up to a bedding of snow across the upper reaches of the mountain that reached almost to his hip.

That year's journey to the winter plateau had been a horrible ordeal. They had lost an uamhas, and nearly her tender, in an icy slide down a steep ravine.

He climbed back down the rocky outcropping and started again up the mountainside, at first swiftly, that he might get to the encampment before they had set out.

His pace slowed soon after, though, as he considered things.

He had no desire to help with breaking down the tents and packing the supplies, and more importantly, if he was not there when they left, many Usgar would be staring out at the lower reaches of Fireach Speuer, seeking some sign of their Usgar-laoch, fearing that perhaps he had been wounded or killed out on the dangerous mountain.

His heroic return would be more dramatic.

"Aye," he said with a nod. He rolled in the soft and moist dirt at the side of the trail, then, and even cut himself in a few places. He wanted them to see him entering the camp, dirty and battered, but carrying such a trophy as this.

He found some blueberry bushes then, and an apple tree, so settled in for some dinner, then curled up under a shady tree and took an afternoon nap.

The sun was almost down when he awakened, dusk had fallen, but that meant little to Tay Aillig. The moon would not be full this night, and it would not be red, in any case. There were creatures on the mountain that could kill him, of course—bears and great cats, packs of wolves and coyotes, even the giant condors called rocs, and deadly mountain vipers. But Tay Aillig knew them, as he knew this place, and so he knew how to avoid them.

Not far from the rocky outcropping, he backtracked and began to climb once more. He grew curious as he neared the top, coming around the side of the stone hill enough to catch a glimpse up the mountain, and to see the glow of a bonfire in the area where he knew the encampment to be.

They hadn't yet broken camp, he realized, a bit disappointed.

That turned to curiosity a heartbeat later, though, when the Usgar-laoch noted a line of small fires, torches, higher up on the mountain.

"What are you about, Mairen?" he whispered, suspecting, rightly, that this was her game.

The twelve current members of the witch's Coven of Usgar sang softly as they made their way slowly up the mountainside, each carrying a torch, each wearing nothing but a simple smock to mid-thigh, each dancing with every step, often turning about, arms high and wide, to draw circles of fire in the air with their torches. Three warriors accompanied the procession, including Egard, nephew of the Usgar-laoch, and one older man, Ahn'Namay, considered the highest-ranking man among the elders and the likely successor to Usgar-forfach Raibert when Raibert at last crossed from this life.

At the back of the line, the three warriors formed a triangle around Aoleyn, who was tied and gagged, her wrists each bound to a pole held by one of the warriors, while Egard stood behind her with a nasty scourge, ready—nay, eager—to punish her if she moved in any way not prescribed by her captors.

Between the warriors and the witches went Ahn'Namay, supported by an uamhas woman who had been tasked with helping him along the difficult hike. Not just any uamhas, but Innevah, the mother of Bahdlahn.

Aoleyn squeezed back tears watching the woman marching before her. Aoleyn was certain of her own fate, but she didn't think the choice of Innevah to accompany them this night a coincidence. When Mairen had been inside her thoughts, she had seen the memories, the images of Aoleyn's time flying in the body of a bird, and seeing through the eyes of that owl, when she had witnessed Innevah sneaking out of the tent belonging to the witch, Caia. She couldn't be sure that Mairen had seen or deduced what Aoleyn had come to believe about that incident, but she was very afraid. For Aoleyn was fairly certain that the white snake that had killed Caia had not entered her tent by accident.

Or perhaps the tribe had learned of Aoleyn's secret relationship with Bahdlahn! He was up there, working on th'Way. Were they going to grab him, too, for this awful journey?

A million fears assailed the poor young woman, none of them for herself. She accepted her fate—what choice did she have?—and took comfort in the truth of what she had done. She had destroyed the demon that had haunted the mountain for time untold, the demon that had slain her father and had ripped the mind of her mother. The demon that had killed Brayth, and had nearly destroyed Aoleyn—and would have, had not Seonagh interceded, at the cost of her own mind.

Aoleyn had watched the ceremony when Seonagh had been thrown into the holy chasm, Craos'a'diad.

She knew what to expect.

And she knew what was down there, awaiting her in death.

But so be it.

She looked at Innevah and grimaced. Her legs went weak beneath her, but the two strong warriors holding the poles bound to her wrists yanked her upright immediately.

Egard's whip bit into her back, her own simple shift offering little padding against it.

Even through the gag, Aoleyn cried out, a muffled whimper, but one that caught the attention of the last two witches, Mairen and Connebragh.

"Halt and break," Mairen called, and she turned back to face Aoleyn. She took one of the binding poles and motioned for Connebragh to take the other.

"Go and piss in the woods," she told Egard and his charges. "Back down the trail fifty paces. Make sure that we are not being followed."

With a nod to Connebragh, Mairen dragged Aoleyn to the side of the trail, and there pushed her up against a stone, that she could sit upon it.

Mairen seemed nervous, pacing back and forth, scratching at her hair and tossing glances that seemed somewhere between anger and disappointment at her captive.

"What a foolish girl you be," she said at last, bending low to put her face very near to Aoleyn's. "Everything was there for you. The Coven awaited. The Usgar-laoch called you his wife—what woman in the tribe would not wish to share a bed with the great Tay Aillig?"

I! Aoleyn thought, but did not reply.

"It was all there for you, right before you," Mairen continued. "How well you heard the song of Usgar. You could have served me for many years. Perhaps you would have become Usgar-righinn!"

To Aoleyn's surprise, Mairen pulled the gag away. "Do you not understand this?"

"I did nothing wrong," Aoleyn whispered, lowering her gaze.

"You killed Ralid," Connebragh said, coming forward, but Mairen held her back.

"He was torturing a man," Aoleyn whispered.

"Uamhas!" Mairen corrected.

"I did'no mean . . ."

Mairen grabbed her by the chin and yanked her head up to stare into her eyes, those black eyes of Aoleyn, so unusual and striking. At first, Aoleyn thought the woman would hit her, but Mairen's face softened, and she seemed more sad than angry.

"I believe you did'no," the Usgar-righinn said quietly. "But child, there is so much else."

"I killed the fossa," Aoleyn said, or almost said, before Mairen's hand slapped her hard across the face.

"You killed Ralid!"

"And after, I hunted the fossa and found it in its cave," Aoleyn insisted. "And there, I destroyed it. I can show you the place, and you will know."

"Then why did you not return its head, or some evidence?"

Aoleyn licked her lips, trying to figure out how to explain. "I can show you the cave," she repeated. "'Tis not far."

"I do'no want to see your cave, child. Why did ye no' bring its head?"

"When I destroyed it, it changed," Aoleyn started to explain. "I burned out the darkness, but a cloud leopard was left . . ."

Mairen's sigh told her to stop.

"'Tis true," she whispered under her breath, lowering her gaze once more.

"And if you went in there, you would know—oh, but you could not not know!"

"Fool girl," she heard Connebragh say.

"Recant," Mairen said. "All of it."

Aoleyn looked up, not understanding.

"Admit your guilt to cleanse your heart," Mairen explained.

"I did," Aoleyn protested.

"Not about Ralid," Mairen snapped. "All of it. Your lies about the demon fossa. Your heresy in breaking sacred crystals."

"No, not a lie . . ." She wanted to continue, but she had clearly pushed Mairen as far as the Usgar-righinn would go, for the older woman shoved the gag back in her mouth and secured it tightly, extra tightly, and with the last yank on the cord done only to inflict pain.

Mairen grabbed one pole, Connebragh the other, and together they tugged Aoleyn to her feet and dragged her back onto the trail, handing her off to Egard and his guards before taking their places in the line again and taking up the song and dance.

Up the mountainside they went.

Many of the Usgar watched the procession leave the encampment earlier that day with a combination of surprise and trepidation. Activities were underway for breaking the camp and heading up the mountain, but to have the entire Coven leaving, along with the highest-ranking man in camp and the nephew of the War Leader, was quite unusual and disquieting.

"Where is the Usgar-laoch?" many asked as the sun set across the lake far below.

"Why is the girl bound?" others inquired.

The warrior Aghmor watched it all with torn feelings, for he, unlike any others in the camp, understood what this was about. Mairen had promised that they would return in three days, to accompany the migration to the winter plateau, but Aghmor realized that they would come back with one less Usgar, and likely without the uamhas, too.

The prospect of that bothered the man more than he expected. He was no friend of Aoleyn, or the uamhas, and Aoleyn had confessed to possessing the bear that had killed Ralid. But he didn't want to see her executed, for her explanation of why she had done it had been quite accurate. Tay Aillig and his hunting party were torturing the man down the mountainside, and intended to kill him if the demon fossa did not, and, knowing Tay Aillig, not pleasantly.

The warrior had no idea of what he might do, but he found an excuse and left the camp soon after the procession had departed. He knew the trails well to the winter plateau, and he followed carefully, off to the side of the main paths and far enough back so that if he stepped on a stick or rustled some leaves, he would not be discovered.

They were easy enough to see, with their torches, and since he suspected where they were going, but not so easy to follow, he realized, for their pace was great. Aghmor believed that the witches were using magic to get them up the mountainside, and his suspicions were confirmed when he watched them float up a fairly sheer cliff face.

The man grew anxious, fearing he would lose them.

He grew anxious, too, because he still didn't know why he was shadowing them!

That didn't slow him, though—quite the opposite. Yes, he knew these trails well, and so Aghmor ran through the darkness as fast as he could and caught back up to the procession on the other side of the cliff face.

He was close enough to watch them when Mairen called for a rest, and crept in close enough to hear most of Mairen and Connebragh's conversation with Aoleyn.

Then he knew, beyond doubt, that this procession would not stop at the winter plateau. They were going higher.

He thought of Aoleyn, and nakedly, removing his anger and frustrations with her from his thoughts and simply viewing her recent actions through the lens she had offered. Perhaps he was being honest with himself for the first time in years, allowing his heart to press him though his fears of breaking tradition or going against Usgar order.

Perhaps it was more than that, even, now that he allowed himself to view Aoleyn away from her dangerous and frowned-upon eccentricities, to see her with his heart instead of his Usgar traditions.

Aghmor considered his options—if they caught him out here, the punishment would likely be severe. The Usgar-righinn was not known to be lenient with men who crossed her, and Egard wouldn't likely protect him.

Aghmor didn't trail the procession when it started once more, for he was long gone.

Now he was leading the way, running with all speed, determined that they wouldn't catch up to him. He passed by the winter encampment, off to the side, not wanting to be seen by the lone resident. Confident of where Mairen was leading that procession, Aghmor moved on to the east of the camp, to a trail that was now a stair leading higher up the mountainside.

The procession of witches and their escorts and prisoners came onto the winter plateau soon after dawn to find an old man waiting for them, heavily leaning on a walking stick in the middle of the flat, mostly stony ground set before the sacred grove of pines that shielded the physical manifestation of Usgar.

Old indeed. It seemed to Mairen that the man, Elder Raibert, had aged greatly over the summer months. He had always been lean, but now he looked emaciated and sallow, older than old, as if he had died and was rotting away, propped on a stick.

Mairen instructed the others to wait at the edge of the clearing, then started toward Raibert, to find Ahn'Namay moving beside her. She looked to the man to scold him, but then caught herself, reminding herself that she had no say over this one, whom the tribe had already decided would replace Raibert as Usgar-forfach when Raibert died.

Ahn'Namay would be a powerful Usgar in short order, she realized, and one whose voice could have deep implications regarding her own dreams of power.

"We had heard that you would be descending to the summer encampment," Mairen said to Raibert as she approached.

The Elder snorted. "You walk on these feet," he chided with a wheezing cackle. "Oh fie, but I have grown thorns inside them!"

The Elder's laugh had always annoyed Mairen, but thankfully the man had never been particularly mirthful. That had apparently changed, she realized as he continued on, cataloguing every pain and infirmity, as every sentence seemed punctuated by a cackle now.

Less annoying than his wheezing laugh was the stench coming from the man, which seemed in line with his words as he explained his inability to control his basic bodily functions.

"I'd be a week trying to get down there," he said, and laughed, and kept laughing, seemingly uncontrollably, as he added, "You'd have found me dead on the path not halfway down."

Mairen and Ahn'Namay exchanged curious looks.

"What's taking it so long?" Raibert cried out suddenly.

"What?" Ahn'Namay asked.

"Death!"

Again, the two Usgar glanced sidelong at each other.

"You have heard?" Mairen asked.

"Heard?"

"Of the trouble?"

"Aye, and the trouble of my feet!" he replied, shaking his head vigorously, and sneering more than laughing. He looked past the pair to the rest of the entourage, and snorted. "The one you've brought bound in vines will likely outlive me."

"Elder . . ." Mairen started.

"Been a long summer," he said, ignoring her. "Too hot. And now's too cold. Don't remember the last time it was a good day. And I know every coming rain days before it falls. In every bone."

Mairen tried futilely to interrupt as the Elder rambled on about every happenstance, every pain, that had befallen him since the tribe had moved down the mountainside the previous spring. She wanted Raibert's blessing before ascending th'Way to Craos'a'diad, but the man seemed incapable of discussing the matter, or any matter that didn't directly involve him. At one point, she just rolled her eyes and sighed, which was a very rude thing to do to the Usgar-forfach, and very ill-advised.

Raibert was too immersed in his current tale of woe to notice, however.

"Will you journey up to Craos'a'diad with us, Elder?" Mairen finally managed to ask.

Raibert just laughed and shambled past her, leaning heavily on the walking stick. Mairen and Ahn'Namay looked at each other and shrugged as the old man went by, then fell into his wake and followed him to the edge of the winter plateau, looking out to the north, to the huge lake far below and the lines of mountains surrounding it. The day was dawning bright and clear, affording them a long, long view.

"The land is flat and dry," Elder Raibert said, shakily lifting one arm and indicating the area to the east, the region known as Fasail Dubh'clach, the Desert of Black Stones. "All the way to the horizon. I have walked it, long ago, in my youth. I would like to see it again."

Mairen shrugged. She had also seen the desert—had seen more of it than most Usgar ever would, as she had once spirit-walked as far across the desert as she could manage. Miles and miles, all the way to the horizon. She knew that Raibert was speaking of something more tangible, though. The poems of the tribe's skalds depicting Raibert in his youth claimed that he had actually gone down there, off the mountain and off the great Ayamharas plateau. Indeed, he was the last known Usgar to do so.

"Those days are behind us, Elder," Mairen said.

"Aye," Raibert replied. "And ahead of us, fewer days than we'd like. Fewer than we know, both of us." Again, the man issued that grating cackle.

"I look only to today," Mairen insisted. "We have walked through the night and have all the morning ahead of us for our journey up th'Way. I must be off. If you'll not join, then give us your blessing and we'll be on our way."

"You look much further than today, child," Raibert said gently. He turned to Mairen and locked her gaze with his own.

That image took Mairen's breath away. For the first time in many seasons, she saw a clarity in Elder Raibert's eyes. He did not seem old to her in that moment, just venerable.

"You look too far ahead," Raibert warned. "Our days are not as long as we would like. None of us. The mountain knows. The mountain is *carn*. The guardian is destroyed."

Mairen stared at him blankly, trying to wrap her thoughts around his strange words—words that he was speaking with surety, it seemed. *Carn*, she mused? An old word, meaning herald. The mountain is herald?

"But for today, I will join you," Elder Raibert said with another laugh, a different sort of laugh, one that signaled absurdity and futility. "I will give my blessing for what must be done."

Without another word, he snorted and cackled, then turned and walked off, dropping his walking stick to the ground. His stride was long and strong then, so strangely. The other witches fell in line, Mairen no longer leading the procession but bringing up the rear, replaying those last words of Raibert.

What did he know? And how had he suddenly found such vigor?

And that clear look in his eyes?

She tried hard to seem confident and serene regarding the dark business of this day, but inside was turmoil.

The old man had shaken her deeply, and worse, she didn't even know why.

6

WHEN LIGHT DIED

Talmadge didn't really want to do this, but the villagers of Car Seileach, the first tribesmen of the region who had accepted him and opened up this world to him, had asked it of him. And they had given him a throwing axe and a fine sword—one he had traded to them years earlier, in fact.

"*Eirigh'ti*," they had called the one he was seeking. "The sun man."

At first, Talmadge had thought the man must be blond-haired, but as he thought about it after he had set out from the village, along the bank to the north, it didn't make sense. Many of the villagers in the towns around the lake had light brown or yellow hair, and so that didn't seem like much of a point of differentiation.

It didn't really matter, he supposed, as he had been assured that he would understand when he saw the stranger.

He crossed through an area of short weeping willows, all bright and yellow in the morning sun, their small leaves turning with the season. Tall grasses spread out wide around the area.

"Great place for an ambush," Talmadge told himself under his breath. Preferring to be the ambusher, not the victim, the skilled frontiersman went down to his knees and crept through. He held his sword in one hand, the hand axe in the other, using the longer blade to part the tall grass before him.

He wasn't too far from the spot where he had killed a man, Badger, after a vicious fight with one of the large lizards of the lake, the ferocious *clo'dearche*.

That memory weighed heavily on Talmadge's shoulders, suddenly, and each movement came hard to him.

But he persisted, and moved up a bluff, and when he parted the last line of tall grass before him, he was afforded a wider view, finally, of a meadow beyond.

"Eirigh'ti," he whispered breathlessly at the amazing sight that presented itself before him—so amazing, and out of place, that it took him a long while to sort it out, to even realize that it was a human, and one Talmadge knew, outfitted in a breastplate of shining silver and trimmed in gold, shining brilliant in the sunlight. The visitor to Loch Beag was gathering wood, logs for a raft or a shelter, it seemed, chopping branches with a gleaming sword, red gems sparkling when the man turned it in a way that caught the sunlight. So perfectly crafted were the breastplate and short metal greaves that the man, Bryan Marrawee of Dundalis, made no sound as he moved and twisted, and if he was hindered at all by his garments, he didn't show it.

Talmadge thought back to that day by the river when he had met this strange character. When he had found the opportunity, he had peeked into Bryan's large sack and seen this armor, but never had he imagined how brilliant it truly was!

Bryan brought his sword down on a branch, then again, and a third time, the chopping finally taking it down.

Three swings, just three, and it was not a thin branch.

He broke it apart into small pieces, then tossed them on a small pile of wood beside a flat stone, with several fish lying atop the rock.

Too much wood to start the cooking fire, Talmadge thought, and the pieces were too large. He considered showing himself and helping Bryan to collect some more appropriate starter kindling, but then the surprising man surprised him again. He began to glow as if limned in some white light, then thrust his sword down into the piled wood and ignited the weapon's gleaming blade!

Flames danced from the shining metal, curling about the wood, and within a few heartbeats, gray smoke began rising from the wet wood.

Bryan didn't seem to care about the smoke. And not about the flames, either, as it began to catch, for he reached down with his free hand, wearing no gauntlet, and rearranged the now-burning wood without so much as a flinch.

Talmadge spent a moment catching his breath and considering how he might approach this strange man, whom he had met only once, and only briefly.

"There's enough fish for two," Bryan called out then.

Talmadge put his face down and sighed. He wasn't really surprised that this particular man had noted him. He pushed up to his knees, then stood and started down the other side of the bluff and onto the meadow.

"Well met again, Mister Talmadge," Bryan greeted.

"And to you, Bryan Marrawee of Dundalis," he replied, and the man stared at him curiously for a few moments, his hesitation reminding Talmadge of the fact that Bryan Marrawee was not really his name, not his given name, at least, as he had admitted in their earlier meeting.

"The fish is fresh," Bryan replied at length. "Join me for a fine meal and finer talk?"

"What are you doing up here?" Talmadge asked, approaching.

"What are you doing up here?" Bryan replied.

Talmadge stopped short and stared at him. "You know."

Bryan flashed a disarming smile and nodded. "You intrigued me. Did you slay your monster?"

Talmadge tried to sort that out for a bit, then started in surprise. "No," he stuttered. "No, I could not dare try. It is no . . . truly, it is a monster, and beyond any man . . ."

Bryan was patting the air with his hands to calm Talmadge.

"The monster in your heart," he clarified. "Did returning to this place you so love slay the monster of fear that lived within you for the woman you lost?"

"Aye," Talmadge started to answer, but he stopped and admitted, "I do'no know."

Bryan replied with a "hmm," spitted a fish on a stick, and tossed it across to Talmadge.

From up on th'Way, Aghmor noted the pause of the procession, and was encouraged to watch the Usgar-righinn and Ahn'Namay conversing with Elder Raibert. Perhaps Raibert would put an end to this madness, he dared hope.

His hope was short-lived, though, for it became clear that Raibert was going to come along with the group up the trail to the sacrificial chasm. He would slow them, and that would give Aghmor some extra time at least.

"For what purpose?" the warrior quietly asked himself. What exactly did he think he might do up here? What could he possibly do up here against a dozen witches and three warriors?

Those thoughts perfectly relayed to Aghmor the futility of his journey. Why was he even up here? If Mairen meant to throw Aoleyn into Craos'a'diad, there was nothing he could do to stop it. There were no words he could say to change any minds here.

He put his face in his hands in frustration, wondering why he would even want to stop the sacrifice if there was a way to do so. Why would he even care?

He thought then that he should quietly slip away into the shadows and get back to the summer camp, and he stood up tall and looked all around, seeking the best route.

Only then did he realize that something was missing here on th'Way. Where was the uamhas worker? Why hadn't he heard the young slave's hammering?

"Aoleyn," he mouthed, and now his tone was more suspicious and even angry. She had been here with the uamhas on the morning after that fateful night a few days previous. If the uamhas had run off, then maybe Aoleyn deserved to be thrown into the chasm!

Aghmor started up the trail, hoping to find the slave, and thinking that if he did, he would be acting on the side of mercy to get the young man off the trail and out of the way, that he wouldn't witness this sacrifice. He would probably do something stupid and get himself thrown in beside her—in beside them, if the other slave, this one's mother, was to be fed to the Crystal God as well.

His focus was on the trail, his thoughts questioning why he wasn't hearing the uamhas at his work, and so he didn't even notice when the young man slipped onto the trail behind him, a huge rock in hand, and lifted high, ready to crash down upon Aghmor's head.

"Why aren't your hands burned?" Talmadge asked his host.

The armored man looked at him curiously.

"You grabbed the flaming logs. I watched you. And why are you wearing that armor?"

In response, Bryan drew out his sword.

Talmadge's eyes went wide and he reflexively leaned back, fearing that he had possibly gone too far here with his questions. But Bryan quickly flipped the weapon over to show him the hilt, the red gemstones, rubies, then the milky white gem set into weapon's crosspiece.

"The blade flames," Bryan explained.

"I saw."

"Well, it would do its wielder no good if it burned him with its own fire," the other man laughed, against indicating the crosspiece. "It is all the magic of the ring stones, of course. Like the monks perform."

Talmadge nodded. He hadn't witnessed such displays in a long time, but he remembered when the monks had come to his plague-ravaged village . . . and had failed.

"These red gems, rubies, create the fire," Bryan explained. "This one on the crosspiece, serpentine, shielded me to protect me from that fire."

"And those on your chest plate? Are they magical?"

"Oh, indeed," said Bryan. "They aid in defense, in turning blades, and make the suit lighter—it is no more encumbering than a heavy vest. And some are there to heal me, even in the midst of battle." He winked at Talmadge. "I'm a tough one to kill."

Talmadge stuttered over a few words, trying to make sense of it all. He had never heard of such things, and couldn't even imagine the workmanship and magic involved, or the cost. He fumbled trying to ask a few questions, finally settling on how Bryan kept the plate so polished out here in the wild lands.

"Lizards," the man said, which confused Talmadge.

"You polish your armor with lizards?"

That brought a laugh. "Your earlier question," he explained. "I'm wearing it because there are many large lizards about. They seem formidable."

"They are," said Talmadge, who had battled one and didn't really want to think about it.

"And there's no need to polish it," Bryan added. "Or the sword."

"Silver?"

"Silverel," the man corrected. "Elvish silver. It will never lose its shine, or edge, or strength, and there is no greater metal in all the world."

He bent over and retrieved his helm then, and plopped it over his head. It was bowl-shaped, tapering down the back of Bryan's head, and closed in front only to just below his eyes, where a strip of gold crossed under his eyes, temple to temple.

It looked like a mask and simple hood as much as a helm, Talmadge thought, for there was an added ridge of metal, almost like the brim of a hat, running around the helm from behind Bryan's eyes, and upon that ridge were set yet more gray stones.

"What?" Bryan asked, smiling, at the man's dumbfounded expression.

"I have never seen such a thing," Talmadge said.

"Few have, and none beyond those who have seen it on me," said Bryan.

"But how? Who are you?"

The other man laughed, then sighed. "It is a long story."

Talmadge started to respond, but noted Bryan looking past him, then, and upward.

"What?" Talmadge asked, and followed the gaze, looking up into the sky on this day, the autumnal equinox, to see the bright sun, not a cloud near it.

But it was not round, and an arc of blackness had stolen the bottom edge of the brilliant circle.

Talmadge climbed to his feet. Bryan was already up, moving beside him.

"What is it?" the frontiersman asked.

The armored man had no immediate answer.

When Aghmor spun around, he saw the most horrified expression he had ever viewed. The slave he had always called Thump stood mouth agape, eyes wide in shock and terror, and with his arm up high.

Looking up at that lifted hand had Aghmor falling back fast with a gasp, for the young uamhas was holding a stone, heavy and tapered on the end he was apparently about to smash down upon Aghmor's head!

The Usgar warrior leveled his spear, but the uamhas flung the rock to the ground and began flapping his hands and shaking his head in complete denial, and fortunately for Bahdlahn, Aghmor realized then that the uamhas was as surprised as he by the truth of the encounter. He noticed, too, that the young uamhas carried a vicious wound in his shoulder.

"What are you about?" Aghmor demanded.

"Thump, no," came the reply, the slave lowering his gaze deferentially.

"You meant to kill me!"

Thump shook his head vigorously.

"Then explain!" Aghmor demanded.

The slave looked up at him sheepishly, winced and grimaced and shrugged helplessly.

"You do not fool me," Aghmor said.

The slave glanced all around, held up his hands helplessly, as if he couldn't understand, but then swallowed hard, a clear tell.

"I heard you speaking with Aoleyn," Aghmor stated bluntly, and when the uamhas didn't answer, he mimicked Bahdlahn's voice and said, as Bahdlahn had said to Aoleyn, "You should go to my mother. She will give you new clothes."

He didn't think the uamhas's eyes could get any wider, but he was wrong.

"And now you wish you had just hit me with the rock and killed me," Aghmor said.

The uamhas seemed frozen with fear for another couple of heartbeats, but then shook his head again.

"Who did you think I was?" Aghmor demanded. "I know you can speak. Who were you going to kill, slave?"

Bahdlahn slave pointed to the wound in his shoulder. "The golden man," he said. "The monster."

"Golden man? Monster?" Aghmor quietly repeated. "A goblin? A sidhe?"

Bahdlahn nodded, but paused and shook his head again. "I thought . . ." he stammered. "Yes, sidhe. Maybe. But no, not like I have ever seen."

Aghmor rocked back on his heels. Yes, he knew this supposedly simple slave could talk, but the sophistication in his words and inflections rocked Aghmor back on his heels.

"Its face," Bahdlahn began, fumbling for words. "Colors. Red, bright red, on a huge nose." He ran his hand down the center of his face, brow to upper lip. "And blue, like the lake in the sun, on the sides."

"What do you mean? What are you babbling about, fool uamhas?"

"Too bright! All of it!"

"Its skin?"

Bahdlahn nodded vehemently.

"Painted?" Aghmor asked, making a motion in front of his face like he was rubbing war paint on, as the Usgar sometimes did. But the slave was shaking his head.

"Just skin," the uamhas explained. Bahdlahn turned quickly and rushed across the path, pointing back to a sheltered tree and bush that served as his home. "It was in there, and stabbed me. It would kill me."

"The sidhe?"

Bahdlahn shrugged. "Its spear . . . Fine and smooth and strong. Not like an Usgar spear, but fine. Its clothes . . ."

"It wore clothes?"

"Fine," Bahdlahn insisted. "Finer than Usgar clothes. Finer than lake-man clothes."

Aghmor was shaking his head, having a hard time deciphering any of this jumble.

"But you ran away?" he asked.

Bahdlahn slave picked up a rock and flung it hard against a larger stone. "I hit it. I hit it again." He motioned repeatedly as if throwing a rock.

"You chased it off?" Aghmor asked, and before he had even finished the question, Bahdlahn was running up the trail, waving for him to follow. They came to a place where the brush at the edge of the path had been bent and broken, and blood showed on the last stone at the edge, right before the ground gave way for a long and fairly steep fall.

"You chased it off and it fell down there?"

The slave nodded.

Aghmor leaned over and looked down the slope, but could see no sign of anyone. He had no reason to doubt the story, and the man's wound looked like a spear stab, and there was blood here on the edge of th'Way. That would have been a grand concoction of a story, he thought, and one that would have required a lot of preparation. And for what? Obviously, Thump hadn't meant to kill an Usgar, or Aghmor would be lying back down the trail with his head caved in.

Or perhaps, Thump had meant to kill another Usgar. Aghmor glanced down the slope, and thought about Tay Aillig, who, as far as he knew, was still out of the summer encampment below.

Perhaps Thump had already killed an Usgar.

As he considered the possibilities, Aghmor thought this a fortunate turn of events. He didn't want the uamhas up here to witness the passing of Mairen's column . . .

The Usgar sucked in his breath, a distant memory coming back to him. "You told Aoleyn to go to your mother," he said. "Who is your mother?"

Thump swallowed hard.

"Tell me!"

"Innevah," the man admitted.

Aghmor rubbed his face at the confirmation. No good would come of this one witnessing the procession. Mairen was going to kill Aoleyn, his friend, and it seemed to him very likely that the slave woman, this one's mother, would also find herself cast into Craos'a'diad.

"Come," Aghmor said, starting over the edge of th'Way. He paused, though, and looked back. "What is your name?"

"Thump!" came the predictable response, in the same phony and goofy simplicity Aghmor had heard from this one for years and years now.

"No," he snapped back, frightening the uamhas. "What is your name? What does Aoleyn call you?"

The slave moved from foot to foot and cast his gaze down.

"I know she doesn't call you Thump," Aghmor scolded. "Just tell me your name, because I don't want to call you that, either."

The slave looked up at him, clearly overwhelmed. "Bahdlahn," he said softly.

"Bahdlahn," Aghmor repeated, nodding, and as he considered the meaning of the word, a less insulting synonym of the word "thump," it made sense and brought a smile to him.

Aoleyn was ever the clever one.

Too clever.

"Come, Bahdlahn," he bade the young man. "Let's go see this sidhe you slew."

They moved carefully down the hill and searched around for a body. They didn't find one, but there was enough evidence—broken branches and crushed shrubs, along with some blood—for Aghmor to believe the basics of the uamhas's tale.

He found a trail, as well, uneven footprints which suggested a man, or a sidhe, staggering away to the southeast around the mountainside.

Off the two went, with Aghmor now determined to keep this uamhas away from Mairen's procession. The trail wound around, then down into a vale, but right back up, along a broken stone path. Aghmor, for all of his time on the mountain, did not know. It meandered this way and that, but not far enough from th'Way, the Usgar warrior only realized when he, and his uamhas companion, heard the singing of the witches.

Bahdlahn looked at him curiously.

"The Coven, I'd guess," Aghmor said with a shrug.

"What do you know?" Bahdlahn asked, his voice thick with suspicion.

Aghmor just shrugged again, and Bahdlahn looked at him for just a few heartbeats before turning about and rushing up the side of the hill, up toward th'Way, toward Craos'a'diad, Aghmor believed, and feared.

The Usgar warrior rushed to keep up, calling out softly for Bahdlahn to wait, then, when that didn't work, ordering the slave to stop.

Bahdlahn did pause, but only long enough to look back at the pursuing Usgar, shaking his head, his expression twisted in confusion.

Aghmor realized that his own reaction had tipped the young man off that something was amiss here, and no doubt, Aghmor knew, Bahdlahn had connected it to the one Usgar about whom he cared: Aoleyn.

"Don't," Aghmor warned, but quietly, for the singing was not that far away. "On pain of death, I warn you, slave, come back down."

Bahdlahn's face seemed to melt, then, with conflicting emotions. But again, he shook his head, turned, and scrambled up the mountainside, a steep grade that had him using his hands as much as his feet.

Aghmor pursued, cursing under his breath. He saw a better route and rushed ahead, soon paralleling the uamhas. He might catch Bahdlahn in time, he thought.

But only briefly, because as he came back around to intercept at the top of Bahdlahn's climb, Aghmor discovered that he was up above the sacrificial chasm, and with Craos'a'diad in view, along with the Coven, their guests, and their prisoners!

He dropped low behind a stone and motioned frantically for Bahdlahn to come to him, tapping his finger across his pursed lips, demanding the slave be silent.

It occurred to the warrior then that if they were caught, Bahdlahn probably wouldn't be punished—he belonged here—but Aghmor surely would.

Bahdlahn joined him at the stony ridge and together they peeked over.

The uamhas sucked in his breath at the sight, and Aghmor slapped his hand over Bahdlahn's mouth, whispering, begging, him to be silent.

Down below, the witches danced a semicircle around Aoleyn, and with the gaping chasm behind the young woman.

To the side of it, Aghmor noted Egard and his fellows, along with the Elder and Ahn'Namay. They were in front of another person, one the warrior could only hope Bahdlahn had not yet noticed, or at least, had not recognized.

He saw Mairen motion to Egard, and he quickly diverted Bahdlahn's attention—and a good thing, and just in time, as Egard so casually shoved Innevah into the chasm. The woman screamed, but only very briefly, more in shock than in terror, it seemed, and both the onlookers turned back to the scene.

Aghmor ground his teeth in frustration, surprisingly angered by the sheer callousness of his people. Was it because of this uamhas beside him, he wondered? Because he was having a harder time in reducing this one, and thus, others, to mere animals or monsters? Or was it because of her, Aoleyn, he had to consider, looking down.

Aoleyn was crying then, looking at the chasm, shaking her head, stamping her feet helplessly. Her hands were bound behind her back and she was gagged, but Aghmor and Bahdlahn could hear her muffled wails.

Bahdlahn started over the ridge.

Aghmor grabbed him and yanked him back. "There is nothing you can do," he whispered harshly into the uamhas's ear. "If there was anything . . . I'd help you. Aoleyn does not deserve this."

Bahdlahn was shaking his head in denial, his bare hands clawing at the stones, but Aghmor felt him relax a bit, as if coming to the realization that there was nothing he could do.

"If you go down there, they'll kill you right in front of Aoleyn, then do to her as they would have anyway. Are you thinking that would make her happy? Are you believing that would make her better able to accept her fate?"

Bahdlahn slumped even more.

"Do'no do it," Aghmor said bluntly, and he let the man go.

He shook his head as Bahdlahn stared, but then the uamhas jerked his head back suddenly, looking upward, his expression curious for just a moment before he turned away and shielded his eyes.

Aghmor, too, turned about and looked up at the sky, and his eyes went wide when he realized that a piece of the sun was missing!

Aoleyn watched the witches dancing about her. She could have been one of them. Had she behaved as expected, performed without causing so many so much trouble, she would have been inducted into the Coven and would be one of those dancers.

She was glad, then, that she had failed, for others less deserving of this fate than she would have been brought here.

And she would have been dancing, and singing, and praising Usgar, when the unfortunate was murdered.

Better this. Better she face her own death than be a part of inflicting such an injustice upon someone else.

The notion had her turning to regard poor Innevah, swept up in this tragedy, she feared, because Mairen had looked into Aoleyn's mind and had seen the uamhas fleeing the tent of Caia shortly before the snake had killed the witch.

She hoped that was not the case, hoped that Innevah being here was just coincidence, or because Mairen suspected that the woman was a friend to

Aoleyn, perhaps. Aoleyn's hopes had been bolstered when they had set her in this spot near the chasm and had begun their sacrificial dance.

If Mairen meant to kill Innevah, wouldn't she do it first, after all, to heighten the pain she inflicted upon Aoleyn?

So Aoleyn turned to regard the older uamhas woman, and just as she did, she noted Mairen's nod, then saw the look in Egard's eyes, and she knew.

Oh, she knew!

Seemingly without care, Egard, staring back at Aoleyn and smiling wickedly, reached out and put his hand on Innevah's shoulder, then simply shoved her into the chasm.

Aoleyn's legs went weak and wails escaped her through the gag. She started to fall to the ground, but was caught by an unseen hand, by Usgar magic, and hoisted from the ground, lying horizontally waist height from the ground.

Mairen was soon there, roughly tugging the gag from her mouth.

"The world was yours," the Usgar-righinn whispered. "And now there is only death."

"You killed her . . ." Aoleyn stuttered, or started to. But she heard something, then, or felt it within her, a vibration, the notes of Usgar, she presumed, but altered. Yes, different, the notes sounding discordant.

A chill went through her, but not from a winter breeze. No, it was a deeper coldness, like she had felt in the pit beneath this chasm when the spirits of the dead had gathered about her and touched her.

Now they weren't gathering, she somehow understood. They were passing her by, floating up from Craos'a'diad.

And the music was . . . wrong.

"Do you hear it?" she gasped. "Do you feel it?"

"Shut up," the woman hissed at her through gritted teeth, her seeming unbalance letting on to Aoleyn that she most certainly did sense whatever might be happening.

"Usgar-righinn!" Aoleyn heard Connebragh say, and she twisted her head to regard the speaker, who was staring up at the sky, as were those near her.

Mairen gasped, and pulled the gag back over Aoleyn's mouth as Aoleyn, too, turned to look up, to see the sun being consumed, it seemed. Parts of the light became darkness, utter blackness, and the witches gasped as much as sang, and none were dancing.

Half the sun was gone!

Then more!

The whole of it was being consumed before their eyes!

"Usgar is angry," one witch dared to cry out.

"No!" Mairen said. "No."

But more of the sun, the giver of light and life, the goodness to Iseabal's dangerous nighttime orb, went utterly dark. It seemed twilight, then, the gloom growing.

"Sing!" Mairen demanded, and they did, and Mairen shoved the gag fully back into Aoleyn's mouth. The poor young woman struggled and thrashed, and Mairen roughly punched and pushed the floating Aoleyn out over the chasm.

"Sing!" the Usgar-righinn cried again. "Sing for the glory of Usgar! I give you this heretic, Crystal God!"

Aoleyn felt the music of the witches flowing through her, holding her up. She tried to grab at it with her thoughts, with her spirit, but alas, there was nothing to hold on to. She even clenched her bound hands, as if trying to physically grasp the strands of magic.

And then the sunlight was fully gone, the land cast into darkness, save the stars that reappeared in the heavens above.

And then the music was gone, just gone, the magic pulled from beneath her, and Aoleyn followed Innevah into the chasm, into the darkness, into death.

Far below the Mouth of God, where the witches sang and stared in awe, where Aoleyn silently fell, and where Aghmor and Bahdlahn huddled in fear, Tay Aillig entered the dark Usgar encampment.

All the tribe came out of their tents, staring upward with great fear, cowering beneath a spectacle that they believed could only be a harbinger of evil.

Many cried out that Usgar had died, that the light would never return, and many simply cried.

None seemed to take note of Tay Aillig as he walked to the middle of the camp, his gory trophy in hand. He didn't know what to make of any of this, of course, and he was no less afraid than the others. Mairen had imparted something to him of Aoleyn killing the demon fossa—was this tragedy a following event to that?

He wondered if he should drop his misshapen bear-head trophy, or if he would do well to insist that it was simply the bear that had killed Ralid.

Where was Mairen? He looked around but couldn't find her in the darkness, couldn't see any of the witches at all.

A torch was struck, then another, but no, Tay Aillig saw none of the Coven.

He looked up at the sky, and thought that this must be Mairen's doing.

And when a sliver of light, a sliver of the sun, returned, the Usgar-laoch took heart, and smiled widely, and held up his gory trophy.

"Behold," he roared at the gathered tribesmen. "I have slain a monster!"

All looked at him, to him. All looked back up at the sky, at the sun that was returning.

So many fell to their knees, and most of those, Tay Aillig noted, were facing him.

No, not facing him, for they didn't dare. They prostrated themselves, faces to the ground before the great man.

Tay Aillig almost laughed aloud, so thrilled was he. He wasn't even certain of all that was going on. He had no idea of why the sun had been stolen, or why it was now coming back.

But he felt confident that most of those gathered would think it all some-how related to him, to his proclamation.

Tay Aillig felt like more than the Usgar-laoch at that moment, more than the Usgar-triath he hoped to become, even.

He was a god.

It was strangely silent as she fell, no wind in her ears. But with that cold-ness of the dead permeating her every pore. She flailed wildly at first, but settled fast and swiveled her head, searching, but all that did was tilt her downward, falling head first.

Aoleyn didn't know why—for what did it matter?—but she didn't want to land that way and splatter her head all over the floor.

She listened for the music and heard the song of Usgar, and it was loud in here, so powerful.

She sifted through the melodies, finding one she thought would catch her and slow her, as she had done before.

Perhaps . . .

A blast of wind hit her and sent her spinning, and she wound up with her feet pointing downward, at least. She did find the green stones of weight-lessness then, but distantly.

She grabbed at them for all her life, desperately. She had accepted her fate when she had no hope, when she thought she had no choice. But now, with the song so near and so strong, Aoleyn really didn't want to die.

She heard the music. She sang the song.

But it was too late, and she hit the floor with bone shattering force. She felt the explosions in her legs, ankles, knees, hips cracking and popping. Straight down went Aoleyn, poor Aoleyn, and the explosions all became one great catastrophe.

And there was quiet. And darkness. And she didn't know.

She didn't know who she was.

She didn't know what she was.

She didn't know where she was, or who she had been, or that she had ever been. She didn't know the darkness or the quiet.

She didn't know . . . anything.

7

THEY SAY AND IT'S BEEN TOLD

More than two-score mountain goblins milled about in a mob, brandishing their crude spears and clubs in all directions. They were not of the same tribe. Some were the remnants of a fight with the Usgar, others had lived not on Fireach Speuer, but in other mountains near to Loch Beag, or in dark holes deep underground.

But they had all come to this place, all compelled by voices in their heads, and all at the same time: the morning following the red moon.

They didn't know why. They didn't know how. But none could ignore the compulsion. They had been called, and so they had come as fast as they could.

Now that they had arrived, however, those inner voices were no more, and they found themselves in a red stone valley almost completely encircled by high cliffs and crowded by other mountain goblins they did not know.

Soon after, the howling had begun, all around them, yipping and melodic choruses singing words they did not know. The songs and cries echoed off the stone walls, surrounding the gathered goblins, closing in on them.

They backed against each other for support, unsure and afraid.

Forms appeared atop the cliffs, but only briefly, rushing about. Graceful forms, leaner than the mountain goblins, the humanoids more resembled men, and yet did not, and seemed to be something else. The mountain goblins tightened their defensive formation, glancing about nervously, expecting spears to rain down upon them. There was only one way out of this box canyon, a narrow trail between high walls that could be easily turned into a slaughter zone.

Ropes came flying over the cliffs, bound at the top and winding down to the ground, and lines of those lean humanoids followed quickly, flipping about on the ropes with practiced ease, and rappelling down into the canyon. Wearing overlapping flaps of dark green and golden-brown armor, the newcomers looked down as they rappelled, showing their bright faces to the group below. Others came over the ledge riding lizards, slowly picking their way down the nearly sheer cliffs, sitting way back in their saddles that they wouldn't overbalance and flip their sticky-footed mounts from the cliff side.

On one especially large lizard came two riders, the driver in front and a passenger dressed in black, wearing a mask made of a huge vulture's skull.

All about the canyon floor, mountain goblins looked to each other with surprise, and more than a few nodded in recognition. To the humans on the other side of the mountains, the mountain goblins were also known as the sidhe, but that was a misnomer, a misunderstanding of the name, which had been coined by the humans not for the mountain goblins, but for these graceful, bright-faced humanoids now filtering down the cliffs.

But that was all long ago, eons ago, before the fossa had come to Fireach Speuer, even, and the mountain goblins had little knowledge, only folklore, of these strange-looking humanoids, with their bright red, huge and flat noses, and bright patches of blue or white on the cheeks beside.

The mountain goblins, no strangers to warfare, did understand, however, that these approaching humanoids could have simply rained rocks and spears upon them. If these newcomers had wanted a battle, it would have been a simple slaughter. Yet, they were coming down.

And so gracefully. They slid to the ground on their ropes, landing lightly and turning about. The last down were the lizard riders, the last of them the driver carrying the black-robed one, and as the others settled about the edge of the canyon floor, he alone approached the gathered mob.

Scores of crude spears were leveled at him, but he seemed unconcerned. "My cousins," he said in the mountain goblin language, and in a voice that echoed throughout the canyon, a voice that every mountain goblin in that canyon knew well, for it was indeed the same voice that had sounded within their heads compelling them to come to this place.

The spears and clubs lowered.

Skath-mi-Zahn, the God-King of the Xoconai, was neither a god nor a king, but a child, a young xoconai. Descended from a long line of God-Kings, the youngster had never seen the outside of his pyramidal temple, and his only interactions happened with the augurs who tended him, and the supplicants they occasionally brought before him.

This day, like all days, the God-King sat on his throne, a beautiful and elegant golden seat, polished and shining. Perched on the precious chair, atop a marble dais in the center of the voluminous, shining, beautiful circular room, he waited. He had become quite adept at waiting.

All about the floor of the room, in their black robes and animal skull *condoral* masks, a bevy of xoconai augurs swept across the room, and several others swept the other way, crossing through doors, parchments under their arms, attendants in tow, going about their business without acknowledging Skath-mi-Zahn. This was normal; the augurs only ever acknowledged the child God-King when they needed something from him—a signature on a decree, a formal recitation of an edict they had crafted for him—or on those much rarer occasions when Skath-mi-Zahn demanded something of them (something the clever old augurs would inevitably mold to fit their own desires).

The bustle in the great chamber of the xoconai city was unusual this day, with an air of urgency rarely seen. The augurs, so practiced in their ways, so mundane in their daily rituals, rushed about with eagerness and determination, but the God-King, so insulated and caught within the dullness that had been trained into his mind, hardly noticed.

He knew not what time it was—time was hardly a concept that occurred to the God-King, who spent his days and nights inside and had rarely glimpsed the sky—when an augur, who was titled and so named *Pixquicauh*, or High Priest of the Xoconai, entered and moved up to the base of the throne to address him directly.

He waited patiently, but Pixquicauh did not immediately speak. A second black-robed, skull-faced augur shambled up to stand beside the first, then another, and another. Five more, ten more, and soon, it seemed as if all the augurs of the great temple stood there before Skath-mi-Zahn.

"A momentous day, God-King," Pixquicauh said behind his condor skull condoral.

"Speak!" the God-King commanded in a petulant voice, one full of frustrations so profound that the young servant, who thought himself a god, could not begin to comprehend.

"The sun was eaten this day. Vomited anew, for us," said Pixquicauh, with great gravity and drama in his voice, a triumphant roar that made the naïve God-King think he should understand that something was important here.

"Vomited?" the young xoconai God-King asked, crinkling his face with disgust. "To me, why would you tell such a disgusting thing?"

Behind the grayish condoral, Pixquicauh sighed. "By the mouth of Kithkukulikahn shall the Shining Orb of Skath-mi-Zane's day be taken. Kithkukulikahn, God-King. Your dragon."

"My . . . dragon?" The child knew that his face was full of trepidation, but he couldn't help it. He had been taught every day for his entire young life about who he was and about the glories of his previous life, when he had ridden a great winged serpent and conquered the world. He believed the stories, of course—it was all that he knew—but those lessons put such tales of heroism and brilliance far in the past, and spoke of any return to glory only far in the future.

"Let it be told that Kithkukulikahn is returned, oh Glorious Gold," Pixquicauh insisted. "Tonalli was taken, the fiery orb of light returned. The light of day was taken, the light of day returned. It is the time."

"The time?"

As one, the gathering of augurs turned about to face a door at the far end of the chamber. It swung open, and two more of the temple augurs entered the room, flanking a third augur in black robes, but one, the only one, who was not wearing a condoral.

The God-King sucked in his breath at the sight, for it was forbidden for any to approach him without wearing the appropriate death-mask!

But his loyal augurs ushered this one—this very old one, he realized—up to the throne.

The God-King stood, and all the augurs fell to their knees immediately.

Even the newcomer, the stranger with the old face bared to his god, knelt.

Skath-mi-Zahn leaned forward. "Stand," he ordered, and all of the augurs began to rise.

"No!" he shouted. "No! No! No!" And they all fell back to their knees. "Just this one. Stand!"

The newcomer rose shakily on his old legs.

"Where is your death-mask?" Skath-mi-Zahn demanded.

The impertinent old xoconai snorted.

"He is of the old scrolls, Glorious Gold," Pixquicauh explained, though it was hardly an explanation to the child pretender, who didn't even know what the "old scrolls" might mean.

It didn't bother him much, though, because Skath-mi-Zahn believed that he was going to have some fun soon enough. Sometimes when he ordered sacrifices, he was allowed to sever the head, slowly, easing the serrated knife back and forth while the victim wailed, then gurgled. He thought it very funny. In the case of this old and impudent augur, he would insist upon wielding the jagged knife.

"Upon my glory, you stare, without a death-mask," Skath-mi-Zahn said. "You must die."

The old, old augur wheezed and coughed in what Skath-mi-Zahn came to realize was a mocking laugh. The youngster started to squeal, demanding immediate execution, but none of the others rose. Wearing a sinister smile, the old augur said, "I am the Last Augur of Darkness, as was foretold. Through my line, my ancestors, my temple wall—and only there—were the signs remembered."

"You wear no condoral!" the God-King screeched.

"I approach naked, as was foretold," the Last Augur of Darkness replied. "For this day have my visions come to be. My eyes alone foresaw this day, my words alone warned. This day, through the unshaken faith of my line, when Cizinfozza, guardian of Teotl Tenamitl, has thinned to nothingness. When Kithkukulikahn then arose to tell us of the great happening by eating Tonalli. Days ago, my heart heard the departure of the evil beast. The dark fiend who slept upon the Teotl Tenamitl to watch over the flood and hold fast the land with the power of dead souls is no more. By mine eyes did I see, by my temple wall did I know, and so, forth I sent my mundunugu scouts."

Skath-mi-Zahn swallowed hard, confused, and more than a little afraid. This augur wasn't shying from him, wasn't intimidated by him. For all the lessons and all the compliments and all the claims of his power, the child understood something, or feared it at least: his power rested fully upon others obeying him.

This one wasn't.

"Kneel!" he commanded.

The old, old augur, the proclaimed Last Augur of Darkness, did not.

"Scouts, you claim. What did they find?" Skath-mi-Zahn screamed, because he did not know what else to scream.

"They have not returned," came the naked-faced xoconai's calm reply. "But we do not need them. We have been shown. Your dragon ate the sun."

"My dragon will eat you!" The God-King turned to Pixquicauh. "I want him to be killed! Now!"

"Glorious Gold, it is not the time," Pixquicauh dared to reply, and dared to rise. "I say and so it has been told. There is one more thing we must do."

"Must?"

"To confirm the words of the son of Bayan, who is the Last Augur of Darkness."

Skath-mi-Zahn sputtered, having no idea of what Pixquicauh was babbling about.

"The signs have come to be," Pixquicauh explained. "Glorious Gold, your beauty will shine greater than all who have worn the throne before you. But you must take up *Tezacuit.*"

"The Golden Rod?"

He knew of what Pixquicauh was speaking. In a dark room within the catacombs of the great temple, surrounded by the open tombs of the line of Skath-mi-Zahn, was a second throne, a dark and ugly seat carved of obsidian. Skath-mi-Zahn had only seen the place once, and that was years before, but he would never forget the sight. Or the feeling of that cold dungeon. For the black throne glowed, or un-glowed, he thought, casting an aura of dusty blackness that reduced even the largest torches to pinpricks of light.

Just enough to see the red veins shot through the seat—the veins of all the God-Kings, the blood of Skath-mi-Zahn—and the brilliant reflection of the throne's deadly trap. For yes, set within that seat was a bejeweled golden rod, Tezacuit, a scepter which protruded between the legs of anyone seated upon the throne like some glorious and erect cock. A weapon, the God-King remembered then, that would strike mortally at any who dared sit upon the obsidian throne.

"Take it up?" he asked under his breath, having no idea what that might mean.

"Rise!" the Last Augur of Darkness commanded.

"You do not . . ." Skath-mi-Zahn started to argue.

But Pixquicauh intervened, seconding the call with a resounding, "Rise!"

The gathering of black-robed augurs stood up and parted, forming a double line, and Pixquicauh ushered the God-King between them, the procacious, unmasked old augur following close behind.

"Cizinfozza has gone," the augur said to his commander, a warrior, or ma-cana, so named for the war clubs they typically carried, fabulous flat-barreled bats of greenish brown, streaked with fine silver veins and lined with the teeth of giant lizards.

"They are his smelly children," the disgusted warrior replied, indicating the growing camp of the gathered mountain goblins, now some hundred strong. "The goblin god's stench remains."

The augur gave a low growl behind his condoral. It was true enough, to some extent, and he, too, could hardly hide his contempt for these bastard creatures, though he constantly reminded himself that they were created, according to xoconai lore, because their own god demanded that his children love the children of Cizinfozza, and so improve their pathetic bloodline with that of the xoconai. The goblins were the children of the demon god, and so should be killed, but these creatures, which the xoconai called *xelquiza*, or half-bloods, were a more complicated lot. For they were descended of goblins, and descended of xoconai.

Children of Skath-mi-Zahn.

Children, too, of Cizinfozza.

"Our mercy would be shown in killing them," said the macana.

"Our wisdom would be shown in letting the humans do it," the augur replied. "The xelquiza know the passes about Teotl Tenamitl and many have navigated Tzatzini. Their hatred of the humans is more than our own. Let them lead the way. Let them be destroyed while destroying our enemies, that they may be of some value to we who made them stronger."

"When?" the macana demanded. "More we will need to guard them than we would to guard against humans, or great cats, or bears, or the black-winged totot. They will kill us if they can."

"They will not."

"They will, augur."

The augur shook his head, but let it go. "Tonalli was eaten and vomited. The Glorious Gold will rouse and gather the armies of Tonoloya. Soon. Soon."

"Before the snows?"

The augur did not answer, other than to stare hard. The snows were al-ready beginning in some of the higher passes, after all.

The macana didn't seem pleased, but he let it go at that.

Later that afternoon, they learned that more xelquiza had been rounded up by other xoconai far to the south. These intended shock troops were already marching north to the foothills to join with the augurs here.

The augur and the macana together looked to the wall of mountains they called Teotl Tenamitl, hoping the scouts of the Last Augur of Darkness, an old xoconai they had thought mad not so long ago, would soon return. No, not the actual scouts, actually, for the journey from the mountain they called Tzatzini to this place would take weeks.

But the xoconai knew how to pass the words much more quickly, shout to shout, or using smoke signals and reflections of the sun off polished golden surfaces. Their spies were scattered about those mountains from time untold, replaced every two seasons.

The augur and the macana looked back the other way, to the west and the wide basin that led to the sea where the fiery orb of Tonalli extinguished its fires and slept each night, toward the great cities of their people, though none could be seen from this particular area.

Word would pass through those cities, from sovereign to sovereign to their xoconai constituents, east to west.

That word, that call, would bring the armies from the west, to follow in the steps of these leading xelquiza forces, the steps that would take the xoconai back home.

It would be a glorious day.

Who knew how many thousands of seasons had passed since the golden scepter had been placed in this stone? It was beyond the ancestral memories of the oldest xoconai bloodlines, beyond the chants, prayers, and visions of the augurs, even the Last Augur of Darkness.

In this dark and rarely visited place beneath the great pyramid, set in the obsidian stone, amidst the eternal lava dust that stole the glow of torches, the golden scepter named Tezacuit was not held by chains or ridges. It simply was, as if it had grown from the seat of the throne, protruding as solidly as if it was part of the stone itself.

Many had tried to take it, tugging futilely. The strongest xoconai macana had grasped the scepter and pulled until their arms and backs ached, or until, it was told, the scepter had tired of them, and so had melted them to ash.

Only a century before, a sovereign of a great city, emboldened by the landslide of a vote that had placed her upon her seat of governorship, had thought herself the embodiment and so had grasped Tezacuit, and had been reduced to bone, then to ash, before her devoted officers. That event had thrown xoconai society into turmoil, for how could so many have voted so wrongly?

In the more distant past, wars had been fought among the xoconai nations over the scepter. In the dark days of Tumult, ten thousand xoconai had died in or about this very temple, as sovereigns vied for the prize.

Yet, here it remained, unbothered, divine, beyond them.

The augurs formed a circle about the dais. Pixquicauh and the old augur flanked the young God-King as he approached.

Even in the muted torchlight, the scepter shone. No dust could touch it—never did it need to be polished.

"Sit," Pixquicauh ordered the God-King.

The child looked at him, suddenly very afraid.

"What if we are wrong?" he asked, barely able to get the words out.

"Then Tezacuit will eat you," the Last Augur of Darkness told him, and nothing in the old one's tone suggested that he was speaking in jest. Both the God-King and Pixquicauh stared in horror at the unmasked old augur of the line of Bayan.

"It is true" was all that he would say to those expressions.

"But we are not wrong, God-King," Pixquicauh prompted, but there was no missing the doubt in his voice.

"We are not wrong. It has been told," agreed the old augur, with full confidence. For it was he, and he alone, with knowledge passed from his great grandsire, who had foretold the event. He alone was the "we" of whom Pixquicauh spoke.

"You do it, then," the God-King insisted.

The old augur wheezed out a laugh. "Whether the prophecy is right or wrong, any but the Glorious Gold who grasp Tezacuit will fail, and will be consumed," he replied.

"Then I shall make you do it . . ." the child began to demand.

"God-King," Pixquicauh interrupted, and when young Skath-mi-Zahn snapped around to regard him, the high priest motioned to the obsidian throne. "Sit."

"It will kill me!" the child cried and hesitated.

But the old augur took hold of him and hoisted him up, dragging him over to the seat. The high priest reflexively grabbed the old augur to stop him.

"You doubt?" the Last Augur of Darkness accused, and all about the dais, the xoconai augurs gasped behind their condorals, and Pixquicauh fell back, shaken, and began to pray.

The old augur dropped the child into the seat, his legs straddling the scepter far too short for his feet to come anywhere near the floor.

"Now is the time," the Last Augur of Darkness told the God-King. "Now is the Cuowitay, the Day of the Xoconai. It is said and it has been told."

The child stared at him.

"Grasp it!" the old augur yelled, so suddenly and so forcefully that poor Skath-mi-Zahn had the scepter in both hands before he even consciously registered his own movements. A horrified look came over him and he pulled back, trying to let go.

But he could not, and arcs of blue lightning began to crackle about his fingers and shoot up his arms. He screamed—how he screamed!—and he thrashed, but the scepter would not let go.

A great wind howled through the underground chamber, blowing out the torches and scattering the black lava dust. But the dungeon did not go dark, far from it, for Tezacuit began to glow, bright white flames swirling about it, over Skath-mi-Zane's child hands.

He screamed louder, though whether in horror or agony, the gathered priests could not tell.

The white flames grew, climbing up his arms, but his screaming changed to singing, a most beautiful song, its light notes full of promise and hope.

As one, the augurs shielded their eyes from the blinding light and heat as the white flames climbed higher, engulfing the child, growing.

The fires came alive. They leaped away from the God-King, reigniting the torches.

And on the obsidian throne sat no child, but a xoconai man, a tall and glorious xoconai, his head framed in hair made of sunshine, his nose the brightest red, lined by blue so brilliant that it would shame a crisp autumn sky, and that framed by white purer and more profound than the midwinter snow on the peaks of Teotl Tenamitl. These were more than mere colors, it seemed, as if the being's face itself was the personification of those hues, in brilliance unmatched.

No more was the golden scepter, Tezacuit, set in the chair, and the hole where it had been, if there ever was a hole, was healed, the seat simply a plane of polished, unblemished, shining obsidian, with no sign that it had ever been anything else.

The beautiful creature held the last notes of his song, and they hung in the air for a long while after he had stopped singing.

He turned to face the high priest, who fell to his knees and prostrated himself, shaking uncontrollably, as did all the others in the chamber, even the stubborn and proud old augur of the line of Bayan.

"Who am I?" the being demanded.

"Skath-mi-Zahn!" Pixquicauh cried, and others followed.

"Scathmizzane!" the true xoconai God-King corrected, changing the inflection and emphasis of the name. "Rise!" he ordered, and the augurs climbed to their feet.

The God-King stood up and motioned for the high priest to come to him. Pixquicauh moved slowly, so obviously terrified and awestricken.

"You did not believe this day of prophecy," Scathmizzane said.

"I did, Glorious Gold!" he shrieked, falling to his knees and dropping his masked face into his hands in shame.

"You tried to stop the Last Augur of Darkness from placing the child I was onto the throne," Scathmizzane said simply, and Pixquicauh wailed.

"Only you knew," Scathmizzane said, looking to the old augur, who stood perfectly at ease.

"They said and it has been told," he replied with confidence.

Scathmizzane lowered the end of his golden scepter under the down-facing condoral of the high priest, and without effort, he used only that to lift the xoconai to his feet, then tilted his face so that he could look into his eyes.

A wave of the God-King's hand sent Pixquicauh's condoral and black robes flying away.

The God-King kissed the high priest. And held the kiss. Pixquicauh groaned and moaned in undeniable, almost unimaginable, ecstasy. It went on and on, and the others in the chamber stared and gasped, and cried at the beauty, and prayed they would one day know such divine joy.

But the timbre of those orgasmic moans shifted, became cries, became shrieks.

And the high priest's face and form seemed to shrink, as if all the fluid in his body was being taken from him, shriveling him into a desiccated husk. And it continued, and his skin began to peel and shrivel, and roll apart to flow, too, into the mouth of Scathmizzane.

White bone showed in patches all about the naked form of the xoconai high priest, then more still, emerging from the melting flesh.

When he was just a skeleton, Scathmizzane relented and pulled away, and the high priest, somehow not yet dead, clattered about as if in confusion, waving his bone arms, and turning his bare skull this way and that, his eyeballs, the only thing left of him that wasn't bone, searching desperately.

Then he fell apart, a pile of bones, and two bulging eyes—eyes remaining as if to forever look upon the error of his doubts.

But no! For Scathmizzane waved Tezacuit and summoned the skull of the high priest to his grasp. He turned to the old augur and bade him to come forward.

Without the slightest hesitation in his step, the old augur walked up, and accepted the kiss of Scathmizzane.

And he knew divine joy. On and on it went, but when it stopped, when the God-King pulled back, the augur remained intact. Scathmizzane's glory had not melted him.

Scathmizzane smiled and nodded, but then, so suddenly that none could even follow the movement, the God-King shoved the skull of the high priest against the face of the old augur, whose arms went straight out to the sides, shaking in agony, grasping helplessly at the air.

And he screamed as if the fires of Tonalli itself were burning within him.

Then it was over, so quickly, and the old augur still stood, except that now he wore the bone mask and bulging, fleshless eyes of the dead man.

No, no mask, he realized, and so did the others, for it was fused to him, surely.

This was his face now.

"No more are you the Last Augur of Darkness," Scathmizzane proclaimed. "Now you are the First Augur of the Light. I name you Pixquicauh, High Priest of Scathmizzane."

"It is said and so it has been told," the new Pixquicauh recited obediently, and there was strength in his voice, power beyond anything he had ever before known.

Scathmizzane stared at him for a few long heartbeats. "You know what to do," the God-King prompted.

Pixquicauh spun about to address the whole of the gathering, and they saw that the jaw of his fused xoconai condoral did not move when he spoke, though his undead, bulging eyes did roll to scan them as he commanded.

"Go!" he told them. "Tell the sovereigns of Cuowitay. Gather the armies."

8

KING'S ARMOR

"What was that?" Talmadge asked when the shadow finally crossed over and past the sun.

Bryan could only shrug. "Whatever it is, it has passed. A giant bird?"

"We would now see it, yes?" reasoned Talmadge, for the sky around the sun was perfectly clear and perfectly empty. "Might it have flown into the fires of speuer?"

"Speuer?"

"Heaven," Talmadge clarified.

"It flew into the sun? I suppose that is a possibility, but the shadows seemed more as if something had passed across . . ."

He stopped and jumped, and so did Talmadge, when there came a tremendous "ka-thump," like the sound of a cupped hand being shoved down into water, only a thousand times louder.

Both turned to the lake and rushed to the ridge for a better view, and together they gasped at a huge swell, a circle of waves rolling out from the south-center of Loch Beag, not too far offshore. They watched dumbstruck as the moments passed and the great, lazy, rolling swell moved toward them, dissipating as it went, but then leaping when it hit the shallows, to roll over into a crashing wave. It rushed up onto the shore, rolling in for some distance before quickly receding, and taking with it trees and brush, even large stones, in that retreat.

"What?" Talmadge asked.

"Something fell from the sky?" Bryan asked more than answered. "A giant threw a stone, perhaps, one that crossed the sun and fell into the lake."

From the man's face, Talmadge realized that he didn't believe his guess any more than he expected Talmadge to buy it.

No matter, though. They waited a bit longer, but the lake soon flattened and seemed to return to normal. And above, the sun was shining.

"I hope it didn't do much damage in Car Seileach," Talmadge remarked, and when Bryan looked at him curiously, he added, "The village just to the south. Fine people."

Bryan smiled warmly. "I admit that I was hoping to find you up here," he said. "I expect that I am a bit . . . unusual, for the experiences of the tribesmen around this lake."

"Loch Beag," Talmadge said reflexively, and Bryan smiled again.

"You see? Another reason I am glad to find you."

"You don't even speak their language."

"Did you, when first you came up here?"

It was a good point, Talmadge had to admit, to himself at least. It had taken him several journeys up here to be able to easily communicate with the lakemen. Bryan's path would likely be easier, since Talmadge had also taught many of them common words of the language of Honce-the-Bear.

"You can be my guide," Bryan said enthusiastically.

Talmadge almost agreed, but after a short consideration, answered, simply, "No."

"No?"

"Why are you up here?" Talmadge knew that his tone had changed, had become less friendly, but it couldn't be helped.

"To see the world. Why are you?"

Talmadge didn't blink.

"My life is an adventure," Bryan said. "You made this place seem an adventure."

Talmadge dropped his gaze, just a bit, to the fabulous breastplate Bryan wore. Even aside from the magic in the gemstones set in the metal, this silverel, whatever that may be, it seemed pretty obvious that no ordinary man, not even a man of noble birth, could be wearing such a suit, or holding such a sword. Talmadge had never even heard of such treasures, and though his experience with the lands to the east was limited, the Matinee each year on the frontier was full of stories of treasure and adventures and great heroes.

"No," Talmadge said again, still shielding his eyes and staring out at the lake to see if anything more was to come. "There is too much unknown. I cannot . . ."

"Risk your friends," Bryan finished with a nod. "I have great respect for that."

"No ordinary man would wear such armor," Talmadge said bluntly. "It is the badge of an order—Allheart Knights, perhaps? What designs might such a warrior order have on the villagers of Loch Beag, I wonder? Nothing good, and nothing I would aid in inflicting upon them."

"No knightly order inspired this suit," Bryan said. "The armor is unique. It was crafted specifically for me, just for me, by the finest blacksmith in Honce-the-Bear, using the greatest metals in the world. There is no equal to silverel, I assure you. This sword will hold its edge when you and I are dust. And both armor and sword were crafted with the greatest gemstones found, too. No minor magic, these."

"Then you have even more to explain."

"Sit," Bryan bade him. "It is a long tale. Perhaps shorter, though, if you have heard of King Aydrian of Honce."

The name was known to Talmadge, but not well. He knew that a young man named Aydrian Boudabras had assumed the throne more than a dozen years before, and the result had been a great civil war, both within the kingdom and within the dominant Abellican Church. By that time, though, Talmadge had been in the frontier, and so had heard some stories, but nothing that had mattered much to him.

"I have heard the name."

"He was a young man, too young," said Bryan. "And corrupted, both by the evil lurking within the Abellican Church and the demon dactyl itself. He failed, miserably, and the kingdom was plunged into darkness."

"All because of him."

"No," Bryan quickly replied. "And that is why I can rise each morning with hope."

Talmadge looked at him curiously after the strange answer.

"He . . . I, was merely a tool for greater and darker forces to work their evil." The man looked off into the distance, his expression one of profound sadness.

"What do you mea . . . ?" Talmadge began, but he bit it short and stared hard at the man. "I?" he asked.

Not turning back to regard him, Bryan slowly nodded.

"You were a part of that? A friend of King Aydrian?"

"This is Aydrian's armor," Bryan explained. "Made to fit Aydrian perfectly."

"Then how do you have it?" Talmadge said, but haltingly, for the truth was coming plain now, as unbelievable as it seemed.

"Do you know the end of King Aydrian's tale?" Bryan asked.

Talmadge tried hard to remember. "I heard of a battle at a church."

"A monastery, a great abbey," Bryan corrected. "And not just any abbey, but St.-Mere-Abelle itself, the greatest structure in all the known world, a fortress beyond compare. The battle was worthy of that place, I assure you."

"You were there?"

Bryan laughed and nodded. "Did you hear of a dragon entering the battle?"

"There is always a whisper of some ridiculous . . ."

"There was a dragon there," Bryan interrupted. "A real dragon, a tremendous and great flying beast that breathed fire, and with claws that could grasp a man and crush him with ease. A beast with such strength that it could lift a fat ox in each claw and fly away without hindrance." Bryan sighed and settled back. "A dragon, a true dragon, and that was not the only marvel of the Battle of St.-Mere-Abelle. The air was filled with magic. Lightning bolts and fireballs." He winced and whispered, as if his voice was failing him, "So many valiant men killed, on both sides. Ghosts pulled from their graves . . ."

Aydrian stopped and heaved a great sigh, looking past Talmadge, looking to nowhere, Talmadge understood, except back to that long-ago day.

"Who won?" Talmadge asked.

"Aydrian's reign was ended that day."

"And Aydrian?"

"Your King Aydrian Boudabras died that day."

Again, there came a long pause, and Talmadge sensed a great sadness within the man.

"He was your friend?"

"My mortal enemy, though I did not know it at the time."

"Then how have you come by the armor of dead Aydrian?" Talmadge dared to ask.

"Because Aydrian Boudabras was killed, but Aydrian Wyndon reborn," the man explained. "This sword . . ." He lifted the blade and Talmadge shied away just a bit. "This sword was crafted by the elves."

"I've never seen an elf," Talmadge said, his tone more than a little dismissive.

"Few have. They train the rangers who roam the lands."

"'I've never seen a ranger, or heard of one."

The armored man laughed a bit at that. "The sword was gifted to Mather Wyndon, and from his ghost, won by Elbryan Wyndon, hero of Honce-the-Bear, trained by the Touel'alfar, the elves. This was his sword, and his bow, Hawkwing, made for him."

"You seem to have collected some fine items . . ." Talmadge began.

"Elbryan was my father," the man interrupted.

Talmadge considered it for a moment, then said softly, "Elbryan, Bryan . . ."

"My name is Aydrian," said the other. "Aydrian Wyndon. I was born as such, and raised as such, until taken by dark forces and given the title of Boudabras. Then I was King—nay, Tyrant would be a better title."

He smiled again, and Talmadge knew it was at his expense, for his own face was screwed up indeed at that moment.

"I thought I would never again admit that," the man, Aydrian, went on. "I know not why. Perhaps as part of my penance, or because I feared that I would never be worthy of the name Wyndon."

"Or because King Aydrian still has enemies?" Talmadge offered, but Aydrian shrugged and shook his head.

"If that is so, then so be it. I did not flee the battlefield. Those who defeated my armies that day at St.-Mere-Abelle granted me leave, with my mother, Jilseponie, who had once been Queen of Honce-the-Bear, and who, on that day, had twice been the hero of the realm."

"It seems that you have many stories to tell," Talmadge said, and Aydrian laughed and nodded.

"Too many for now. But I have told you the one that matters most."

"And what now for Aydrian Wyndon?"

"The world. Helping where I may, and harming no one."

The two stared at each other for a long while then.

"We should go and see to your friends in Car Seil . . . ?"

"Car Seileach," said Talmadge, and Aydrian nodded.

Off they went, and this time, Talmadge led the conversation. "You have seen much of the world?"

"More than most."

"Have you ever been to To-gai?" Talmadge asked. "That is where I will go."

"They are not the most welcoming of people," said Aydrian, and Talmadge flashed a scowl. "I have been there," Aydrian went on.

"Tell me the way."

"East," Aydrian replied. "East until you see the mountains looming in the south. That is the Belt-and-Buckle. If you can cross, you will find the steppes of To-gai."

"And if you cannot cross?"

"Then you travel east for many weeks, to the coast of the Mirianic, and there sail south around the mountain spur from the city of Entel to the port of Jacintha."

"And you are in To-gai?"

"No, then you are in Behren. You travel the weeks again, the other way, across scorching deserts, keeping the mountains to the north, until you reach the plateau."

Talmadge hesitated. But he had made up his mind. "How might I cross these mountains? Is there a pass over them?"

Aydrian shook his head. "Well, perhaps there is, but the way I know is not over them, but under, through a deep tunnel known as the Path of Starless Night. But it is guarded by the doc'alfar, the dark elves. If you are elf-friend, they may let you pass. If you are not . . . then you should not approach their homeland, or the entrance to the path, for they will find you, and you'll be given to the bog."

That sounded unpleasant. But so did crossing all the way to the coast, across Honce-the-Bear, a land Talmadge had not seen in years and to which he never planned to return at all.

"Why do you want to know about To-gai? Do you plan to go there?"

"I knew a woman once," Talmadge said cryptically, with a movement that could have been a nod, or maybe a shrug. "It is . . . it was, her homeland, and I would like to see it."

"What happened to her?" Aydrian asked.

"She died." He looked to the left, to the great water. "On the loch, two years past. I was with . . ." His voice failed. "I did not think I would ever return here."

"That would seem to be a common theme with the man called Talmadge," Aydrian said, and Talmadge looked at him with confusion for just a moment, until he remembered that the other time he had met this strange man, by a river far to the east, he had also been avoiding the plateau, because of the terrible incident with the man called Badger.

"You run from more than you run to," Aydrian said. "That can never be a good thing."

Talmadge didn't answer, but the question reverberated in his thoughts along the way to the village. Yes, he was leaving again, as every year, but if he went to To-gai, as he was thinking, he thought it unlikely that he would ever return to Loch Beag.

He thought of the Usgar woman he had met a few nights earlier, who had saved him from her tribesmen, and who had dared to enter that cave, a demon cave. Aydrian might know something of that, he told himself, and so decided he would talk with this strange man about it in the very near future.

He shook his head. Why should he care? He was leaving and not returning.

But he couldn't shake the image of that small and dark-haired, dark-eyed woman, Aoleyn. So full of spirit and surprising power. So much like Khotai.

Talmadge stopped, and Aydrian went many more steps before turning back to regard him.

Talmadge had left that woman, like he had left Khotai, like he had left his village when the rosy plague had come calling.

That was indeed the story of Talmadge.

But the Usgar woman on the mountain was still alive, he believed. He had offered to take her from this place, but she had refused.

Perhaps he should not have left her, should not now leave her. Not now. He looked to Aydrian again, in that splendid armor and with those fabulous weapons and mighty gemstones, and he wondered.

His hand reflexively went to an inner pocket of his trousers, feeling around for an item he once had, but knew he had lost: a lens held within a brass ring and magically empowered by two small quartz gemstones. How he wished he had it now. He could look up the foreboding mountain, magically and from afar, and perhaps find the young woman, to at least learn if she was well.

Perhaps this strange man who claimed to be a king, and who certainly was dressed in armor and magic befitting such a station, could replicate that far-seeing crystal. Talmadge even started to ask.

But there came a wail, and such a cry that it froze both men in their tracks.

"Car Seileach?" Aydrian asked.

"It is at the end of a cove . . ." Talmadge stuttered. "It should be protected from the wav . . ."

"Shallows," Aydrian breathed, and started to run.

Talmadge, who had never encountered the activity of large waves, wasn't sure what that might mean, but between Aydrian's gasp and the wail of the distant woman, he didn't need to have an explanation then. He sprinted behind the man, and was amazed that he could not keep up. Aydrian was running in plated armor, and unarmored Talmadge, a man who spent his life running the trails of the frontier, could not keep up.

And the man's stride! Talmadge was taller than Aydrian, his legs much longer, and he was thinner. Talmadge glided when he ran, with long loping strides.

But Aydrian almost seemed like a springing deer, his strides covering nearly twice the distance as Talmadge's.

Another question, another thought, Talmadge filed away as he caught up to Aydrian at the top of a bluff beneath the blowing branches of a willow, a bluff, he knew, that looked down upon the village of Car Seileach and the sheltered cove that housed it.

It was not a large village, perhaps a hundred houses and a few common areas, for village meals, for building boats, for councils, for prayers, and the like.

Now it was a hundred shattered structures of thatch and wood floating mish-mash in the cove, many pieces bobbing under the weight of shocked and desperate villagers hanging on.

Men and women ran all about the shoreline, which had mostly reverted to its pre-wave levels, Talmadge could see. They wailed and they cried, screaming for children or other loved ones who were missing.

"Their heads," Aydrian stammered, for, despite the devastation before him, it was impossible not to notice these people, their skulls elongated and shaped from birth—in this particular village, most usually into two distinctive humps.

"They are just men and women," Talmadge yelled at him, running by and down to the shoreline, calling out and trying to find some way to help.

Any disappointment he might have felt at Aydrian's reaction wouldn't last, though, for the armored man ran past him, seemed to almost fly past him. Aydrian didn't go into the water, he went onto the water, running across it as if it was solid ground!

A woman nearby struggled in a tangle of flotsam and jetsam, and Aydrian rushed to her, bending low, offering her a hand, then hoisting her effortlessly from the water, quickly running back to shore to drop her on dry ground. Right back out he went, returning soon with two more.

And so it went, tirelessly, and when a wailing woman screamed for her child and indicated a bobbing corner of what had been a house, Aydrian ran to it, patted a green strip of cloth he had tied around his left arm, and, armor, sword, and all, dove under the water.

The eyes of every villager not involved in a desperate struggle went to that spot, to the strange-looking eirigh'ti, this sun man, so unexpectedly pulling their kin from the waters.

For many heartbeats, every noise, every movement, everything seemed to stop. Aydrian's gleaming helmet appeared, then all of him, strangely, crazily, as he lifted up out of the water in a rush, to stand upon it, with not one, but two children cradled in his strong arms.

He ran to the shore, to the wailing woman, and placed her children, crying and very much alive, on the ground before her, then turned and ran right back out.

Talmadge pulled a rope from his pack and ran along the shore, throwing its end to nearby villagers to help pull them to shore. He had never seen, had never imagined such a sweeping devastation as this—the wave had run up through the village, then simply pulled everything back out with it.

He put his emotions away and helped where he could.

So it went for a long while, everyone trying to help each other, Aydrian running about the water, sometimes diving under, sometimes bringing out half-drowned, or drowned, villagers to carry to the shore.

As the immediate and obvious tasks diminished, the wails began anew, drawing Talmadge to one small group, kneeling and crying over a horribly wounded man. A splintered log from a shattered house had skewered him, just blow the ribs, and he groaned in pain, still pouring blood, somehow still alive.

One older woman—Talmadge knew her as one of the village healers—reached for the natural spear, but as soon as she touched it, the man howled in agony. Her hands shaking, for there really was nothing she could do, she placed a torn cloth about the impalement to try to stem the bleeding. Perhaps she was, Talmadge thought, but only outwardly. Inside, the man continued to bleed. Everyone there understood that he was in the last moments of his life.

Aydrian pushed through the circles of the gathered villagers. Many shied from this strange man, despite his previous and continuing efforts, while others calmly ushered him by. A couple tried to hinder him, but he pushed them aside with incredible ease, finally falling to his knees beside the dying man. He pulled off his helmet and placed it on the ground, then put one hand over the gemstones set in his breastplate and the other on the man's wound.

He chanted softly—Talmadge could feel the energy and warmth building around him.

A wave of healing came forth, silencing the complaints of a few villagers and bringing enough calm to the dying man that he breathed more easily, the rattle and rasp clearly diminished.

Gasps arose as Aydrian grasped the impaling log, but then let go and shook his head. Looking up at the others, he took up his helm and placed it on the head of the wounded man. Then he placed one hand on that faceplate, on the gemstones crossing above the man's nose, and grasped the log with the other. He chanted again, another wave of healing, then again, but for something different, something that jolted the poor, wounded man. Before anyone could react, more especially that poor fellow, Aydrian yanked out the log!

Blood poured behind it, but Aydrian's hand was there, suddenly, and more healing came forth.

"Usgar," Talmadge heard one of the onlookers whisper, and not complimentarily or congenially.

"No Usgar!" the frontiersman loudly countered, standing tall. "No Usgar! From the east! A friend!"

Whatever anger the claim that Aydrian was Usgar might have brought could not gain traction in that crowd at that time. This strange newcomer had helped tremendously, selflessly, perhaps even placing himself in danger repeatedly by diving under the water.

And now this mortally wounded villager was alive and awake, and he even managed a bit of a smile when Aydrian gently removed the helmet.

He was still in pain, obviously, and still seemed on the edge of death, but he was certainly more comfortable, and appeared much stronger already.

Aydrian clasped the man's hand and nodded, then let go and stood up.

"Inform me if he begins to weaken again, or bleed again," he said, and all the villagers looked at him curiously, most shaking their heads and shrugging. Aydrian turned to Talmadge, who translated to the villagers in the language of the plateau.

Then he went off, with Aydrian and most of the others. There was still so much to do, still so many missing. They spent the rest of the day erecting shelters, trying to get a few boats upright and out into the cove, searching the water, and the land nearby—and indeed, they found a group of villagers far back of the cove, much further inland, having been washed there and deposited by the giant wave.

When darkness fell, Aydrian brought up a magical light from a diamond on his necklace, and walked again onto the water, searching.

It seemed impossible that he would find anyone else alive, of course, but it didn't matter. He had to try, and even if he only found bodies, having that evidence and closure would be better for the families.

Talmadge didn't miss the decency in that effort.

Neither did the villagers of Car Seileach.

9

GLORIOUS GOLD

The grand temple had taken on a different feeling in the days since Scath-mizzane's ascendance. It was lighter somehow, brighter, as if the mere pres-ence of the true God-King of the xoconai had brought with him an aura of lightness, of heart and soul and, it seemed, actual daylight. He was called the Glorious Gold among other things, after all, and all the augurs and others who came to the great pyramid temple now understood that title more fully. As his dragon had vomited the sun, the God-King had returned to them a different sort of light, no less warming and blessed than the orb above.

The God-King had taken up his place on the throne, the same seat oc-cupied by the xoconai children whom the augurs had revered before him. Much had changed, though, and immediately. No longer was the throne room merely ceremonial, a place to keep the God-King while the augurs went about the business of overseeing the Tonoloya nation of the xoconai. No more did those augurs hustle to and fro about the temple, passing through the throne room as if it was any other chamber, paying only a cursory glance and offering only a customary, but hardly deferential, bow or salute.

No more. Not the augurs nor any other xoconai would dare ignore the tall and beautiful being seated atop the golden throne on the high dais in the great room of the great temple. They could not! Simply looking upon this being of unspeakable beauty compelled them to lower their gaze, to genuflect, and to take great joy that they were alive in this time of Scath-mizzane's true return.

Scathmizzane took it all in without vanity. He didn't need it. The defer-ence simply was, as it simply should be. Scathmizzane was beyond them, as much as they were beyond the green-speckled, golden-headed cuetzpali they rode as mounts, and so he was their God-King, as it should be. Only days before, this throne had been warmed by the ass of a child, a young and innocent xoconai, revered for his bloodline and not for any accomplishments, certainly, or intelligence, certainly. That, of course, had been a lie—the xoconai child had been no more than a placeholder in a long line of place-holders, a promise of the return of the true god being, and of himself, of themselves—all of the child's ancestors—they had been nothing of conse-quence. Mere figureheads keeping warm the golden throne and reminding the xoconai of their duties and deference to Scathmizzane.

"Word has fingered through the passes and to the sea, God-King," one of the younger of his attendant augurs told him one dusty morning, the desert-like hot winds howling down from the eastern slopes of Tyuskixmal.

"Word that is doubted?"

"No, God-King, there is no doubt!" the augur said with great enthusi-asm. "How could there be? All watched Kithkukulikahn eat the sun and vomit it back as your gift to us."

"How could there be?" Scathmizzane echoed in a tone that drained the blood from the young augur's face, though it was covered by a buzzard skull condoral and so was not witnessed. Still, the way the xoconai shuffled from foot to foot, and from a puddle forming between his feet, those around understood well that this impertinent fool expected that his life was about to meet a horrible end.

The room went deathly silent.

"Is this how you spoke to the child, Skath-mi-Zane?"

"No, God-King."

"Do you bear false testimony to me?"

"No . . ." His voice failed him.

Scathmizzane stood up tall upon the dais and let his gaze flow about the chamber, and every augur in there felt naked before this great and powerful being.

"I am not without mercy," he said. "You have all witnessed this one." He pointed to the young augur, who gave a pathetic mewling sound and shook so badly that it seemed as if he would simply fall over.

"He questioned me," Scathmizzane said simply, and a collective inhale ensued. "Perhaps he should offer himself for sacrifice."

"Yes, God-King," the pitiful young augur squeaked.

"It is not accepted!" Scathmizzane boomed suddenly and violently, and the chamber shook under the sheer power of his voice.

Many heartbeats passed in absolute silence, before Scathmizzane added, "This time. None other who stand before me will be forgiven this sin."

As one, a score of augurs bowed.

"Finish your message to me," Scathmizzane told the young augur.

"God-King, none dare doubt," the flummoxed augur stammered in that high-pitched, edge-of-shrieking voice so typical among the xoconai. "They come! From every city, the pilgrims come, hoping to gaze upon your beauty."

Scathmizzane sat back down and nodded as the young augur finished, "We await your commands of how they may look upon you."

"They will process through this very chamber, singly, in a line," Scathmizzane told them. "They will gaze at the floor before them."

He paused.

"It is said and so it has been told," all of the augurs chanted in unison.

"They will each look upon me only once."

"It is said and so it has been told."

He stood up again and walked to the edge of the dais. "You know what my return foments. Cizinfozza is destroyed. Our way home is clear and cleared."

"It is said and so . . ." some of the augurs began to cry out in joy, but Scathmizzane kept speaking and so they all fell silent, elation turning to sudden horror.

"Cleared of the god of death, but cleared not of our enemies. What remains upon Tzatzini and beyond is our task."

Now he paused and the chorus was raised appropriately.

"Hear this, my children. Let no pilgrim come to me without his macana and atlatl. None! Not the women, not the children. All must be prepared to kill. All must be glad to die."

He paused but held his hand up, demanding no refrain, demanding silence.

"But I promise you, my children, that all will not die, and that we will go home."

The augurs then cheered, just cheered, too overwhelmed to worry about forming words or refrains. They cheered on and on, and Scathmizzane let them.

When it ended, the young augur stood before the dais still.

Scathmizzane sat back down on his throne. "You have more to tell me?"

"I offer myself in sacrifice, for the glory of Scathmizzane!" he cried.

"Remove your houtic-condoral," the God-King ordered, using the formal name for the augur mask, which translated to "cleaner of the dead" in the colloquial xoconai language.

With trembling hands, the young augur complied, revealing that his cheeks were stained with tears of joy, for he was happy, and he looked upon his God-King with tears still pouring down his face.

"Not now, child," Scathmizzane told him. "You are the example of my mercy. The living example. You will not err again, will you?"

"I will die before I . . ."

"Good, then be gone and remember ever that my mercy is with limits."

The poor, overwhelmed young augur started to leave, then stopped and bowed repeatedly and foolishly as he tried to put his condoral back on. Finally, he collected himself to begin to depart, but he had gone only two steps when Scathmizzane yelled for him to halt.

"Turn," the God-King ordered, and the young augur slowly swung about to face the beautiful and terrible god once more.

"You sin again?"

The young augur sucked in his breath, obviously at a loss.

"Has it been that long?" Scathmizzane told him, told them all. "Has the disrespect for the line of God-Kings led to such sloth?"

The augurs had no answers.

"When you depart my presence, henceforth, you will do so backing and bowing, every step."

"It is said and so it has been told!" they all cried.

The young augur bowed and backed, then bowed again, but Scathmizzane pointed to the floor before the dais where he had originally been standing—or more particularly, pointed to the puddle of piss on the floor.

The young augur swallowed hard.

"Clean it," the God-King ordered.

"It is said and so it has been told," the young augur recited, and glanced around for a broom or a bucket, or a cloth, or anything he might use.

"Now," Scathmizzane warned.

The augur hiked up his black robes and fell to his knees, as if to use the robe to sop up the puddle.

"Do not dare soil the robes of my priesthood," Scathmizzane warned.

Now so obviously and thoroughly flummoxed, the poor young augur glanced sidelong at some of his more venerated and experienced fellows, but alas, none could offer anything to him.

"Now," Scathmizzane said calmly, too calmly.

The augur fell flat to the floor and cleaned the puddle, with his mouth.

Scathmizzane sat back on his golden throne, quite satisfied, and didn't give the young xoconai, his living example of his merciful manner, another moment of thought.

The old augur, now named Pixquicauh, glanced at the great temple often, but rarely visited. He didn't have to, even though he had been named as the High Priest of Scathmizzane, for he understood his god's needs without having to be told. Perhaps it was telepathic, or perhaps—and the old augur wanted to believe this—it was simply instinctual to him due to the purity of his soul. His family had followed the old ways, the true ways, without interruption since the old times. He understood Scathmizzane's desires, he thought and hoped, because the will of the xoconai God-King was the lesson of his life. The only lesson, the only way.

Scathmizzane believed that, too, he knew, because the God-King had anointed him as Pixquicauh. The name itself didn't much matter to him, or at least, he knew it shouldn't matter to him. His purpose, his joy, his very reason for being, was to serve Scathmizzane, however the God-King demanded. If asked by the Glorious Gold to offer himself for sacrifice, the old augur would happily and without hesitation throw himself upon the altar and open his robes, inviting the dagger.

But the title did matter to him, and it was a failing that he knew he had to simply accept in himself. His line, his father, his grandfather, and many before that, had held true to Scathmizzane, and had known the substitute xoconai God-Kings called Skath-mi-Zahn for what they were. They had known that the dragon would return to eat the sun and announce the glorious return of the true god.

His family had suffered for their faith—for their stubbornness, so they had been told. They had suffered the barbs of the other augurs, telling them to move into the great present and let go of the superstitious past. They had suffered the bare coffers, for so few xoconai would adhere to their teaching, the old ways, which were not as comfortable and gratifying as the new.

Xoconai civilization had become corrupted around him, and he, and his ancestors, had been forced to suffer that indignity and sinfulness.

So this title, this name of Pixquicauh, which shouldn't have mattered to him, did matter, because it was a validation of his family's generations of suffering, of frugality, of denying great pleasures and great accolades, of abstaining from love, other than love of Scathmizzane.

Now it was all worth it, he thought, then immediately chastised himself for that thought.

"It was ever worth it," he whispered. "There is no other way."

Later, he must scourge himself bloody for the momentary transgression, he knew.

He shook the thought away, remembering his most important task this day. Into a common room he went, where more than a dozen xoconai adults sat drinking the wine that had been brought in trade from the northwestern valleys, chatting, and playing various games.

The atmosphere grew tense immediately when the black-robed augur wearing a gruesome skull, an actual xoconai skull, as a condoral entered, and grew more anxious still when the old augur lifted his arms out wide and high, revealing the many black feathers that had been added to his garb, signifying his penultimate rank.

The xoconai revelers fell all over themselves in trying to get down quickly to their knees, even the tavernkeeper, who disappeared behind the bar as he sank low.

The old augur pulled a wrapped object from a wide pocket on the side of his black robe. With great reverence, he unwrapped it, revealing a circular frame with a golden plate inside it, suspended top and bottom by leather cords.

A third cord, a handle with a loop to fit over the bearer's finger, marked the top of the obdiji, the aura spotter. The old augur hooked his crooked finger through the loop and lifted the obdiji aloft, holding it out from his body as he moved to the first kneeling woman, holding the item beside her head. With a puff of breath, he sent the gold plate spinning within the frame.

Around and around it went, and the augur stared into the spinning, polished surface, seeing more than the reflection of the woman's profile, seeing the colors she carried, signifying the level of purity of her devotion to Scathmizzane.

He did this for each of the patrons, measuring them, then selected three from among them.

Three worthy to carry the word of the God-King.

And so he went through the vast city, and late that afternoon, he entered the throne room of the great temple with two dozen porters in tow, each pair of them carrying a heavy wrapped parcel.

The God-King smiled at him. "My child returns," Scathmizzane said, and the mere sound of his melodic voice brought a great warmth to the old augur, and to everyone else in the room, he could tell from their smiles, and even the mere posture of the other augurs, whose faces he could not see behind their condorals. The sound was simply so uplifting that none could help but be joyful.

"Come forward," Scathmizzane bade him, and he moved to stand before the dais. When he arrived and bowed low, Scathmizzane said, "What have you borne to this sacred place?"

"Gifts, God-King," he answered. "The gifts you desire." He turned and motioned to the two nearest porters, who quickly complied by laying their parcel upon the floor and pulling back the wrappings to reveal a stack of a half-dozen shining sheets of polished gold, expertly crafted and gleaming in the few shafts of sunlight that permeated this chamber (or perhaps the light was emanating from Scathmizzane, the Glorious Gold, himself).

On another motion from the old augur, the porters lifted the top sheet and tilted it up on end, showing it to be a full-length mirror.

"Seventy-one?" the God-King asked his High Priest.

"Seventy-two," the old augur answered. "One for each of your temples, and the finest for the eyes of Glorious Gold alone."

Scathmizzane laughed, a beautiful airy laugh that echoed around the room and once again widened the smiles of all in attendance. It struck the old augur how at ease were the porters, common men and women all, and at how brilliant the reds and blues of their facial skin seemed to glow in the presence of this great being.

"I need no mirror for myself," Scathmizzane said. "I see myself in the eyes of my servants, and need no better view."

The augur bowed low, but he did not fear that he had disappointed his deity.

"Take the last one, my servant, to your old temple, on the far foothills, and consecrate it. You will place one atop, of course, to follow Tonalli's flight each day, but this will be your second, set inside the temple, beside your altar, before the grand mural of the line of Dayan. That place in its humbleness shall be known as my greatest temple of them all."

The old augur nearly fell over at that pronouncement, yet another commendation of his ancestral fealty.

"The greatest until . . ." Scathmizzane added teasingly.

The old augur was confused for just a brief moment, then remembered his station as High Priest, and realized that Glorious Gold had just confirmed a plan to him of reclamation and renewal.

"I will bear the mirror personally over Teotl Tenamitl, God-King," he replied, and his heart was so full at that moment that he believed he could indeed make that journey, bearing the heavy item.

"One priest to each pair of porters," Scathmizzane told them all. "In your hearts, you know the way, that these shining sheets of glory are placed at the top of the pyramids at each of my temples. Go now with all haste."

The gathering went into sudden motion, but it was quite organized and efficient, for indeed the voice of Scathmizzane rang in the heads and hearts of the augurs as they each gathered up their pair of porters, knowing exactly the road before them.

Pixquicauh knew, too, that he was to depart the city, back to his temple. He would not continue from there, however, and so a second priest joined him and his chosen porters, to carry on from that location.

Winter was coming. These shining symbols of the Glorious Gold would show the way when the passes of Teotl Tenamitl began to open once more.

"Many will die to the snow and the freezing winds before they ever cross the parapet," a young and swift macana named U'at remarked to Halfizzen, the augur overseeing this mission.

The pair stood on a high ridge, overlooking a long and narrow valley. Down below, the valley floor was dotted with tents and lean-tos, and shorter, thicker forms milled all about. Mountain goblins, the children of Scathmizzane, corrupted with the blood of the children of Cizinfozza, had gathered to the call in numbers rarely seen. Seven hundred strong, they filled the valley, and even from here, the watching xoconai could detect their anxiety and unease. They seemed as if they would simply bust out of the canyon, or murder each other trying.

"Their purpose is to die," Halfizzen replied. "Their only hope of salvation is to give their lives in fealty to the Glorious Gold, else the darkness of Cizinfozza will consume their eternity. Even to the snow and the wind should they fall, it will be with purpose."

U'at, who had been to Tzatzini, the Herald, and indeed had been in battle with a strong human there upon the mountain and had barely escaped, surely understood. He looked to the west, toward the ancient temple of the old augur, on whose commands he had set out to the east, and to whom he was expected to return.

The pair watched as other xoconai passed them on either side, moving in lines, riding their sure-footed cuetzpali down the steep and rocky slope with ease.

"They will deliver the word," Halfizzen remarked. "They will tell the xelquiza the path to their salvation."

"And if the half-bloods do not hear?" U'at dared ask.

"Most will hear. What choice is before them? And those who do not accept the truth will become the sacrifices for the victory of those who do."

U'at smiled and nodded, glancing down at the gathered army of the brutish xelquiza. Most would hear, and so would slaughter any who did not, which meant, of course, that even more would suddenly see the light of the Glorious Gold.

Few fights erupted among the disparate mountain goblins that day in the valley, and those that did were ended quickly and efficiently and with severe finality. In the trailing lines of the westering sun, the half-blood force broke ranks and began its march up the Tyuskixmal slopes of Teotl Tenamitl, a few dozen xoconai observers trailing upon their beautiful and deadly lizard mounts.

"Soon, they will crest the peak," the augur Halfizzen said to U'at, "and rush like the flood of the God-King down the other side, the bringers of death, the forebears of doom."

The High Priest of Scathmizzane reached his weathered temple in the foothills of Teotl Tenamitl some days later. He watched the porters scaling the sides of the small pyramid to place one of the divine golden mirrors as instructed at its apex.

And when they had, it seemed to Pixquicauh as if the temple itself had shed some of the ravages of time. The edges of the rounded blocks of the pyramid appeared straighter once more, and sharp-cornered, and the whole of the place seemed quietly limned in golden light.

On sudden inspiration, the old augur moved past the returning porters and himself scaled the side of the pyramid, confident that the God-King would not let him fall.

He neared the pinnacle mirror, nodded appreciatively at the care the porters had taken in setting it in place, large stones tight about the base so that the winter winds would not topple it.

He reached the apex easily, a climb he knew he could not have made mere days before, when the pathetic child, not the true Glorious Gold, had sat upon the golden throne. Somehow, the emergence of Scathmizzane and the God-King's kiss had given him renewed strength and energy. Arriving, he looked at his reflection in the golden mirror. He felt as if he must look younger. He could not see his face, of course, since the front of the skull of the apostate augur had been fused upon it.

With great reverence and trembling hands, Pixquicauh grasped the edges of that condoral, thinking to remove it.

He paused.

Scathmizzane had put it there.

His name had been Dayan-Zahn, but was now Pixquicauh, a name given to him by Scathmizzane. He would never use his old name again. And this was his face, a visage of bone and bulging dead eyes, given to him by Scathmizzane. He would never use his old face again.

He peered more closely into the golden mirror. His hair seemed thicker, shining more silvery and less dull gray. And fewer wrinkles did he see along his temples and those parts of his jowls visible around the edge of the death-mask.

He sought behind the teeth of the skull, but he could not see his own teeth, and when he talked, as he did then, praying for guidance to Scathmizzane, he realized that the condoral mouth did not move with his words, but neither did any real mouth he might have had behind the mask. Did he even still have his old mouth and teeth?

When last did you eat, my child? rang a voice in his head.

Pixquicauh paused and gasped. He didn't eat much anymore. Food had long ago lost its flavor to him, but only now, before the mirror, did he realize that he had not eaten anything, anything at all, nor had he sipped wine or water, in many days. Too many days!

He should be dead, but he was not, nor was he hungry or thirsty.

"Glorious Gold," he whispered, and cried.

He lingered more than he should, staring at his new face, at the image that showed him to be more than a mere mortal xoconai. Finally, he reminded himself of humility more than once, more than a dozen times, but still he stared and pondered.

He knew not how much time had passed when at last he became so satisfied, so humbled, so grateful to his ancestors for imbuing upon him the power of unflinching faith, that he turned to climb back down.

He heard a voice in his head once more, and this time, less preoccupied with his own image, he recognized it as the whisper of Scathmizzane.

He spun back to the mirror, delighted once more as he came to fully understand this newest miracle. For these were more than shining badges to mark the temples of the God-King. They were portals of clairaudience, through which Scathmizzane would call to his augurs, and they, in turn, would relay to his children.

Pixquicauh noticed then lines of xoconai walking the trails about his temple, coming to see the shining golden mirror, to bathe in the beauteous light of Scathmizzane, and to listen to . . . him.

Truly to hear him, for perhaps the very first time, to comprehend his homily as never before.

To ready for the renewal, for the expansion of Tonoloya, the nation of the xoconai, from sea to shining sea.

He looked into the mirror again, and his reflection faded, replaced by an image of what would be, he realized.

He saw the trails about his temple, all through the foothills. He saw the great army of xoconai, under waving golden banners, lines and lines of lizard riders with shining lances, lines and lines of walking warriors, beating their macana against skin drums, the western slopes of Teotl Tenamitl echoing with the cadence of the army, with the mighty fist of the Glorious Gold.

Tears flowed freely then down his face. His auguries, his father's visions, his grandfather's prophecies, would all be realized.

The march for renewal, the march to war.

10

USGAR-TRIATH

He felt as if his arms weighed as much as boulders. He could find no strength, no energy, no reason.

Though the sun was shining above him once more, his world was dark now, and without hope.

The deamhan Usgar had taken Aoleyn from him.

The sun was up in the sky, but would it ever really shine for him again? He was nothing now, without friends, without hope. He was a slave, only a slave, ever a slave, until he worked himself to death. He was not Bahdlahn anymore, either, he believed, and the pit inside of him grew deeper and darker.

No, he was Thump again, just Thump, and to be anything but, to hint at anything more, meant that he would be horribly tortured and surely murdered—probably thrown into the same pit that had taken Aoleyn!

But that Usgar deamhan knew the truth of Bahdlahn.

Bahdlahn chewed his lip, trying to come to terms with this new reality. The Usgar named Aghmor knew. Was he to trust this deamhan?

"I am strong," he whispered, nodding, thinking that he was stronger than Aghmor, certainly. Perhaps he could throw the Usgar off a cliff, or into the same hole where they had murdered Aoleyn.

"Yes," he decided, but hearing the word aloud brought him a fit of panic. If he killed this deamhan Aghmor, where would that leave him?

Alone.

Alone and working until he died, or until he slipped and revealed himself to the deamhans and they murdered him.

The day was cold, very cold, but Bahdlahn felt a sweat upon him as he lay in his hidey-hole, staring at nothing. The air was crisp and dry, but he felt like it was suffocating him, closing in on him, holding him there in a state of helplessness and emptiness.

He gasped aloud when he heard movement just outside, and held the breath that wouldn't come when the branch-fashioned door was pulled aside and Aghmor's face appeared. The Usgar nodded and moved in enough to sit at the entrance, half-in, half-out, for the space was not large. He brought his arm around and dropped a bundle at Bahdlahn's side.

"Food," he explained. "Make it last a few days. My tribe is breaking camp tomorrow and will climb to the winter plateau, not far from here."

Bahdlahn forced himself to sit up and nodded.

"I will get you away from here before they arrive," Aghmor added, surprising him. "I have found a cave, not so far away, where you can huddle through the winter. I will bring you food when I can—you will have to forage some, perhaps."

"Why?" Bahdlahn didn't even know where to begin. What was this surprising Usgar even talking about?

"We must get you away," said Aghmor. "This is likely our last chance."

"Why?" Bahdlahn asked again, but mostly because he couldn't find his sensibilities enough to form any other words.

"They will know you. And they will kill you. Even if they do not discover the truth of Thump, they will not keep you alive much longer. You are strong. You are a threat. Tay Aillig is not merciful and the Usgar will be his. We can move you now, before they arrive on the winter plateau, and hide you until the winter season breaks. By that time, perhaps they will have forgotten Thump, and so you will get down the mountain."

Bahdlahn winced at that, remembering Tay Aillig's overt threat to him not so long ago.

"Why?" he asked a third time. "Why are you helping me?"

Aghmor's expression revealed to Bahdlahn that the man didn't even seem sure of any answer. "Aoleyn," he finally decided. "She'd want you to live, and to live free. I will make the Usgar believe that you were killed by some animal, or that sidhe creature you chased off. Oh, but they'll hunt you to make sure, but they'll not be finding you, not before the snows come deep and strand them upon the winter plateau. In the dark of winter, they will forget you, and then you can leave."

Bahdlahn didn't reply, other than to stare, as he tried to wind his thoughts through this shocking development. He still didn't trust this Usgar, of course, but if the man had wanted him killed, he certainly wouldn't need to go to these lengths.

He could have just let Bahdlahn go over that ridge atop the mountain, to be thrown into the pit after Aoleyn.

Eventually, Bahdlahn managed a nod.

Aghmor did not leave the cave where he had hidden Bahdlahn feeling better about the situation, or even remotely confident that he could pull off his plans for the uamhas. He remained determined to try, though, and every time he replayed in his mind the image of poor Aoleyn going into that chasm, it strengthened his resolve a bit more.

That image haunted him, night and day.

He came down to the winter plateau and started to cross, when a shaky old voice called out to him from across the way.

"I will know the darkness," said Elder Raibert.

Aghmor turned to see the man standing in the doorway of his hut, or rather, slumped against the side of the jamb. He moved over quickly to stand before Raibert, offered a hand to help.

"Why?" Raibert laughed at him, feebly, slowly, waving the offered hand aside.

"I'll be helping you to your bed," Aghmor explained.

"The darkness is there. The light is coming, but I'll not see it!"

Aghmor stared at him curiously. The man sometimes seemed quite confused, after all, but this was somehow different. He noted that Raibert wasn't looking at him at all, but was looking past him. He glanced over his shoulder, but nothing was there, and yet the man kept staring off, nodding, grimacing, shaking his head, mumbling.

"The spring of the swarm," Raibert said.

"The swarm?"

"Covering the mountains, covering Fireach Speuer."

"What swarm?"

"Numbers beyond count! Riding, marching . . . the dragon flying . . ."

"What darkness, old man?" Aghmor yelled, grabbing Raibert and shaking him.

"Darkness?" Raibert answered directly, his face locked in a seemingly maniacal grin. "No, none. No darkness. The light. The swarm of sunlight!"

"What nonsense do you speak?"

"Nonsense?" Raibert began to laugh then, wheezing and coughing with every sharp and mocking chuckle.

"Now I see," the Elder remarked, his gaze drifting past Aghmor again. "At last and in the last!" He shouted with surprising strength, and he grabbed back at Aghmor powerfully, more so than the man would ever have believed possible.

"Now, at last I see, and only in this last moment."

Elder Raibert slumped into Aghmor's arms. The man shook him and demanded an answer.

But the dead do not speak.

After settling Raibert's body upon his bed and covering him with blankets, Aghmor started fast down the mountain to report the great event. The Elder of Usgar, the Usgar-forfach, was dead. That would open a path for Tay Aillig, perhaps, unless Ahn'Namay could claim the title and stop him.

Strangely, Aghmor found that he didn't care. This death would alter the tribe, surely, but to no better way, as far as he could tell, whatever might happen next.

A steady snow began to fall as he made his way, slowing him, slickening the ground, chilling him.

It seemed appropriate, he thought.

It was almost nightfall when he at last made the encampment, or what was left of it, for the preparations for the journey back up to the winter plateau were nearly completed. One tent that remained was Tay Aillig's, and as he approached it, Aghmor heard the voice of the War Leader, and that of Crystal Maven Mairen, as well.

"There is nothing to explain," he heard Tay Aillig say.

"There's a time of mourning expected," Mairen replied.

"But not demanded. We'll be married on the morning, a celebration to lead the journey up the mountain. We'll consecrate the union at the sacred form of Usgar, the Usgar-righinn and the Usgar-triath. It's fitting and right."

Aghmor wasn't surprised by the statements, including Tay Aillig's titling of himself as Usgar-triath, as Chieftain—until he realized that Tay Aillig was already presuming that old Raibert was dead. How could he know?

Had Mairen seen it with the magic of Usgar?

"War Leader," he said, announcing his presence. "I must speak with you."

Tay Aillig pulled back the inner flap and motioned Aghmor inside.

"Sad news comes with me," Aghmor said. "Elder Raibert has passed on to Corsaleug."

He watched their faces as he told them, and neither seemed the least bit surprised, for a moment. Then both appeared shocked, and given the last few remarks they had made before they had known he was there, Aghmor knew they were feigning surprise.

"And the Usgar slave, too, is dead, I fear," he added.

"The boy?" Tay Aillig asked. "How?"

"We did not see him when we went to Craos'a'diad," Mairen told him.

"He was off gathering stones, then," said Tay Aillig.

Aghmor shrugged. "He is not there, and has not been for some time. I found blood. I think him dead."

Tay Aillig let out a little growl.

"He would have become dangerous," Mairen said. "His mother was given to Usgar."

"I wanted to kill him," Tay Aillig replied, then to Aghmor, "You found his body?"

"Just some blood."

"Then he has run off," said Tay Aillig. "Find your witches, Mairen, and find him."

"There were sidhe tracks near th'Way," Aghmor said.

"We should have killed him years ago," Tay Aillig grumbled.

"He is stupid," Mairen reminded him. "If he ran, he is on a main trail down the mountain or he will get lost in the wilds and killed by a beast. He can'no evade us." She left the tent and Aghmor heard her call for Connebragh. They would search the lower trails magically, but they wouldn't find Bahdlahn, Aghmor expected, and hoped.

Once again, the man wondered why in the world he was taking this great risk, and for the sake of an uamhas.

Tay Aillig led the way out of the tent, then, and shouted for the tribe to gather around him. He pulled Mairen to his side.

"We have word that Elder Raibert is dead," he said, and gasps and wails arose, followed by many chants and prayers.

"This is time for the fist of Usgar to tighten," he declared, holding up his clenched hand. "The traitor Aoleyn was given to Usgar, and the Usgar-forfach is delivered into the hands of our god. This day, I take Mairen, Usgar-righinn, as my wife."

There came cheers, lots of cheers, but many murmurs, too, and more than one glanced to Ahn'Namay, who all believed to be next in line to replace Raibert.

"I take these signs from Usgar," Tay Aillig shouted. "He is pleased." He stared straight at Ahn'Namay and smiled. "I am Usgar-triath, and Usgar-righinn is my wife."

More cheers, more gasps, and one shout of "no!" followed immediately. The gathered folk looked all around as if not quite knowing what to make of this startling claim to power. There had been no Usgar-triath, no Chieftain, since Raibert had forfeited many of the duties of the position many decades before. Most of those gathered weren't even old enough to remember that day.

But now Tay Aillig had named himself as such, and had claimed a wife, though his own sacrificed wife's body had barely cooled.

"Let any who would deny this speak now," Tay Aillig said, an obvious warning. As if on cue—and it probably was on cue, Aghmor realized—more than a few young and strong Usgar warriors, led by Egard, nephew of Tay Aillig, moved to stand beside the man, the Usgar-triath, in open and threatening support.

An uncertain gathering began to whisper, to cheer, to complain, but as the moment moved along, as more warriors moved to Tay Aillig's side, as the other eleven witches of the Coven moved to join the Usgar-righinn, the cheers began to outweigh any other sounds.

These were the finest warriors of Usgar and the witches of Usgar united.

None in the tribe would stand against them.

Aghmor wasn't surprised by any of this, other than the suddenness and boldness of the move. The harsh justice swiftly enacted upon Aoleyn had cleared the way.

So had the timely death of Elder Raibert.

Coincidentally and conveniently.

"If he is not dead, find him and return him to me," Tay Aillig whispered to Mairen as the chorus of cheers mounted around them. "I would know my greatest pleasure in killing that uamhas."

"The greatest pleasure, you say?" Mairen whispered back teasingly, and she squeezed Tay Aillig's hand.

The man managed a smile and a wink at his new wife. Let her believe what she needed to believe to lend him her power. He gripped her arm tightly, and his free hand went to the secret tab in his breeches where he kept the sunstone he had gained in a raid on a lake town years before.

The sunstone which could defeat the witch's magic wholly.

The sunstone which could poison an already-feeble old man quite effectively.

11

THE SHADOW IN THE DEEP

"You keep looking to the east," Aydrian noted late the next day, when he found Talmadge halfway up the same ridge from where they had first seen the destruction of Car Seileach. Down below, the work of rebuilding the devastated village and preparing the dead for burial had already begun. "Do you search for the monster?"

Talmadge gave a curt shake of his head, if that's what it even was, and didn't otherwise respond, obviously distant and distracted.

"If there is a lake monster," Aydrian remarked, figuring that would get the man's attention.

"There is." Talmadge didn't even look Aydrian's way when he spoke the words.

"Tell me of it," Aydrian bade him.

"There is a monster, a huge and terrible beast. It lives in the lake, and only in the lake from everything I have ever heard. And I have heard much, for the folk of all the villages know of it, and they fear it, but they know how to avoid it and so it rarely kills anyone."

"It is a great fish?"

"No . . ." Talmadge paused and shook his head, as if trying to convince himself. "Not a fish, or unlike any I have ever seen or known. Nor is it akin to the giant clo'dearche lizards that swim the waters of Loch Beag."

"But you believe that something has changed?"

"The villagers speak of the lake monster causing this great upheaval." Talmadge replied. "Some say that the beast swam up with the great wave and bit their houses apart."

Aydrian looked back at the ruins of the lake and put on a doubtful expression. "In a time of great tension and fear, the last thing to believe might be the words of those so afraid."

"There is a monster," Talmadge repeated. "And it is huge and terrible."

"You have seen it," Aydrian remarked.

"Once," Talmadge said, his voice faltering. "Only once."

"But you lived to tell the tale." Aydrian paused, studying Talmadge's face, recalling their earlier conversation, before they had come running to Car Seileach. "Two years ago," he added. "You survived."

"My beloved, Khotai, did not."

Aydrian and Talmadge fell silent as the sun sank behind them, its last rays sweeping the still, still waters of Loch Beag.

The lake was calm again the next morning. Too calm, perhaps, with nary a ripple showing on this windless day. Even the way the paddles of Talmadge and Aydrian sank into the water seemed exceptionally quiet to both of them that overcast morn as they paddled out of the cove which held Car Seileach. They had done all they could there, or all that they could do which the resilient villagers could not do for themselves.

They were a long way out, moving south and east across the lake, but close to shore as Talmadge had insisted, before the frontiersman even found the courage to speak. "They showed you a great honor in allowing your use of the magical gems," he told Aydrian. "To the folk of Loch Beag, magic is the evil way of the Usgar."

"They were in desperation," Aydrian replied. "Several more would have died if not for the magic of the soul stone, and many others would have remained badly crippled to the end of their days."

"They lost many," Talmadge agreed. "A score dead, a dozen missing. But they will survive and go on."

"There is no other choice," said Aydrian. He was in front of Talmadge, kneeling and paddling, so the frontiersman couldn't see his face. But the tone of his voice revealed a grimace, and Talmadge knew that Aydrian's last statement was also the fallen king's reminder to himself.

And one to Talmadge, one that pained him and reminded him of that fateful journey across the lake, when he had seen the monster and had lost his beloved Khotai.

The lake was so silky smooth, so deceptive, such a perfect cover for the horrid monstrosity which lurked below.

It wasn't until Aydrian glanced back at him that Talmadge even realized that he had not put his paddle in the water for many, many heartbeats.

"Would you prefer that we walk?" Aydrian asked.

Talmadge shook his head quickly, before his fears could overrule his good sense. He would have vastly preferred walking around the lake, but knew that such a journey was not without its own dangers and would take much longer. He had to get to Fasach Crann, to his friends, to the village that had taken him in as one of their own so many times over the years. The villagers of Car Seileach had thought it unlikely that the other villages between them and Fasach Crann had been hit nearly as hard, because of the geography of the lake and the areas where those villages had been built, sheltered and often up on rocks, and, of course, Clach Boglach, the town in the backwaters, with houses built on stilts and protected from the wave by many thick groves.

But Fasach Crann had been built right on the waters of Loch Beag, with a long and open beachfront and many houses very near the water. They were not prepared for such an event as this great wave, and why should they be?

Talmadge was afraid of what he would find, but knew that he had to go and look, and help, if there was anything left of the village to salvage. He owed it to the folk, a hundred times over. That realization alone allowed him to dip his paddle under the too-still waters of Loch Beag and more forward.

He let his mind drift back to the happier times when he and Khotai were running the frontier together. There had been no better time in Talmadge's life! So immersed did he become in those daydreams that he didn't even realize how rapidly the canoe was moving, gliding along the water with barely a wake, almost as if it was floating above the lake, yet still being propelled by the paddling.

He glanced all about, unsure, and finally, his gaze fell upon Aydrian.

"What are you doing?"

There came no answer, other than a low chant whose words Talmadge could not decipher. He couldn't get up close enough to look around the front of the man, but if he had, he realized, he would have seen the energy of a gemstone of some sort.

Aydrian's paddle went into the water, and a great stroke sent them soaring along. Then to the other side of the canoe went the paddle, and again, the canoe lurched forward.

Talmadge kept up his own paddling, but watched the shore now more than the lake ahead, his jaw hanging in disbelief at the shoreline sliding past at great speed.

It ended a short while later, and Aydrian lifted his paddle and held it across the canoe and leaned on it, giving a big exhale, as one might after a great physical exertion.

"Magic?" Talmadge asked.

It took Aydrian a moment to catch his breath. "I wasn't sure if I could manipulate it that way, to take the weight from myself, the canoe, and you all at once."

"Impressive."

"At the same time, I was giving both of us greater strength for our pulls," Aydrian went on. "I don't know it you felt the gusting tailwind, but that, too . . ."

He paused and laughed, and added, "I am quite weary."

"But we are near to Fasach Crann already," Talmadge informed him. "In a single day! You see those rocks ahead, and the bend to the south beyond? From there, we will catch sight of the village."

Aydrian continued to rest for a bit, but Talmadge picked up the pace behind him, and even without the magical enhancements they made good time in rounding the rocky peninsula. Talmadge held his breath as they turned toward the south, then gave a great sigh of despair when Fasach Crann—when what used to be Fasach Crann—came into view.

The wave had reached up to the back edges of the village. Talmadge could clearly see the line where it had reversed, taking all the vegetation, and all of the structures, with it. As his initial shock wore off, he took some comfort in noting that the rebuilding of the village was already under way, and that there was much activity and many villagers working.

"They saw it coming," he whispered hopefully.

"The ground rises swiftly not so far back from the shore," Aydrian remarked. He put his paddle into the water and helped drive them to the water's edge, and soon both were out of the canoe and dragging it forward.

A mob of villagers, spears and clubs raised, their faces twisted with outrage, came rushing down at them, others whooping and calling out alarms. The mob slowed, though, and put up their weapons somewhat, when they recognized Talmadge.

"Talmadge of the East," said an older man, stepping out before the others. "That is not my boat!"

"It is not, friend Memmic," Talmadge replied. "The great wave took your boat. This is a boat from Car Seileach, who gave it to me to cross the lake back to you."

"What of Car Seileach?" asked another villager, a young woman named Catriona with golden hair, thick and braided, and a growing reputation as a superb fisherwoman.

"Ruined, like here . . ." Talmadge started to reply.

"And who is he?" Catriona insisted, prodding her spear toward the stranger, who couldn't, of course, understand any of this chatter.

"Where did Talmadge find more coin for such a boat?" Memmic wanted to know.

"He is . . . I did'no," Talmadge said, turning to an answer far easier than explaining King Aydrian! "They gave me the boat because of my . . . of our, efforts in helping them after the great wave. Many died, and many homes were washed . . ."

"Who is he?" Catriona demanded again.

"A great hero of the eastern lands," Talmadge replied quickly.

"Come at the same time as the great wave?" Catriona asked.

"At the same time as the darkness in the day?" another man from further back in the gathering added.

Talmadge realized that this was not going well. He turned to Aydrian and warned, "Make no move to threaten."

Aydrian shrugged, seeming fully at ease.

"We came to help," Talmadge told Memmic, and particularly Catriona, who seemed as if she was taking the lead here. The frontiersman looked about, hoping to spot some of the other noted leaders of the tribe with whom he was on better terms. Judging from the size of the gathering, it seemed to him that most of Fasach Crann's tribe was out here, and unlike with Car Seileach, few of the people here seemed to have been wounded.

"How did you . . ." he started to ask, but paused and shook his head. "I feared that I'd be finding many dead."

"We've got missing," said Memmic.

"Take their boat," Catriona told some of the others, who advanced immediately.

Talmadge moved to intercept, as did Aydrian, and that brought the spears and clubs up high again.

"I am no enemy," Talmadge reminded them.

"Take the boat," Catriona said more insistently, her stare locked on Talmadge.

"We lost two boats on the lake," Memmic explained, pointing out to the north. There, far out on the lake, loomed the angled mast of a sunken fishing boat. "The wave took them and flipped them—that is how we first saw it coming, and in enough time to flee the village to the higher land."

"What are they talking about?" Aydrian asked, and Talmadge stepped aside and pulled Aydrian with him, then surrendered the canoe while he translated the conversation.

Aydrian looked out to the lake, then glanced back to see the villagers, turning the canoe to paddle out.

"Stay here," Aydrian told Talmadge.

"Don't," Talmadge warned, but Aydrian shrugged him aside, and pulled off the cloak that had been covering his fabulous, shining armor.

That elicited more than a few gasps, notably from Catriona, who started to say something—likely a command to attack the man, Talmadge thought—but stopped and gasped instead as the stranger ran to the water, then began running across the water!

The two men at the canoe dropped it to the sand and stood gawking, as did all the rest.

"Talmadge?" Memmic and Catriona said together.

"Not Usgar," Talmadge said immediately, thinking it wise to get that out there right up front. "He is, he was, a king from a land called Honce, a land I once called home."

"He was your king?" Catriona asked.

"No, well, perhaps yes," Talmadge stuttered. "I knew little of the greater . . ." He fumbled about, trying to recall the lakeman word for "cities," but then gave up the hunt. Did they even have such a word?

"I knew little of the great Honce villages," he said.

"You didn't know your king?"

"I was already in the west when Aydrian ascended," Talmadge explained, but just waved his hand and let it go at that. There would be plenty of time for explanations and proper introductions later.

He turned to see Aydrian running far from shore, that fabulous armor gleaming.

"What made the wave?" Talmadge asked Catriona, who was also obviously entranced by the sight of the man running atop Loch Beag.

"The monster," Memmic answered for her.

"How does he run on water?" Catriona asked.

"Magic," said Talmadge, and he quickly added, "Not Usgar!"

"This is the magic of the east?"

Talmadge nodded. "He can heal, too. If you have wounded, prepare them for Aydrian's strong hand."

"You speak like a fool," said Catriona.

"That is why Car Seileach gave us the boat. Aydrian healed many. Many who would have died, now live. They rebuild homes instead of funeral pyres."

"He is strong with magic?" asked Catriona.

"Very."

"Strong enough to hide the sun? Strong enough to lift the waters of Loch Beag?"

Talmadge stuttered. There was no missing the threat there, and the man almost expected to be assaulted then and there! "No, no!" he sputtered. "No, he was with me when the sun hid, and with me when the lake waters rose."

"In Memmic's boat, and you survived?"

"No, on land, near Car Seileach. They had seen him. They sent me to find . . ." He took a deep breath, realizing that he was veering all over the place here. "Aydrian of the East was with me when the sun hid and the wave came," he said more calmly, trying to exude confidence, trying to elicit confidence. "I came upon him in a meadow near the willows," he said. "He is known to me."

"He was your king."

"I did'no know that. Not then, and not before when we met by a river far from this land. But I did know that he was no enemy, and so I found him once more, and together we watched the sun hide, and together we watched the water rise, and together we ran to Car Seileach to help them as we could. And we did, all through the day and night."

"And night?" Catriona asked doubtfully, and murmurs arose around her.

Talmadge understood, and could only heave a sigh. He had just claimed to have spent the night across the lake in Car Seileach, but that story would hold little sway because it would make little sense to the folk of Fasach Crann, who knew that to get to the western village would take much more than one day of canoeing.

Talmadge answered the only way he could, by turning and sweeping his arm out to Aydrian, running across the water, already far from shore.

His hand glowed with a yellowish hue as he clutched a magical bit of amber, calling upon its powers to keep him above the waters. Of all the magical gems, this one most unnerved Aydrian, even more than flying with moonstone, for the feel of a watery cushion beneath his feet, not only supporting him, but lifting him in his bounds (which were accentuated even more by the weight-reducing powers of the malachite) seemed very strange to him indeed.

He glanced back to see the canoe launch behind him and that only spurred him on faster. If there was something bad out there, he wanted to discover it and be away before any more of the villagers could be caught and killed.

Another sprint, great, leaping bounds, moved him far from shore, and when he glanced back then, the canoe was a distant speck, while before him, the capsized boat loomed large. The beauty of the amber water-walking was that it barely left a ripple on the water, so the ranger let it all settle quickly about him, then peered through the translucent haze.

He was surprised to learn that he could see no hint of the bottom anywhere about. This mountain lake was clearly very deep.

He moved to the boat and knocked on the hull, then put his ear against it, quietly called out, and listened.

He could hear the water slightly lapping at the wood inside, but nothing more. He drew another gemstone from his belt pouch, a green agate, and sent his thoughts into it, that he could detect life.

He saw nothing, other than an occasional flitter that he knew to be a fish.

Still, Aydrian wasn't satisfied. Anyone inside might simply be too exhausted or frightened to call back, or even unconscious and lashed to the rail. Aydrian rolled up the sleeve of his fine shirt to the edge of his breastplate and checked the knot on a green band of cloth that he had tied there.

He sent his thoughts into that band, feeling the magic of the elves ready and waiting for him.

Simply out of habit, for there was certainly no need, he took a deep breath and let go of his amber magic, sliding under the lake waters, under the edge of the boat and around to come back up inside the overturned craft.

No survivors were waiting for him. Just an empty hull.

He knew he couldn't stay under the water for long, for it was very cold, but he wanted to explore more. He came back up to the surface, took another deep breath, simply out of habit, and dove again, this time swimming straight down and releasing the malachite magic of his armor, so it weighed on him like an anchor. The elves had taught him to be careful of his descent in deep waters, so he used the malachite, even the amber, to slow himself, and to pause more than once. Breathing underwater was no problem with the green armband of purity.

Down he went, and it began to grow darker all about him. Still, he could see, much farther than from the surface, and gradually began to make out shapes far, far below, to the lake's deep bottom, he supposed.

He made out one shape—it seemed an underwater mountain, huge and even-sided.

How he wanted to go and investigate further! But he could feel the press of the water upon him and knew that he could not. For all his magic, he could not dive that deep, and worse, the cold of the waters was beginning to creep into his limbs. He feet grew numb.

He called on the malachite to fully free him from the weight of his breastplate, then began to slowly swim upward, going just a few feet, then pausing to let his body acclimate to the lessened pressure. In that moment, he threw as much of himself as he could into the green agate, widening its range in detecting living creatures.

Fish, fish, and more fish. Something else, then, which Aydrian came to realize as a rather large lizard. But no people. He had cast a wide net, and if any of the missing villagers from Fasach Crann were in that net, they were not alive.

Up he went some more, continuing to power the agate most of all, searching to the very end. He had moved for some time, though was still far below the surface, when he sensed something.

Something not human.

Something much greater and more powerful than any human.

He paused in his ascent and followed the sensations of the gemstone, peering down, down, into the gloom.

Then he saw it—not the creature, but its shadow, its snake-like silhouette going on and on, wider than a team of fat oxen standing side by side, longer than a caravan of wagons stretched end to end.

Larger than Agradeleous, the dragon of Behr, a great and gigantic snake-like shadow slithering through the water far below!

It couldn't be. Aydrian could not wrap his sensibilities around something this . . . huge, swimming about in an inland lake. Or even in the Mirianic Ocean. He had heard the tales of journeys to the distant island of the ring stones, and never had even those obvious exaggerations come close to the reality of the shadow beneath him.

He thought it might be a trick of the water, some distortion that made this creature, whatever it was, seem larger. Or a giant school of fish, swimming in tight formation.

But no, the agate was screaming in his mind. The sheer power of this living being, this singular living being, overwhelmed everything else.

He saw it. He couldn't deny it. And then, as it turned, Aydrian realized that it saw him.

His hand went reflexively to his sword hilt, but even as he touched the weapon, he felt himself a fool.

He couldn't fight this thing with a weapon, any weapon, not even Tempest, his sword, or Hawkwing, his bow. He would need magic, powerful spells—spells that he knew to be beyond him.

Aydrian shook himself from his stupor.

"Magic?" he said skeptically, though it came out as merely bubbles.

He would need an army, and probably a dragon of his own!

But the beast had seen him and had turned, and he felt its approach. He would be swallowed whole, and perhaps that would be the best possible outcome.

Hardly even thinking of the movement, Aydrian threw himself into his amber, the stone of water walking, and flung its magic all about. Upward he shot, slicing through the water like a fired arrow. He drew his sword and put it up before him, thinking the narrower leading tip would give him more speed and some measure of control. He saw the daylight approaching fast, and then he was in it, but breaking the surface didn't stop his ascent, no, for the amber would not be satisfied until he was out of the water, above the water.

He shot up into the air like a graceful Mirianic dolphin, rising above the water a dozen feet and more before he played out his momentum and dropped back down—but down only to the top of the water, where he began to run.

For all his life, Aydrian ran, maintaining the amber, calling upon the malachite, leaping and bounding, twenty feet, thirty feet at a stride. He couldn't know if the monster was in pursuit, if it was right behind him, even, because he had released the magic of the agate out of necessity, to focus all of his energy on the two gems that could get him out of there the fastest.

He spotted the canoe, far ahead of him, not so far out from shore.

"Go back!" he yelled, waving his arms. "Turn about! Turn about!"

They couldn't understand him, of course, not his words anyway, but neither could they miss the frantic waving, or the fact that this stranger, so splendidly armored, was running for his life. They began to turn the canoe, but as skilled as they were on the waters, Aydrian could see that they'd never get it turned about and back to shore in time.

So he ran for them, and he fell deeper into the malachite, and he called upon the bloodstone set in his armor to enhance his strength, and he grabbed the turning canoe by the prow, and he pulled. For all his life he pulled. For both of their lives, he pulled.

The villagers paddled wildly, trying to help, but there was no doubt of what, or who, was propelling this boat as it sped along, as fast as if it had great and wide sails that were full of a wintry gale!

As they neared the shoreline, the gathering there, almost all of the tribe, began to cheer them on, begging for speed. A quick glance over his shoulder told Aydrian why, for a large swell was following the craft.

He knew what it was.

So he ran faster, driving his legs, pushing his feet against the water and leaping off. As he neared the beach, the gathering broke apart, retreating, screaming, and so, when Aydrian hit the beach, he kept running, and kept pulling, and used his malachite to steal most of the weight from the raft and its paddlers behind him. But then they were out, and running by, and Aydrian dropped the boat and sped away.

A swell rolled up onto the beach and broke apart harmlessly, the monster, if it was the monster, not showing itself above the water.

Aydrian stumbled and let himself fall to the sand, thoroughly exhausted.

Talmadge came to him soon after, along with the man he had called Memmic and the woman named Catriona.

"Was it?"

Aydrian nodded. "There are no people alive out there," he said. "Tell them that their friends are lost. And tell them to stay off the water for a long while."

"It was the lake monster?" Talmadge asked.

Aydrian nodded again.

"A dragon? A demon?"

"I have seen a dragon," Aydrian said. "A true dragon, terrible and breathing fire. I do not think it more terrible than this beast."

Talmadge stared at him, then turned to translate for his Fasach Crann companions.

"Tell them to stay off the water," Aydrian said breathlessly. "Just stay off the water."

Aydrian and Talmadge, too, stayed off the water, when they left Fasach Crann the next morning. They had helped as they could that previous night, clearing debris, and Aydrian using his soul stone to heal many minor wounds—but only minor, to the great credit of the folk of the village, who had fled without question or pause when the wave had been spotted. In this regard, they had found a huge advantage over the victims in Car Seileach, for that town, in a sheltered cove, did not have so wide and clear a view of the open lake waters.

Nor did the next village over to the west, Carrachan Shoal, they were told, and so, with the gratitude of the folk of Fasach Crann, the pair headed straight out to where their efforts and magical healing might prove more critical.

But not on the lake. None were going out on the lake, except one boat Aydrian towed out from shore and anchored, a boat flying a flag of warning to all the other villages.

Even by land, it was not a long journey to Carrachan Shoal—it was actually shorter in distance, though the terrain was much rougher. It would have taken a villager more than a day to make the crossing over the rocky ridge that separated the communities, but with Aydrian's magic, he and Talmadge scooted up in short order, and from the top, they spied the village of Carrachan Shoal, and saw, to their relief, that the wave had not done considerable damage there. For while the cove itself was shallow, as with Car Seileach, the bend of it had sent the bulk of the wave off to the western side, where there were no structures.

"Hopefully, you will be back in Fasach Crann tomorrow," Aydrian said.

"Hopefully, we both will."

"Teach me their language."

"It would take months," said Talmadge.

Aydrian held up a soul stone. "I know an easier way, but let us discuss that another day."

Talmadge looked at him curiously as Aydrian led the way down the other side of the ridgeline. He knew that stone as the one Aydrian was using for healing. He didn't know, however, that it could also be used for possession, or a spiritual, mental link.

The greeting at Carrachan Shoal was the same as at Fasach Crann—colder, even, and more threatening, for while Talmadge was known there, he was not nearly as friendly with these villagers as with those in the town over the ridge. Still, it was going well enough as he introduced them to Aydrian and explained that this was the man who had brought the boat with the warning flag out upon Loch Beag at the request of Catriona of Fasach Crann.

"He can heal your wounded, as well," Talmadge was saying. "He is possessed of great magic from the east. Not evil and destructive, as the Usgar, but gentle and warm."

Many nods came back at him, and whispered conversations went on all about as the villagers tried to come to terms with these two visitors after so devastating an event on their precious lake.

Talmadge took in as much as he could garner from the whispers, giving them time, and looked over at Aydrian with a smile and a nod.

A nod that froze halfway through.

A smile that fell with a figurative thump into a frown.

For there, past Aydrian, was another of the villagers of Carrachan Shoal, though hardly a native.

There, on a roller cart, rested a one-legged woman.

"Khotai," Talmadge mouthed, but hadn't the strength to say aloud, and then he toppled and would have hit the ground had not the agile and strong Aydrian caught him in mid-fall.

PART 2

CIZINFOZZA'S

BASTARDS

They say and it's been told that Miczilan, the Time of Great Darkness, engulfed Zala-natl, the world between the seas. In this time did the mict children of Cizinfozza roam the lands, killing all they could find: Xoconai, human, animal, it did not matter. They served their god of darkness. Darkness is death.

And Cizinfozza fed on the souls of Xoconai, and on the bodies of the humans and animals, who have no souls. And his children were fruitful. Like the broods of mice were the litters of Cizinfozza's children, the mict, that the humans call the goblins.

The god of darkness and death did thus grow stronger, and the darkness deepened, and the world knew despair, and the skies above did weep, and the golden light from above could not get through the deep weeping veil of Cizinfozza. The sky itself did cry, echoing the lamentations of the countless dead.

They say and it's been told that there is but one way through despair to enlightenment, and so did the whispers of Scathmizzane burn in quiet hope. Scathmizzane saw the darkness and was sad. He freed the bright and fiery sky orb, Tonalli, from the shadows of Cizinfozza, and in so doing made the day, and each day grew longer, and every shadow lightened. But the children of Scathmizzane were few, and those of Cizinfozza uncounted! For a thousand years, the gods battled for Zalanatl, the world between the seas, light to burn the darkness, darkness to dim the light, ever to dim the light. Scathmizzane ruled the day under the fire light of Tonalli, and the dark nights bowed to Cizinfozza.

Scathmizzane was not pleased, and his anger grew great, but he is one of mercy, and anger is not of mercy, and so he excised the darkness within himself.

"Do not kill the children of Cizinfozza," Scathmizzane commanded his children, the Xoconai. "No more to war, but to love."

And with that love did we Xoconai accept the mict, and together we did multiply, and though the xelquiza, these half-blood children, were ugly to we Xoconai, they were beautiful to the goblins, and bigger, and stronger.

But then did Cizinfozza of the Darkness see his doomed future, as the light brightened on the world, and every day did the fires of Tonalli shine, brightening all the lands of Zalanatl. And then there came Citalli, specks of light twinkling in the dark nights of Cizinfozza, and then did Metzalli, the young sister of Tonalli, rise in the night sky, *with pale light to lessen the darkness of Cizinfozza. The god of darkness and death could not escape.*

They say and it's been told that Cizinfozza burst his own body, to destroy Otontotomi, and we Xoconai cried, for this was the greatest temple of Scathmizzane, the heart of Tonoloya. The skies did weep, the fires of Tonalli hidden behind the smoke of Cizinfozza's burst form, and so was Otontotomi buried in a cold and airless tomb, and there, too, was the living Kithkukulikahn interred. Cizinfozza's spirit then did wickedly turn the xelquiza against his own children, to drive the goblins away, and in their hatred did the half-bloods come to see the love we Xoconai held for the goblin mict to be an evil thing, and so they hated, too, the Xoconai, and so they fought us, the children of Scathmizzane.

They say and it's been told that in that onset of the greatest war, in that darkest moment, Scathmizzane accepted the truth of the world between the seas.

Then from the vast plain did he raise, and we Xoconai did cross, Teotl Tenamitl, and the great mountains did then end the war. And here in Tonoloya did we Xoconai multiply and grow stronger, while in Mictlan, the east lands of Zalanatl, the humans did battle the mict of Cizinfozza, and in the divide among the mountains did the xelquiza half-bloods roam, godless, hopeless.

In the east, the humans won, and did multiply and grow stronger, and their kingdoms crawled to Ayuskixmal, the eastern slopes of Teotl Tenamitl, scattering the few xelquiza, claiming the land.

And we Xoconai did wait, and we were promised that Cizinfozza would meet his end, and in that moment would Kithkukulikahn rise and eat Tonalli, and vomit Tonalli, to tell we Xoconai of the light renewed.

In that glorious moment would begin the march.

They say and it's been told that in this moment Tonoloya will stretch to the eastern sea once more.

Necu Tonoloya, it will be called, and all of Zalanatl will be Scathmizzane's, ruled by the Xoconai, between the seas. In the east, we will watch Tonalli ignite her fires as she rises from the great sea. In the west, we will watch Tonalli quiet her flames as she goes to sleep beneath the waters.

Zalanatl will know light.

—The Last Augur of Darkness

12

SALVO

"It will snow today," Talmadge told Aydrian, the pair moving up the mountain southwest of Carrachan Shoal.

"Are you sure that's not just your mood speaking?" Aydrian replied, giving Talmadge pause. The frontiersman stopped and regarded his companion.

"She was not pleased to see you?" Aydrian asked.

"She hates me and I do'no blame her," Talmadge replied. He closed his eyes, both reliving the memory of his shocking encounter with Khotai and trying to excise it from his mind all at once.

"Do you believe her less surprised than yourself? Given your description of the encounter with the lake monster, she thought you dead, of course."

"I left her."

"You found her leg! How could you . . ."

"It matters not. I should have looked. I should have summoned the courage to find her."

"In the belly of a dragon?"

"But she was not, was she?"

Aydrian sighed audibly. "How could you know?"

"I left her. It is what I do. It is what I did in my home. It is what I did to Khotai. It is what I do." He looked up the mountain and thought of that unusual and powerful Usgar woman, Aoleyn.

Aydrian's laugh surprised him.

"You mock me?"

"Or myself," Aydrian replied. "It would seem that I am able to forgive myself much more easily than is Talmadge."

"Who did you abandon?"

Aydrian laughed again. "I waged war on the world. Against my own mother. I should have been hanged, or drawn and quartered, after the defeat of my army, and am alive only through the sufferance of those I wronged."

"And you can so easily dismiss your guilt? What does that say about Aydrian, I wonder?"

"Dismiss it? No, my friend Talmadge, I do no such thing. I bear it as my weight and as my reminder. I wish I could go back and undo all that . . . it does not matter, because I cannot. What I can do is be better, make what amends I might. You, though, wear a frown of judgment for an action that was not evil, nor cowardly, nor even a slight bit unreasonable. You found her severed leg, Talmadge. Who could have expected that she would survive such a wound?"

"She hates me."

Aydrian shrugged. "Her surprise . . ."

"I know, but after the surprise, last night when we were alone . . . I could feel it. She wanted me to leave. She told me to leave. I tried to argue . . ." He closed his eyes. He could see Khotai's face, still beautiful, but twisted into a profound scowl as she yelled at him to leave her alone, to be gone from Carrachan Shoal, her new home forevermore. "I tried to argue."

"Thus, you led me up here this morning. To find something, you said, but was it really to run away once more?"

Talmadge gave a dismissive snort and spun away. "These trees all look the same," he said with no small anger.

"They are trees, after all," Aydrian answered, and Talmadge turned back to see the man smiling. "Likely they feel the same way about men."

Talmadge stared at him blankly.

"You learn these things when you are among the Touel'alfar," Aydrian explained. "Are you actually searching for something?"

"There is a place, somewhere about here," Talmadge replied, glancing all about. "But it was dark—the forest looks much different at night." He didn't add that everything also looked different when one was being dragged around by a gang of Usgar warriors.

"I was not alone," he did say. "And there was a bear. Even though some days have passed, there should be tracks."

"It has snowed and rained, and the snow melted," Aydrian reminded him. "The ground was near frozen a few days ago, so no tracks would have been deep."

Talmadge couldn't deny that. He had thought it would be easier to find the spot where he had been tied and tortured. He should have come right back when he first realized his loss, but so much had transpired in between.

"We won't find it," he said, his voice thick with resignation.

"You still haven't told me what you seek," Aydrian reminded him.

Talmadge hesitated, but what did it matter? "I am looking for something I dropped," he said. "A lens."

Aydrian cocked his head. "What sort of lens?"

"The sort that lets me see far."

"A spyglass?"

Talmadge shook his head. "Smaller." He held up a hand to indicate the size.

"And it lets you see over distances?"

Talmadge nodded.

"Great distances?"

He nodded again.

"Magically?"

Talmadge didn't answer, but his expression told Aydrian all he needed to know.

Aydrian laughed again. "You should have said so!" He reached into his pack and pulled out a small red stone, polished and round. He focused his eyes on the stone for a moment, then looked up. "I am no stranger to magical items, my friend Talmadge. The Abellican Church in the east, for all of their claims that the gemstones were gifts from God and so sacred and to be in the hands of the monks alone, would often sell stones to noblemen and wealthy merchants, who could not use them as the monks might, but who could have them crafted into items usable by any, like my own sword and armor."

Aydrian clenched the red stone in his fist, which began to glow slightly as the magical power of the gem grew. Then he held it up to his eye.

The smile disappeared from Aydrian's face. He blinked a few times, looking around.

"What is it?" Talmadge asked.

"It's . . . your lost lens is this way," Aydrian answered and started off.

Talmadge paused, staring at the man, suspecting that Aydrian was not telling him everything. He said nothing, and followed, and in a short while, they came to a clearing Talmadge recognized.

He saw the tree to which he had been tied, and off to the side, followed Aydrian's movements to a pile of leaves, and the glint of crystal.

Aydrian picked it up and held it aloft, studying it. "It is a fine piece."

"More trouble than it's worth," Talmadge said, taking it back.

"You came to find it," Aydrian reminded him.

"I need it now, but that does'no mean I trust it."

Aydrian seemed confused by that.

"I am not always sure of what I am seeing. I do'no think the lens always shows me true."

Aydrian held out his hand and motioned for it back, then inspected it again, more closely, before tossing it to Talmadge. "Perhaps the problem is with the user, not the item. It seems a fine piece to me. Perhaps I can offer you some training to better understand what it shows you."

"Be quick, please."

"You need it," Aydrian said.

"There's a woman . . ." Talmadge began, nodding.

"In Carrachan Shoal."

"No, not Khotai. Another," Talmadge explained and looked up the mountain.

"You are full of stories, my friend."

"My book grows thick," Talmadge agreed, for that was the way Khotai had always described a full and adventurous life. He thought back to those days with that wonderful woman, and it was some time before he looked back at Aydrian, who seemed not to understand the reference.

Before he could explain, though, they heard a noise, distant and sharp, a scream.

"Carrachan Shoal?" Aydrian asked, spinning about.

Talmadge could only shrug. He ran past his companion, moving for a high spur nearer the lake that would let them see.

The brothers, Asba and Asef, and their friend Tamilee had learned how to make even their sentry duty enjoyable, this day, playing a game of "sixes."

They took turns rolling cubed dice into a tin, six to start. Whenever a six came up, but only once in a turn, that die was removed, and the next roller had to roll five. Then four, if that next roll showed a six as well, and so that die was removed, and all the way down to a single die, if needed.

The first player who rolled without getting a six lost the round. They gambled for baubles, for stones, for food treats, for extra watch duty through the night, even for clothes when they were really bored. But it was just for fun, and just to pass the time.

The three always took their actual purpose seriously, though, and even when playing, rotated the watch, ever vigilant.

That sense of duty saved their lives this day, when Asba, at the window of the small treehouse they had built on the perimeter, noted movement up in the foothills. At first, he thought it the strangers, Talmadge the trader and the man with the shining armor and deamhan-like magic, but before he even said that to his companions, he noted more movement.

Much more movement.

"Sidhe," he whispered. "Lots of sidhe."

The others scrambled to their feet, Tamilee rushing to the window while Asef, who hadn't found much luck in rolling this day, quickly pulled on his shirt and shoes.

Tamilee didn't have to wait long for confirmation of Asba's observations, for the foothills ahead of them suddenly swarmed with the thick-bodied mountain goblins.

"We can'no fight that," Tamilee whispered.

"Run," Asba told her and his brother. "Just run. Out the back and run!"

He paused, crossing the floor, to usher Tamilee by him, and helped the struggling Asef get up after finally getting his shoes on. Out the back of the treehouse they went, dropping down to the ground and sprinting away.

Behind them, a sidhe screeched, and others joined in from nearby slopes, and the chase was on.

"The lake! To the boats!" all three screamed as they neared the town. Some villagers stopped and stared, while others, veterans of Usgar raids in past years, just dropped whatever they were holding and ran to the southeast, to the cove that held the village watercraft.

As the trio moved to the village proper, many of the sturdiest folk had gathered, men and women with weapons in hand. The three skidded up to them.

"Usgar?" one of the older veterans asked.

"Sidhe," said Tamilee. "Many!"

"Too many," Asef added. He could see the doubts on the faces of the gathered. The folk of Carrachan Shoal fled the Usgar, as was the custom in all the villages. But the Usgar were great warriors, and carried magic that the lakemen could not withstand. The sidhe were not so powerful.

But neither were the sidhe often seen in such numbers as were now approaching Carrachan Shoal, Asef knew.

"Too many," he said again, shaking his head, imploring the leaders to order a full retreat.

"Form! All defenders!" the village leader shouted. "To the boats, all the rest!" His expression changed and the blood visibly drained from his face then as the sidhe horde crashed into the southernmost houses of Carrachan Shoal, more sidhe than any of those gathered had ever seen before.

Screaming and scrambling, most of the town ran for the boats, but the warriors, Asef, Asba, and Tamilee among them, stood their ground and lifted their spears and clubs.

"Give me a weapon!" came a voice from behind the forming line, and Asef turned to see Khotai on her roller board, holding her hand.

"Woman, run . . . err, crawl!" he shouted at her.

"A spear!" she shouted back. "A club. Anything! I'd rather die in a fight than flee a stinking goblin."

"Get her out of here," the village leader told Asef. "Go, to the boats."

Asef paused, not wanting to leave his brother and dear friend, and not wanting to do anything to save this wretched woman. He didn't even want to touch her.

But another did, a large man, breaking from the ranks, scooping the surprised Khotai from her board and hoisting her high as he sprinted for the cove—with Khotai cursing him and punching him every step of the way.

Asef nodded and turned about, then nearly jumped out of his shoes as the first wave of mountain goblins came charging in. For a brief moment, the line held, with coordinated spear thrusts and support among the villagers. But they weren't used to this many sidhe, or the sidhe demeanor, for they charged in fearlessly, fanatically even, and the second wave broke through and sent more than one man or woman spinning down to the ground, to be covered by clawing, biting, stomping goblins.

Then it was chaos, purely so, as Asef and Asba and Tamilee and many others had never before seen, had never even imagined. The three friends tried to stay together in mutual support, but the goblins got between them, between all of them, pushing relentlessly forward.

Asef turned aside a crude spear at the last moment, got scraped hard across the side by a second one, but managed to backhand punch that sidhe hard enough to drive it back and buy him enough time to retreat from the first attacker. He called for Asba and Tamilee, but they had their own problems at that moment, each engaged with a capable foe.

The first goblin pursued with abandon, and Asef managed to keep his composure enough to properly defend, and even managed to cleverly set the butt of his spear against the side of a house right before his nearest opponent leaped at him, impaling itself.

Asef's thrill of victory proved short-lived, though, for the stabbed sidhe went into a frenzy, spinning all about and tearing the spear shaft from Asef's hands. The monster went rolling away, but the other one came charging in at the now unarmed man.

"Khotai," Talmadge breathed, looking down at Carrachan Shoal from on high. A fire had started in the town, where the activity was still high, a battle clearly raging. Shouts and cries of pain carried up to the high ridge. They could barely make out the combatants, but enough to see that the villagers were fighting a retreating action, and seemed as if they would be overrun at any moment.

Many boats were already out on the lake, at least, pulling away from the town.

"We've got to get to them," Talmadge said, glancing all about. The two men stood on a rocky bluff and the path before them was far from promising. "Back around," he said, turning in the direction they had come.

But there, he froze.

"What?" asked Aydrian, who glanced over at his companion, to see him standing there, blood draining from his face. He spun about to see what Talmadge was looking at, and he understood.

Not far from them, mountain goblins streamed down the trails, but not toward Carrachan Shoal, not east of the ridge upon which Aydrian and Talmadge now stood. They were moving down the mountain in the west, straight for Fasach Crann.

Aydrian leaped over and pulled Talmadge down low. "What is this?" he asked. "You said nothing . . ."

"In all the years I've come here, I've seen few of these monsters," Talmadge replied. "Nothing like this."

"We have to get to your friends."

"Khotai."

"No. We can beat this group to the other town," Aydrian explained. "A warning may save many lives." As he spoke, he pulled that bow with its feathered end off his back, and in one easy movement bent and strung it.

Talmadge glanced back the other way. "My Khotai," he said, but he nodded to Aydrian.

Aydrian took the lead, hopping agilely down the back side of the ridge, which was not nearly as treacherous as going the other way. On the lower ground, he sprinted ahead down to a copse of trees, trying to discern how far ahead the leading goblins might be.

It looked to him like he and Talmadge could get ahead of the invaders, but they were going to have to cross open ground to do so, and once spotted, they'd be chased all the way, no doubt.

"We're going to run down that way, and they'll see us," Aydrian decided. "You're going to keep running, all the way to the town."

"What are you doing?"

"Making sure you get there well ahead of the invaders."

"You can'no!" Talmadge argued, but Aydrian grabbed him by the arm and, with frightening strength, tugged him out of the cover, running down across the open field. They hadn't gone halfway when the mountain goblins began to hoot at them. As soon as they entered the trees across the way, Aydrian shoved Talmadge along, then drew his sword and looked about, surveying the battlefield.

"Go!" he shouted at Talmadge, who hesitated.

"You'll die!"

"Then you'll die as well if you stay, and your friends in the town are doomed!"

To Aydrian's relief, Talmadge sprinted away. And not a moment too soon, the man who had been king realized, for the lead mountain goblins were in sight, closing fast for the kill.

"Here we go, then," Aydrian whispered, and he rolled his shoulders and stretched his neck and realized it had been a long time since he had been in a fight.

He called upon the bloodstone and dolomite set into his breastplate, infusing himself with toughness and strength, and set an arrow. As the first mountain goblins came into sight, he drew back the darkfern bow with its silverel string, leveled quickly, and let fly. The broadhead arrow hit the goblin in the chest and sent it flying backward, dead before it hit ground, tripping up two more coming in behind.

Aydrian let fly again and a third time, and those two, as well, went spinning down to the grave. Then a fourth, but now a swarm was closing.

Aydrian dropped the bow and drew forth Tempest, the blade made by the elves for Aydrian's great uncle Mather, one of the famed rangers. The sword alone was nearly without equal in craftsmanship and materials, yet Aydrian had improved upon it, adding gemstones, because Aydrian, like his mother, could use these magical gems with great proficiency.

In came the next goblins, leaping from on high to fly down at Aydrian, who turned, ducked, slashed left, and stabbed ahead, all in perfect balance, leaving one mountain goblin crashing down behind him, a second falling off to the side, grabbing at its slashed hip, and a third impaled.

Aydrian backpedaled quickly, sliding his blade free, the goblin dropping to its knees, grasping helplessly at the air.

Ahead went the man, angling by the skewered thing, which he did not even bother to finish, for the wound was surely mortal. The next pair came in at him more cautiously.

But they wouldn't fare any better. Aydrian pointed his left foot forward and put his back foot perpendicular to that, and moved at them swiftly, never crossing his feet, never losing his balanced posture. Ahead he went, then back, then ahead once more, where he snapped off a sudden stab, too fast for his opponent to even realize the attack.

This was *Bi'nelle Dasada*, the elven sword dance, a fighting form that allowed the small Touel'alfar to battle much heavier and stronger opponents. Forward and back, always balanced. Strike with the speed of a serpent and retreat.

Aydrian was no lithe elf, though, and so the dance was but a part of his fighting repertoire. As he retracted his blade from the mountain goblin's chest, he broke from the dance pattern and brought his weapon out hard to the side, slashing more conventionally, as he would with the heavier weapons more common in the land, and with devastating effect, chopping the goblin down.

More were already there to take its place.

Further down the mountain, Talmadge came around a boulder and paused for just a moment to catch his breath. He glanced back with great concern, and saw the first exchanges, saw the goblin flying over his companion, saw a second veer out and crumble, a third kneeling and looking dead.

He watched the second fight, his jaw dropping open at the speed of Aydrian's blade and movements—he was still trying to sort out the stab on the first of this group when the second went spinning suddenly under the weight of a sword slash.

But more were coming and Talmadge grimaced and almost cried out, then did yelp in startlement as Aydrian's sword became a line of bright flames!

The mountain goblins shrieked and skidded to a stop before the surprising man.

Talmadge ran on, leaping stones and roots and ducking branches, and nearly cracking his skull on one low branch that crossed his path. Not long after, he began calling out, for Fasach Crann came into view.

"To arms! To the boats! The sidhe are upon you!"

To his relief, the folk were already astir, for sound carries well across the water, and the battle in Carrachan Shoal had alerted them, along with the fleet of that nearby village putting out to the open water.

"Sidhe!" Talmadge kept yelling all the way into the town, where the warriors were gathering and many others were fleeing for the beach and the boats. "Too many!" he added breathlessly. "Run! Flee!"

"How many?" demanded Catriona, rushing over to grab him and halt his run. Talmadge could see in her eyes that she had no intention of running from such beasts.

"Too many," he answered.

"There is no such number," said another man, and while all those of the village too old or too young to fight headed for the boats, the warriors, men and women alike, formed into groups and moved for cover, crouching behind one house or another.

Despite the dangers of the lake monster, despite the flooding tide that had just struck several of the villages and had devastated more than one, Loch Beag served as a sanctuary for the lakemen. When the Usgar came, with magic they could not fight, the men and women of the targeted lake town piled onto their boats and rowed and sailed out onto the loch. Let the Usgar take some supplies, and yes, sometimes an unfortunate person who could not get to the boats, but the village would survive.

This time, though, the sanctuary seemed far less secure for those first fleeing Carrachan Shoal.

Khotai watched helplessly, so outraged by her inability to join in the battle ashore that she wasn't even terrified of being out on the open water, something she had not done since that fateful day those years ago.

She thought of Talmadge, and of how she had treated him, sending him away coldly, not even allowing her shock at seeing him alive diminish enough to express her love for him.

No, she could not. She was no woman anymore, certainly no wife. She was a beggar on a rolling plank, ever dirty and usually helpless. And now he was probably dead anyway, for he had gone up onto the mountain, where the sidhe had come from.

More boats splashed out of the cove, with bloodied warriors, but so few! Just a handful, though near to a hundred warriors had formed the defense in the town. Gasps and moans rolled from the first wave of those fleeing, from people who feared they would never see their loved ones again.

"So few!" one woman wailed.

And the mountain goblins were still about the town, where smoke was now rising from burning houses. Ominously, the sounds of battle had all but died away.

Sighs of relief were heard as more boats showed around the edge of the cove, rowing awkwardly and with slapping oars for the open water.

Short-lived, they were, for some of those boats were not crewed by the rest of the defenders, but by mountain goblins.

"Sails! Sails!" came the cries, from the waiting boats and from those few approaching. "West, west, to Fasach Crann!"

Fighting began back at the mouth of the cove, boat to boat, man and goblin tangling and tumbling and splashing into the water. The few boats nearer the main flotilla did not turn back to help their kin, but kept coming with all speed and calling for retreat across the waters.

Khotai's boat began to turn.

"No!" she shouted at the same burly man who had carried her to the craft and was now manning the rudder. "No, we have to help them!"

"Help them how?" he snapped back at her.

Khotai had no immediate answer. She turned back to the unfolding tragedy, and noted one boat of villagers floundering nearer to the shore, and with a smaller boat overloaded with several heavy mountain goblins closing in.

"There!" Khotai yelled to the big man. "There! We can help them. Your brothers and sisters. Would you leave them to die?"

"Bah!" the man snorted, but he did indeed turn for the shore, and even leaped forward, pushing a much smaller man out of the way and grabbing up the oars. "You're to get us all killed, fool woman," he complained, but he rowed, how he rowed, with all of his great strength, lifting the prow so violently that Khotai almost pitched over.

The lakemen of Carrachan Shoal, like those of the other villages, were expert sailors. Their oars did not splash at the water like those of the goblin-crewed craft, and those steering the boats knew the angles to take to intercept schools of fish or other boats.

It quickly became apparent why this one boat of fleeing warriors was having such problems. They had lost more than one oar, and carried nearly ten villagers in a craft designed for half that number. They were near to the shore because they were looking for a place to beach the boat and run off to the west along the lakeshore.

But they weren't going to make it. The pursuing boat stayed with them, apparently well aware of their troubles and eager for the fight.

Now a second boat, Khotai's boat, closed, but the mountain goblins did not relent, and rather howled with anticipation, even veering a bit as if hoping to engage both craft, one on either side.

"So, we're in for a fight," the burly man growled. "Good enough, then."

Khotai had a different idea, though. She focused solely on that enemy boat, noting how low it was running, surprised, actually, that it hadn't already tipped under.

"Try to come alongside," Khotai called back to the big man.

"What do you think we're doing?" he yelled back at her.

"Not our sister boat," she corrected. "Alongside the goblins!"

The man's rowing slowed as he turned about to stare at her incredulously.

"How high can you throw me?" Khotai said with a wry smile.

He stared a bit longer, then seemed to catch on and offered a nod before digging his oars in once more, driving the boat as instructed.

They drew closer now to both. Khotai recognized some of those in the fleeing Carrachan Shoal boat. Not her favorite people, truly, but that didn't matter. She had wanted her fight and now she was getting it. She had wanted to die in battle, and now, that seemed all but certain.

"Help us!" the ten in the fleeing boat called out.

"An oar! We need an oar!" one man yelled.

But Khotai's boat veered away from them.

Spears flew out from the goblin boat, bouncing all about. Khotai slapped one aside with her flailing arm, good fortune alone saving her. But she didn't flinch.

"So be it," she said.

The boats were barely five strides apart, the goblins trying to turn so that Khotai's boat didn't go right past them. But Khotai's rowers put up oars suddenly and the big man grabbed Khotai under the arms and so easily hoisted her up into the air.

"One shot," Khotai said to him. "Aim well and then be gone."

And she was flying, high into the air, thrown like a sack. She fought to right herself, to keep her focus. She saw spears lifting toward her, and indeed got one through the shoulder as she crashed down, but the burly man's aim had been true, and she fell just to the side of the overloaded boat, turning and grabbing the rail as she splashed down, her momentum pulling the side of the craft with her just enough before her grip faltered for her to take that rail beneath the water.

The woman flailed as she sank from the sunlight, but she took heart and knew joy, for she had surely swamped the mountain goblin boat.

The light suddenly disappeared, lost in the shadow of a thick enemy, leaping in after her. She wasn't as deep as she had thought, she realized when the creature grabbed her and began thrashing her about.

Blood filled the water, pouring from her wound, and all about was turmoil and slapping sounds. Khotai tried to get her hands in the monster's face, to gouge out its eyes or just to hold it under with her, drowning it beside her.

Farewell, my love Talmadge, she silently recited.

More splashing, more slapping, more darkness.

The goblin holding her let go, but did not flee, just hung there weirdly in the water.

Khotai didn't know what to think when more hands reached for her.

She fought back, punching, scratching. Good, she'd kill two!

But she was grabbed and hugged too close, and it was not a goblin, but a man, a young man named Asef.

Her sensibilities left her then, and the world grew darker still.

Talmadge gave up trying to convince the villagers to take to the boats—they had sent the infirm, the young, the old, to the beach—but no more. Once the fighting began, the frontiersman was glad to be in their midst, glad to be a part of this defense of a place he believed worth fighting for. He wasn't afraid and he didn't shy. He took a hit, more than one, but he fought through the fear and didn't even really feel the pain.

He believed in this fight, and so he waged it beside Catriona and the others willingly, and with every turn of the tide that seemed against them, he actually came to fear that Catriona or someone else would call for a retreat to the lake. Better to bleed, better to die even, than to surrender Fasach Crann without a fight.

In the midst of all the other jumbled thoughts and tension and immediacy of peril, it did occur to Talmadge that this was the first time in his life he had ever felt such a thing. He had heard of it before, so many times, but he had never felt it. Not like this.

Like when he felt love for Khotai.

The book of Talmadge's life grew much thicker this day, and he acquitted himself well on this battlefield, more than one mountain goblin falling before his sword. He fought for Fasach Crann, that it would not die. He fought for Khotai, whom he feared had died. He fought for Aydrian, who must be dead, he feared, since the sidhe had come on and Aydrian had not. Still Talmadge suspected that the goblin horde was thinner than it had been on the mountain, and he knew that to be the work of the man who claimed to have once been a king in the east.

Around the back of one building, Talmadge and a handful of others, including Catriona, found a short reprieve.

"Catch your breath and bind anything that's badly bleeding," Catriona told them. "Many more's the sidhe that're about."

"We've lost a score and more," one man said.

"And a hundred sidhe and more lay dead!" another woman countered. "Oh, but we'll win the day."

Talmadge wasn't sure of that, or what that even meant. The losses here were mounting, and what of the sidhe who had probably overrun Carrachan Shoal? Perhaps the folk of Fasach Crann would win the day, but what about tomorrow?

"More on the ridge?" one woman asked, moving to the far corner of the building to get a view to the east of the village.

"Not a sidhe," said another. "His sword's aflame!"

Talmadge was up and moving quickly, pushing past Catriona and the others to join the two at the far corner.

"It's that man, your friend, who walked the water," the woman at the corner said as he arrived.

Talmadge hardly heard her, too engrossed in the view of the distant fight, and it was a fight indeed! Aydrian stood high on the side of a rocky bluff east of Fasach Crann, the same ridge the two had climbed upon to first view the trouble in Carrachan Shoal, though that vantage had been much farther back from the water and the town.

There was Aydrian now, his sword seeming like some magical torch, the blade wrapped in flames that danced and flowed as he brought it side to side, sweeping clear the nearest sidhe. As soon as he had put some room between himself and his foes, he changed his stance, changed his style of fighting altogether, it seemed, and began a forward-and-back approach, stabbing, lightning fast, with that flaming blade.

A sidhe stumbled back, grabbing its chest. A second charged, thinking it had an opening. But Aydrian had retracted and so struck again, his fiery sword burying itself so fully in the brute that the witnesses from the village at first thought the fires had gone out. Aydrian drove the blade to the side, though, and snapped his arm down and about with frightening strength, sending the powerful mountain goblin flipping and spinning from the rocks.

More enemies poured in at the man. Others moved along the ridge up above Aydrian and began throwing rocks down at him, and so precarious seemed his perch that Talmadge almost cried out for him, and might have, except that Adrian simply leaped away, jumping down twenty feet or more to the ground.

He dropped fast and Talmadge and the others winced, expecting him to land hard, but right as he neared the ground, he slowed and landed lightly, and in a run. Coming straight for the town, he sheathed his sword, pulled out that strange bow, and had it up and ready in a heartbeat, announcing his arrival with a line of well-aimed arrows that sent several sidhe spinning to the ground.

"To his side!" Talmadge yelled, and he rushed around the building to intercept the charge of Aydrian. So, too, did the others, and with Aydrian in their midst, his sword aflame once more, the lines of mountain goblins began to dissolve.

The Battle of Fasach Crann turned toward clear victory, and just in time, as several ships from the neighboring village came into view, sails full of wind, oars working hard the water.

"Go!" Aydrian told Talmadge. "Go and see, and get them all off the water."

Talmadge offered an appreciative nod and sprinted away. Aydrian stayed with Catriona and the others, moving house to house, joining in wherever they could to help their comrades overwhelm the scattered groups of enemies.

As he neared the water, Talmadge began to wave frantically, motioning for the boats to come in—those of Fasach Crann and of Carrachan Shoal. He understood Aydrian's fear here—anyone who had seen the lake monster up close would certainly understand Aydrian's fear.

The first boats in were those of Carrachan Shoal, their warriors leaping out to prepare any defenses that might be needed.

"They took some of our boats and chased, but I do'no think they're coming," Asba told Talmadge as the frontiersman splashed into the water to get beside the man at the front of his boat and help pull it further in.

Others jumped out and helped, grabbing at the sides.

"Still some fights," Talmadge told them. "Avenge your villag . . ."

The word stuck in his throat, as he happened to glance over the side of the boat, to the rear bench, and to the one-legged woman lying upon it. He breathed her name—he couldn't even find the strength to speak it—and he pulled himself over the rail awkwardly, tumbling down hard as the craft bounced with the tugging and splashing.

Talmadge clawed at the wood and forced himself back there, falling over Khotai, and now calling to her softly and repeatedly. She looked dead, her face blue, and so he was elated when she at last opened her eyes.

"My Khotai," he said. "I am so sorry. For leaving you. For leaving you then and leaving you now."

He was rambling, and thought he sounded quite silly, but the words poured forth before he could begin to even think of what he should say.

Finally, Khotai lifted her hand gently to his face, then grabbed him more forcefully. "Promise me that you'll never leave me again," she whispered, and it sounded to Talmadge as the most beautiful song he had ever heard.

13

CUOWITAY

"The village is secured," Aydrian said, walking over to join Talmadge and Khotai. He offered a smile when he saw the two up close, Khotai behind Talmadge and with her arms wrapped about Talmadge's neck, and also with a rope tied about both of them, so that if Talmadge stood, he would lift the woman up with him.

"I see that you have shed your fear of being a burden to this man you love," Aydrian said rather bluntly, drawing a look of confusion from Khotai and a scowl from Talmadge.

"That is why you sent him away, is it not?" Aydrian bravely pressed on. "You weren't mad that he left you—how could he have possibly known better with your leg in his hand . . ."

"Aydrian!" Talmadge scolded.

"It is the truth," Aydrian replied. "You could not have known that she might be alive, and she left you as much as you left her. Did you not?" he asked Khotai directly, and she still seemed confused.

"How many times did you inquire about him, if he had been seen?" asked Aydrian.

"I thought him surely dead," Khotai admitted, and Aydrian looked Talmadge in the eye and held up his hands as if that answer ended the debate.

"She was never angry at you, my friend Talmadge," Aydrian explained.

"She was as shocked to see you as you were to see her. And as elated—which didn't last for either of you. You saw what had happened to her and were horrified, and she knew almost immediately that it would not be fair to you to so burden you with a crippled partner, one for whose condition you would no doubt feel responsible."

"Shut up," Talmadge warned, and seemed as if he meant to leap up and attack Aydrian. "Why are you doing this?"

"Because he's right," Khotai answered, eliciting a gasp from Talmadge, but not surprising Aydrian in the least.

"My friend, the only way to face pain is to admit it, and, well, face it," Aydrian said. "I do not know you so very well, and yet I recognize this truth about you better than you do, it would seem. You run from pain, and hide from pain, better than any I have ever known. That way leads to shadows where there should be light, I assure you."

"Now you're my teacher?"

"Someone has to be," Khotai said with a laugh—a wonderful laugh that none had heard in a long, long time—into Talmadge's ear.

Talmadge's expression shifted instantly, and he reached up to put his hand over that of his beloved and turned to look into her brown eyes and into that brilliant grin.

"The village is secure?" Khotai asked Aydrian.

He nodded. "The folk of Fasach Crann are even now planning to pursue the sidhe who overran Carrachan Shoal along with the survivors of that town. To retrieve the supplies before winter comes on in full."

Talmadge stood up, taking Khotai with him. "Will you join?"

"A chance to kill goblins," Aydrian replied with a wry grin. "What do you think?"

"Join him," Khotai said, and Talmadge glanced back doubtfully.

"If you reverse our fates, I'd drop you in the mud and pick you back up when I returned," Khotai assured him.

That brought smiles all around. The three started for the center of the town, where Catriona and the others had gathered to plan their assault to retake Carrachan Shoal, or chase down the sidhe to take back the supplies. Before they arrived, though, there came a flash high up the mountain, bright and sharp like a bolt of lightning.

"Ah, but I told you it was them deamhans!" a man near Catriona shouted, shaking his fist at Fireach Speuer.

"They set the sidhe on us," another chimed in.

As he finished, the thunderous report echoed down from on high, rumbling about the town and turning all eyes up to the mountaintop, where flames then leaped, and another crackle of lightning.

"Not so sure," Catriona, and some others, said quietly.

"Your lens," Aydrian said, holding his hand out to Talmadge.

Talmadge handed it over and Aydrian wasted no time in putting it up to his eye and calling upon the far-seeing magic. He knew immediately that the villager's assessment of the situation could not have been more wrong.

Twenty to a side they sat, glancing about uncomfortably, expressions revealing their distaste for their surroundings, for though this was a temple to their beloved Glorious Gold, and the family temple of the line of Bayan, of Pixquicauh himself, no less, these wealthy, pampered augurs and the sovereigns of the greatest score of xoconai cities were not accustomed to such sparse surroundings and dirty stone. Nor were they pleased about the difficult journey in merely getting to the place, far in the east for most, and in the less-traveled foothills of the towering mountains that, to the xoconai, separated the world of light from the darkness and death of Cizinfozza's realm.

The pyramidical temple around them was constructed of simple gray stone, and had not been built to hold this many. Bundled together on benches that had been brought in for this occasion, the city sovereigns were not used to such crowded proximity, which forced unusual and demeaning informality. These xoconai women and men, elected to leadership, were not used to being touched by any who were not given explicit permission to do so, but in here, they were bumping up against each other with disquieting frequency.

An altar of simple granite rested along the back wall, beneath a mural of faded paints depicting a great victory of old. Before that altar stood the High Priest, and beside him, a propped sheet of polished gold, which seemed so out of place in this otherwise drab structure. Even the dusty air could not dim the luster of that golden mirror.

"The Glorious Gold will take joy in our attack," Pixquicauh told them.

From the sides of the chamber, the augurs raised their fists in apparent agreement, but among the central twenty, the pragmatic sovereigns who governed the cities and who could be voted out of power at any time, the reaction was much more ambivalent, and more than one hiss of disapproval was heard.

"The armies gather," one of the sovereigns said.

"Every day brings more macana," another added, using a word that referred to the tooth-edged war clubs of the xoconai warriors and to the warriors themselves.

"The mundunugu ride from every corner of Tonoloya," said another.

"If we wait, we will become unstoppable," said a third.

"Our army is already unstoppable!" cried one of the augurs. "We have the power of Scathmizzane behind us. We cannot lose on the battlefield."

"You must never think that way," one of the sovereigns, an older woman, scolded.

"To suggest otherwise is heresy," the augur retorted.

"Heresy!" the priests called in agreement, and several sovereigns joined in.

The old woman sovereign bowed low, conceding. "It is not said and was not told that we are not already superior," she said apologetically.

"Then it is not wise to imply it," boomed the stern voice of Pixquicauh. He and the old woman exchanged glares then, hinting to the others that there was personal history between them. There was indeed history, and they were indeed contemporaries.

The sovereign sat down and lowered her gaze, which pleased the High Priest greatly, for this situation between them had been reversed decades before.

However, another city sovereign, a younger woman with a strikingly bright red nose and brilliant sky-blue beside it (such colors were usually not nearly as bright in the women as the men) stood up quickly, and with clear determination.

"More macana every day," she said, her voice loud and strong. "But they are more mouths to feed. Food is not so plentiful. We need more to feed the army of Glorious Gold, and more still if we would have our army march into the mountains against the coming winter."

"If they march, we will have more food," said another sovereign. "For all our cities. My citizens are so busy with the needs of the macana that they are not gathering as they should."

"How many citizens will be needed to ferry food to the marching army?" an augur argued.

More voices joined in. Up by the altar, Pixquicauh grew angrier by the moment. "Voices without recognition!" he finally yelled above them all, for indeed, protocol said that speakers should be recognized by him, as the one leading this gathering, before any word was uttered.

The temple quieted.

"I have seen," the High Priest declared, indicating the golden mirror beside him. "Scathmizzane has shown me the mountain lake and the humans. Food is plentiful beyond Teotl Tenamitl."

"We do not know snow," the old woman sovereign dared to argue. "Not here. Or very little in the hills. That is not the way of the tall mountains! The snow in the mountains will stop an army, and the winds freeze the blood. To go is a great risk and all could be lost."

Pixquicauh stared at the sovereign with his bulging dead, borrowed eyes. The orbs didn't blink, of course, but he was twitching, so great was his anger. This one, Sovereign Disu Suzu Ixil, had ever been a bane to him. It was she, a mere child, who had sent her macana to these foothills demanding a tithing of food in the Summer of Barrenness, when the old augur's father was still presiding at the temple.

The temple's flock had eaten little that year. Many had left, not to return, reducing the tithing to the augur's family. It was she, this one, Sovereign Disu Suzu Ixil, who had begun the fall of the augur family of Bayan.

It was possible that she knew what she was speaking about—hers, Tavu Tavu, was the easternmost city of Tonoloya, nearly as high in the foothills of the Tyuskixmal as this very temple, and her citizens were known to wander the higher passes. But Pixquicauh didn't allow that possibility to dissuade him here, not against this one, not when he, not Disu Suzu Ixil, had spoken to Scathmizzane.

"I have made my decision," he declared, lifting his right arm before him, palm down. "I speak for the Glorious Gold." He held his pose as a murmur of complaint wafted through the crowd. If he turned his hand palm-up, it would be a call to wait; a clenched fist meant a call to war.

He closed his fist.

The priests cheered, as did some of the city sovereigns. Those who had spoken against this course said nothing aloud, but the eyes of Disu Suzu Ixil spoke loudly to the High Priest.

Loudly in disagreement.

That only made him more certain of his decision.

"I speak to the macana when the dawn's rays shine upon the mountaintops," he declared. "To war!"

Good fortune alone had saved them, Tay Aillig believed. Had not Aghmor been out on the mountain that particular morning, up high and in the only region allowing him to see past Fireach Speuer to the south and west, the Usgar would not have seen this force of monsters crawling up those southwestern slopes with wicked intent.

Had Tay Aillig understood the truth of why Aghmor had been out there, circling around to conceal that he had been bringing supplies to the missing slave, he probably would be holding a significantly different opinion of the day's "hero."

The Usgar, fittingly with Tay Aillig as their leader, did not lack confidence in battle, no matter the odds. They saw themselves as godlike compared to the lesser creatures skittering about them, like the lakemen, and particularly the mountain goblins, whom they called sidhe. But the tribe numbered around three hundred—not three hundred warriors and witches, but three hundred in total, and more enemies than that were coming over the high ridges of Fireach Speuer against them this day.

Caught by surprise, the tribe might have been overrun before they could organize any defensive posture. Caught out in the field, away from this sacred place, even the great warrior Tay Aillig might have been forced to order a full retreat so as not to engage such a mass of enemies as was now approaching.

But here, with time to prepare, the Usgar-triath did not want to run. With the witches so close and attuned to their warriors, Usgar spear tips gleamed and crackled with power. The bond was strong, the proximity to the source of power so important that Tay Aillig expected Mairen to heal his wounds as fast as he received them.

Even without that, though, the proud man willingly and often uttered, "They are just sidhe."

He glanced to the sacred pine grove, hearing the song, for in there, ten witches danced about the God Crystal, and others, former witches, or those training or having shown some affinity with the magical song, sat about the perimeter of that dance, basking in the power of Usgar being brought forth by Mairen and the others. There were only twelve in the Coven now, for Aoleyn had not been replaced—and the thought of Aoleyn did send a pang of regret through Tay Aillig. Not because he was sad about killing the troublesome little wretch. On a personal level, he cared not at all for her, but her prowess in the joining ritual, where a witch sent her magic out to the attuned warrior, could not be denied, not after the display she had put on with Brayth against these very same enemies, and even against the demon fossa.

Two other witches had gone out from the sacred grove, positioning themselves as Tay Aillig and Mairen had determined, one up above a narrow ledge rounding the mountaintop on the west, the other at the base of a decline thick with snow, down which the sidhe would likely swarm.

They would know soon enough, as the first sentries began calling out that the enemies were in sight.

You think I would fail you? he heard in his head, a sharp reminder that Mairen was in there, telepathically joined with him, and had realized, obviously, his regret over Aoleyn.

Tay Aillig could only laugh, but he stopped in surprise when he felt the power of Usgar suddenly flowing through him, strengthening him, toughening him, and his spear began to thrum with power beyond anything he had ever felt before.

We are near the God Crystal, Mairen explained in answer to his unspoken question, to his surprise, really.

The leading monsters came rushing down the bottom steps of th'Way, between the caves which normally housed the uamhas, though they were all huddled in the main encampment now, and in sight of the eastern edge of the winter plateau, where stood Tay Aillig and the main group of Usgar warrior defense.

The Usgar-triath began to bark out an order, but stopped before he uttered a word, finding a sudden impulse to hurl his spear at the oncoming enemies.

Not the spear. Throw the magic, he heard in his mind. Tay Aillig had never experienced anything like this before, never anything this intense, and it unsettled him somewhat, so much so that he thought of grabbing the sunstone he had in the small pocket he had secretly sewn into his pants.

He felt Mairen's questioning at that notion and worked hard to dismiss it before she could solve the puzzle here. He focused immediately on her instructions and followed his instincts through the call and flow of the magic. His eyes went as wide as those around him, though not as much so as the eyes of the charging mountain goblins, when a tremendous blast of lightning exploded out of his speartip, blinding all with its searing flash, and crackling into the monster ranks.

Down went the lead sidhe, rows and rows, some falling into lumps, others down and jerking about in spasms.

Now Tay Aillig called for the charge, the Usgar warriors launching themselves into the sidhe ranks before the monsters could recover. Several more spear tips erupted in smaller bursts of magic, some fire, some lightning, and more monsters died.

Up on the mountain to the east, Tay Aillig heard screaming, and he glanced that way and couldn't help but grin wickedly.

Up on a narrow ledge, a witch had magically brought forth a field of ice, and the sidhe were struggling to hold their footing on the edge of the cliff. That grin became a mocking laugh, and one of approval to Mairen, surely, when the witch cast a second spell, a great burst of wind down at the enemy holding so tenuous a position. Over they went in a tumble, a dozen and more plummeting down the rocky, windblown cliff face.

And those sidhe behind, not yet in the magically iced area, turned about and fled.

Some distance to the west of the winter plateau loomed another, more round-about approach, but one that the sidhe had decided to use, with their second line coming in opposite those charging down th'Way. It was a clever play—or would have been, had not the Usgar, who knew every slope, every stone, every gully on this part of Fireach Speuer, anticipated it.

The mountain path ended in a long snow-covered decline that emptied into a gully west of the camp. At the base of that slope, burrowed into the snow, hid a trembling Connebragh, who was second in power in the Coven, behind the Usgar-righinn. She clutched two crystals, one filled with milky white flecks, the other thick with red, like tiny embers floating within the clear crystal.

She wore multiple skins, but even so, she had been buried in the snow for some time now and the cold was creeping in. So, she was both happy and afraid when she finally heard the enemy, whooping and coming fast down the steep snowy decline.

She hoped this devilish plan would work as she fell into the first crystal, enacting a white shield about her—at least, that's what it was supposed to do, and so Connebragh had to trust in it, since she couldn't see the white glow when she was buried in the snow.

She went to the second crystal then, exciting its magical power, bringing it to its highest point possible, a point beyond anything she had ever experienced.

The mountain goblins were close then, she could hear, but with their ranks still stretching far up the slope.

Connebragh released the magic, released the fireball, and felt the flash of heat despite her serpentine defensive shield. The witch wisely burrowed in deeper, pushing up against a rocky overhang, and just in time, as the entire hillside began to tremble and shudder, a river of snow beginning an inevitable and deadly slide.

Down came the sidhe, tumbling with the avalanche.

Connebragh curled up tighter and yelled, but she couldn't even hear her own voice as the river of snow roared past, full of tumbling monsters screaming and rolling boulders grumbling.

"Beyond the mountains lies the promise," Pixquicauh told the great gathering of warriors. "Beyond the mountains live the enemies of Scathmizzane. No more does Cizinfozza protect them. No more are the souls of their dead haunting the caves and the passes. Our time is come, my brethren.

"We saw Kithkukulikhan bring the short night," he cried and the gathering cheered. "They say and it's been told that the wide-winged totot are few in the west, that the high lakes of Tyuskixmal have dried. But I have seen, and Scathmizzane has shown me. The great waters of Ayuskixmal remain, awaiting.

"Let them wait no more! We are called, my brethren, to Ayuskixmal, to the herald Tzatzini, to bring the light of Scathmizzane beyond Teotl Tenamitl!"

He ended with his arms held high, and with the cheers of thousands of xoconai: augurs with their polished mirrors of gold and bags of healing herbs; the mundunugu riders astride their cuetzpali; the anqui deerstalkers with their javelins and soft shoes; the macana footsoldiers in their wooden armor, spiked macana and spears waving.

What a glorious gathering, he thought. What could stop them?

"We will cheer Tonalli awakening from the sea beyond our eastern shore, and pray for her return when she douses her fires to sleep beneath the waves beyond our western shores," he chanted, and a thousand voices took it up.

The High Priest glanced over to the right-hand side of his pyramid temple's steps, where the twenty city sovereigns stood. He wanted to see if any remained with doubt.

Perhaps he could have them sacrificed to ensure a greater march, he mused, and smiled at the thought.

That grin didn't hold, though, for these were elected leaders, and murdering them would cause great distress among the citizens of Tonoloya. The entire preposterous thought flew from his mind even further when he noted another xoconai standing unexpectedly among their ranks, a woman of great reputation who could not be denied.

Noting the look, that woman had the temerity to step forward and cross the empty steps to join Pixquicauh near the center of the stair.

"I would speak with you, if you please, High Priest," she said, her voice strong and low. She was middle-aged, not very much younger than the old augur, but none looking at the pair would ever guess that. For this woman stood straight and was filled with vitality, her eyes clear and sharp, her muscles solid and hardened by years of adventure and battle.

Before he could answer, Pixquicauh heard the name of this legendary xoconai commander being whispered all throughout the gathering.

"Tuolonatl," they said. There was no title accompanying the name, as with Pixquicauh, because like Pixquicauh, the name itself served as such. Tuolonatl, hero of the xoconai, a mundunugu unparalleled on cuetzpali or even on horse. Tuolonatl had been a part of every major conflict in Tonoloya for four decades, and of late, her role had become nothing more than signing on as mercenary commander of one city or another that was being threatened by an aggressive neighbor. That act alone had averted three wars, at least, for none desired to fight an army led by Tuolonatl.

And all desired to fight for Tuolonatl.

"Then speak, great mundunugu," Pixquicauh responded.

But Tuolonatl glanced about and shook her head. "Not here, before all," she said.

Pixquicauh began to scoff at that, but Tuolonatl quietly added, "I would not embarrass the High Priest of Scathmizzane before this important gathering."

Under his permanent condoral, Pixquicauh seethed. He considered his options here, one of which would involve an immediate condemnation of this legendary warrior for her impudence. But this was Tuolonatl, and many of those thousands in attendance would follow her across fields of burning coals. Condemning her, even embarrassing her, could prompt an uprising before the army could begin its march up the mountain trails.

Without another word, Tuolonatl turned and started up the steps for the temple entrance.

Trying to appear composed and in control, the High Priest followed.

"You cannot speak to Scathmizzane's High Priest in such a manner!" Pixquicauh scolded as soon as they were alone inside, the door closed behind them.

"You offered me no choice," Tuolonatl said simply. "The march must be stopped, and so I must stop the march."

"Stopped? Did you not see Kithkukulikhan eat the sun?"

"I did. It is Cuowitay, I do not doubt."

Pixquicauh cocked his head in confusion.

"The wind blows from the north across Teotl Tenamitl," Tuolonatl explained. "The trails will be clear and then they will not be clear, and you will strand an army in a place where they will find no shelter and no food. You will kill us before a spear of our enemies ever could. I have been there, High Priest, to the high passes. We cannot go until the days grow long once more and the winds blow warm."

"The way is clear. I have seen," Pixquicauh insisted.

"The way will not be clear for long enough," Tuolonatl replied without hesitation. "The mountaintops seem so close, but they are far. I have been. We cannot cross."

"I am the voice of Scathmizzane," the High Priest reminded her. "Do you doubt the word of the God-King?"

"I doubt the wisdom of his High Priest in this," Tuolonatl calmly replied.

No other would have spoken to the High Priest with such aplomb. He fashioned a reply, but before he could begin to argue, Tuolonatl nodded her chin to the back of the room, to the side of the altar, where stood the tall mirror of polished gold.

At first, Pixquicauh thought it a trick of the sunlight, as that glossy surface shimmered and shone. When he realized the truth of it, he, with Tuolonatl close behind, rushed to stand before the magical mirror, arriving just as an image of Scathmizzane filled it.

"Now you will see," the High Priest whispered to the warrior, who still seemed not at all concerned.

"God-King," Pixquicauh began, "the army of Glorious Gold stands ready."

Scathmizzane turned his gaze to regard Tuolonatl. "You question this?" he asked.

"I do, Glorious Gold," the mundunugu said, and the High Priest gasped audibly.

"How dare . . ." Pixquicauh started to scold her, but Scathmizzane held up a hand for him to see, motioning him to silence.

"I have been to the mountains in my youth, God-King," Tuolonatl explained. "I have spent my life, in service to you, in observance of the land, the wind, the seasons. We will not cross Teotl Tenamitl before the snows fall thick about us and in that winter, we are surely lost."

Scathmizzane did not reply for many heartbeats, then turned to regard Pixquicauh.

"You do not agree?" he asked.

"This is Cuowitay, the Day of the Xoconai," the skull-faced augur said. "Even now, the xelquiza do battle with the humans about Tzatzini."

Outside the temple, the gathered crowd began to cheer wildly, and both Pixquicauh and Tuolonatl turned in surprise.

"I have shown them my image in the mirror you placed atop your temple," Scathmizzane explained. "Let them not think of conflict, unless it is war for the glory of Scathmizzane."

"Then we march," Pixquicauh reasoned.

"No, my loyal augur," came Scathmizzane's surprising answer.

Pixquicauh's shoulders slumped. "God-King . . ."

"Use the counsel of Tuolonatl," Scathmizzane instructed. "She has been to the high mountains. She bathes in the light of Scathmizzane."

Before Pixquicauh could begin to argue, the image in the golden mirror shimmered to nothingness.

"Come, High Priest," Tuolonatl offered, and there was no taunt in her steady voice. "Let us go and speak of our enemies. The winter will not be long, and the spring will see the first march of the xoconai."

Pixquicauh followed Tuolonatl out of the temple, two steps behind. He kept glancing back at the golden mirror, uncertain for the first time in many days.

He knew the heart of Scathmizzane, so it was said and so it had been told by the God-King himself. How could he have made this mistake?

"What is it?" Talmadge asked Aydrian, translating the heart of the questions coming fast at the strange man from the east. Most of the survivors of Carrachan Shoal and the villagers of Fasach Crann crowded around the three outlanders, and they seemed more than a little agitated—rightfully so, but with their scowls aimed right at Aydrian.

"A fight on the mountain," he said, and Talmadge translated to those gathered.

"Mountain goblins," he went on, but slowly, so that Talmadge could quickly translate and Khotai could confirm. "Many came against the tribe up there."

"Deamhan Usgar," Khotai said to him, and he nodded.

Many voices reached out to Talmadge all at once, and he tried to hush them, then explained to Aydrian, "They hope the sidhe rid them of the deamhan Usgar."

Aydrian shook his head. He hadn't seen everything up there on Fireach Speuer, just glimpses, but enough to know that the mountain goblins had been routed there more thoroughly than in Fasach Crann.

"The mountain has quieted," he said to Talmadge. "I did not glimpse many fallen Usgar, but the sidhe dead are piled."

Talmadge stood up straight, and his movement brought a silence from the villagers. He turned and somberly informed them.

That brought more anger, more agitation, and more fingers pointing Aydrian's way.

Talmadge spoke back at all of that, as did Khotai, and Aydrian understood that they were defending him here, telling the villagers that he was no Usgar and no deamhan. Of course, Aydrian understood their anger and trepidation, and wondered if he might have to find a quick way out of this place. Finally, though, Khotai turned about and sighed.

"Talmadge reminded them of your help," she explained. "And many of them are grateful enough to the strange man in the shiny armor to accept that you are no enemy."

"But they'll watch you closely, do'no doubt," Talmadge said, and he was more serious than lighthearted, even though he was grinning.

Aydrian smiled back at him and nodded. If these villagers, or even Talmadge and Khotai, knew the truth of his past, of the things he had done in all their gory detail, they probably wouldn't be so accepting.

The weight of the snow pressed in on her, but they had chosen her location well and it would not crush her or suffocate her, she knew. It would not kill her.

But the cold would.

Connebragh could feel it seeping into her bones. Her toes and fingers burned as if a thousand fiery needles were being stuck into them. She had tried to call upon the crystals again, enacting a shield, even bringing forth some flames. But that had only settled the snow more fully upon her, and had left her wet and miserable.

She could breathe, her face remained clear, though pressed uncomfortably against the stone, but that didn't matter.

Because the cold seeped in, taking the warmth of her life bit by bit.

She heard the muffled screaming nearby, but she was too far gone then to even realize that these were the death screams of those sidhe that had survived the avalanche. The Usgar were upon them, as they lay helpless and broken in the piled snow, finishing them off with spear thrusts.

It didn't matter to Connebragh. All that mattered was the cold, and the sleep it invited.

A bright light shone in her face. She thought it Usgar welcoming her to the eternity of Corsaleug.

A hand roughly grabbed her and hauled her out of the snow, and she was up there, lying on the pile, for many gasping breaths before she even realized that she was still alive, that the warriors had found her.

They didn't tend her, though. Not then. She heard them all about, calling out that another monster sidhe had been found and was still alive.

Not for long.

She heard the discussions, but barely registered them.

"A great victory," one man declared. "Only seven dead, and the many wounded already mending. Glory to the Usgar-triath. Glory to the Usgar-righinn."

"And the sidhe bodies will pile high and make a great fire."

"A pity you can'no eat the things," said a woman Connebragh could not see.

"Fifteen sidhe dead by Tay Aillig's hand," the first man said.

"Thrice that number dead by this lass alone!" the woman said back at him, and it wasn't until she knelt near and stroked Connebragh's hair that the half-frozen Connebragh even realized that the woman had been speaking about her, about her avalanche that had worked so well in laying low the sidhe flanking force.

"We won?" asked Connebragh, still not opening her eyes, for the light stung her so badly. "The encampment is secured?"

"Aye, and let us get you near a fire," the woman replied. She yelled to some men to help her.

A few moments later, Connebragh was lifted from the ground. Finally, she opened her eyes and glanced about the shining white hillside.

The Usgar warriors were finishing their gruesome work—she saw a sidhe dug out of the snow and hauled up within a circle of warriors. She saw the look on the monster's face, one of stark terror, as the warriors began to prod it with their spears, all of them smiling.

They would take their time.

Connebragh looked at her frozen hands and was surprised to see that they were not covered in blood. She shook that thought away immediately, though, reminding herself that these were monsters, and that they had attacked the Usgar, not the other way around. And she, Connebragh, had killed many of them—more than two score if the woman's claim was to be believed.

Usgar-righinn Mairen would be pleased.

Usgar-triath Tay Aillig would be pleased.

14

THE VIEW FROM YESTERYEAR

There was . . . nothing.

No firmament against her back or hands.

No light—more than that, the absolute absence of light, a darkness more profound, more endless, than anything ever imagined.

No sound, no magic song.

No pain, no warmth, no cold.

No wind, no breath.

No dreams.

No thought but emptiness.

And a fear that this was eternal death that barely registered in the woman's nothingness.

She existed and she did not, caught somewhere between life and death, without consciousness, except that it was there, somewhere unknown, chewing at the dark and pervading unconsciousness.

So, it went, through days and nights that did not exist here, in this emptiness, in this fugue state.

A lick of chill tickled her neck. She thought it the coldness of death, surely. She was dead, of course she was dead! How could she not be?

The fall.

The impact.

Conscious thought. A sense of self.

There was more beyond the grave!

But she had no body. She could feel no body. She opened her eyes, or did she, for there was no light, not a speck, not a hint.

Aoleyn, she thought. *I am Aoleyn. I was Aoleyn. I am dead.*

She heard a whisper in her mind, a gentle call, *My child!*

Elara, she somehow knew. The mother she had never known.

Elara, who was long dead. In this place of emptiness.

Aoleyn, said another whisper in her mind, one she certainly recognized.

Seonagh, who was dead, who had been broken by the fossa in her efforts to save Aoleyn, and had then been given to Craos'a'diad, the Mouth of Usgar.

Help us, my child, Elara's spirit imparted to her. *We are leaving. We can'no stay.*

Diminishing, Seonagh added. *The demon fossa has no grasp to hold us.*

Cizinfozza, the ghost of Elara thought, and Aoleyn heard, and knew it to be a demon name.

The others are gone, my child. All gone. And we are leaving. We can'no stay.

There came a sharp crackle and a flash of lightning, from directly underneath Aoleyn, though she did not feel it. It jolted her body a bit from the floor, and when she settled, she lay at a slightly different angle.

She did not understand. She felt nothing beneath her back.

"Why?" Aoleyn asked, and audibly with her voice, and she heard! She was alive! She could feel the stone floor against the back of her head, could feel the brush of her hair—and the scrape of it against her cheek. Dried blood, she thought.

She brought her hand up to move the hair aside.

No, she did not.

She could not.

She could feel nothing except . . . could feel nothing below the sensation of the cold floor on the back of her neck. That and the general chill. So cold.

But no more like the cold of death, she thought. This was the bite of winter on her face and ears and neck. Physical, not spiritual.

Help us! she heard both of the spirits scream in her mind.

Aoleyn began to piece the bits together. She thought of the chasm, this dark and deep gorge, and of the many spirits she had encountered when she had been exploring the crystal caverns in her trial for the Coven. She couldn't sense those many spirits now, not at all, beyond these two, her mother and her aunt, the woman who had birthed her and the woman who had raised her.

"Help?" she asked, and then, only then, did Aoleyn fully grasp their pleas.

She had fallen, mortally. She was fast dying, and would be dead, but for these two spirits, Elara and Seonagh. They were singing the song of Usgar within her, catching the magic of the wedstones caught in the many crystals in this most magical complex of caverns and tunnels. They were healing her—no, they weren't strong enough to do that. They had been sustaining her tiny thread of life.

We are leaving. We can'no stay, Seonagh's spirit said yet again.

And they were, Aoleyn realized. Already their thoughts were thinner, more distant, less substantial. Through those thoughts, Aoleyn heard the music of Usgar, and she grabbed at it, how she grabbed at it!

She brought the warmth to fight the coldness, and it did seem to diminish—nay, the cold began to spread.

But that was a good thing, Aoleyn suddenly realized, for she could feel the cold stone on her shoulder now, and down one arm, which was awkwardly angled beneath her back. Hardly even thinking of why that might be, she yanked the arm out wide and brought it across to begin touching the rest of her body, to ensure that it was all still there. She reached down as low as she could manage, but yes, her legs seemed to be there, intact.

Why couldn't she feel them?

She reached for the music again and again, but to less effect. Much less. Elara and Seonagh were also singing Usgar's song, but their voices grew more distant, and the song became a hum and nothing more, and ineffective against Aoleyn's maladies.

Aoleyn knew that she was alone again. She sent her thoughts out to the cavern, calling for her mother, for her aunt, for the magic of Usgar. Her renewed hopes quickly turned to desperation, for there was nothing upon which she could hold. The warmth was gone. The spirits were gone. She had no idea of the extent of her remaining injuries, other than the growing pain in her forearm, for she couldn't feel anything beyond that limb and her uppermost body. Those wounds would kill her, though, she was certain, or the coldness would.

She lay there for a moment, trying to compose herself, trying to find some solution. There was just the hard floor beneath, one she could only feel on the back of her head, her neck, and her right side to her fingers. She brought that hand in to touch her face and felt the wrist tie hanging from it, and could smell the burning rope.

The lightning crackle? Had the dead witches freed her hands with a jolt of lightning?

She whispered her thanks, but then recanted, for this seemed the cruelest trick of all. To let her awaken, to tease her with the spirits of her mother and aunt, and to leave her, helpless, in a deep, deep, and black hole, too far from the magical gem-filled caverns above for her to hear the song, or at least, to hear it enough to access the magic. For it was there, far in the distance, and that seemed crueler still.

She walked her fingers back toward her side, bending her arm, and with great effort, pushed off the floor to lift her head and one shoulder, just a bit. She tried to look around, but no, there was just blackness.

Aoleyn felt tears welling in her eyes. She didn't want to die like this. It would be slow, she feared, and now she was feeling pain in her unnumbed shoulder and arm, and she had to ease the limb back down, realizing that her arm was almost certainly broken.

She called out, but so weakly that her voice carried not at all.

Who would hear her, anyway?

So she lay back and waited to die.

The cold emptiness began to creep in once more. She called for her mother, both with her voice and with her thoughts. But no, the spirits were gone, diminished to nothingness or flown away—she could not know.

It was the demon that had trapped them here, they had said. She had freed them, then, by destroying the fossa. She had freed them and thus, had unwittingly doomed herself.

She thought of the fossa's cave, where she had battled the beast. She had felt the ghosts there, too, and it was not far from this place, though higher up, she sensed. Much higher up than this pit.

The cold crept in. She wore only a slight, almost sheer, short shift, one torn in many places, and hardly protection against the winter's bite.

Panic grabbed the broken young woman. She could not die like this! She reached for the song.

But no, it was too far.

She swung her broken arm with all her strength, somehow managing to turn somewhat on her side. Then she reached out into the darkness, clawing at the floor, looking for something to hold on to. She found a slight lip in the stone, and she pulled. With all her desperation and all her anger, Aoleyn crept.

She understood that she had moved barely a finger's breadth, and that she had turned herself more than she had actually moved from the spot, but it didn't matter. There was no point, but there had to be!

She reached again and pulled again. Pain shot through her arm, burning and awful, but she gasped against it and reached farther into the nothingness around her.

And her hand touched upon something, at first startling and frightening. But then it seemed familiar, and Aoleyn grasped the small item and brought it in.

An earring, her earring, with a red garnet gemstone, and more critically, with a strand wound of wedstone. She clasped it tightly in her hand and listened for the music, focusing on the gray strand, the magic that would bring her healing.

With all her strength and willpower, Aoleyn washed that healing through her broken and battered body. Over and over again, she called upon it, and by the time she had to lay back in exhaustion, the feeling had begun returning to her other arm.

She attached the earring to her ear, healing the wound around the wedstone wire, making it, as it had been, a part of her.

Hope did not return to poor Aoleyn, though. Not yet. Even if she could somehow manage to heal the rest of her shattered body, how might she fend off the cold? She couldn't maintain the healing magic forever, after all, and if she slept now without the spirits of Elara and Seonagh feeding her the magic of Usgar, she would surely freeze to death.

She rested as long as she could manage, until her ears and fingers began to sting, then she fell back into the magic of her earring, but this time into the garnet, the stone that would let her sense and see any nearby magic.

She glanced about. The more energy she was able to pour into the stone, the wider her net was cast.

She saw! Two other pieces of her jewelry, and nearest lay her ring.

She had to crawl, but now she had use of both her hands and so she could manage it. She got to the ring, and fell over it, hugging it close and letting go of the earring's magic. She pushed herself against a wall, propped herself to a sitting position, then took a deep breath, trying to find her calm, her center, her balance.

She gathered her mental strength, then called upon the white stone of the ring to create a magical glowing barrier about her. Into the other stone she sent her thoughts, building its magical energy. She found some loose stones about her as she did, and she pulled them in close.

"Please work," she whispered, and she released the energy of the ruby, creating a fireball around her of considerable power. It only lasted a heartbeat, but as the flames wisped away, the glow of the stones lit the area, giving her a good view.

A good view of very little, for all about her was dark stone, and not like the fabulous crystals in the caverns up above her. She saw upward for quite a distance, and noted that the shaft turned and twisted, which was probably why no daylight could find its way this far down. She saw, too, her legs, sticking out of the bottom of her shift, and her feet were there and all her toes.

She tried to wriggle them. She could not.

Aoleyn released the protective barrier of the serpentine, and let the warmth of the heated rocks seep into her body.

It felt good indeed, but it wouldn't last, and she would have a hard time keeping up with the bitter cold using fireballs, which greatly taxed her magical energy. She called upon the ruby again, to see if there was something else she might manifest from the gem's magic. She did hear a different path for the song, but wasn't sure of what it might be, and alas, she couldn't seem to access it.

She had to get out of here. There was no other way. But how?

She took a deep breath again and settled back, curling as tightly as she could against the heated stones, even putting a couple of rocks atop her, grasped in her hands as she tried to keep the feel of her fingers.

She started for the ring's power again, to enact the shield, but changed her mind and went instead to the earring and the magic-seeing garnet. After some time, she heard the whisper of a song to her right, but far away. With no choice, with time moving against her, Aoleyn crawled hand-over-hand into the darkness. She jammed one finger, cut another, and was sure she was tearing the skin of her legs and lower torso even as she was further tearing the light fabric of her smock, but she knew that she couldn't afford the time to stop and try to cast some healing spells.

No, she kept her focus and she found, first, her anklet, and heard the song of her belly ring further along in the darkness.

The anklet was stronger in the wedstone than either her earring or her ring, though, so she clutched it close and felt the songs within. It could cast lightning, she knew, and had a myriad of uses that produced cold and frost, even an icy field. Perhaps that coldness could be reversed.

When she searched the magic within the gem, she didn't find that, though.

She couldn't reverse the flow of the song, and using that bluish stone of the anklet, the zircon, would only make it colder around her.

Something else intrigued her, though, for on that anklet, in addition to the wedstone band, the zircon, and the graphite bar, were also some chips of a purplish gem. Searching through so many riddles of how she might survive, Aoleyn got the sense that she could shape the magic of the other gems differently with those specks of sapphire. She went again at the zircon.

No, she still could not revere its effects, but on a sudden thought, she went instead to the ruby in her ring.

The alternate songs of the ruby seemed far clearer then, various bars playing parallel to each other. She followed one and found the magical notes, then nearly screamed in surprise and fear as flames erupted all over her body.

She batted at them reflexively, and they stung her hands a bit. But they didn't burn her body. They weren't consuming her or her smock. It was as if she was wearing a cloak of fire, one that warmed her, but did not burn her. And it took only minimal magical energy to maintain it.

She allowed herself to rest there, happy that she could see the area around her in the light of her flaming cloak, and could see her own body, bruised and bloody though it was.

For now, she just pulled herself to the wall, sat back, and basked in the warmth, allowing herself a much-needed reprieve.

A short while later, the cloak of flames disappeared. Still enjoying the warmth of the heated stones, Aoleyn pulled herself over her legs and worked the anklet back into the skin of her left ankle. Now, with the ring, the anklet, and the earring, she could access much more of the wedstone.

But she was exhausted.

Instead, when she started getting cold again, Aoleyn called up a second cloak of flames, for that enchantment cost precious little energy. She could do this for a long time, she understood, and while recuperating from her efforts. She even managed to nap for a short while. Only after, feeling determined and refreshed, did Aoleyn call upon the wedstones, bringing their collective song to a growing chorus and harmony. She was afraid, truly, for what if she could not heal these greater wounds?

She didn't want to die down here.

With a growl, she pushed through the song and called upon the wedstones, and felt a great wash of warm and comfort coursing through her, and she held it as long as she could, casting repeatedly.

When she was done, exhausted once more, she wore a wide smile, for she could feel her torso again, and the hard floor against her buttocks. She still couldn't feel her legs, but she would again, she was confident. Still, after her next period of rest, and another short nap, Aoleyn didn't immediately go back to her healing. Instead, she called up a cloak of flames, reached into the garnet for guidance, and, with the better mobility provided by a warmed and awakened body, she moved off along the chasm.

She hadn't gone far when she saw that she was not alone, and after the shock wore off, she scrabbled her way to a body, crushed and broken in the fall.

"Innevah," she breathed, and she fell over her friend and cried. The spirits had saved Aoleyn. Why had they let Innevah die?

Desperately, Aoleyn fell into her wedstone, hoping there was some life to be found here.

But no, she realized before she even cast the spell, and only then did she come to understand that not only was Innevah already dead, but she had been for a long time. Her body was frozen and fully discolored and bloated, and in this profound cold, that process would have taken many days.

How long had Aoleyn been down here? Why hadn't she starved?

Aoleyn gave thanks to the magic of Usgar. She kissed Innevah on the cheek, and forced herself to crawl on. Her other ear jewelry, the turquoise cap set with a cat's eye, was not far away, and putting it on gave to Aoleyn the vision of a hunting feline, and the darkness seemed not so deep. Finally, she found her greatest treasure, her belly ring, and in that moment, Aoleyn knew she would survive this ordeal.

For it was intact, thick wedstone bands holding a thicker gray lightning bar that created four strands. One held a diamond, which could bring light. A second held a beautiful purple stone that enhanced her health and toughness. The third was striped in varying green hues, and with this powerful stone Aoleyn could eliminate her own weight and could climb these walls.

She wouldn't even have to, though, she knew, for the fourth strand held a soft blue, cloudy moonstone, and with that one, Aoleyn could fly.

She decided not to wait, for it was too cold down here. She called to the moonstone, bringing it to its full power, then willed herself into the air, climbing fast near to a wall, her dead legs dangling below her. To her surprise, though, as she ascended, it grew colder.

She came around a bend, a second, then a third, and saw light far, far above, and saw, too, snow on the small shelf of the winding chimney. There, Aoleyn paused. Winter had come to Fireach Speuer.

How long had she been down here?

Her belly growled. She felt light-headed. She needed food and water. Up she went, flying, then, as she tired, using the striped malachite to free her of her own weight, that she could physically scale the wall, hand-over-hand. She thought to go to the caverns below Craos'a'diad, where she had explored as her test for the Coven, but she found a lower level of tunnels, and glancing down with the cat's eye enchantment, then with the magic-sensing garnet, she heard a different Usgar song, but one quite strong.

She settled just inside a corridor off the deep shaft, wrapped herself in her cloak of flames, and closed her eyes. Physically and magically exhausted, she was soon fast asleep.

The hand went up before her, feeling the way from tree to tree. No, it wasn't her hand. It was his hand. The moment of confusion passed as she sorted it out. She was one with him. She was in his thoughts, seeing through his eyes, feeling what he was feeling. Like with Brayth in that battle with the sidhe, then the fossa, on the field, when she had joined with him spiritually, and worked through the magic to heal him, to enhance his battle prowess, even to make him fly.

But that had been planned, prepared, undertaken through a magical ceremony. This wasn't Brayth. It wasn't a memory—not her memory, at least.

She didn't know this man.

That thought lingered, stuck with her, prodded her and teased her.

She could feel the physical strength of this man, an Usgar warrior. She could see his hands and forearms as he reached out to move from tree to tree, and the easy way he handled his heavy spear.

He was afraid, particularly so right now, because he knew that he was in a precarious and disadvantageous situation. He had to get through the tangled copse quickly and back out under the red moon that hung full in the sky.

The red moon. The Blood Moon!

Its light could not get through these thick boughs—Aoleyn could feel the conflict within him over that fact, the emotional against the practical. He was glad of the concealment on a purely human level, but the trained warrior understood that such darkness was not his ally, and truly favored the demon.

His name was Fionlagh, she somehow understood.

Fionlagh!

Her father!

She felt his fear and understood it. The reputation of the fossa was not ambiguous on the matter of concealment: the demon's victims rarely if ever saw its approach in time to react. She was in his thoughts as he tried to bolster himself, seeing the ceremonies, hearing the compliments offered to him by the leaders of Usgar. He reminded himself that he had been among the most highly heralded warriors in the tribe, that the whispers said he might one day be Usgar-laoch, even.

"Because you are with me," he whispered, and only then did Aoleyn realize that she was not alone with him in his thoughts. Fionlagh clutched his crystal-tipped spear tightly, feeling the magic and the spiritual connection to his beloved.

"My love, my life, Elara," Aoleyn's ghostly host whispered.

Aoleyn knew that name, of course. Elara and Fionlagh? Her parents, but it could not be. Was she dead? She tried to reach out to them, to contact these spirits, but no, there came no response and their magical melding continued on around her, as if she wasn't there—because to them, she sensed, she wasn't.

"I'm needing you," Fionlagh quietly whispered as he neared the open and rocky mountainside once more.

Aoleyn wanted to answer that call, wanted to help, but she knew not how.

But another did. A witch of the Coven, who sang the song of Usgar with clarity and strength.

"Elara," she said again, or tried to, for she couldn't hear her words, nor could this young warrior. She knew that her guess was correct. Somehow, she knew.

The crystal tip of the warrior's spear came alive with magic, enchanted from afar by the woman to whom he had bonded.

Aoleyn understood, and felt the magic streaming through Fionlagh's limbs and into the crystal tip of that weapon, and knew that the giver of the enchantment, Elara of the Coven, Elara, who was her mother, was not far away.

She felt Fionlagh relax and heard his exhale, Aoleyn felt him leaning on a tree as tangibly as if it was her own body against the bark, and peered out at the night through his eyes. The full moon, shining red, seemed huge as it hung in the sky above, painting a surreal tint to the gray shadows of mountain jags and trees, limning the many ridges.

Knowing the significance made Aoleyn terribly afraid. What was this nightmare upon which she had intruded? This was the Blood Moon, the face of Iseabal, consort of the god Usgar. Iseabal, the goddess, ruled the moon. Usgar, the god, ruled the world. When Iseabal rode the full moon to Usgar's realm, the barrier between the worlds thinned and Usgar raged. For Iseabal's red face was a taunt to Usgar, a reminder that she had fled him and her wifely duties.

And so, when the moon was red, Usgar screamed.

And so, when the moon was red, the fossa heard.

And so, when the moon was red, the witches of Usgar danced wildly.

Aoleyn above all others understood Usgar's demon creature that would answer his call. Only then did she realize the truth of this encounter, or one of the possible truths of what she was witnessing here, and she became terribly afraid.

No, it had to be a dream, a terrible nightmare.

She knew that she was sweating—that she was, and not just this warrior who stood awaiting the arrival of Usgar's demon rage. He seemed calm to her. He trusted in Elara. But too calm!

He should not relax.

No, he must not.

She called to him, screamed at him, but he couldn't hear, nor could she. Her screams were silent to all but her.

She tried to grab him, but her hands went through his corporeal form. She scrabbled and slapped and tried to yell again.

But she saw his face, and followed the pain there to his thoughts, and surrendered her impossible attempt. He was thinking of Elara, of the witches, and then of his own failure. The memory, too, came clear to Aoleyn.

This very same spiritual connection with Elara had brought Fionlagh to disgrace in the recent past, Aoleyn understood from their silent communication. For on the rainy day the Usgar had raided the village of Carrachan Shoal on the shore of the great lake at the eastern base of great Fireach Speuer, the warriors had been discussing the coming arrival of Iseabal.

The raid had been executed perfectly. At least for the Usgar, but Aoleyn recoiled at the memories of the warrior and his witch bride, for the raiders had silently moved like shadows through the perimeter of the village, felling the sentries in silence, then had slipped into the village proper without notice and slipped into the outer ways of the village without notice. Fionlagh and his fellow warriors had before them an easy win against the unwitting uamhas, for most of Carrachan Shoal's strongest adults had been caught far out on the lake in their fishing boats.

The victory had never been in doubt. They would quickly and easily get the furs and food, perhaps even a few child slaves, and without enough resistance to seriously threaten any of the raiders.

What a glorious day it would be! Fionlagh and all the others flowed through Carrachan Shoal in pursuit of the fleeing villagers, all the way down to the lakeshore. There at water's edge, the village stragglers, the old and the young mostly, desperately tried to launch their small boats out onto the safety of Loch Beag, where the Usgar would not go, and it seemed like all might make it, that the raid would garner supplies but none of the prized slaves.

The scene in Fionlagh's thoughts, and so in Aoleyn's thoughts, became distinct. So young and swift, the promising young warrior had sprinted off to the side, to a hidden inlet, and there Fionlagh had caught a villager trying to shove a craft from the sand and onto the waters of a hidden cove. He came upon the man in fury, sweeping his spear down across the man's arm as the terrified villager turned to meet the charge. The blow knocked the filleting knife from the villager's hand, and he stumbled, nearly toppling into the craft. In that moment, Fionlagh brought his spear up and angled, stabbing for the man's belly. Aoleyn gasped, she was sure, when the tip penetrated the soft flesh and this fierce warrior, her father, called upon the gray magic within the blessed weapon to bring forth a burst of lightning that jolted and flipped the poor villager over the side and into the rowboat.

There he lay, helpless and terrified, and Aoleyn wanted to scream out, but could not, when her father moved to murder the innocent.

Helpless and terrified and shaking his head in denial and despair, the poor victim tried to shield another in the boat.

His child. His daughter.

Fionlagh had a great prize before him, a young slave.

But he felt the spirit of Elara through his blessed spear, and with that sensation came a reminder that he could not dismiss.

Aoleyn's father looked at the ugly villager, but did not see the obvious differences—the man's weakness or misshapen head. Nay, he saw instead the man's eyes, and there a thread of commonality, for in this man's expression, in the sheer sadness, Fionlagh realized that he was seeing himself as he would appear were the roles reversed.

How that touched Aoleyn, who had seen the commonality between Usgar and uamhas in the slaves, in poor Innevah who lay dead down below, and in Bahdlahn, who had become so dear to her. She didn't know what had sparked such a twang of conscience in that particular moment for her father, until she followed his thoughts from that spot, just a brief flash of a memory.

For Elara was not alone back up in the village awaiting Fionlagh's return. Tucked at her side lay Fionlagh's infant daughter, their first child.

Watching this . . . what was this? An event? A memory? A demonic trick?

It didn't matter, for Aoleyn looked upon something that seemed real enough, and true enough, and that meant that Aoleyn now looked back on herself, a newborn.

Her father's spinning thoughts came clear. From the moment he had seen his little girl, Fionlagh had come to know fear. For the first time in his life, the invincible Usgar warrior had come to understand that his spirit could be truly destroyed.

And so Fionlagh recognized the vulnerability painted on the face of this doomed lakeman, not for himself and his own impending death, but because this man knew that his young child was also surely doomed.

The spear's tip hovered just before the prone man's chest. A simple thrust would end it.

Aoleyn could not understand if that was happening, or if this had happened, but it didn't matter. She couldn't watch a murder. She screamed, with everything she could manage. Physically, with her mind, with her spirit, with her magic, with anything and everything she could manage, she screamed.

Fionlagh hesitated.

And he withdrew the weapon and lowered his shoulder against the high prow of the small boat and pushed it out onto the water.

He hadn't even thought about it. It was a ridiculous thing to do. It went against everything the Usgar had come down to the lakeshore to achieve, everything the Usgar believed, every tradition that had sustained the tribe through the generations.

Even as the boat caught the current and drifted away from him, Fionlagh could hardly register what he had done. He did not feel the blessing of mercy bestowed in that moment, or the relief that Aoleyn was feeling, or the jumbled emotions she sensed within Elara at that fateful moment.

Just confusion for Fionlagh.

Confused, too, was the Usgar warrior who had come up beside him a moment later, head shaking, eyes wide with surprise. The boat slipped out into the cove, not far, but by all tradition and a reminder in the form of an edict of the Usgar-righinn, the Usgar warriors were strictly forbidden from entering the waters of Loch Beag, not even a step.

"Dead," Fionlagh lied to the man.

But the other warrior snorted and shook his head and motioned with his chin, and when Fionlagh looked back to the boat, he saw, Elara saw, and Aoleyn saw, that the wounded villager was sitting up and trying to set an oar. And as Fionlagh began to weave a lie of excuse, the man's young daughter had also appeared, staring back at the beach, at Fionlagh and the other Usgar.

Aoleyn lost herself in the swirl of Fionlagh's thoughts as he tried to concoct a story, an excuse that he hadn't seen the girl, that the child must have been covered by a dirty blanket.

The words never passed his lips, though, for the returned expression screamed at Fionlagh that this other warrior knew the truth, knew his failure.

And so it was that Fionlagh had been disgraced, and that he would nevermore accompany the hunters or the war parties, and that he would not be allowed to claim paternity of his dear little girl.

He was shunned. After the raid and the return to the mountain, only Elara, beautiful Elara, would even speak with Fionlagh, and even then, only secretly.

Back in the forest under the Blood Moon, Aoleyn felt the warrior steady himself. His beloved and his new daughter deserved more than this, more than the shame of his failing. He had to regain his status in the tribe, had to become proper Usgar once more, for their sakes, for their very lives, most likely, because life on the mountain was difficult and the wind was already beginning to blow fast with winter's coming bite. There were times, after all, when the tribe had to make sacrifices to Usgar, or had to decide who would eat and who would have to go without.

Fionlagh considered that his wife was a member of the Coven, one of the thirteen witches who blessed the weapons, but he couldn't count on that to protect his family after his heresy, he knew.

And Elara knew, too, Aoleyn realized, for she was a part of this desperate plan. If Elara hadn't thought Fionlagh's fears valid, she would never have agreed to let him come out here to hunt the demon fossa. The folk of Usgar did not stray from their defensive crouch within the perimeter of their camp when the taunting face of Iseabal leered from the sky above.

Moving boldly, determinedly, the warrior left the cover of the trees. His steps were silent and light, for the magic of the speartip included the green stones—so clearly could Aoleyn hear that song.

Elara's presence filled him, her spiritual joining to him strong and complete. She sent magic to expand his senses and add her own cues and clues to his. Aoleyn felt it all, keenly, and tried to be a part of it. Aoleyn knew the way of the fossa. She knew how to defeat the fossa!

"Give me time to stab the beast," Fionlagh whispered with his voice and his thoughts.

He meant to strike first, to kill the beast.

To redeem himself.

Aoleyn awoke, shivering, hugging herself and trembling, with tears streaming down her cheeks. What had she just witnessed? She feared she had become unbound in time, a collection of disjointed realities and memories, or, more likely, that she was actually quite dead.

Of course, she was dead. She had been fed to Craos'a'diad. How could she not be?

"The child," she whispered into the darkness. "Aoleyn."

Her father had thought of her, lying beside her mother back at the camp, and that had stayed his hand at the lakeshore. She was glad of that, glad that he was possessed of mercy, but with her relief came, as well, no small amount of guilt.

In her father's mind, she knew, he had failed, and that failure had driven him out in desperation to hunt the tribe's most feared enemy, the demon fossa itself.

"No," she said aloud, needing to hear the denial. "No." She didn't know anything. It was just a dream.

"No," she said yet again, and more times after that, as she fell into her wedstones and brought forth the true power of Usgar. She washed herself with warm healing once more, more powerfully, more determinedly.

The dream kept tickling at the edges of her thoughts, but she fought it aside and kept her focus.

She felt a profound tingling in her legs, and drove on harder.

Then she slumped. She brought forth a cloak of flames again, and quickly, because her mind was fast flying away as she passed again into unconsciousness.

The hairs on the back of Aoleyn's neck stood up. She could feel it, the predator, coming for her, coming to chew her flesh and crunch her bones, and worse, to devour her soul.

She could feel it, it was not far. She had to run.

But he resisted and would not run, and only then did Aoleyn realize that it wasn't the hair on the back of her neck that was standing, but on his.

The predator was coming for him, this Usgar warrior, Fionlagh.

She felt Elara calling out to him in warning, directing him. Elara had sensed the demon with her magic and guided him now, that he could get that first strike.

Her energy flowed through him, into the spear, and the song was loud and strong and beautiful, and reminded Aoleyn so much of her own magic, and of a situation very much like this. For a moment, the young woman took heart in that, and pride in powerful Elara.

But Aoleyn remembered that similar encounter, remembered Brayth.

Her mind filled with the image of Brayth flopping about, broken, as the fossa dragged him away.

She could feel the magic building from the tingling in the fingers of the man whose body she now inhabited. The energy arced and crackled, ready to explode with the power of a lightning bolt when Fionlagh drove the weapon home.

He crouched low as he came over one angled rock, working to keep the line of the horizon as clear and close as possible in the uneven terrain, so that he might glimpse the silhouette of the beast.

Every sense screamed at him, at Elara, at Aoleyn. The demon fossa was close. Fionlagh didn't know how he knew it, but his instincts screamed the truth of it. The Usgar tribesmen, raised on the mountain, traveling the mountain trails on the darkest of nights, had been trained by bitter experience to trust in those instincts. They would hear, they would see, they would smell, the hints of danger before any clear confirmation.

Fionlagh eased himself down the side of the angled rock, to an almost-flat stretch of ground where some chokeberry bushes had taken root. These were only about mid-calf to the man and Aoleyn could feel them scratching at his legs, stealing his silence. He accepted that as he moved to the center of the large spread.

The bushes would slow the demon fossa. The bushes would shake with its passage, revealing the charge, and Fionlagh would strike first.

By the time he had centered himself in the chokeberry patch, the Usgar warrior crinkled his nose, and Aoleyn, too, shared his disgust at the foul smell, like a combination of rotted flesh and burned hair.

"Do you know?" the man whispered.

Before Aoleyn could answer, for she could not, she felt Elara's spirit confirming. As the fossa could sense the magic, so Elara could sense the foul demon.

Aoleyn remembered, too keenly, and she felt herself recoil at the violent recollections.

Fionlagh heard a growl and spun about in a crouch, spear at the ready.

He saw the dark night and nothing more.

And the night had grown silent.

The smell nearly overwhelmed.

A slight breeze blew past and the stench grew stronger, and Fionlagh spun again, facing the breeze, certain that it carried the smell of the approaching demon.

The chokeberries shivered and the man danced, straining, seeking. It was near. He knew it was near.

A low growl came from the brush before him. But how could the demon be beneath the bushes? They were too short!

He moved to prod.

Behind you! Elara's thoughts screamed in Fionlagh's mind, and in Aoleyn's mind.

Fionlagh whirled, but too late, as the demon creature exploded into a leap from under the brush behind him.

The spear tip crackled with lightning power.

The demon fossa landed before him—to look upon it again nearly sent Aoleyn cowering—but shied fast, cutting sharply across to stay ahead of the spear.

Fionlagh almost had it. And now he followed it with his spin, trying to catch up, knowing that when the fossa turned back or slowed, he would have it.

But the tail swept across and Fionlagh felt it slam against the side of his ankle, pitching him into the air to land hard in the bushes.

He rushed to bring his spear to bear, but did not despair, for the demon was out of reach and he had time to recover his defenses.

"An Usgar does not fear," he recited, rolling as if to stand—and he would have tried to do exactly that if not for the shock he sensed within his spirit, the silent wail of Elara.

Fionlagh didn't understand. His arms and face were scratched, yes, but he had the demon fossa in sight, and he didn't plan to let it get away.

Oh, my love!

And through Elara, Aoleyn, too, understood, and heard her own wail, Oh my father! Fionlagh got to his knees and brought one leg forward, and only then did he understand his beloved Elara's dismay, only then did he realize the truth of the fossa's strike.

Only then did he realize that both of his feet had been severed by the sweep of that awful tail.

He saw them, one of them at least, atop a chokeberry bush just to the side, and he started to reach for it, to reach for his own foot, before he realized that it would do him no good.

He growled through the fear, he didn't feel the pain, to Aoleyn's amazement. Her respect for Usgar warriors multiplied in that horrible moment, for Fionlagh did not despair. He set himself firmly and resolutely on his knees, took up his spear in both hands.

"Come, then!" he yelled at the stalking demon, who glared back with those fiendish orbs, part cat-like, part fire. The fossa moved in a perimeter about him slowly and deliberately.

I will kill it, Fionlagh silently assured Elara. I'm no' afraid to die, but the demon fossa's to be destroyed, and you'll not be shamed. And then, aloud, he declared to the fossa, "My daughter will'no be shamed!"

The creature paused in its stalk and stared at him, mocking him.

Its malevolence overwhelmed Aoleyn.

"Come on!" Fionlagh cried at it.

The demon creature sat down, watching, waiting.

Fionlagh's spirit heard Elara's wail.

She knew, and he knew, too, then, for his lifeblood poured from his shorn ankles, and, the moment of surprise passed, he felt the fiery pain, felt the stabbing of the tendons rolling up at the backs of his legs.

He brought the speartip in close, silently calling to Elara, and she responded, giving him the strength to excite the healing magic within the blessed weapon. They had to stem the bleeding.

The warmth of magic filled him, taking the pain, restoring his hope. He closed his eyes, basking, centering, but only for a moment.

For the demon fossa was gone.

Fionlagh strained to peer deeper into the darkness, glanced left and right. It was just there—it couldn't have moved far.

"Under the bushes," he decided.

But no, the demon fossa slammed Fionlagh in the back, its fangs closing on the back of his neck. He started to swing about, wanted to turn, but suddenly, his body would not answer his demands.

Aoleyn, too, felt nothing, felt as she had when had first awakened on the chasm floor, far below this tunnel. Numb. Helpless.

Fionlagh and Aoleyn didn't feel it when the fossa let him go, didn't feel himself falling, even, until his face crashed through the branches of a chokeberry bush, tearing bloody lines. He had to get up! He had to lift his spear! Did he even still have the spear? For surely he couldn't feel it!

He wanted to roll.

He couldn't.

Aoleyn knew.

Aoleyn awoke with a start, and climbed to her feet before she was even aware of the movement. It wasn't until she got there, standing in the tunnels fanning off the deep shaft, that she realized her legs would not work, would not support her.

Down she tumbled, painfully.

"Where are you?" she cried out helplessly as she floundered about on the floor. "You are here! You are in my mind! Help me!"

Nothing. She felt no presence about, spiritual or physical. She heard the song of Usgar beyond the gems she now wore, but it remained distant and of a melody she had not before heard.

This whole situation didn't make sense to her, though. If that was Elara, or Seonagh, or both, then why would they waste time imparting a long-ago memory to her, when they could be helping her with the great physical healing she still needed? And these memories, or dreams, or whatever they were, remained cryptic and elusive.

"Mother!" she called. "Elara of the Usgar. Come to me if you are near. I need you!"

She waited, letting the echoes of her call filter along the passageways until the halls went silent once more. Silent, still. She fell into her wedstone only briefly, only to attune herself more fully to the spirit world.

But there was nothing. Aoleyn had encountered many of these ghosts when she had come down here in her test for the Coven. And she knew the two who had saved her in her fall. She had no doubt that the spirits of Elara and Seonagh had caught her descent with the magic of Usgar, and had flowed the healing magic through her for all the time—days?—she had been unconscious. There could be no other explanation, for certainly she should now be dead.

Or maybe she was dead. Perhaps she was drifting through the confusion of the first moments of the afterlife, seeing time out of sequence, hearing the echoes of memories she should not have.

How could she have such a memory as the one she had just witnessed? She had not been there . . .

An image flashed in her thoughts, that of a young mother with an infant girl lying beside her.

That thought rocked the poor and battered young woman. She leaned back to consider the implications and possibilities, and fell deep into her thoughts, until the coldness about her began to sting her fingers and her toes—her toes! She could feel her toes! The sensation of pain brought her back to her senses, to the here and now, and Aoleyn immediately fell into her gemstone magic, first creating another fiery cloak to warm her and the stones about her, then into the wedstone with renewed determination.

Soon after, she stood back up, and this time, Aoleyn did not wobble. The pain was gone, cured by the power of Usgar.

Except for the pain in her growling belly.

She thought to go back the few strides to the chasm, to call to the green-striped malachite to help lift and climb out to the world above. She shook her head, doubting that she had the strength to manage that at this time, with so much of her magical energy already spent in the heating and healing.

"Not this time," she told herself, putting her hand over her belly to try to settle the growling.

Standing strong and sure, Aoleyn called upon a different gem, the most minor of enchantments, and enacted the magic of the cat's-eye that was set in the turquoise of her ear cap. Now she could see, and off she walked down the tunnel, following the music of Usgar's magic.

The turquoise on her ear, too, offered her some unexpected insights, alerting her of other creatures in her area.

Fish.

There were fish.

Aoleyn followed the call and noticed the tunnel growing warmer—so much so that she dismissed her cloak of flames. She heard rushing water and continued tentatively, as thirsty as famished as she was. She didn't know of any rivers in this part of Fireach Speuer.

It was no river, she learned soon after, but a waterfall, cascading down the rocky wall, kicking and spraying wide as it hit the jags of stone, but forming a wide pool in the middle of a large, warm cavern. Aoleyn moved to it, trying to sort out the riddle. Why was water running fast from above?

She moved to the pool, using the turquoise to sense the fish, and saw, too, all about the place, various mushrooms she knew to be edible. She dipped her hand in the water, to find that it was very warm, and grew warmer as she moved closer to the waterfall. With a thought, she brightened the light from the diamond on her belly ring, and fell deeper into the turquoise to better scour the various living things in the crystal-clear pool.

Just fish, some as large as her forearm, but nothing menacing. And some lizards, she noted, small and harmless, scampering about the back wall bordering the pool.

She focused on the fish—so many! Fish that would come to her call. Fish she could catch, and cook with her ruby. Water she could drink.

Nothing had ever tasted better to poor Aoleyn.

She ate her fill, drank more than that, then, on a thought, pulled off her smock and slipped into the warm water. It wasn't deep here near the ledge, but Aoleyn played it safe, since she had never learned to swim. She called on the striped malachite, though, and found herself floating effortlessly. The warm water felt good on her cold and bruised body. She went toward the waterfall, where it was warmer, and kept following the heat until she was standing right under the cascading flow, which was so warm, hot even, that it tingled when it kissed her skin.

And there, too, Aoleyn understood. This was no river, but snow melt. She was directly under Dail Usgar, she realized, directly beneath the warmth of the crystal god that was melting the snow falling on the winter plateau and the sacred grove. The water was flowing down from there, to this place, and likely out of this place and down the mountainside, perhaps underground, to feed Loch Beag. She felt truly blessed in that moment, as if she was bathing in the glory of Usgar, and so she remained in the shower for a long while.

She had barely climbed back out of the pool before curling up on a mossy bed, and didn't even consider, as she closed her eyes, that her dream was still there, waiting for her.

She was within the mind of another again, but no longer her father. For a heartbeat, she feared him gone, a notion only reinforced by the sniffling and tears she noted rolling from the eyes of her host, Elara.

But Elara had not given up. Aoleyn felt her mother tighten her resolve and redouble her efforts through the gemstone flecks encased in Fionlagh's crystalline spear tip, which the man had fallen atop, fortunately.

Elara fully gave herself to the gray wedstone, falling wholly into the melody of Usgar's most beautiful song, transporting her life essence across the mountainside, to these gray flecks in this magical crystal, to this man she so dearly loved.

Elara jolted, spiritually and physically, when the demon fossa rushed back in, slamming Fionlagh and sending him spinning and tumbling away from the spear. Elara tried to reach out, thinking the creature would go and finish her beloved husband.

Aoleyn, who had learned that the real hunger of the demon fossa was not manflesh, but magic, recognized her mother's error. Elara did, too, but too late!

The beast attacked the spear, and while its fangs chomped against the crystal, its spirit flowed into the flecks within, into the connection between the witch and warrior. Elara felt as if something sharp slashed at her own life force when the fossa's powerful maw closed on the crystal spear tip. She felt the crystal crumbling beneath the mighty crush of that bite, and felt, too, to her amazement and dismay, the beast consuming the gems within that crystal, consuming the magic.

Elara should have left then—Aoleyn screamed for her to do so—but she could not. She called upon the gray graphite to spark, and took some fleeting hope in the howl from the demon fossa.

But no, Aoleyn knew, again from her own experience, that this was no howl of pain. She recalled the battle with this creature and Brayth, when her own light-

ning bolts had struck at the beast from on high. The powerful strokes of crackling energy would have killed any known living creature, but no, not the fossa.

Quite the opposite.

Its shriek now was no cry of pain or fear, nay, it was a cry of joy.

An epiphany came to Elara: Don't fight the dark, embrace the light! Aoleyn, who was thinking of exactly that, wondered for a moment if she had somehow gotten the message to her mother from across the years. She dared hope for a moment that somehow this magical bond might be changing the course of events, that perhaps she had given Elara the key to defeating the fossa, and so Aoleyn would not grow up orphaned.

But no, she realized as Elara's thoughts worked through the problem. The witch had come to realize, all on her own, as Aoleyn would learn two decades later, the paradox of the demon creature. Elara had come to understand that she could not defeat it with destructive magic, for it was already wounded beyond life, almost an undead thing. You couldn't break what was already broken.

You had to fix it.

Elara knew that now, and Aoleyn took hope, fleeting hope. She had not changed the course of events. This was playing out exactly as it had those years ago. Aoleyn was no more than a helpless witness to the death of her father and the shattering of her own mother's mind.

Elara embraced the light, and sang the internal magical harmonies with power that seemed so pure and akin to Aoleyn's own, and Aoleyn knew then that she had come by her gifts with the stones because of this wonderful woman. It was too late for Elara, though, for so deep into the darkness of the fossa was she by then that there was no light to be found.

And so the fossa ate.

At the sound of another wail, this one human, Elara's spirit reached for Fionlagh, carrying with her healing magic.

But the magic was dissipating, surely, the vibrations, the song, drifting to nothingness. Both women could feel the struggle of Elara's Usgar magic against the darkness of the demon, and could feel the power of Usgar falling further and further away, the conduit gemstones being absorbed by demonic darkness.

Yet through sheer determination, Elara stayed with Fionlagh, whispering to him telepathically, promising her love, comforting him in his last living moments. She was with him when the fossa bit him by the scruff of the neck and so easily dragged him away, with him when the demon dragged him into the cave—Aoleyn knew that cave, and felt herself faltering when they all entered it—and to the narrow crawl space, tugging and sliding the groaning warrior across the angled stone.

And Elara, and so Aoleyn, were with her doomed father when the fossa dragged him to the other side of the crawl space, where the mighty demon beast so easily took Fionlagh in its jaws and jumped down into the pit that was the heart of its den, the heart of darkness itself.

Aoleyn cried for her father, and for her mother, for she knew that Elara could sense the dead here, could hear the bones rattling underfoot, could feel the edges of those bones under the skin of Fionlagh.

Together, they had found Ifrinn. Together, they had found hell.

Elara stayed with Fionlagh, all sensibility cast aside, when the fossa began to eat, lapping the blood, gnawing the bones. The demon took its time, expertly devouring the man so that he was alive and aware for a long, long time.

And Fionlagh felt Elara, too, and was comforted, she knew. But then he grew horrified and mentally assaulted her, trying to push her away.

For Fionlagh saw what Elara could not. Fionlagh saw what the helpless, onlooking Aoleyn knew to be true.

Elara was as caught as he. The fossa would devour him, would kill his mortal body and consume his spirit.

And consume her spirit.

Aoleyn could only watch.

The couple shared tears. They shared wails, they sank together into darkness.

Fionlagh died without hope.

And in her tent in the Usgar encampment, Elara lay on her back without hope, and stared blankly, seeing only darkness, her magic consumed, her life force diminished, her mind shattered by the horror.

Aoleyn awakened in a cold sweat. She had hoped to change the course of events, to somehow go back in time and save her parents from that awful fate.

She had failed.

She screamed into the darkness of the cave around her, cursing Elara, or Seonagh, or whomever it had been who had foisted that horror upon her.

"To what end?" she cried. "To what gain?"

She rose and called upon the diamond to light the area. "No," she said, her thoughts going in a different direction. "Did you think I could save you? Did you bring me back, hoping I'd be giving you the strength to win? How could you . . ."

Aoleyn stopped, and stood there dumbfoundedly for a long while, replaying all three dreams in succession.

Finally, she understood. Elara hadn't pulled her back in time. Nor had Seonagh. No, she hadn't gone back in time, nor was this a vivid tale imposed upon her by the dead witches.

No, this was a memory, and not one caught within the cavern by some twist of Usgar's magic, and no residual ghostly memory offered by Elara.

But it was a memory—it was Aoleyn's own memory.

She had been there, she realized, in that very time and place, not only physically lying beside her mother, but within the song connecting Elara to Fionlagh. While not giving to her something extraneous, something—the echoing songs of magic in these caverns, the ghosts of Elara and Seonagh— was bringing Aoleyn's adult sensibilities back to the reality she had witnessed on that distant, terrible day. She had seen it then, through the song, but with an infant's mind, not capable of understanding any of it.

That memory remained, though, somehow, and now she could see it again.

Aoleyn sat there, thinking. She couldn't be sure of any of this, of course, and perhaps it was just a dream.

"No," she decided, shaking her head. It was more than a dream. It was, or had been, real.

A smile, one of gratitude, found its way to her horrified and heartbroken face. She hadn't given the answer, the riddle to defeat the fossa, to Elara.

Nay, Elara had given it to her. Elara had found out too late to save herself or Fionlagh, but in that last, desperate moment, Aoleyn had learned the truth, and would later use that truth to save herself and destroy the demon fossa that had haunted Fireach Speuer for time untold.

Even as she sorted that information, it seemed impossible to Aoleyn.

So many things seemed impossible, and she was learning every day that they were not.

"Thank you, my mother," she whispered.

That was her decision regarding the dreams in the dark cave when she should have been dead but was not. And that decision, and its implications, would guide her now when relevant. She had no time to unravel any of this further.

But she did have the time, and now had the strength as well, to explore these lower caverns and discern the source of that strange Usgar melody.

15

SHE WHO MADE HIM HUMAN

He saw them, then, his tormentors, two boys, almost men, of the Usgar tribe, kicking him, punching him, taunting him.

How he wanted to strike back. But he could not!

How he wanted to run away. But he could not!

He was helpless. He was nothing, just an uamhas. If he struck back, they'd kill him, without remorse and without recourse. If he tried to run, they'd catch him and torture him until he was dead.

He was just an uamhas, unworthy of anything but this slave life, and he'd never escape, as his mother would never escape.

So, they beat him, and he could do nothing but accept it, and the taunts, always the taunts!

Even his name was a taunt.

Thump.

He saw the face of that particularly vicious one, Egard, fist raised, smile wide, and all the wider when that punch landed.

But then that smile was gone, wiped away by a countering punch, and as Egard turned, he got a knee lifted into his groin, and as he doubled over, a left hook took him in the jaw and laid him low.

And she was there, Aoleyn, who was around the same age as these boys.

Thump watched her, marveling at the way she moved, at her ferocity. These

boys were no match for her—she was too spirited and they knew she would em-
barrass them.

She chased them off, then lifted the uamhas to his feet.

But he was not an uamhas, not to her.

And she spoke to him, "Bahdlahn."

"Aoleyn," Bahdlahn whispered as he awakened from that dream. "My
Aoleyn."

He was shivering, cold and alone in the cave the Usgar named Aghmor
had found for him. It was long past dawn outside, but was hardly bright inside the cave. The shelter was not large or particularly deep, but at the back
of the entry area, which was no more than a shallow alcove beneath the lip
of a large boulder, a small channel moved behind a natural rock wall, deeper
under the stones. That second, inner chamber was sheltered from the bite of
the winter wind, and in that place Bahdlahn could make a fire without fear
that its light would be seen by his captors.

Sitting now near the ashes from the previous night's fire, Bahdlahn
wiped a tear from his eye, replaying the dream, remembering that long-
ago incident that had inspired the dream. Remembering Aoleyn, his
Aoleyn, his dearest friend, and more than that. Much more than that, in
Bahdlahn's heart.

Few were the moments of the last years when he wasn't thinking about her,
picturing her, imagining her, and in ways that he had never dared mention.
He often felt the sexual urges of a man, and always when he saw or thought of
Aoleyn. The sound of her voice made him nervous, but in a good way. A
glance at her eyes made him feel as if he was lost, and found, all at once.

He conjured an image of her and he held it fast, never wanting to forget
a bit of her—her black hair and eyes, her crooked smile, those wonderful
curves of her compact and powerful form.

In years, he had not seen her without wanting her, without desiring her,
without feeling an overwhelming lust for her.

Except once, he thought, and he winced profoundly at the most recent, and
most horrible, memory. For on that occasion, seeing his dear Aoleyn helpless
above the chasm, all Bahdlahn wanted to do was cover her back up, and pull
her to his arms to protect her. He would have wrapped her in himself and let
his splattering flesh and broken bones shield her fall if he could have.

If he could have.

What in his entire life could Bahdlahn have done about anything?

The young man sat up and rubbed his face, feeling the tears. He felt as if he had lost everything up at the chasm atop the mountain. The woman he adored, the only one he could talk to, the Usgar who had protected him and healed him and spoke to him.

Without her, what was he? Was he even still Bahdlahn, or was he again, simply, Thump?

"Oh, my Aoleyn," he whispered into his hands.

"Your Aoleyn?"

Bahdlahn snapped his head up at the unexpected response, eyes wide with terror. He relaxed when he saw the speaker, Aghmor, moving through the narrow channel to enter the small inner cave. He carried an armload of food-stuffs, and had more firewood tucked under one arm.

Bahdlahn chewed his lip.

"Your Aoleyn?" the Usgar warrior asked again, quite sharply. He dropped his bundles and brought the spear from his back.

"I . . . I . . ."

"You are uamhas!" Aghmor reminded him with sudden and surprising anger. "A worthless slave. You are nothing. She was . . . she was Usgar, a strong Usgar woman. A witch of Usgar, who is not your god. I should strike you dead for such words. Your Aoleyn?"

"She was my frien . . ."

"Shut your mouth!" Aghmor yelled at him, and flipped his spear over, pointing it straight at Bahdlahn's head. In that moment, with the look on Aghmor's face, Bahdlahn had no doubt that Aghmor would kill him.

The young slave sat there confused for a few heartbeats, trying to figure out where this level of outrage had come from. It made sense that Aghmor wouldn't want someone he considered lesser, someone he considered not even a man, with any Usgar woman, but this . . . this went beyond that level of anger. The man seemed beyond thought here, his face twisted so fully that Bahdlahn wondered if the forced movement actually hurt him.

A thought came to Bahdlahn, and then he understood. It all made sense, even Aghmor's apparent generosity toward him in helping him get away from the murderous Tay Aillig. Aghmor wasn't doing any of this for Bahdlahn's sake, and indeed, he probably thought very little of anyone who was not Usgar. No, he was doing this for Aoleyn, for her memory, and for his own feelings for the young woman.

Bahdlahn referring to Aoleyn as "my Aoleyn" had stung him greatly for reasons beyond hatred of anyone not Usgar. It had, and would, bother Agh-mor to think of anyone else as partnered with Aoleyn.

"Only my friend," Bahdlahn said, and to his relief, Aghmor did seem to be calming down.

Aghmor kicked the pile of food and furs that lay beside him. "I'm not knowing how long it will last, but you'll find little else to eat through the whole of the dark season. The snows are falling heavy now, the passes fast closing. The Usgar are not far, yet I've walked the morning through just get-ting here."

Bahdlahn rose and moved past Aghmor to the narrow channel, then eased through to look out the shallow alcove. It had snowed hard the pre-vious night, and still did. Very hard—Bahdlahn saw the trail Aghmor had made in entering the sheltered area, but even that was already beginning to disappear.

"You should be on your way at once," he said when he went back in.

"And I'll be lucky to make it," Aghmor said. "Eat little. As little as you can. Unless we're finding a thaw, I won't be making this journey again."

The Usgar warrior paused at the entrance to the channel and looked back at Bahdlahn for just a heartbeat, scowling. Then he snorted and moved through.

Bahdlahn accepted that scowl, and shook away the man's insults and threats. He could only be grateful here. Without Aghmor, he would have been killed by Tay Aillig. That was a courageous act, Bahdlahn knew, for if the Usgar learned of Aghmor's betrayal, his life would almost surely be forfeit.

And now this, trekking through deep snows to bring food and furs and wood to the sheltered uamhas.

Bahdlahn sorted the items, placing the wood with the other kindling on one side of the small cave, piling the furs on his bedding right beside the fire. Except for one, an old and ragged, but quite large bearskin, which he bundled about himself, sighing in relief.

He gathered up the food and carried it through the channel. At the side of the shallow alcove was another small opening, into a second cave that was really just a hole. The cold out here would better preserve the meat, he knew, so he stuffed it in, moving it to the back of the small morsels already in there.

The young man stood tall and stretched, staring out at the whiteness, the snow blowing sideways in the mountain winds, and so thick that it was hard to tell where the fallen snow ended and the new-falling snow began.

"You should not have come out," he said, though the words were drowned by the howling wind. He meant it, though. This was not a day to be walking on the mountain.

That realization reminded Bahdlahn of the desperation of his own situation. If Aghmor had not come out this day with supplies, would he have been able to get back to Bahdlahn before the spring thaw?

Bahdlahn had spent his entire life on the mountain, very high on the mountain in the winters. Since he was an uamhas and not Usgar, and so very expendable, he had been out of the protected Usgar encampment in the winter snows many times before, running tasks. He remembered his shock on each occasion. The warmth of the God Crystal protected the Usgar winter encampment from the snow and the wind, creating a small patch of perpetual springtime for the tribe. Just outside of the perimeter of the small plateau, the pine grove, and the lea holding the crystalline form of Usgar, loomed another world, one of winds that could freeze a man solid in short order, and of snow drifts so deep that Bahdlahn hadn't been able to push through them. Worse, the whiteout of Fireach Speuer concealed the many ravines. More than once had Bahdlahn sunk down suddenly, grasping desperately to catch himself from a long slide that would have left him trapped and freezing.

Looking out at the blizzard, he couldn't help but appreciate Aghmor, despite the man's scowl and insults.

He wondered if he would ever see Aghmor again.

That grim thought followed him back through the narrow channel to the inner cave.

He heard a scream, and turned back and moved into the alcove once more, listening.

Had it been a scream?

He heard another, but no, it was the wind. He wanted to believe it was the wind, whistling through the stones. The storm blew more fiercely now, a curtain of whiteness whipping before the cave.

Bahdlahn winced. He rushed back into the inner cave and began selecting furs to wrap his legs and feet.

Back out at the alcove, he shook his head at his own foolishness.

But he knew something was wrong. Perhaps it had been a scream, or maybe it was simply his own fears of the dangers he knew to be out there. He owed it to Aghmor to look.

Out he went into the snow, trudging through, trying to follow Aghmor's tracks exactly—but already, the storm was taking them!

Still, he pressed on, breaking branches when he could, then sticking them into the snow, turned to indicate the way back to his shelter. He turned back repeatedly to get his bearings. He had only gone around fifty strides, but already the rocky ledge that formed his cave was lost to the blowing snow.

He had to go back. His teeth were already chattering.

Stubbornly he pushed on, following Aghmor's trench in the snow, which was now no more than a slight depression. Despite the danger, he yelled for the man, but the wind grabbed his voice and scattered it to nothingness.

A gust of wind knocked him from his feet sprawling in the snow. He pulled himself up and stumbled forward to a tree, grabbing it for support.

"Aghmor," he whispered, shaking his head, certain that the man would not be able to make it back to the Usgar encampment, and certain, too, that if he went on, the blizzard would claim a second victim.

So be it, he thought. He could not dismiss his debt to this man, Aghmor, and what did he risk, anyway? Without Aghmor, where was he to go? How would he even survive the winter, or know when to flee safely down the mountain from the deamhan Usgar?

Growling against the merciless winter, Bahdlahn pressed on into the thickening whiteness. He looked back repeatedly, trying to spot his shelter, but soon dismissed that notion, realizing that it was just slowing him down.

He didn't have time for that. He was wet now from the blowing snow, from falling into the snow, every bit of it getting through his wrapping, melting against his skin. By all reasoning, he had to turn back and hope he could find his way to the cave.

But he didn't. He pressed on.

He moved through a copse of thin, bare trees, and the scraggly things gave him some bearings at least, and in here, the wind and snow lessened just a bit, and he could see Aghmor's tracks.

He followed them out the other side, where they all but disappeared immediately.

"Aghmor!" he called, then paused and listened.

Nothing.

On he went, calling every now and then, and the storm thickened about him.

Finally, Bahdlahn could go no further. He had to get back to the cave, had to hope he could find it quickly, or he knew he would die. He was almost halfway to the Usgar encampment, he believed, though that second part of the trip would be far more treacherous, scaling rocks and crossing deep dells.

"Aghmor!" he called one last time, and when he heard no response, he turned about and made all haste, hoping to be quick enough to follow his own trail. At least no predators would be out in this miserable winter storm.

He had barely gone ten strides when he heard a call. His name!

No, it was just the wind, he thought, and he listened for many heartbeats. "Just the wind," he whispered.

"Bahdlahn!" he heard.

The young slave whirled about and crashed through the snow. He came to the edge of a bowl, and there Aghmor's tracks ended, for there, Aghmor had tumbled or been blown to the side, where the new snow had given way, sending him sliding down a steep decline.

Peering through the blinding blizzard, he thought he spotted the man, or something at least, half-buried below and waving frantically.

"Bahdlahn," he heard more clearly when the wind swirled into his face, carrying desperate Aghmor's plea.

Bahdlahn looked all around. He had no rope, and there was nothing apparent to throw down to the man. He couldn't get Aghmor out of there.

At least not on this end of the bowl, he thought, and tried to remember this area more clearly. Then he didn't hesitate further, and just hopped to the snow beside Aghmor's descent, and rode the mini-avalanche down into the bowl, landing right beside the fallen man.

"My leg!" Aghmor yelled, but it seemed barely a whisper to Bahdlahn, who stood right beside him.

Bahdlahn looked down at the twisted limb and knew that it would not support the Usgar warrior. He glanced around, up the slope. Too steep that way.

Bahdlahn shook his head, and before Aghmor could say another word, he grabbed the Usgar by the arm and hoisted him across his shoulders, then bent and retrieved Aghmor's spear as well.

Aghmor began yelling at him, but he didn't listen, and just pushed on through the deep snow, back in the general direction—he hoped—of his cave, veering as he went so that he was not paralleling his own tracks. He had to hope that the dell exit would be less steep there, and it was, so much so that Bahdlahn was hardly aware that he had come out of the dell, when he crossed . . . his own tracks!

He had to make better time, even with his burden, he knew, so Bahdlahn ran. He could hardly feel his legs any longer, but he ran. For all his life, for Aghmor's life, he ran, the Usgar warrior bouncing about his shoulder. More than once, he stumbled down to one knee, but without hesitation, without complaint, Bahdlahn growled and pushed back up, running, stumbling on.

Aghmor groaned and grunted along the bouncing way, and tried to call out continually, but to chatter that didn't matter to Bahdlahn. Not then.

All that mattered then was running on, keeping the trail before the wind and snow took it away. Somehow, some way, Bahdlahn kept going, and when he finally fell, exhausted, he was close enough to see the rocky ledge, and knew that his shelter was nearby. He didn't even try to pick Aghmor up again, just dragged the half-frozen, injured man along, into the shallow alcove, then down the narrow channel and into the sheltered cave.

"Get out of your wet clothes," Bahdlahn told him, laying him beside the firepit. Bahdlahn rushed to the wood pile and set up a pyramid of his driest kindling, then placed some of the dry hair he had pulled from his scalp earlier beneath it, and took out the wooden hand drill Aghmor had given to him.

Within a short while, he had a fire going, and as soon as he was certain that it had caught fully and would not die out until the wood was consumed, he went to Aghmor and helped him finish undressing, taking great care to get the pant leg over his obviously broken shin. Bahdlahn wrapped the injured man in dry furs, then stripped off his own wet wrappings and lay beside Aghmor, both of them resting there for a long time, letting the feeling return to their wind-bitten, frostbitten bodies.

When he woke up, Bahdlahn found Aghmor sitting, huddling under his furs, shivering.

"I'll set more wood," Bahdlahn said.

"You need to carry me back to the camp," Aghmor replied.

Bahdlahn stared at him incredulously.

"I'll tell them that I freed you from goblins, and that you then saved my life," Aghmor explained. "I do'no think Tay Aillig will kill you."

"We can'no."

"You are uamhas," Aghmor sharply answered. "You will'no disobey me. Carry me to the winter plateau."

Bahdlahn shook his head. "I could'no get there alone. The snow . . ."

Not about to continue the argument, with Aghmor's scowl growing by the word, Bahdlahn went over and scooped the man up into his strong arms, then walked him through the narrow corridor to the front cave.

They could barely see above the snow, snow deeper than Bahdlahn was tall.

"We'd be down and dead before we neared where you fell," the uamhas explained, carrying Aghmor back to the inner cave. He settled the man by the firepit, then went and gathered a few logs to restart the fire.

"We've not enough food," Aghmor said. "We've no' passed midwinter, and have barely the food to last one man."

Bahdlahn shrugged, having no answers.

"You will get more," said Aghmor.

Again, Bahdlahn shrugged.

"I could kill you and eat you," Aghmor warned. "Usgar do not frown upon such things!"

Before he had even finished the sentence, Bahdlahn had the spear in hand, tip pointed at Aghmor's face. "You are hurt. If you try, I will be tasting man-flesh, not Aghmor."

The horrified warrior shrank back from that prodding spear. "You dare?" he breathed.

"I will," Bahdlahn promised. "And you can'no move well enough to stop me."

"Do you know what I could do to you for such a threat?"

"Are you knowing what I could do to you right now?"

Aghmor started to respond, but instead just licked his lips and stared hard at the surprising young man.

"We will take care the food and melt much snow to drink," Bahdlahn explained. "When the storm is settled, I will seek food. When the paths clear, I will take you to the Usgar—near them, where you can call to them and be found. But I'll'no be going back there. I'll be dying out here, but not there. Never there!"

There was no room for debate in his tone, and to his relief, Aghmor offered none, and instead merely nodded and said, "We will need food."

Bahdlahn nodded and moved out of the inner cave, carrying the spear. He set it up high, on an interior ledge above the cave opening, out of sight and up so high that Aghmor would have little chance of reaching it with that troubled leg.

He went back in and got the fire going, sat across it from Aghmor, and stared at the man with hardly a blink, and with a warning scowl.

Bahdlahn had wondered if life was worth living after witnessing the sacrifice of his dear friend Aoleyn, but now, under the threat, when the possibility of his death had become so real, he had found his answer.

He would kill Aghmor if he had to. He probably would even eat dead Aghmor's flesh if he had to.

He would live or he would not, but he would fight to live until he could not.

She felt herself growing healthier by the day, and the song of Usgar grew stronger in her mind. There was something about this place, this secret pool and waterfall, that seemed truly calming and magical to Aoleyn. For a while, it was enough for her to simply bask in the warmth and cleansing water, enjoy her meals, and hear the song, but as the days slipped past, her curiosity mounted as her wounds diminished.

Was she really under the God Crystal? She knew in her heart that she was, but in her mind, she kept trying to find other explanations for this possibly natural cave.

She used the moonstone in her belly ring one day—she had no idea if it was morning or night—to fly up to the top of the cavern. Exploring the ceiling, she found, very near the waterfall, the strongest song of Usgar, and a vein of quartz crystal within the rock. Indeed, it thrummed with the power of her god, so she fell into its song and found herself suddenly looking out on the surface world!

It took her many heartbeats to realize the truth of it: she was looking out from the sacred crystal itself. The day about it was bright and sunny. The wind blew the pines this way and that, and there was a bit of snow in the air, though whether it was falling from some unseen cloud or simply blowing about, she could not tell.

Aoleyn went back down to the floor to regather her strength and sort through this new puzzle. Was she truly looking through the eyes of her god? She thought of the quartz-flecked spear tips, of how the witches could use them to look far down the mountain for returning hunters, or escaped uamhas.

The song had never been this pure and strong, however. What else might she do through this vein of magic, she wondered?

She flew back up and fell through the inviting quartz magic once more. She studied her surroundings. Hardly even aware of her action, she called to her turquoise ear cuff, and sent that magic through the God Crystal.

A mouse. Several more. An owl.

An owl.

Aoleyn remembered that day, which seemed like years before now, though it was not, when she had entered the mind of an owl and flown about the mountain.

Could she?

She sent her thoughts out through the God Crystal, reaching for the mind of the owl. She became disoriented, then, and nearly banged her head on the stone, for she was suddenly looking back on the crystal from a nearby pine. The sound around her magnified intensely, as well, the howling wind, the crackle of a fire, the murmurs of human voices. The Usgar camp.

As she had on that long-ago day, Aoleyn easily took control of the bird and flew from the branch, gliding on rising winds to gain some height.

Fireach Speuer lay thick with snow. Deep snow. Midwinter snow. She had been down here not days, but weeks.

She glided down part of the way to the camp, taking care to stay out of range of any spears, then swooped back again, using the owl's amazing hearing to eavesdrop on this conversation or that. The owl couldn't understand the words, of course, but Aoleyn certainly could, so when she heard Tay Aillig referred to as the "Usgar-triath," she understood that he had indeed taken full control of the tribe. She learned, too, that Mairen was now his wife, their hold on the tribe secure.

She wasn't surprised nearly as much by the information as she was by how little she cared. She wasn't even sure she considered herself Usgar anymore, although she certainly had come to hear the song of the tribe's professed god more clearly.

She flew all about the camp, looking for one person in particular, and when she didn't find him there, she swept up to the southeast, to th'Way, riding the winds all the way to Craos'a'diad.

She found no sign of Bahdlahn, no sign that he, or anyone, had been up there in some time, for the trail was deep with trackless snows.

Back down by the encampment, at the entryway to th'Way where lay the uamhas caves, Aoleyn settled the owl and listened, hoping.

She could hold this enchantment for a long, long while, she knew, but not so much the flying, or even levitating enchantments that had brought her up to the quartz vein. She tried to continue the connection to the bird as she floated away from the ceiling and was thrilled to learn that she could indeed maintain the telepathic bond from the floor.

There she sat, in the dark cave, but seeing the bright sunlight on the deep snow, and hearing the sound of the Usgar and the uamhas.

There, the owl sat when the sun had set and the uamhas had all returned to the caves, with no sight, or sound, of Bahdlahn.

Back in the cave, released from the owl's sensibilities, Aoleyn feared for her dear friend. She was exhausted by then, though, and so she just curled up and went to sleep, determined to find the owl or some other animal host the next day.

The same owl was there on the pine, almost as if waiting for her.

Aoleyn took flight again, about the camp, up th'Way, then, frustrated, she just soared about Fireach Speuer. Through the keen eyes and ears of the owl, Aoleyn took in the sheer majesty of the mountain and its winter blanket, and heard the scurrying of the various animals, and heard the bark of a coyote far off, even heard a bear snoring in its winter cave.

Truly, she was enjoying this day, soaring from tree to tree to rocky ledge.

Unexpectedly, she saw another form, a human form, dark against the snowy backdrop, and what she saw more keenly was the spear the fur-wrapped man held, with its distinctive crystalline tip. Why would an Usgar, any Usgar, be out from the winter plateau and the protective warmth of the God Crystal?

Aoleyn moved her host closer, taking care, and settling in a tree. The man was hunting, or trying to, but he didn't handle the spear very well, and seemed to be floundering about the snow more than purposefully stalking some prey.

At one point he stopped, and looked about, then threw back his heavy hood for a wider view.

Aoleyn was sure that her corporeal form back in the cave had gasped, and that her heart had skipped a beat.

Bahdlahn!

He moved more pointedly then, pushing back to a rocky ledge, and into a shallow cave. She watched him slide behind a slab of rock in the back, out of sight, and she flew in close and perched, tuning her owl ears.

She heard him talking, then heard someone else—it sounded like Aghmor—complaining that he had returned without food.

"I can'no go more than twenty strides," Bahdlahn protested. "The wind covers my trail too fast and I'll lose my way."

"And we'll both be starved if you do'no get some food!"

The owl flew away. Aoleyn wondered if there was some way she could use the turquoise right through this animal's sensibilities, to sense other animals so that it could better hunt. Not now, though, she knew—if it was even possible, such a feat would have to be enacted at the beginning of the possession.

She had another idea.

She flew to the Usgar encampment, and there waited, watching. Some women brought out a slab of meat to the central fire, and there began cutting it into small chunks.

Through the eyes of her host owl, Aoleyn looked all about and saw her chance.

With a flurry of feathers and talons, the owl descended upon the cutting board, sending the Usgar women and a pair of uamhas diving away. Meat in hand, the owl flew off, gone before anyone could react.

"Today will be the day," Bahdlahn promised later that morning, wrapping his heavy furs and hoisting the spear.

"It has to be. Every day has to be," Aghmor growled at him.

Bahdlahn couldn't hold his optimism against that scowl, so he just shrugged and moved out of the inner cave, to find, strangely, two hefty slabs of meat and a pile of sticks on the ground in the shallow alcove of his cave.

He looked all about, even went out into the snow, clenching the spear in both hands, then carried the prize back to Aghmor.

"How can this be?" he asked.

"Someone knows we're here," Aghmor answered, shaking his head as he did, for it all seemed ridiculous. "The wood, too?"

Bahdlahn nodded.

"We have to leave," Aghmor reasoned.

"There is no place to go."

"The Usgar camp . . ."

"We can'no make it."

"Carry me!"

"No, I can'no," Bahdlahn yelled at him. "We'd not get halfway. It's all ice and wind and blinding snow. Twenty strides and I can scarce see the rocks behind me. There's nowhere to go."

"Someone knows we're here," Aghmor repeated.

"Or someone's thinking to make this their home."

"Guard the front cave!"

"I can'no for long. It's too cold."

Aghmor spat into the fire and grumbled something undecipherable.

"Are you not wanting the food, then?" Bahdlahn asked, and he moved over and spitted the meat, placing it carefully on the flames.

Aghmor glared at him, but stopped complaining.

Bahdlahn did go back to the front cave often after that, spear in hand, ready to defend this shelter, or to share it, perhaps. And later that same day, he found another present, a dead rabbit, marked with what looked like the talons of a hunting bird.

And more small pieces of wood.

There was another prize the next morning, and the morning after that. On one occasion, he spotted an owl, watching him from a distant branch. On another a white fox watched his every move, even barked at him as he moved back into the cave.

He didn't understand it, any of it, of course.

But none of the food went uneaten.

16

BODY AND SOUL

There was no place she had ever been that she'd rather be.

For Aoleyn, the music of this cavern, the feel of the divine song vibrating in the air, enchanted her, and more importantly, it made her feel as if she was growing in her understanding of the magic, the notes coming clearer to the point where she could anticipate them and predict them with great accuracy. And she felt as if that, in turn, was allowing her to grow personally, to better understand her place in the world, to better appreciate the bonds between her physical being and her spiritual, magical being.

Every now and then, she put all of her thoughts into the graphite bar set in her anklet, and with a stomp of her foot, released the thrumming energy in the form of a blinding shot of lightning. She had been able to do this for a long time, of course, had even sent her energies across great distances through her connection with Brayth that long-ago day to shoot lightning from his crystalline spear tip.

But nothing like this. Nothing of this power. She could imagine ranks of goblins falling dead under the strength of the strokes she was sending forth now, in this place. She had never imagined the thrill of having such energy coursing through her body, leaping out from her in such brilliant destructive beauty.

Yes, this was the place she wanted to stay forever. She had all the drinking water and food she could want, protection from the winter's cold, and heated water, too, for relaxing and bathing. From here and through the God Crystal, she could go out into the wider world, possessing owls and foxes and coyotes, even a cloud leopard once (and she hoped it was the one that she had saved from the grip of the demon fossa, but she had not been able to tell). With this freedom and help from the animals, she caught food, or stole food from the Usgar, and delivered it and firewood to Bahdlahn in his snowbound cave.

He seemed to be doing quite well, appeared healthy and content, and indeed, more than once, he had called out thanks to the "spirit of Aoleyn."

If only he knew the truth!

One day soon, he would, she had determined. One day, as winter let go of Fireach Speuer, she would leave this place and go to him in his cave.

She looked forward to that day very much.

But for now, she was content, she was warm and safe, and she was happy. And even more than that, Aoleyn was intrigued, for even above the greater power she was finding with the gemstones in this place, there resonated something else, some type of magic she had not known before, and so she spent hours each day trying to find the source.

When at last she determined the exact area, on this very level and not many corridor twists from her cavern, she understood why it had taken her so long to properly locate it. This power wasn't coming from a visible gem, nor, as she was more accustomed to, from a crystal growing out of the floor or wall, as were prevalent in the tunnel complexes higher up. No, this power was within the wall itself, behind the mundane stone.

Aoleyn had no tools with which to mine, of course. But she did have the gray bar of graphite on her anklet.

She feared sending that first lightning bolt into the wall, thinking that she might be despoiling the gift of Usgar in some blasphemous way. But after that blast, where many flecks of stone flew aside and a crack appeared in the wall, Aoleyn felt the strange song more keenly.

It was in there, not too far away.

Again and again, she blasted the wall, until finally she slumped down in exhaustion. Catching her breath, she moved to the wall, and was surprised at how little damage she had actually done.

She ran her hands on the stone, and could feel the power behind it. Somewhere in that wall lay a treasure, she believed, a new and exciting magic. It tantalized her and taunted her because she could not get to it.

Over the next couple of weeks, Aoleyn returned to that spot many times, and even assaulted the wall again with blasts of lightning, to no avail. Thinking that perhaps there was another way to get behind that stone barrier—a secret passage, or one of the many corridors she had not yet explored, she set off more determinedly along these under-chambers of Fireach Speuer, her diamond light shining brightly.

On one such excursion, she found something truly remarkable. She came into a T-intersection, higher up than her cave, she believed, but not so far away. Stepping into that perpendicular passageway, she felt a noticeable increase in the warmth. She turned right and started down, but quickly reversed direction, letting the heat guide her.

The temperature around her rose with every step. Soon, she was sweating, even with the minimal exertion. She nodded, remembering her trial to see if she was capable of joining the Coven. She had been left in these very tunnels, though higher up the mountain maze, and she had found a room of crystals, huge crystals, alive with energy and generating enormous heat.

She called upon the milky white stone set in her ring and brought a translucent shield of white energy about her. She could still feel the warmth of the area, but now, at least, her bare feet weren't stinging on the too-hot floor.

She went on eagerly, wondering what glorious and divine beauty she would find. Around the next corner, she had her answer, for down another long hallway, there shone a bright orange glow. Aoleyn sprinted ahead, but slowed and moved close to the wall, the glow just beyond, around a sharp corner.

Aoleyn was sweating again, and every breath pained her, despite her serpentine shield. She knew she had to hurry, that this heat would find ways to get through her shield and do her great harm. She poked her head around.

A large chamber lay before her, thick with gigantic crystals of an orange-white gemstone. They reminded her of the God Crystal, and she expected that these contained some of the same powers.

She moved in, quickly, for again, she could feel the warmth under her feet, right through the protective barrier. She glanced around, searching, left and right, looking for something, anything, that she could bring forth from this place to examine. She thought to strike at a crystal with a bolt of lightning, but dismissed that notion immediately, for it seemed wrong to her, disrespectful, blasphemous even.

She rushed about, to and fro, feet moving fast to keep them from any prolonged contact with the hot floor, eyes darting all about, searching. She could hear the thrumming in the air, as if the crystals themselves were singing aloud, and she stopped just briefly, to listen.

She heard, too, a tap-tapping sound, off to the side near a wall.

She had to go—her lungs were burning!

But she ran to the wall, and there saw a small tumbling stone in its last bounce into a pile of orange-white stones. She looked up and saw a red-glowing hole in the stone wall. At first, she thought it a red-colored gem, but then realized that it was not, that it was something different. She called upon her moonstone and flew from the ground, battling the overwhelming heat to get nearer.

It was a hole, not quite wide enough for her to crawl through, and she wouldn't have, anyway, for the redness edging that hole wasn't coloration. No, the stone itself glowed like the embers of a great bonfire, and the heat here burned at the woman's eyes. She stayed as long as she could, peering in, trying to discern.

Far down the hole, for it was more a tunnel than a cubby, she saw a distant crystal, like those in the room, but there was no way for her to get to it.

And no way for her to stay here any longer, she realized, when she nearly swooned and almost lost control of her magical flight—and almost grabbed the edge of the hole for support.

She retracted her hand at the last moment, certain that her serpentine shield would protect her from that.

She went down fast to the pile of orange stones at the base of the wall. Using the power of the red gem on her earring, she saw the magic within them, all of them. A quick search guided her to the one shining brightest with magic, and she grabbed it, expecting it to burn her hand.

It was warm, but her shield sufficed, and out she ran, around the bend and back down the corridor.

She was gasping for breath when she finally stopped, and had to slump down and sit there for a long, long while, regaining her strength. She placed her new gemstone on the floor beside her and let her serpentine shield lapse. The heat had sapped her—she could not have even entered that room without the magic of the milky-white gem set in her ring.

After a while, she dared reach down and touch the light-orange gem. Still it was warm, but not uncomfortably so.

She cupped it closer and listened for its song, then, hearing the pattern of the notes, she sent her thoughts to them.

She didn't understand.

She glanced around, her gaze falling over a small stone jag in the tunnel for no particular reason. But that view gave her insight into the gem, and she brought forth its magic and slid over to reach out for the jag with her other hand.

It had been solid rock, but now, at Aoleyn's command, it became malleable, putty in her fingers. She twisted it, she pulled off a chunk of it. Then she played with that chunk, rubbing it and rolling it, making shapes.

She set it down and ended the magic of the orange gem, and almost immediately, the malleable stone with which she had been playing hardened once more, but held the shape Aoleyn had forced upon it.

She had shaped stone. She had torn a piece of stone from the wall and had reshaped it!

Aoleyn fell back, gasping. She felt like a god, like some creature that could create and destroy the world itself. She could build mountains, or tear them down, she believed.

And she feared.

Shaken by the revelations, Aoleyn went back to her cavern home.

The next day, she took up the orange gem once more and began to test its limitations, her limitations.

She was not as powerful as she had believed, not nearly, and she was no god.

That came as a relief.

Still, she had found yet another new and wonderful magic, and with the orange gem she could shape small bits of stone, could draw pictures in it, could break it apart or meld it together with other magically affected stones.

"I could build a most wonderful house of stone," she whispered, standing under the waterfall of hot water late that day. "I can shape it to pleasing curves and build thick walls and doors to keep out the wind and the wolves."

Aoleyn rubbed the splashing warm water through her thick and long black hair.

The smile left her face.

"Or I can tear down a wall," she whispered.

So entranced by the orange room had she been, so consumed by the possibilities, that she had nearly forgotten about the tantalizing, unreachable magic in the other wall, not so far away.

She gathered her smock and ran off, coming before the wall she had cracked with her lightning.

Smiling, she brought forth the orange gem and called to its magic, then took the wall apart, handful, by handful. When she grew exhausted, she lay down right there and slept. She couldn't leave, for she could feel the magic keenly now, and knew that it would be hers the next morning.

She had barely begun her digging, clawing away the stone as if it was thick mud, when her hand closed on something harder, something the magic of her orange stone had not affected. Holding her breath as surely as the item, Aoleyn retracted her arm and pulled forth a clump of stone. Holding strong the magic of the orange gem, she scraped away the mundane stone, revealing a flat, round gemstone as wide as her palm. She released her magic and blew aside the stone dust remaining when the rock hardened once more.

With the edge of her smock, she brushed this new gem clear, marveling at its glisten in the diamond-created light.

She set it down on the floor and bent over it, reaching deeper into the diamond to brighten the light so that she could get a good view.

She had never seen anything like it. It was smooth, very much so, and flat, no thicker than her thinnest finger. It was almost perfectly round, and fit in her palm. Aoleyn lightly ran her fingers about it, hearing its magical song. It seemed thick with wedstone, and she saw some quartz, but there was more, for the bulk of the striated disc was gray with hints of white, but black splotches, four small ones arched about a larger, central one. Like the paw of a large gray and white cat, she thought.

Smiling at that, she picked it up and listened for its magic, then let herself fall into the song.

She thought of the cat again, giggling, but then felt a pain unlike anything she had ever experienced. Deep inside her arm and the hand holding the gem, she felt her muscles twisting and tightening, but too much so! Her bones felt as if they were bending under the stress, then cracking!

She moved her hand as if to fling the gem away, but nothing flew, for there was no gem.

And that thought only lasted the moment it took Aoleyn to realize that her arm wasn't her arm at all anymore, but the arm of a giant cat, like a lynx, but larger, like the greater cats the Usgar called cloud leopards.

"The fossa!" Aoleyn shouted and she fell away, trying to retreat from the arm, the cat's paw, her arm! She had turned her arm into that of a cloud leopard!

Screaming and crying, Aoleyn shook her head and thrashed her arm, trying to shake away the magic. The pain was gone, but it would consume her, she feared—she would become a deamhan, like the fossa, hunting under the Blood Moon, drinking blood and eating the souls of her victims.

She scrambled, she ran, she grabbed at the arm and cried for the magic to stop. She made it to the pool in her own cave and dove in without hesitation, slapping at the water as if it could wash away the curse.

And it did.

Her arm became her own, and the disc-shaped gem fell from her hand, sinking to the bottom of the pool, as Aoleyn swam and kicked her way to the edge of the pool, scrambling onto the stone floor once more.

She sat on the bank of the pool the rest of that day and into the next, staring at where she believed the gemstone to be.

"It was just magic," she told herself repeatedly, trying to calm her fears. "It wasn't the fossa. I am not the fossa. It was magic, nothing more."

She tried to reason through all that had happened. Had the excitement of the magic melded her with the gemstone? It had been gone, after all, when her arm had been that of the cloud leopard.

She went about her day. She went out with her spirit, through the channel to the God Crystal and beyond, and found her friend owl in the pine tree. Then she flew, far and wide, and found, to her joy, a real cloud leopard.

She watched it for a long while, marveling at its beauty and grace.

The fossa hadn't been a cloud leopard, she reminded herself. It had possessed a cloud leopard, but had withered and burned the beautiful cat from within, making it something ugly and evil-looking.

Back in her cavern, Aoleyn had her dinner then lay down upon her mossy bed. But only for a moment, for the gemstone called to her, and she dove again into the pool, bringing forth her diamond light. She came back out soon after, the flat, round gemstone in hand.

She set it down near her moss bed and fell asleep staring at it.

Her dreams were full of cloud leopards, of being a cloud leopard, leaping about the deep snows with graceful joy, playing along the ledges of sheer cliffs, lounging in the soft late-winter snowfalls.

"It is magic, nothing more" were the first words out of her mouth when she opened her eyes again, and before she went to wash, before she went to find her breakfast, Aoleyn picked up the stone and lay it flat on her right palm. She lifted the hand up high and called to the magic, then winced as she felt the pain of transformation.

Then she marveled at her hand—no, her paw. She bared her claws, then retracted them. She bared them again and swiped across—and wouldn't Tay Aillig's face melt under the scrape of this arm!

Aoleyn let the magic go soon after, and watched with relief as her arm twisted and wrenched and became just that, her arm, once more.

She thought of the fossa. It was connected to this, she believed, but distantly.

Perhaps another had used a gem such as this, had become a cloud leopard wholly with the power of Usgar. And that man, or woman more likely, a champion of Usgar, had then done battle with the spirit of the fossa, and so had become possessed, and corrupted, by the deamhan's magic.

Aoleyn held her breath as she considered that line of thinking. Where had she even gotten such ideas, she wondered?

But somehow, some way, there was a measure of truth there, or there certainly could be.

"Is it any more crazy than calling a red moon the bloody face of a goddess?" she asked aloud, giggling, but she bit that back, fearing that some power in this place, in the sacred tunnels of the God Crystal, of Usgar himself, would strike her dead for her impudence.

"What secrets do you hold?" she asked the disc-like gem resting on the floor beside her. "Are you the essence of leopard? The mother goddess of leopardkind?"

Aoleyn giggled again at her silliness, but again, it was short-lived.

How could she know, after all? With magic, she could make lightning and fireballs, could fly, could walk free of her body, could make fields of ice, could soften stone into putty.

Was anything truly outlandish? Was anything impossible?

She left the disc there by the mossy bed and went about her day, later moving to the far wall of the cave to play with her other new toy, the orange gem. What piece of jewelry would she make of this, she wondered, and what other magic tricks might it play?

She found one when using the orange gem on a patch of floor later on, intending to draw pictures to recount her time here. She sketched the body of poor Innevah, and an image of herself kneeling beside the fallen woman. She drew an owl, a fox, and, of course, a cloud leopard.

Then, sitting back, admiring her work as the stone hardened once more, Aoleyn had another idea. On a hunch, she called, too, upon the red ruby in her ring, and brought forth the power of the orange gemstone once more, winding the magic together.

Aoleyn's eyes sparkled in reflection of that before her: a hot field of stone, smoldering, streaked with liquid red like that which she had seen at the hole in the hot crystal room. It crackled with heat, sharp dots of white-hot light glistening about the hardening black stone as it cooled once more.

It took her a long while to find her breath.

Back at her mossy bed later on, Aoleyn studied the disc-shaped gem intently. She used her diamond, then her wedstone, anything to find some hints, some clues.

"What else have you for me?" she whispered to the stone, for she was certain that she was missing something here. She thought she should tear a strip from her smock, to make a hand-wrap that could hold the gem.

But no, that wouldn't suit her.

What would she do with this strange gem? She would make a second ring for the orange stone, she had decided, but this one was too bulky for anything like that.

On a whim, Aoleyn tickled the leopard-paw gem with lightning energy, froze it with the blue stone of her anklet, heated it with her ruby. She could feel its power, calling to her, beckoning to her, with each touch of her magical energy.

Aoleyn brought forth the orange gemstone, focused on it and on the ruby in her ring, as she had done earlier, and threw all of that energy into the leopard-paw disc.

There came a sharp crackle, like the snap of a giant tree, and a burst of power, of pure magic, flashed through the room, throwing Aoleyn backward. She came up coughing, her mouth and throat tingling as if she was inhaling stone dust or some other grating substance.

Stone dust?

Horrified, Aoleyn ran back to the spot, searching frantically.

The disc was gone—she knew that she had inadvertently, had foolishly, had stupidly, blown it apart!

But no, she saw it, and her heart fluttered, then sank again when she fell over it, to see that it was no more a singular gemstone, but was, instead, powder of that same stone, looking the same as it had before, except that instead of a single, solid disk, it was a conglomeration of a million million tiny crystals, arranged to perfectly replicate what the disc had been.

She put her hand near to it and felt for the magic, and felt, indeed, the magic, and more acutely, as if all the mundane elements of the gemstone had been removed, blasted away, leaving just the pure magical elements behind.

But what was she to do with this?

Was there some way she could reverse that which she had done, to make the tiny crystals into one again?

She didn't dare try. Not then. Feeling quite the fool, Aoleyn went over to the pond and plopped down on the stone ledge, putting her feet into the warm water. There she sat for a long while, the whole day through, mulling, considering what she had done and what she might do now.

She called upon the wedstone and used its magic to fall deeper into herself, finding a place of pure serenity and meditation, considering all while considering nothing at all.

A long while later—and so deep was Aoleyn's trance that she had no idea of how long—she opened her eyes and said, "It's only magic."

The revelation seemed obvious to her now, as she stripped the implications of judgmental divinity out of the equation. She had never thought of the magical crystal, or gemstones, in this manner before. She had been brought up, and then specifically trained, to believe these to be the powers of Usgar granted through his priestesses, but how could that be?

For Aoleyn had been able to bring forth powerful magic before her encounter with the fossa, before her turn from the tenets of the tribe—a turn that Mairen had called heretical, and for which Aoleyn had been fed to Craos'a'diad.

Why, then, was Aoleyn able to bring forth magic of even greater power now? If Usgar was the arbiter, if the magic god-given, then how could Aoleyn and Mairen both wield it proficiently while taking ethical viewpoints which seemed so diametrically opposed?

It was a puzzle she'd need a long time to resolve, she was sure, but for now, the thought that it was only magic, that it was but a force to be taken and shaped by the wielder, led her to a sense of great relief and serenity. Was a lightning bolt brought from the gray stone any different from the fire created by a bow drill?

She loomed over the pile of pulverized gemstone bits, inspired that even in so many bits, the gemstone had retained its shape and appearance. And its magic. She could feel the power all about the pile, even stronger, it seemed to her, than it had been when the leopard paw had been whole.

Aoleyn chuckled at herself, still thinking she had been reckless in so experimenting with the strange powers. It seemed like she hadn't done too much actual damage, to the magic at least, but what could it mean? How could she hold this magic together? Should she put the tiny crystals into a bag, perhaps, or could she somehow melt stone around them and re-form the item, albeit clunkily?

What could be the binding force in this magic that had worked within Aoleyn, had transformed her arm into that of a great cloud leopard?

A smile came to the woman.

Aoleyn winced as the needle-like crystal, a tiny fragment of wedstone, pierced her skin yet again. Her palm bled, just slightly, with each successive jab; at this point, there were several dozen stabs, and the blood was starting to add up. But the last piece of the image was taking shape—what had been only in her mind was now clear for her to see upon her palm. She would be finished soon.

She smiled at the fresh pain. Among the Usgar, tattoos were forbidden for all except warriors, or, rarely, women claimed by warriors who wanted them to wear a tattoo badge. In the Usgar tribe, only men could be warriors.

But Aoleyn fancied herself a warrior anyway.

She jabbed the wedstone needle in again, sending her thoughts into it to excite the magic and make it vibrate, to fully set the tiny crystals of the leopard paw gem. She retracted the wedstone, but called more fully upon its powers to heal the wound around those tiny pieces, setting them forever in her hand.

She took a deep breath, hoping, then leaned over to the pool and washed her blood away. She brought forth her hand, palm up, shining in the diamond light. The image seemed perfect—she had been guided in their placement by the magic of the leopard paw.

Now she had a tattoo, on her palm, of that paw.

She looked to the pile. Many more crystal bits remained.

She had another palm.

But for another day, she decided, and she went to her moss bed, weary from her magical efforts. She couldn't sleep, though, tossing and turning repeatedly as her imagination tickled her. She had to find out.

She rolled to her back and lifted her arm above her so she could see it in the dim lichen and glowworm glow.

She listened, not with her ears, but with her heart, and found this newest song, intimately. She called to it, her spirit sang the notes. She felt the discomfort, the twisting muscles, the popping bones, but it passed quickly.

Aoleyn lay there, admiring her limb, the paw of a great cat. She dismissed the magic, then waited and watched, and giggled when her arm reverted to its natural form.

It wasn't a sigh of relief, or a burst of laughter to relieve the tension, either, because she had known it would happen. She understood now.

It was just magic, so she told herself.

She went back to the powdered gemstone the next day and took up her wedstone needle, thinking to put a paw on her other palm.

But no. Something happened when she coated her needle with the bits, something within her, some magical compulsion.

She was afraid now at the stark reminder that making a lightning bolt was not quite the same thing as rubbing sticks together to light a fire, but she couldn't resist.

Her hand moved, seemingly haphazardly, poking randomly, it seemed. She stripped off her smock and kept going, jabbing, calling bits of healing.

She went to work the next day, and the day after that, and the days became a week, then two. She hadn't gone out to Bahdlahn, and wanted to, but she could not. She barely ate and drank, and her sleep grew restless. She thought she should stop and consider all of this, whatever it might be. Had she been wrong? Was she making herself into the deamhan fossa?

But she couldn't stop. The compulsion was too great, for Aoleyn understood that she was becoming more intimate with the magic now than she had ever imagined.

The powder pile was almost gone. Aoleyn's hand moved tentatively now, as she moved the needle about her face, reveling in every sting, followed by the warm rush of healing magic.

That night, the powder depleted, Aoleyn slept, more soundly than she had in weeks.

She awakened the next day, if it was day, for she couldn't know down here, refreshed, but unsure. Unsure of everything, wondering if it had all been a dream.

She moved to the pool, but far from the waterfall, where the water was mostly still. She brought forth diamond light to view her reflection. She couldn't make out much. She did see some lines, like an outline of some sort, but it was too dim in the watery mirror.

Aoleyn had a better idea. She strengthened her diamond light so that it seemed like a midsummer day within her cave, then fell into her wedstone, fell through her wedstone, stepping out of her body, just enough to look back at her naked corporeal form.

Had her spirit still been in that body, it would have taken her breath away, surely.

For with the powder, Aoleyn had made the markings and delicate outline of a cloud leopard. Her body had been a canvas, the powder her ink.

She went back into her body and listened for the song of the leopard paw, and heard it, so keenly, so beautifully.

Aoleyn called it forth, looking again to her reflection in the water.

The image of the cloud leopard glowed silvery, even the cat's tail, which she had traced down the side and back of her left leg. Her own reflection faded behind it, and for a moment, she wondered if she had actually transformed into a great cat!

To bolster that thought, her senses became more keen—she had known this sensation when she had possessed a cloud leopard one day on her spiritual travels—and her muscles tightened. She felt as if she could pounce, could spring up and touch the distant ceiling.

She focused on the first tattoo, the paw print on her right palm, and called forth the magic there more powerfully. Her arm transformed, but that was all, as the rest of the enchantment dissipated.

There was more she needed to learn here, she understood. Much more.

But for now, there was nothing more to be done with this.

She left the cavern that day, spiritually, climbing up through the veins of magical gem to the God Crystal. She found her owl and she possessed it and flew off, gliding about the mountainside, feeling refreshed, feeling free, feeling confident.

And feeling quite happy when she saw Bahdlahn again, out foraging near his cave. Winter's grip on Fireach Speuer had greatly diminished, Aoleyn realized. The lower regions, down near the lake, showed pines free of snow and patches of bare ground.

She had been in this cavern for an entire season! She couldn't know the exact time of year, of course, but it seemed clear to her that spring was drawing near.

She caught a rabbit and dropped it by Bahdlahn's cave entrance. She stole some food from the Usgar, and brought it to her secret friend.

She flew back about the Usgar camp. They weren't yet making preparations to go down the mountain and the snow was still deep up here, but not as deep, she believed, something she confirmed when she flew past the winter plateau, over to the east.

Aoleyn's shock nearly threw her from the owl's mind. She saw a long slope, snow-covered, but covered, too, with bodies. Mountain goblins, the sidhe, she realized as she flew past low to the ground. They were frozen in the snow, most showing garish wounds Aoleyn suspected to be from an Usgar spear. It appeared as if she had missed a great battle.

Who might have died in that skirmish, she wondered?

She realized that she didn't really care, and that indifference shocked her, but only briefly.

She released the owl, then went home, to her mossy bed, and slept soundly.

The next day, she studied her tattoos in her reflection again. She called upon the magic, and as it was enacting, spirit-walked out of her body, just a bit, to look back upon herself, to see the silvery glow of the cloud leopard image.

She thought it beautiful, but more than that, Aoleyn thought her body beautiful. She saw it in a way she had never imagined before, as *her* body, the vessel of her being, of her spirit, of her thoughts.

When she had started the tattoos, part of the action had been in defiance. It was forbidden for an Usgar woman to tattoo herself. Only a man could do that, and only a man could instruct his woman to do that.

But no, the defiant mood didn't seem to fit her now, Aoleyn understood. The image she had painted upon herself had nothing to do with the warriors, with Usgar, with anyone who was not . . . Aoleyn.

Just Aoleyn.

This was her canvas, her clay to be molded. Hers, only hers, to be given by her, to be withheld by her.

By none other.

Now she truly looked at herself under this new understanding, at the play of her muscles as she danced about, at the beauty of form.

The unanticipated effect was not lost on the young woman. By scarring herself, she had claimed herself, wholly, completely.

And now she knew. It wasn't *just* magic, as if something as mundane as coaxing fire from dry leaves by running a bow drill. This was a different power, an inner clarity, a spiritual strength.

Her tribe named that Usgar. To the lakemen, it was the work of a deamhan.

Aoleyn shook her head. None of that mattered. Nay, she rejected it.

This was *her* power, a manifestation of *her* spirit and will.

And this was *her* body, just *hers*. It did not belong to a warrior, any warrior.

That thought gave Aoleyn pause, as she remembered the ritual she had endured before her spiritual joining with Brayth, when he had pushed her over and raped her.

Just remembering that brought forth the power of the tattoo once more, turning her arm into that mighty leopard paw.

Aoleyn nodded, her face grim, but she was satisfied.

She had never been more at home in her mortal coil.

The thought of leaving this cave did not sit well with Aoleyn. A big part of her wished she could spend the rest of her days here, basking in the music of magic—she could not bring herself to call it the song of Usgar any longer—and learning about herself as she learned the power of the enchanted gemstones.

But spring was coming up above, she knew, and Bahdlahn was out there, alone and probably afraid, and likely very soon to be in grave danger.

Besides, when Aoleyn actually considered the whole of her situation, she knew that there was more for her to learn, about herself and others and the wide world, out there than in here.

A few days after her journey with the owl—it was impossible to track time accurately down here, but Aoleyn had slept three times since creating her tattoo—Aoleyn once more went forth from the place spiritually.

She found her owl friend and set off, but this time focused more keenly on the Usgar encampment. The day was warm and sunny, and most of the tribe were out and about, beginning the earliest preparations for their move down the mountain.

Aoleyn knew the routines quite well, and so it was easy for her to quietly fly into an empty tent and steal a few odds and ends: a small knife, a pair of metal spoons, and a silver necklace the tent's occupant, Connebragh, sometimes wore.

The owl flew up above Craos'a'diad and dropped the stolen pieces into the chasm.

Aoleyn let the bird go free.

Down the corridor she went, back out to the main chasm. She held her breath and looked back many times, but held her nerve, called upon her diamond for brilliant light, then called upon her malachite and jumped into the blackness. She enacted the levitational magic almost immediately, not having the nerve to trust the distance of the fall.

Before she even got to the bottom, she found one of the spoons, caught on a small ledge. Down at the base of the chasm, she found the other spoon, the knife, and the necklace.

Now she used her malachite more powerfully, climbing the wall swiftly. Then, when she broke past the last twist in the chasm, she enacted her moonstone and flew up—right past the tunnels she had called home for the last month, and up higher, high enough to see the daylight with her own eyes for the first time since she had been thrown in here, and finally to the landing she had been on before, during her trial for the Coven.

These tunnels she knew, and so she went boldly, calling upon the magic all about her to excite the crystals full of diamond flecks to brighten the way, as if lighting the magical lamps simply with her passage.

She knew what she wanted and knew where to find it, and soon she was hard at work, crafting another piece of jewelry: a chain belt and wedstone wire, thin and delicate, with a single tassel that held a teardrop pendant of wedstone—a more concentrated and powerful block of that most important stone than anything she currently possessed. At the center of that teardrop, she set the orange gemstone she could use for stone shaping.

She felt quite pleased when she tied the belt about her waist, using strands of wedstone to pierce it to her body and keep her intimately connected to the music. She thought to return to her cave, then, but changed her mind, for it was not cold up here at all, and Aoleyn explored and wandered, wondering what she might next craft.

Before anything could come to mind, though, the young witch felt something unexpected.

There was a music to the caves, a vibration, impossibly subtle to those who did not recognize it, but clear as a ringing bell to Aoleyn, attuned as she was to the crystals. On this day, unexpectedly, that typical song changed. Where before it had been a low buzz, now it was much louder; where before she had heard the rhythm only of the crystals themselves, suddenly the music coalesced into a more unified and powerful song, like a choir.

Curious, Aoleyn made her way through the caves, heading toward the surface, toward the bottom of the great pit ceilinged by Craos'a'diad. As she climbed, she felt the music ebb and flow, but mostly she felt it grow stronger. Something on the surface, she decided, was causing this. Or someone, she strongly suspected.

She came to the base of the pit and looked up through the mouth of Usgar. The sky far above was dim. Twilight, she figured. She felt the cold air flowing down from above, and nodded—even long after spring had come, which she believed it had not, the nights atop Fireach Speuer could be brutally cold.

She flexed her leg, felt the last bits of soreness from her tattooing, and told herself that a soak in the hot water below would do her well.

Aoleyn laughed at herself. It was just a deflection, an excuse. Winter was letting go up top, and something strange was occurring on the surface, almost certainly concerning the Coven. Bahdlahn needed her, or would soon—she could not forsake him.

She hoped that she would find the opportunity to return to this place, to the cave below that had been as true a home to her as anything she had ever known. But now, she was ready, she decided.

She called to the magic all around her, then focused her thoughts to those gems intimately pierced about her body. She narrowed her call again, and sought out the vibrations of her favorite stone, the malachite. A smile widened—she couldn't help it—as she felt herself grow lighter and lighter until her feet lifted off from the ground. Up she floated, up into the cold, twilit air atop Fireach Speuer.

She was shivering by the time she exited the chasm, but she didn't dare enact her cloak of flames, for it would have marked her clearly to anyone about. She could no longer feel the vibrations of magic, as she had in the caverns below, but she could hear the song of the witches, and moving to the southeastern edge of this higher plateau, looking down on the Usgar winter plateau and the pine grove that held the sacred God Crystal, she could see them, the witches of the Coven, holding tiny diamond-flecked crystals in their outstretched and uplifted hands. They moved in a circle about the God Crystal, and each rotated as she went, creating tiny circles about the ring of the larger.

Aoleyn maintained her levitational magic, and coaxed the moonstone of her belly ring to life, slowly flying down the mountainside, staying low so as to not present a silhouette against the darkening sky. She came down to the pine grove opposite the winter plateau, then carefully picked her way through, enacting a third gemstone, the diamond, but reversing its effect to create wispy shadows about herself, to better conceal herself.

She could hear again now the music of the gems, the melodic hum of the crystalline energy, blending sweetly with the song of the witches.

Aoleyn knew this song, the song of the holy day, the spring equinox.

She came to the edge of the trees, peering in at the dancing witches, all dressed in short smocks of sheer material, clothing they only wore here in their rituals. She recognized Connebragh nearest her, moving away to the right, and Aoleyn counted until Connebragh had come all the way around.

Eleven were dancing. Mairen stood in the center, near the God Crystal. Within the ring of witches, too, stood another, a young woman, barely more than a girl.

"Moragh," Aoleyn silently mouthed, recognizing her. She understood, then, the significance of this ritual. It wasn't merely the dance of spring, which was no small thing in itself, but the Coven was also using this holy day to fill the void left by the death of Gavina and the subsequent heresy of Aoleyn.

Moragh was to be the twelfth witch of the Coven, twelve serving the thirteenth, the Usgar-righinn, completing the circle.

In the center, Mairen untied the top of her shift and lifted her arms. The God Crystal flared with red-orange light as Mairen's smock fell away, leaving her naked to the night, and, more importantly, to the God Crystal.

The dancing witches began to similarly move, one by one, in sequence down the line, lifting their arms, shedding their slight smocks, baring themselves to their god. The women rhythmically turned and whirled, gyrating and stepping-in, stepping-out from the circle of dancing, as the whole of the group continued its balanced turn about the object of their worship. Whenever one moved close to the centerpiece, the huge crystal protruding at an angle from the ground, she moved back in a deferential way, almost bowing, always with eyes low.

Only Mairen, standing immediately behind the base of the angled crystal, kept her eyes high, to the growing stars in the night sky, and kept her arms high, as if beckoning to a higher power.

And only Moragh wore her smock now, and Aoleyn noted that she had her arms in close before her, as if trying to cover further. Clearly uncomfortable, the young woman glanced left and right, never letting her eyes linger on any of the dancing naked witches for any length of time.

Aoleyn, with her new insights and perspective, almost laughed aloud at that.

The power of the gemstone magic tingled in the air, palpable and exciting. The dance increased in its pace, the song increased in volume.

"Join us," Mairen called above the song.

"Join us," each of the eleven recited in turn, one at a time, while the other sisters kept the melody flowing.

Moragh's discomfort remained, clearly, but she slowly untied the top of her smock, her lips moving only a bit as she slipped into the trance-like rhythms.

That could have been her, Aoleyn thought. This was to be her destiny. She didn't know what to think of that in that moment, however, as regret battled with determination, reminding her that she had come to know a different, and better, way, and a different and more thorough understanding of the crystal magic, and of herself, body and spirit.

Moragh knew that she should be unashamed of her naked body, here in this place and company, and without concern of petty vanity.

She was accepted, fully so, Mairen and the others had assured her.

Still, unused to such a ritual, she felt her cheeks burning, and hoped that the low light would hide her blush.

The song of the night flowed into her heart and thoughts, and so she, too, began to sing—she couldn't help it, it just flowed from her. She let her smock fall, then bent low to retrieve a pair of small crystals as she stepped out of it. They flared to light as she stood back up, lifting her arms, feeling the communal power of the Coven's song and dance. Growing more comfortable with her nudity, she began to mimic the footwork of the others in their dance, and to turn, but she did not yet join the outer ring.

With every turn, the steps of Moragh's dance became less inhibited, and guided by powers unhindered by any of the imposed human modesty. Her whole body tingled with the energy, like little sparks of lightning tickling and teasing her skin, making her feel alive in every bit of body. She couldn't deny the pleasure and the power.

Her arms went out wide as she turned, the wind tickling her bare skin, her thick hair flowing behind her like an extension of her shadow.

A cry of ecstasy surprised her and turned her attention to the center of the circle, to see Mairen wrapped about the God Crystal, hugging it close, her body trembling.

Moragh stopped her dance, eyes unblinking, jaw hanging open, for then she understood. The flush of shame returned to her cheeks, but she fought it off.

A sister moved beside her and ushered her to the outer ring, inviting her to fully join the dance, and Moragh complied and quickly resumed her foot-work, turning and singing.

The witch to her side then stepped in toward the God Crystal, to replace Mairen, who flashed Moragh a brief smile and nod as she fell into the line beside her.

With her turn, Moragh glanced at that second sister, reclining upon the angled God Crystal, her head immediately going back and swaying, her eye-lids heavy and half-closed.

Moragh felt her cheeks flushing once more, and she understood. They would make their way around the circle, one by one, to find their place of worship and ecstasy with their god, Usgar, and her turn would come, last in the line, and then, only then when she had completed the ritual, would she become a witch of the Coven.

The crystal, the phallic crystal.

Aoleyn did not feel a sense of sisterhood here, did not see this as a ritual of mutual pleasure, no. For all their energy and apparent pleasure, this was not a celebration of womanhood, no. This dance worshipped the men of the tribe. The men who thought nothing of beating them or spitting upon them. The men who told them what they could or could not do to their own bodies.

The men who owned them.

In that manner, perhaps this was a brief moment of freedom, but even in that, there was reverence, not to the female form, but to the men. Always and only, the men.

She thought of Brayth again, and what he had done to her, and what any Usgar man who had been joined with a witch would do to her, and to what the Usgar men had routinely done to the uamhas women against their will.

One after another, the witches went to the crystal to worship, to find their orgasm and to credit it, too, wholly to their masters.

Even the witches, even the Usgar-righinn, even in their most personal moments, in a place where no man was allowed, served.

Aoleyn focused on Moragh. She could see the young woman missing words in her song, stumbling now and then in her dance. She was scared—of course she was scared. Her time neared.

Among the notes and subtle words of the song came whispers of encouragement, and even joy from the others in knowing that Moragh was about to become a woman, as well as a witch of their sacred Coven.

The twelfth woman moved away from the God Crystal, stepped toward Moragh, motioning for her to go forward, to the glowing crystal member.

Slowly she moved into the soft red light, fighting, Aoleyn could tell.

Aoleyn was glad that it was not her. The spirit of the evening had flown from her, and she felt this ritual was not what the others apparently believed it to be. It was not freedom with their bodies—surely, Moragh had no freedom here.

Moragh reached out to feel the thrum of the huge crystal, tentatively so, Aoleyn could tell.

Twelve witches danced about her, but then a thirteenth joined the ring, and she was not dancing, and her arms were not uplifted.

Almost bumping into her, the nearest approaching dancer looked at her curiously. The woman's eyes widened with shock and she fell back and cried out loudly with recognition. Those behind her followed suit, and those across from her, as well. Across from Aoleyn, past the God Crystal, Mairen came forth, eyes wide with shock.

"Ghost!" she cried. "What deamhan, you?"

Aoleyn felt her anger rising. She stared hard at Mairen and thought of Innevah, poor, enslaved Innevah, cast into the pit to die by order of the Usgar-righinn. Aoleyn wasn't even aware of the changes that were then coming over her body, wrought by her cascading emotions.

She only became aware, in fact, when the witches nearest her cried out again, this time in obvious fear, and shrank away.

Then Aoleyn knew. Her leopard tattoos were glowing, and it took all of her willpower to stop it there and prevent her arm from transforming.

"Deamhan!" Mairen cried again, pointing accusingly at her. "And in this sacred place, you dare! Take her!"

Aoleyn lifted her arms up before her and lifted one foot from the ground. Several witches came at her as if to tackle her. Others ran to the edge of the lea, to their more typical clothing and the crystals they had left there.

In they came, grabbing at her, leaping at her.

Aoleyn stamped her foot, throwing forth the magic of the gray bar upon her anklet, sending a ring of lightning power flowing out from her, crackling along the ground, sparking into the nearest attackers, tossing them and sending them to the ground in spasms.

And the invoking witch, Aoleyn, never even looked at those attackers, her gaze locked with that of Mairen, who stood beside the God Crystal. The lightning energy rolled right up to her, too, and she snarled as it crackled into her bare feet. But the bulk of the energy was already spent and it did not shake her.

"Ghost!" Mairen accused.

"Quite alive," Aoleyn answered. She surveyed those witches to her sides, a few of whom had gathered crystals now, and all of whom were moving behind and beside the Usgar-righinn, though more than a couple walked awkwardly, their muscles not yet fully responding after the lightning attack. "You didn't kill me, Mairen, though you surely tried."

"You were given to Usgar," Connebragh blurted.

"He didn't want me, then," Aoleyn said with a shrug. "Because he didn't take me." She thought of explaining a bit more here, to taunt Mairen with the fact that the spirits of Elara and Seonagh, her mother and her aunt, had caught her in her fall and had saved her. But she held it back. There was no reason to tell this murderer anything.

"Because here I am," she stated defiantly, to Connebragh and particularly to Mairen.

"What warrior has claimed you?" the Usgar-righinn demanded.

Aoleyn snorted at her. "No man."

"You are marked and adorned," Mairen argued. "What man . . ."

"I did it," Aoleyn admitted.

"Who gave you such permission?" The Usgar-righinn's voice rose, the whispers about the circle sounded less confused and more angry.

"It is my flesh, to mark, to pierce, as I will," Aoleyn declared. She brought her hand to her navel ring to clutch the gemstones more tightly, reached through them to the crystal, reached through them to her own life energy.

"You belong to Usgar. You have no right!" Mairen roared.

"My flesh!" Aoleyn shouted back, and slapped her empty hand against her chest. "Mine!"

"You have no right!" the Usgar-righinn roared again. "You have no soul!"

There it was, the damning curse, the worst that could be said to a woman of the tribe, a curse that would wilt the strongest and shame her to a life broken and despairing.

And yet, in that terrible moment, this young woman Aoleyn found her strength and her heart.

"I am a soul," she growled back, as if the voice had come from the most primal place she could find—and indeed, it had.

Mairen grabbed a crystal from the witch beside her and immediately began to empower it. Aoleyn caught a flash of blue, heard a hint of the song, and even as Mairen launched her attack, a burst of icy sleet falling over and all about her target, Aoleyn called upon her own gemstones, enacting that flame shield to counter the freezing assault.

"Kill her!" Mairen cried to the others, many lifting crystals and beginning their chants.

But Aoleyn was ahead of them, and faster on the draw because of her intimate wedstone connection to her magical gems. She brought the moonstone to its most powerful crescendo and reached into her ring simultaneously.

"You have no soul!" Mairen shouted again.

"I am a soul," Aoleyn answered, her voice full of strength and conviction. "I have a body." The sheer power of her voice brought forth the malachite, and Aoleyn floated up into the air, above the glowing God Crystal, as if proud to be on naked display before them all, her tattoos, her piercings.

And so she was.

"You will be . . ." Mairen started to threaten, but her words disappeared in the flash of a fiery wind, as both the moonstone of Aoleyn's belly ring and the ruby of her finger ring released their magic, as a great burst, full of wispy, dancing flames, flowed forth from Aoleyn, rushing into Mairen and her dozen witches and throwing them backward, leaves in a gale, tumbling and skidding through the grass. One of the robes on the ground behind them lifted up into that wind and caught fire, fluttering and flaming, and so, too, did the grass ignite in places, flaring to life abruptly and flaming out quickly, wisps of smoke dancing circles on the wind.

"I am a soul!" Aoleyn said again, accompanying each word with a feral growl. "I have a body.

"My body!"

PART 3

THE UNSTOPPABLE ROLL OF LIGHT

They are not masks. We thought them masks. The red, red nose, brilliant red, bloody red, with the brightest blue beside it. What beauty and elegance have I seen!

We did not know what to expect when we found these deep graves in the dry desert west of the Wilderlands. We did not know what we had found when we removed the wrappings from the bodies. We believed these barbarian graves, the mortal remains of the tall men who live in the cold north. The bodies were thin. Drained of life fluids, we assumed, as is the practice seen in other parts of the world. But even if thicker in life, these were too thin.

The sacred stones of Abelle alone revealed to us the truth: these were not barbarians of the north. None like we would know. They were not human, but neither goblin. Neither anything known to us.

Our surprise was great to find the clues in the songs of Skald Djono'orsen, who traveled west from Vanguard in the days long before the birth of Abelle. His sagas, carried down in barbarian tradition, named this people. Little is known beyond the face coloring. They are tall and lean and stronger than they appear. They are not goblins and not human. They are something different, something lost to the world.

Once they were mighty, so claim the poems. Once they built the greatest cities in all the lands, greater than the desert cities of Behren.

They are lost to the world now. I feel a deep sense of regret. I would have enjoyed their golden temples and unusual ways.

They were the Sidhe, who called themselves Xoconai.

FIRST DIARY OF THE TOMB OF UNKNOWN ANCIENTS IN
THE RUINS OF HERTEMSPAH
BROTHER GILBERT OF ANNACUTH, GOD'S YEAR 62
(UNREAD IN THE CATACOMBS OF
ST. MERE ABELLE IN MORE THAN TWO CENTURIES)

The war is little recorded, but from my investigation, I believe it coincided with the dactyl wars of the 4th century before Abelle. It can be no coincidence, and so I fear these magnificent creatures, the Sidhe, were of the dactyl's making.

It is confusing, I must openly admit here, because they did battle, too, with the goblins of the demon dactyl. For those who will peruse my tomes, I humbly submit that you take care in assigning this race to those of the demons. A caveat to caveat, I admit my prejudice here, as every record I can find speaks in awesome terms with regard to the creations of the Sidhe, their beauty, and the grace of their movements, so unlike the goblins.

In that war of BA4th Century, the Sidhe and the many kingdoms of Honce did furious battle, most particularly in those kingdoms about and west of the Masur Delaval. The demon goblins did furious battle with the many kingdoms of Honce east of Masur Delaval, and warred with the Sidhe west of the westernmost Honce kingdoms. Was it one war, or four? I do not know. I have seen evidence that some of those old Honce kingdoms did battle with each other at the same time.

The chaos of the demon dactyl did infect the world, so it seems.

The accounts are all vague, and few remain, but still, I conclude:

a) *The goblins and Sidhe were enemies alone and no alliance between them could I find.*

b) *Goblins and the men of Honce did war about the Mantis Arm and from Entel all the way to the city we now call Ursal.*

c) *The Sidhe and the men of Honce did battle for the lands about and west of the Masur Delaval. Here, there were battles of three armies—human, Sidhe, goblin—and none seem aligned.*

d) *The Sidhe were driven west, beyond the Wilderlands, and there eliminated from the world.*

My conclusions are far from conclusive, I fear, and I will garner no more before I am called to my reward. Perhaps Brother Abelle will speak with me there and tell me the truth of these strange creatures, the Sidhe, the Xoconai. How I long to know!

But if not, if their secrets remain beyond my ken for eternity, I do not consider my three decades of searching for the truth of them to be a waste. Nay! For as I have learned tiny hints of the Sidhe, I have so, too, learned more of myself, and of my brothers of Abelle, and of the wide world. A life of learning is not to be mourned.

And so I go, soon I am sure, to explore the greatest mystery of all.

My heart is full.

FINAL AND SEVENTEENTH DIARY OF THE TOMB OF
UNKNOWN ANCIENTS IN THE RUINS OF HERTEMSPAH
BROTHER GILBERT OF ANNACUTH, GOD'S YEAR 93
(UNREAD IN THE CATACOMBS OF
ST. MERE ABELLE IN MORE THAN TWO CENTURIES)

17

THE TRUST IN AOLEYN

Aoleyn felt the cool air against her body, against her fur, and it was glorious.

The cold snowy patches of ground she traversed did not sting her feet, because they were not her feet. Not as she had known them, at least.

Leaving the sacred lea while the witches were all tumbled and disoriented from her powerful blast, Aoleyn had grabbed up a pile of clothing one of the witches had set outside the perimeter of their dance. She had taken, too, as many of the sacred crystals as she could manage, turning the clothes into a large pack before running off. Her magic had led her, leaping from a cliff, using the malachite to drift down slowly, far to the north and east of the Usgar.

She had no plan, except to get away—and to not lead any pursuit anywhere in the direction of Bahdlahn, of course.

She thought of flying with her moonstone, but feared such an obvious display of magic. She did it for a bit, just to get further afield of any who might be chasing her, to show no tracks.

But then another thought had occurred to her. Instead of using the gems directly, which she feared Mairen might detect, Aoleyn had called upon something more intimate.

She had fallen into the music of her tattoo, but not to turn her arm into the paw of a great cat, no. Instead, she had focused her thoughts lower, and her wince carried, too, a smile of satisfaction and wonderment as her legs had transformed.

Now she ran easily about the snow, powerful hind legs, leopard legs, propelling her along. At first, it had been awkward, but Aoleyn had gradually come to realign her balance appropriately for these new, stronger and swifter legs. And there was, too, a teasing desire to fall ever deeper into the magic, to fully transform into the cloud leopard.

Caution had held her back, both because of her horror that she would become as the fossa, her belief that perhaps she couldn't bring forth the magic to that extent, and most of all, her very real fear that the bone-altering twisting and crunching of such a transformation would kill her.

Now her gait was easy and swift, and her tracks were not those of a fleeing heretic witch, surely. She ran down and around the side of Fireach Speuer, crossing to the west far below the Usgar encampment. She looked back up the mountain as she did, to where the glow of the bonfire at the winter plateau lit the sky. Somewhere up there was Mairen, wounded, defeated. Aoleyn remembered the look on the Usgar-righinn's face, one of abject shock, when the searing wind had swept over her and the others, tossing them back across the grass to tumble into and about the pines.

Aoleyn took great satisfaction in the recollection. She had shown them, all of them. But she also knew that she had awakened a great enemy, and the Usgar were neither a forgiving nor merciful bunch.

Strangely, though, Aoleyn did not care. "I will show to you the truth," she whispered repeatedly, convincing herself that she would find some way to transform the Usgar, to reform the Usgar. Those who stood in her way, like Tay Aillig and Mairen, she decided, would learn a more forceful lesson than she had taught to the witches this night.

She picked her way across and then back up, moving gracefully, carefully, feeling the hum of the magic flowing through her.

Maintaining the magic was taking a toll on her, though, and she knew it could not hold.

She needed to find shelter, and soon.

Fortunately, she knew right where to go. She had flown there, in the borrowed form of an owl, a score of times already. She had traveled up these same trails in the borrowed body of a fox, and so she found her way well enough even as the night grew dark about her, for the cat's eye gem on her turquoise ear cuff gave her that marvelous vision. As the moon reached its zenith, she came over the last ridge, and saw the cave entrance below, mostly hidden by a piled snowdrift.

She slipped into the cave silently on padded paws and noted the two forms lying among some piled skins and woven blankets, which confused her. Had Bahdlahn taken a mate? Had he found a friend? Another uamhas escaping?

She moved closer, trying to sort out which might be Bahdlahn.

One of the mounds of furs stirred, the man under it rolling about to lift his head, sensing another presence, it seemed. He let out a cry and scrambled, tossing aside furs.

Aoleyn backed away, recognizing the voice of Aghmor.

Beside the man, the other form stirred, and the first, Aghmor, came clear of his bedding, awkwardly shifting to one knee, lifting a spear before him.

"Where is Bahdlahn?" Aoleyn demanded.

"What? Who?" Aghmor stuttered in reply. "Who are you?"

"Aoleyn?" Bahdlahn cried out, for it was indeed Bahdlahn under the other pile of furs. He moved immediately to throw some wood on the fire, which flared to life, and with that distraction, Aoleyn dismissed her leopard magic, grimacing and stifling her growls of pain as her legs transformed back into those of a human woman.

"It can'no be," Aghmor breathed, lowering the spear.

Bahdlahn started for her, but Aghmor threw out his arm to hold the man back. "She's a ghost!"

Aoleyn giggled. "Hardly," she said.

"We saw you thrown into the chasm," Aghmor protested, but as he spoke, Bahdlahn burst through his blocking arm and rushed across the cave to fly against Aoleyn with a great bear hug.

"Aoleyn! Aoleyn! Aoleyn!" he said repeatedly, tugging her back and forth, lifting her right off the ground in his strong arms, and he began to sob with joy.

Aoleyn looked over his shoulder to Aghmor, who sat there shaking his head. She offered a smile.

"How is it possible?" Aghmor asked. "We saw them drop you into the chasm."

"The place is filled with magic," Aoleyn lied, as she wasn't about to tell them about actual ghosts catching her. "I heard the song of Usgar, and found within its notes the magic to slow my fall. I was hurt, but, well . . ."

As Bahdlahn let her go, she stepped back and held her arms out wide, showing them that she was whole and alive.

"I am sorry, though," she added, reaching a hand to grab Bahdlahn's forearm. "I could do nothing for Innevah."

He looked at her incredulously. "What? What of her?"

Aoleyn turned to Aghmor again, and he was shaking his head emphatically.

"You do'no know?" Aoleyn asked her uamhas friend. "Your mother . . ."

"It was Innevah who cried out?" Bahdlahn balked, the words catching against the lump in his throat. "My ma?"

He began to rock and Aoleyn was quick to him, catching him, steadying him, and now it was her turn to give him a needed hug.

"She wasn't afraid," Aoleyn said to him, though of course, she had no way of knowing any such thing. She pulled Bahdlahn out to arm's length and stared into his blue eyes. "Innevah struck out at them. She killed one of the Coven, one who deserved to die. Her courage . . . remarkable. She loved you, Bahdlahn, above all else. She would have fought back years ago, except that she understood that you would suffer the consequences. She was a warrior in her heart."

The words weren't helping much, she knew, so she went back to the hug and just held her friend close and let him have his moment of grief. She knew he'd come through this, and quickly. Bahdlahn and his mother had been slaves of the brutal Usgar for all of Bahdlahn's life—almost two decades. Innevah had known freedom before that, down at a lake village in the shadow of Fireach Speuer.

The Usgar spoke of the lakemen as weak, cowardly, and simple, but to Aoleyn, Innevah stood as one of the strongest, bravest, and cleverest people she had ever known. Bahdlahn understood that, too, and knew the many sacrifices his mother had made to give him a chance at life. As far as Aoleyn knew, he was the only male slave ever to have been allowed to live past his transition to adulthood. That had been Innevah's doing, with her strict instructions to him that he would be stupid as far as anyone else would know. Feigning the part of the simpleton had made Bahdlahn less of a threat— enough so that he was still alive.

Alive, and out here, for some reason, Aoleyn reminded herself. She pulled back and turned to Aghmor.

"I would greet you with a hug," he said. "My heart's full at seeing you, for sure that I thought you'd been murdered. But I fear I can'no stand." He guided her gaze down to his leg, pulling the furs off it, to show his calf bent halfway down, in a manner that no human leg should ever bend.

Aoleyn rushed to his side, inspecting the garishly broken leg.

"It aches, but not so bad, unless I try to stand," Aghmor explained. "I fell early in the winter and broke it."

"You've spent the whole season out here with Bahdlahn?" Aoleyn looked from one to the other.

"We couldn't get back," both said at the same time.

"But why are you out . . ." Aoleyn bit back the question, for she could figure it out, regarding Bahdlahn, at least. Tay Aillig had promised to kill him, and if Bahdlahn believed that she had been killed, he would know that he had no defense against the merciless Usgar warrior. Why Aghmor might be here, though, she could not begin to imagine.

"I'm weary now," she told the Usgar. "In the morning, I'll tend your wound. Might that we'll be able to fix your leg."

He grabbed her by the forearm with surprising familiarity. "I trust you will," he said, too intensely, she thought.

She wasn't sure what that meant, but was sure that she needed some sleep.

Bahdlahn moved to the skins and blankets and pulled some aside, preparing a bed for her. Gladly, she accepted, and collapsed into them, falling fast asleep.

Tay Aillig pushed to the forefront of the gathering in the winter encampment, nearly the whole tribe out on the northern end of the plateau, staring into the sacred trees, where something strange seemed to be happening.

That array of puzzled expressions only grew more confused when the witches came filtering through the trees, most wearing nothing but their simple, sheer smocks, two of them fully naked. All seemed disheveled and out of sorts, some leaning on each other, with wisps of smoke coming from their smocks or hair.

A pair were helping Mairen, but when she saw the gathering, she tugged free of them and came forward determinedly, though on legs that were far from steady.

She started to speak, but stopped when Tay Aillig couldn't stifle his laugh.

"What?" she demanded.

Tay Aillig brushed her hair back from her face, trying to control his snort. "Your eyebrows," he said. "They're gone. Your face is red. What . . . what?"

She glowered at him. "Aoleyn lives."

The mocking grin disappeared from the Usgar-triath's face. "She survived the sacrifice? No."

"Yes."

"How many could have done so? What does this mean for the favor of Usgar?"

"None, ever," Mairen replied. "Yet she did. She is alive. She attacked us on the plateau."

"You are sure?"

"Of course I am sure!" Mairen growled back at him. She looked around at her sisters. "Aoleyn," they all confirmed, one after another.

"And she is powerful with . . ." Connebragh started to add.

"Shut up," Mairen told her.

"Where is she now?" Tay Aillig asked. He looked back and called, "Warriors!"

"She fled, down the mountain."

Tay Aillig nodded, unsure of his next move.

Mairen pushed right up to him and whispered in his ear. "She is out there, and with great magic. She is a danger to you, to us."

The man nodded as Mairen stepped back. Suddenly this all seemed more serious. "How fared your ritual? Was it ruined?"

"Sure that it was cut short," Connebragh answered him.

"It went far enough," Mairen snapped. "We are thirteen once more. The Coven is completed."

A murmur went up through the witches behind, some voicing their disagreement with that assessment, but Tay Aillig ended the debate simply, forcefully saying, "Good."

"Aoleyn must be caught," Mairen declared.

Tay Aillig rocked back on his heels. "Must?" he asked, his voice calm.

"We are all in danger."

"Or she'll not return," said Tay Aillig.

"A risk we can'no take, any of us," Mairen insisted. "She has found some power beyond the sacred crystals. In her blasphemy, she has twisted the magic to her own evil ends. Usgar is not with her, but she has found a way, a demon way, to be sure. I do'no know how she survived Craos'a'diad, but she has, and her continued existence marks us in the eyes of our god. Usgar will not be content until she is given to him."

"All out and about the camp," Tay Aillig ordered his warriors. "Look for signs. Find her trail, but do'no venture far, and ne'er alone!"

As the gathering began to disperse, forming into hunting groups, Tay Aillig pulled Mairen aside.

"You wear your fear upon your face," he said to her quietly.

"One spell," Mairen answered. "We were surprised, aye, and that is no small thing, but one spell, just one, sent us all bouncing and burning. I've ne'er seen . . ." She paused and took a deep breath.

"We have to find her. We have to catch her. We have to kill her," she said to her husband.

Tay Aillig glanced around at the first spring night, the snows still formidable this high on the mountain, the wind's bite still lethal. "How?" he asked, an all-encompassing question. Aoleyn had been given to Craos'a'diad an entire season ago. How could she have possibly survived? Where had she gone?

"How?" he asked again.

"It was Aoleyn" was all that Mairen could reply.

Aoleyn would have slept the day through, except that anxious Aghmor would not wait. He stirred her, and when she tried to roll over away from him, he grabbed her more forcefully and called her name, shaking her until she pushed his hands away and sat up, rubbing her bleary eyes.

"My leg," the man pleaded. He was sitting on the floor beside her, and he grabbed that injured limb and pulled it around before him.

"Get the crystals," he told Bahdlahn.

"No," said Aoleyn. "I do'no need them." When Aghmor started to protest, she stared into his eyes and held her hand up, bidding him to trust her.

Aoleyn brought one hand to her own hip, to the wedstone pendant hanging from her chain belt, and placed the other upon the wrongly bent section of Aghmor's calf. She knew immediately as she began casting her spell that the bone of shattered leg had long ago healed, but had healed wrongly. She went in with the magical warmth, casting a powerful spell of healing, but there was little to actually repair at that time. The bones had mended, the skin and muscles about them had reset, but in this new and unwieldy manner, and at such an angle that Aghmor could not walk without great discomfort.

She heard Aghmor sigh with pleasure and relief as he felt the soothing magic, but when she stopped and he opened his eyes, he looked to his leg and gasped, for nothing appeared different.

"It's to be more difficult than I was thinking," Aoleyn admitted. "Your bone's solid. There's naught to heal."

"I can'no walk!" Aghmor cried, seeming on the edge of an explosion here. "I need . . ."

"There is a way," Aoleyn said calmly and forcefully. "But you be sure that it's going to hurt."

Aghmor stared at her, mouth open, clearly at a loss.

"Lie down," Aoleyn instructed, smoothing the furs beside him.

He stared at her, his face full of suspicion.

"Do you want to walk?" she asked calmly.

The man rolled down to his back and Aoleyn motioned Bahdlahn over.

"Hold him down," Aoleyn instructed.

"No!" Aghmor started to protest, but Bahdlahn caught his arms even as he started to flail, and pinned him easily, having all the leverage, and possessing superior strength.

The Usgar began cursing then, but only for a brief time, as Aoleyn stuffed a wad of cloth into his mouth.

"You bite it, and with all your strength," she said. "I'll get you walking, not to doubt, but it's not to be easy. If you're wanting me to stop, then nod now and so I will, but you'll be crawling about for the rest of your days."

Aghmor settled and finally shook his head.

"Bite it with all your strength," Aoleyn told him, and to Bahdlahn, she said, "And hold him as best you can."

Aghmor's eyes went wide and he began making strange mewling sounds as Aoleyn grabbed his misshapen calf above and below the badly healed break. She fell into her wedstone then, and sent her spirit searching, searching, while settling back and lifting one bare foot to place it between her hands against Aghmor's leg.

"You think you're strong enough to break it?" Bahdlahn asked, or started to ask, for even as the words left his mouth, there came a sharp crackle, a blast of lightning from Aoleyn's foot, shooting into Aghmor's leg.

The man howled, the scream muffled by the wad of cloth in his mouth. He began thrashing and Bahdlahn struggled to hold him as Aoleyn tugged hard with her hands, and pushed hard the other way with her foot.

Aghmor's other leg came across to kick at her, but Aoleyn accepted the blow and answered with a second lightning bolt, and with it came a sickening crack of the bone as she forced the broken leg to straighten.

Immediately, the woman shifted her magic, falling back to the wedstone, taking another couple of kicks from the frantic, agonized Aghmor.

He calmed almost immediately when the first wave of warm healing magic washed through him.

Aoleyn went at the leg with all of her magical strength, mending the bone, sealing the veins.

She fell back soon after, gasping for the effort. She managed to motion to Bahdlahn to let Aghmor go, for the man, covered in sweat, had stopped struggling.

Bahdlahn removed the wad of cloth.

"Are you okay, then?" Aoleyn asked, and the breathless Aghmor nodded.

"Do'no try to sit up, and do'no you dare try to stand," Aoleyn told him. "We've not near finished here."

"No more lightning," he whispered.

"No more," Aoleyn confirmed. "Just the healing now, and you'll be walking again. Might be a day, might be three, but you'll be walking."

Aghmor flashed her the warmest of smiles, his eyes boring into hers with such intensity that it rocked her back a bit.

"Sleep now," she bade him, and she collected herself and gathered up some more clothes, moving aside and suddenly feeling very exposed.

"I do'no like it," said Sorcha, the oldest witch in the Coven, one who had been considering her journey into the p'utherai, the sisterhood of those retired from actively acting as witches. "There is too much turmoil, too much disturbance."

That declaration from the venerable witch brought a collective hush from the five witches around her, the oldest of the Coven's dancers with the exception of the Usgar-righinn, who was not there, and of Connebragh, who was there and was still quite young, barely into her thirties. They were back at the sacred lea, ostensibly to begin planning the breakdown of the winter encampment and the move back down the mountain, a conversation that had seemed quite trite in light of the recent events.

"Aoleyn will join, Aoleyn will not," Sorcha spat. "She battles the demon fossa on a field of sidhe, and Seonagh is lost to us! Oh, fey!"

Connebragh nodded, knowing that old Sorcha and Seonagh had danced together for many seasons before Seonagh had retired to a quieter existence. Connebragh, too, profoundly felt the loss of Seonagh, who had been her teacher.

"Seonagh is given to Craos'a'diad, following her sister," Sorcha said.

"We do not speak of that," said Annagh, the second-youngest there besides Connebragh, but one who looked much older, for her hair had turned white at a very young age.

"Bah!" Sorcha snorted, waving her hand. "And Gavina will join, but lo, she falls to her death? What witch would so fall with a sacred crystal in hand?"

"But she was not a witch, was she?" Annagh retorted. "And she could not be, so it's seen."

"Another dead," Sorcha continued. "Seonagh, Gavina, then Aoleyn is fed to the god. Brayth is killed, then Ralid. Too much, I say! Too much disturbance. Elder Raibert falls."

"Brayth was killed on the field. All saw," one of the others reminded them.

"By the fossa, and when Seonagh was lost," Annagh added.

"Raibert was an old man," said yet another.

"Seven more lost to the sidhe," Sorcha spat.

"A large force," Connebragh reasoned.

"Aye, and who's e'er seen so many sidhe together as that?" She sighed and sat back, quietly considering the litany of unusual and deadly events that had befallen the Usgar in the last few months.

"All reasonable, aye," she said, talking as much to herself as to the others. "But so many? All at once? And now this? Young and wild Aoleyn returns from the grave to throw us aside as if we are but children? Can it not be a sign from Usgar that he is not pleased?"

"Moragh will be acceptable," said Annagh, who was Moragh's aunt. "She will grow strong in the magic of Usg . . ."

"Compared to Aoleyn?" Sorcha scoffed.

"That was no magic of our god," Annagh insisted. "Demon magic. She fought the fossa on the night Ralid was killed, I have heard."

"She killed Ralid," said one of the others.

"Perhaps she fought the fossa before that," Annagh reasoned. "Perhaps the demon beast overcame her and took her, and it was the fossa, not Aoleyn, who slew Ralid. And the fossa, not Aoleyn, who went into Craos'a'diad, and who came forth from Craos'a'diad to torment us."

The others were following her lead here, leaning in and nodding, except for Sorcha, who leaned away, arms crossed over her chest, shaking her head.

And except for Connebragh, who knew better. "No!" she interrupted harshly. All eyes turned to her and she swallowed hard, her loyalties torn, her thoughts jumbled. "I was with the Usgar-righinn when Aoleyn returned, and before. Mairen believed that Aoleyn had destroyed the fossa—that was Aoleyn's claim. It is possible."

"Then why give the girl to Craos'a'diad?" Sorcha demanded.

"Heresy," Connebragh admitted. "It was'no demon magic, but the gems Aoleyn wore, gems she took from the crystals in the caverns below Craos'a'diad."

That brought a few gasps around the small circle.

"She claimed to have found a new . . ." Connebragh shook her head, for she was getting too far down a line of thought here that she could not begin to explain.

"You do'no believe that Aoleyn should have been fed to the god," Sorcha said.

"She killed Ralid, they say," Connebragh replied.

"But for the rest?" Sorcha pressed.

Connebragh shrugged and blew a long sigh. "The Usgar-righinn speaks for our god. I do not question her judgment."

"The Usgar-righinn, who was tossed like a child by the breath of Aoleyn," Sorcha said.

"Hush!" Annagh warned, and others joined in.

"I do'no know," Connebragh admitted, silencing them all. "There is much I do'no know. But Mairen is Usgar-righinn."

"Who is married to Usgar-triath, who was Usgar-laoch and who was Aoleyn's husband," said Sorcha.

She left the implications hanging out there for the other five, and none could deny the convenience of the spectacular fall of the powerful young woman named Aoleyn.

"Let us plan the journey to the lower camp," said Sorcha. "And let us pray to Usgar that these next seasons will be less . . . eventful."

The pain and exertion of the healing had Aghmor sleeping soon after, leaving Aoleyn and Bahdlahn to share stories of their winter adventures.

"I've been staying in the caves under the mountain," Aoleyn explained to him. "I found a place, a most marvelous . . ." She paused and sighed, shaking her head. She could describe the waterfall cavern, of course, but could she really explain to Bahdlahn the magical and mystical beauty of it, the song of the gems within the crystals, the kindness that cave had bestowed upon her? For that's how she felt, truly, as if the cave itself had welcomed her and given to her that comfort which she most had needed.

"I've not eaten in a day," she said, buying some time to consider her story, and also because she was indeed quite hungry. "Have you any food?"

"We do, but not much," Bahdlahn said.

"I will go out this night and hunt," she said.

Bahdlahn looked at her curiously.

"Trust me when I tell you that I'll be more successful than you at it— more than you and Aghmor together if he was able."

"For some reason, I do'no doubt you," Bahdlahn admitted with a laugh. He found some food and gave it to Aoleyn, and while she cooked it and ate it, he told her his own tale, of how he and Aghmor had watched her be sacrificed, and of how Aghmor then had saved him, shuttling him away to this place.

"An owl has been bringing us food," Bahdlahn explained. "Sometimes a fox, though we've not seen any offerings for a few days."

Aoleyn, a bit of rabbit between her teeth, smiled at him.

"'Twas you," Bahdlahn said, and she shrugged.

"The winter's letting go now and food will be easier to find," Aoleyn said.

"And we'll be easier to find, by the Usgar," Bahdlahn warned.

"What were you to do, then?"

Bahdlahn looked at Aghmor. "All on his leg," he explained. "If he was able, we were to go down the mountain together."

"To the lake tribes?" Aoleyn had to swallow hard to avoid choking on her latest bite.

"Tay Aillig meant to kill me. I wanted to go to my moth . . ." He had to pause and steady himself. "I would leave, down to the town in the shadow of the mountain. Aghmor meant to come if he could, but if not, then he meant to go back to the Usgar and tell them that it was Bahdlahn who had kept him alive."

He shrugged again. "They thought me dead, or long gone."

"You might have made it," said Aoleyn.

"Now we will make it," Bahdlahn insisted.

Aoleyn looked at him long and hard, but then shook her head. "No, we won't have to," she explained. "I'm not done here. Not with Tay Aillig and not with Mairen. I'm knowing so much more now. More about their god than they know!"

"They will kill you."

"I won't let them. And I will show them."

"We can get away. With you . . ."

"We can still get away, but we'll not until I've tried," Aoleyn insisted. "It has to be more, don't you see?" She leaned forward and put her hand on Bahdlahn's forearm.

He shook his head at her question.

"We can change it. We can change it all."

"Change what?"

"All of it. No more slaves, no more raids, no more warring. The Usgar have to learn—I will make them learn!—that the folk about the lake are not our enemies, and not our cattle, to be enslaved and tortured and raped. No, this will end. I will end it."

"You're one person," Bahdlahn protested. "We're two, or . . ." He motioned to Aghmor.

"I will take great care," Aoleyn promised. "And if I see no way, then we will be gone from this place, off the mountain. I promise." She leaned forward, locking Bahdlahn's gaze with her black eyes.

"Will you trust me?"

18

PROCESSION OF GLORIOUS GOLD

"It is arrogance," Pixquicauh's fleshless face said to no one in particular. The other xoconai augurs marching alongside the High Priest knew better than to respond. Pixquicauh had often done this in the weeks since being openly challenged back at his temple, voicing his complaints against Tuolonatl in their presence, but not for their benefit, or even asking them for a response, confirming or not.

"She will not keep it up," he said to himself. "She is showing off, currying favor. When the battles begin, she will not stay with the vanguard. This is a conquest led by the augurs, who hear the voice of Scathmizzane, not by the sovereigns, who cower beneath the protests of common xoconai. The mundunugu and the macana are our tools, our weapons, nothing more."

The augurs marched through a valley. They were at the very center of the main xoconai column. Ahead, along the banks of a river swollen with meltwater, they could see a thousand macana marching; behind them, another thousand. A dozen other xoconai columns traversed this rough terrain, split among the many valleys as they climbed the foothills of the Tyuskixmal, to the peaks of the towering mountain range they called Teotl Tenamitl.

But it was what they could not yet see that remained Pixquicauh's focus. Far ahead, leading all the columns, were the cavalry vanguard, and at their head rode the mundunugu and the legendary Tuolonatl, who had become, in his mind, his greatest rival for Scathmizzane's love.

Pixquicauh wanted no competition for the love of Glorious Gold. Scathmizzane had scarred him, had infused his face with the skull of his predecessor. To make him ugly, Pixquicauh had come to believe, so that no others would covet him, so that he would be Scathmizzane's alone. What xoconai woman, or even man, would not wish to serve every need of Pixquicauh, the augur who had foreseen the rise of Kithkukulikahn to eat the sun, who had predicted the return of the God-King—the true God-King—at the risk of his own life? For had he been wrong, he would have surely been sacrificed.

"She is not as courageous as she wants us to believe," he said with a sneer.

He turned around, continuing to walk backward, but fixing his gaze on the augurs behind him. The eight priests carried a litter, and on that platform had been set a small wooden chair, carved to look like a throne and painted golden. Atop the throne rested a mirror of shining, polished gold.

Pixquicauh saw his reflection in the mirror, and he spoke to it. "Tuolonatl wishes to outshine us," he said, "but in doing so she separates herself from the Glorious Gold. She wishes to place herself above us, but instead she places herself more distant."

He peered into the mirror, as if waiting for his reflection to answer. After a while, he grew satisfied, and turned back around.

The other priests said nothing.

He would hardly have heard them if they had.

Tuolonatl had seen war. War with other xoconai, war with the xelquiza, war with mict, war with the cillipontic, the short and rugged hairy humanoids who wore their bright berets (one of which Tuolonatl kept in her pouch to wear into battle), even, once, war with a band of brown-skinned humans who had come up from the far south. In the last two decades, whenever a xoconai sovereign decided to plunder another nearby city-state, he or she had called to Tuolonatl to lead the charge.

Her scars were many, but mostly old. She could still fight as well as any, but her true value lay in her understanding of the battlefield, of how to attack, where to attack, and when to attack.

Yes, Tuolonatl knew war.

Tuolonatl hated war.

She hated riding lizards, too, much preferring her horse, small and fast and incredibly powerful, a three-year-old she had carefully bred through specific bloodlines for decades. Up here, though, on the slopes of the Tyuskixmal, her green, golden-speckled and golden-headed cuetzpali was far more effective, and a far safer mount. But she hated the thing, hated all the dragons. They could be controlled, but they were stupid beasts, and cared not for their riders, other than the food those riders provided, and the punishments the riders would inflict when the lizard did wrong.

Tuolonatl smiled as she rolled with the long strides of the mount, thinking of her horse, Pocheoya. Such a smelly thing, he was, but such a friend, as well. In battle, Tuolonatl could count on Pocheoya to protect her, she knew, but this mount, this lizard? It would protect her incidentally, at best, eager to attack anything it could and hopefully aiming for her enemies.

The pleasant thoughts of Pocheoya, who was at the rear of the column, riderless and led at the back of a wagon, disappeared when another mundunugu loped his cuetzpali up beside her.

"It goes splendidly," said Ataquixt, a fierce young warrior of great repute, whom Tuolonatl had named as the lead scout of her column. "We will cross Teotl Tenamitl soon enough, and let the battles begin!"

Tuolonatl smiled and nodded, not wanting to dampen his enthusiasm. Inside, though, she knew that more than glorious battles would commence. So, too, would the garish wounds, the deaths of many far too young, the battlefield cries for mantli, as sons and daughters called out for the person who had given them the greatest comfort, as all sense of comfort flew away in the cold pain of death.

Tuolonatl liked Ataquixt. She thought him funny and clever, and very competent as both mundunugu and scout. They had fought together before, though that inter-city war had been more posturing than macana play, with few wounded and fewer dead. She thought him handsome, too, quite. His blue facial colors were narrower than most, but striking in color, just enough so to bring out the hint of golden flecks in his otherwise dark eyes. If she were twenty years younger, or even ten, she knew where she'd be spending her nights.

And every time Ataquixt flashed her his smile, or laughed at one of her jokes, she thought she might entice him to her bed anyway.

She didn't want to imagine him lying broken on the ground, wailing out "Mantli, mantli," to a mother who would never hear.

She had seen too much of that, which was why Tuolonatl was usually care-

ful about not making friends with those who would fight beside her. Ataquixt had charmed her, though.

"To see the sun rise on Ayuskixmal," he said wistfully. "To climb Tzatzini
and look down upon . . ." He couldn't even finish, caught halfway between
a joyful laugh and his words.

Tuolonatl looked around at the many mundunugu, all pressing their
cuetzpali along, all eager to bask in the blood they would spill for the Glorious Gold.

Tuolonatl didn't hate humans. She would happily lead her forces against
any xelquiza half-bloods that might revolt, however, and she took particular
pleasure in killing mict goblins. Other than fellow xoconai, her least favorite enemy were the humans. No, she didn't fear them—most were terrible
fighters—and they were ugly, of course, and didn't particularly smell any better than her Pocheoya. But they were not irredeemably vile, like the others.
This she had learned in her one fierce encounter with them, for when the
humans lay broken and dying, they called out their word "mother," which
Tuolonatl knew to mean mantli.

So, while she would not dissuade, and couldn't even disagree with, her
army, the augurs, all the xoconai, who viewed this eastward march to be the
greatest glory of their God-King, and justified, of course, merely because of
Scathmizzane's word, her heart was not as light as those about her.

Any human she struck down throughout this campaign, she resolved to
kill quickly, before it could call out to its mantli.

At her bidding, Ataquixt continued to ride beside her. The trail was fairly
straightforward here and those leading the column would not likely go astray,
and Tuolonatl enjoyed the company. There were other matters for the two
to discuss, as well. Tuolonatl had assigned the sculpting of the battlefield
model to a trio of older mundunugu who served Ataquixt directly, two
women and a man from Ataquixt's city-state. That small replica of the terrain they would first conquer could prove critical to her, not just from a tac-
tical standpoint, but in giving her solid and tangible counterpoints when
she ran into the inevitable interference by the fanatical High Priest and the
other superior-minded augurs.

Still, the conversation between the two was more lighthearted and personal this day, swapping tales of home, and even stories from Ataquixt
regarding his mischievous youth, which reminded Tuolonatl of their age
disparity.

An interruption came later that afternoon, from a short and bright flash from somewhere far ahead, and much higher, near the peaks of Teotl Tenamitl.

"Code-talker!" Ataquixt yelled, correctly anticipating Tuolonatl's command.

Another flash showed ahead, then a second, from another high peak in the mountains before them.

A few moments later, a mundunugu carrying a small sheet of polished gold rushed her mount up beside the pair, to the other side of Ataquixt, who pointed out the ridge where they had seen the initial flash.

The code-talker maneuvered her golden sheet carefully, catching the lowering sun's rays and flicking the mirror in a series of bright flashes up toward the mountaintops.

Almost immediately came a responding series of flickers.

"What is it?" Tuolonatl asked.

The code-talker moved her mirror furiously, interspersing long and short flashes in a set pattern to spell out words to the distant code-talkers.

A string came back, then a second from the side peak.

"News from Tzatzini, my general," said the code-talker. "Some of those who shadowed the xelquiza forces have returned to the Tyuskixmal."

"Signal them down to us," Tuolonatl instructed, and as the code-talker complied, she turned to Ataquixt. "We make camp here, in this area. Find an acceptable spot."

Ataquixt nodded and tugged his bridle, dropping back between the general and the code-talker, and turning to ride off.

"Defend it well and send word to halt the line," Tuolonatl told him. "Except for High Priest Pixquicauh and his entourage. Bid them to come forward to join us." She looked ahead, back up the mountain. "It should be an interesting evening."

Her tent was set up in the middle of the area chosen for the forward camp long before the High Priest and his accompanying augurs had arrived. Even better, the first of the scouts came into the camp as the last spike on that tent was being hammered, giving Tuolonatl some time alone with the messenger before having to share the information with her rival. She summoned Ataquixt to her war table, and there met the scout.

"You have glimpsed it?" Ataquixt asked as soon as the formal introductions were over. "You have seen Tzatzini? You have seen the beauty of Otontotomi?"

"I have walked the trails of the Herald, yes," the young xoconai named U'at replied. "But no, there was no city below, no temple, just a . . ."

". . . great lake, running long to the north and west," Tuolonatl finished for him, and when both men looked at her, she added, "You should study more carefully the prophecies of the Last Augur of Darkness of the line of Bayan, who is now Pixquicauh, High Priest of Scathmizzane. Otontotomi is no more seen."

"As you will," U'at said, bowing.

"I will do better, my general," Ataquixt promised.

"I have been to the peaks of Tzatzini," U'at explained. "At the bidding of Halfizzen, who served the Last Augur of Darkness, did there I journey, and did there I fight with a human."

"There are not many xoconai alive who can make such a claim," said Tuolonatl.

"Where is your trophy?" asked Ataquixt. "His head? His ear? His hair? Have you nothing?"

U'at lowered his gaze. "He fought well and knew the land. I did not. I thought it better to flee and so return."

Ataquixt started to say something snide, but Tuolonatl interceded. "To know the land is a great advantage," she said. "That is why you are here."

The tent flap opened and three others entered, one an augur, the other two mundunugu.

"Halfizzen," U'at greeted, bringing his palm up over his face briefly.

"My general, great Tuolonatl," Halfizzen said, using that same hand greeting with the general, but then bowing low before her in deference. "These scouts are returned from the battles. The xelquiza did engage the humans on the banks of the lake in the shadow of Tzatzini, and upon the highest reaches of the great shining mountain."

"All of the humans?"

Halfizzen shook his head and looked to the scout at his left.

"Several villages of humans are scattered about the southern reaches of the great lake," that female mundunugu explained. "The humans were too many. We sent the half-bloods to attack two, the two nearest the shadow of Tzatzini, and drove the humans from one."

"Just one?"

"The humans fought well, better than the half-bloods," the scout explained.

"But we have one village taken?" Ataquixt said.

She shrugged. "Perhaps. Or perhaps the humans will take it back."

"They will," said the scout on Halfizzen's right.

"If the xelquiza we sent forth can overtake one, we can destroy a hundred," Tuolonatl said. "What of the mountain? Human scouts or hunters? Were they driven from the slopes of Tzatzini?"

"A village," Halfizzen answered.

"You said the highest reaches."

"Near the very top." He looked to U'at.

Tuolonatl and Ataquixt exchanged curious glances. Tzatzini was, by all accounts, the tallest mountain of the region, and the peaks of the towering Teotl Tenamitl range were not hospitable in the least.

"The greatest village, perhaps," U'at offered. "It is the one I first spied."

"More than half of the xelquiza force attacked that village," Halfizzen added.

"And they failed?"

"They were obliterated, General," U'at explained. "The humans struck them with lightning and great exploding blasts of fire."

"Lightning?" Tuolonatl asked incredulously.

"What nonsense . . . ?" Ataquixt started to add.

"Obliterated," Halfizzen agreed. "Killed, every one of the half-bloods." Again, he motioned for U'at to explain.

"Perhaps some of the humans were killed," U'at offered. "I could not get close enough to learn the extent. But not many fell, if any, I am sure. Never have I seen such power unleashed. If a thousand atlatls were all thrown at once . . ."

"Enough," said Tuolonatl. "And be wise in how you speak of this, all of you." She looked mostly at Halfizzen as she gave that command, knowing that the augurs, above all others, seemed to understand the concept of morale the least.

"The xelquiza scored many kills by the lake?" she asked the woman.

The scout nodded. "Yes, and drove the survivors out in their boats across the waters, and there gave chase."

"Then that is the tale we will tell," Tuolonatl said.

"We must not hide the dangers of the village on Tzatzini," said Halfizzen.

"They wield magic as if they were blessed by Scathmizzane himself," U'at stated, and his eyes widened at the looks that got him.

"Blasphemy!" Halfizzen cried.

"Calm. Calm," Tuolonatl said sharply, interrupting the stream of curses the augur, the other scouts, even Ataquixt, began hurling the foolish U'at's way. "Blasphemy, perhaps, but useful information as well," she said. "Take care your words as you describe this, U'at, who has twice walked the slopes of Tzatzini. High Priest Pixquicauh would not forgive your poor choice. But we here shall. Just once."

"Pixquicauh must be told of the event upon the Herald," Halfizzen said.

"He is on his way to this tent," Tuolonatl explained. "Until he arrives, you mundunugu will go with Ataquixt to the mud trays and work with the sculptors to fashion Tzatzini's slopes and locate the villages of the humans. Go."

The three saluted, palm to face, then scurried away. Halfizzen turned to follow.

"You will remain," Tuolonatl bade him.

He turned to regard her curiously.

"If you please, good augur," she said, sweeping her hand out to a pair of chairs that had been set up to the side, near a small firepit. "I will have food and drink brought to us while we discuss the path ahead."

"I am honored, great Tuolonatl," Halfizzen said with a bow.

The general could sense his unease, and marked his suspicion. She knew, too, though, that her reputation was thick with this one, and that her unexpected invitation had somewhat charmed him. He was just a young augur, an insignificant pawn, and she, the greatest living commander and mundunugu of Tonoloya, had invited him to her table, to dine alone with her.

Still, he was Pixquicauh's man, she knew.

She had to correct that unfortunate circumstance.

Pixquicauh walked about the table, hands clasped behind his back, his skull face never leaving the strange model of mud and dirt that had been constructed.

"I am to believe that this is Tzatzini?" he asked after perhaps his fourth circuit of the muddy sculpture.

"It is a guess, re-created from the memories of those who went there," Tuolonatl answered. "Some who were there at your command."

The old augur just mumbled something she couldn't make out. She did well to hide her smile, for she understood the source of the High Priest's cantankerousness. Back at his humble temple, she had made him look foolish in front of his God-King. Had he been generous of spirit and honest in his love for Scathmizzane, such a confrontation would not have bothered him, or would not linger, at least. After all, Tuolonatl had been correct in the timing of the attack, in delaying, for they could not have marched to the peaks of Teotl Tenamitl before the winter with any hopes of surviving the journey, let alone the battles that might follow.

"And this water," the High Priest went on. "Is it . . . ?"

Tuolonatl shrugged. "We'll not know until we drive the humans from the mountain and the lakeshore. When that is done, we will learn the secrets of the mountain lake."

"The scouts spoke of lightning and fire magic," Pixquicauh remarked.

Tuolonatl slid out her long dagger and tapped it to the high reaches of the sculpted mountain model on the northern face, overlooking the lake. "Up here," she explained. "The one village up here."

"They must die first. They are apostates. How dare they . . ."

"We will defeat them," Tuolonatl interrupted. "But there are many more humans down at the lakeside, with at least five villages, each larger than the one on the mountain."

"They will be dealt with in time."

"They will be dealt with all together," Tuolonatl corrected. "Yet before the assault on the mountain village."

"Blasphemers first," Pixquicauh declared.

The mundunugu leader shook her head. "That would not be wise."

Around the perimeter of the tent room, the other augurs began shifting uncomfortably and whispering to each other. Tuolonatl regarded them with an amused expression, confident that none would speak openly against her, or even in support of the High Priest. Augurs, speaking with the surety of blessing, were unused to being challenged. While they might be quick to punish commoners who dared speak against them, Tuolonatl was no commoner, and had the ears of every sovereign of Tonoloya. These distant holy clerics had no skills at countering such blunt rebuke.

"The lake is more important," she clarified. "We will be marching for long days with few rations. One of the villages down there is already destroyed, another sorely wounded. When we take the southern bank of the lake we will have all the food and water we need as we gather our forces."

"You leave them the higher ground," the High Priest argued. "You leave them the den of power."

"They will have neither if they come down to fight us, and every day they delay, we will only grow stronger, our macana fed and rested. The mountain will prove little hindrance to us with so many mundunugu. Our cuetz-pali will get our army into place quickly."

"If we surprise them up high, the first strike, it will be easier," Pixqui-cauh insisted, and it was clear that he was becoming quite agitated here.

"And if we do not?" She let the question hang there, locking the High Priest's gaze as his eyes widened.

"You doubt?"

"I prefer caution when risk is not needed. Your way is risk."

"Are you not the legendary Tuolonatl? It is said that you move your forces as if they were ghosts, and strike always where you are not expected."

"Much is said," she replied dismissively. "Much is wrong."

"The blasphemers die first," the High Priest decided. "This is the word of Scathmizzane."

"You risk everything," Tuolonatl replied before he had even finished. "You would strike their strongest hold and most powerful magic before we have fully recovered from the march, when an easier way rests before us. If this is the voice of Scathmizzane, then so be it, but the lake towns are the easier prey, and from them, we will grow stronger."

"We march for the Glorious Gold," Pixquicauh yelled at her. "We bear his symbols, we carry his mirror. No enemy is a threat. All will fall before us!"

"The minions of Glorious Gold are in our charge, High Priest. They are our responsibility."

"They are in his hands," Pixquicauh countered.

"Through us," Tuolonatl insisted. "Scathmizzane trusts in you, which is why you are named as High Priest. Scathmizzane trusts in me, which is why I was summoned to lead this march to Otontotomi. What need of either of us if the army is undefeatable?"

"We . . . I am the conduit of his voice. You are the . . ." Pixquicauh paused and fumbled about for a few moments. "You are but an aspiration, a goal for young macana and mundunugu to achieve, to gain glory with the God-King."

"Glory I have gained, because I am no fool and understand the dangers of the wider world. Dangers even to this great army of Tonoloya."

"Do you suggest that Scathmizzane's army could possibly fail?" The High Priest's voice grew shriller still, and he rose to his feet. The general rose as well, but calmly.

"Scathmizzane placed me in command of his army because he is wise," she said simply. "He knows that his warriors must be well managed, or they can indeed be defeated."

"Blasphemy!" Pixquicauh cried, and several of the augurs around the room voiced their agreement.

But the general was not cowed. "Unless the God-King himself tells me, I will lead to the best solution. That solution is to take the villages in the shadow of the mountain, on the lakeshore, and from there, when we are rested and fed, the village high on the mountain."

"I am Scathmizzane's voice on this journey," the High Priest retorted. "We attack the mountain village first. We attack the blasphemers first."

"No," came another voice, silky and deep and beautiful, echoing through the tent as if it were a great hall. All in the room turned to the source of the voice, the golden mirror atop the throne. In it, they saw not their reflections, but the image of Scathmizzane himself, shining golden.

"You both err, and both speak truly," Scathmizzane said. "When the xelquiza attacked, did they not strike at the lake and mountain at the same time?"

"Close, God-King," Tuolonatl replied. "Those at the lake struck first, but only because they arrived first. They were not disciplined in their movements. The half-bloods are too stupid to understand proper tac . . ."

"They performed their service well," Scathmizzane interrupted.

"If we had sent them all against the mountain village, it would be ours," Pixquicauh growled at Tuolonatl.

"If we had done that, then all would have been slaughtered, and there would remain two unwounded villages on the lakeshore," Tuolonatl retorted.

"Are you quite finished?" Scathmizzane asked, in a tone that told them that they were indeed!

"She is impertinent," the High Priest explained.

"In this great endeavor, she is your peer," Scathmizzane corrected, his tone changing to something lower and more sinister, his words a threat. "You are the voice of Scathmizzane, Pixquicauh, by my decree. Speak not words that are not inspired by Scathmizzane."

"Yes, God-King," the High Priest replied, lowering his gaze.

"You will take the lakeshore," Scathmizzane told Tuolonatl. "Spread wide from the shadows of Tzatzini. Chase the humans out onto the lake, that is your charge."

"I understand," she replied, and bowed.

"And you, my High Priest," the God-King continued, "gather a smaller force from my general, one of swift mundunugu riders. They will strike at the mountain village, but lightly, to tease the humans from their defenses. And you, personally, will carry my mirror to the summit, above the human village."

"Yes, God-King. Wherever you command."

"You will know where to bring the mirror when you arrive, and where to cast it."

That had many in the room glancing to those near, shrugging, unsure.

"Cast it?"

"You will understand," Scathmizzane promised.

"Yes, God-King," said the High Priest.

19

A GIFT OFFERED

The next few days came rainy and warm, with just enough of a chill at night to put an icy sheen on the wet snow. Spring was coming fast, but the trio in the cave, particularly Aoleyn, weren't thrilled about it.

"The paths will clear and they will look for you," said Aghmor, standing without support for the first time in months. He was still shaky, but his strength was slowly returning to his injured leg, though it was not yet nearly as solid as the other. "And when they look for you, they will find us."

"We won't be here," Bahdlahn assured him.

"Or we'll find them first," Aoleyn added.

"You mean to get us killed," Aghmor insisted.

"I might well get myself killed," Aoleyn admitted, "but I'll have you both far afield before that. Besides, I know I can win."

"Win? What does that even mean? What do you think you'll win, woman?"

"Woman?" Aoleyn replied with a wry grin, one completely comfortable with the intended, and therefore failed, attempt by Aghmor to put her in her place, meaning some place below him. "We will see, won't we then?"

"I didn't mean . . ." Aghmor stammered, and Aoleyn grinned all the wider.

"Might that we'll be leaving Fireach Speuer," she said. "Might that you'll be leaving without me, or that you'll promise me that you'll get Bahdlahn back to his home on the lake before you go back to the Usgar and weave a story about your missing months—you can use my own name in that tale however you feel it best, since, well, if that's to happen, I'll be dead."

Off to the side, Bahdlahn swallowed hard, and Aoleyn flashed him a comforting wink.

"Oh, but I've met Mairen and all the others, and I've beaten them, and they're knowing it," Aoleyn said.

"Then why do you run? Why didn't you just claim the title of Usgar-righinn?" Aghmor asked.

"A title I'd not want, nay, not under the rules of Usgar."

"What is your plan?" Bahdlahn interjected.

Aoleyn smiled again, but she had to add a bit of a shrug, because, honestly, she did not know. She had to find some way to defeat Tay Aillig, to get him away from the others and truly best him in combat, and in a manner that would keep him from doubting that she'd do it again, more severely, if he did not agree to her terms.

She really didn't care if he remained the Usgar-laoch, or Usgar-triath, even. The titles meant nothing to her—Mairen could even retain the lead of the Coven, and certainly Aoleyn preferred that Mairen remain as Tay Aillig's wife, for it was nothing she desired. One of Aoleyn's biggest reliefs in these months of regrets and trials was that Tay Aillig had never consummated their marriage.

But she wasn't quite sure of how to go about facilitating her designs just yet, and she knew, with more rain than snow falling now, that she didn't have much time.

She remained determined, however. She could get down the mountain with Bahdlahn, even with Aghmor if he so chose, too quickly for the Usgar to catch them. Perhaps that way lay their best course.

But Aoleyn was Usgar. Her mother and father had been Usgar. Seonagh had been Usgar.

Aoleyn had to try to save her people.

The storm relented the very next day, with warm winds wrapping around the great mountain from the east, across the lower deserts, blowing the clouds aside. It would be a dangerous time out on the mountain, with the snow-pack growing very unstable, but Aoleyn went out anyway, late in the day, as the sun began to sink over Loch Beag far below.

She had treated Aghmor's wounds again, and he was feeling much stronger, insisting, even, that he could travel down the mountain if need be.

"Well, you might need to," Aoleyn said, and she gave Bahdlahn a hug, because she saw that he needed it. "I won't be going near them tonight," she assured her dear friend. "Not in any way they could know, at least." Her smile was sincere in this point, and Bahdlahn clearly got it, because his relief was clear to see.

Aoleyn started to leave, but paused and just stood there for a bit, staring into Bahdlahn's eyes. He was such a good-hearted soul, she recognized so clearly, and it seemed to her that if all, or even some, of the folk living along the great lake were of similar weal then perhaps she would enjoy living down there and leaving the Usgar be.

She had to remind herself again of her duty to those she had loved, and who had loved her. She couldn't give up on the Usgar just yet.

In looking at Bahdlahn, sweet Bahdlahn, she was surely tempted. She moved to the narrow natural corridor to the cave's outer foyer considering the young man, and thinking of Brayth, and of what he had done to her. She didn't like to think about that, not ever. It was something that should not have happened to her, should never have happened. Not to her, not to the uamhas, not to any Usgar woman . . . or man. Not to anyone. What Brayth had done to her, whatever the pretty trappings of marriage or ritual, was theft, nothing less, and theft of the highest order in a violation that could find its way into all of her musings, even the pleasant ones that she got in looking into Bahdlahn's blue eyes.

Yes, it was more than theft—it was a theft in which the thief had left something behind, something enduring and dark.

"I'm glad you're dead," she whispered to Brayth's memory as she left the cave, and she was.

Gentle Aoleyn, who did not want to hurt anyone or anything, was truly glad that Brayth had died in the crushing bite of the demon fossa.

She wasn't proud of that feeling, but neither would she deny it.

Off she went, to find an owl. She liked owls the best, liked the sounds of the mountain through their keen ears, and the sights of the mountain through their keen eyes. Inside the owl's consciousness, Aoleyn felt incredibly alive, and alert.

This night, she would need to be alert.

She wanted to hear every conversation, every plan, every reaction.

Much later that night, Aoleyn returned to her body, which she had left settled high in a pine tree, then returned to the cave, weary, but satisfied.

She had eavesdropped on Mairen and Connebragh, and knew that no searchers would be out until the snowpack settled, which would be several days, at
least. She had learned as well that the Coven had no intention of magically
searching beyond the camp and the sacred lea.

Her show of power had unnerved them. They were vulnerable. Now she
had to plot her next assault.

She thought of Connebragh most of all. She was Mairen's second in the
Coven, it seemed, but she had been trained by Seonagh. And Sorcha had
been Seonagh's friend. Perhaps there lay a wedge or two that Aoleyn might
exploit.

She entered the outer cave skipping lightly, then turned into the inner
cave, where the fire burned steadily and Aghmor reclined on some furs, his
repaired leg up and pressing hard against the wall as he tried to regain some
strength.

"Where is he?" Aoleyn said, surprised, glancing around.

"The uamhas?"

"Don't call him that."

"He's out."

"What does that mean, out?" Aoleyn demanded. "The night is halfway
through."

"Our friend knows the mountain night as well as anyone alive," Aghmor
told her. "He did most of his work on th'Way under the stars, not the hot
sun. He's been going out on many nights—clear nights, like this one—
whenever the weather allowed."

"To do what?" Aoleyn pressed. "Where would he go?"

Aghmor shrugged. "He tells me he'll be back. He comes back."

Aoleyn spun on her heel, shaking her head as she made her way back outside. The sky above was indeed clear, a million stars shining, and though
without a blanket of clouds, the night was growing colder, it was hardly in-
tolerable or dangerous. Still Aoleyn did not like the idea of Bahdlahn wandering the icy passes of Fireach Speuer in the low light, where one misstep
could send him tumbling into a deep ravine.

He likely hadn't gone far, she reasoned, particularly if he had a special
place that he had visited on much less hospitable winter nights.

Aoleyn called upon the moonstone in her belly ring and leaped away, flying up above the small trees and rock jags of the area, circling wider and
wider. With the jag of rocks of the secret cave still in sight, she spotted

Bahdlahn, the silhouette of a man, at least, on a high rock spur over to the east. She flew in carefully, moving lower to the ground, then setting down on leopard hind legs, padding her way powerfully and softly toward the spur.

She breathed easier when she confirmed that it was Bahdlahn, and saw that he was resting easily, leaning back against a flat wall, staring out to the southeast around the mountain.

She crept up and reverted her legs to those of a human, then whispered his name.

He jumped in startlement, but settled fast, and shifted and smiled when he saw Aoleyn moving to the spur beside him.

Aoleyn thought to ask him what this was about, but as soon as she made the spur, she found that she understood, for the view up here was truly spectacular, looking down from the mountain, over Fasail Dubh'clach and far, far away. Looking back to the north, Loch Beag lay still and clear, reflecting the stars, but Bahdlahn's gaze, she had noted, had been to the south and southeast. And it was again now, as she settled in beside him.

She didn't ask, said nothing at all, sensing that he was focused elsewhere.

"Sometimes, just as the sun dips below the horizon in the west, I like to look to the south," Bahdlahn said at length.

"Southeast, across the desert."

"No, more to the south," he corrected, pointing to the right of the wide desert plain, where the mountains continued and shortened the horizon.

"Why south?" Aoleyn asked. "I've looked south, and all I've ever seen are the mountainsides, and they're not as grand as those around the other side of Fireach Speuer. It's just the end of the world." She had always found that notion curious, and more so now that she had said it aloud. According to Usgar lore, the mountains running north and south to the west of Fireach Speuer marked the edge of existence, and there was nothing beyond them—nothing, at least, in this world. It was just one of those stories Aoleyn had heard a hundred times and more in her childhood days, and she had never really considered the implications of it. "The end of the world"? What did that actually mean?

Bahdlahn shook his head and didn't look back at her. "Not at the ground." He lifted his arm and pointed up past the most distant visible peaks. "At the sky. It's not always there. It's like a flash, a little flash of green or red or blue. Look." He pointed suddenly, more imperatively, and Aoleyn gave a little gasp and a wide smile.

"It's not just a flash," she explained, for yes, she had viewed this band of color before. "It's a whole realm. You can see it better from higher up the mountain, or when you're flying inside the thoughts of an owl."

That brought Bahdlahn's head around, as he stared at Aoleyn curiously, caught by that last remark. "You've seen it?" he asked. "The third realm?"

"Third?" Aoleyn asked.

"My mother told me that the flash of color is when two of the three worlds meet. The first realm, and the third."

"Three?" Aoleyn had never heard such a thing. "The Usgar know only two. This world and Daonnan, Eternity, with the tents of Corsaleug itself, and the horrors of Ifrinn, where the dead dwell. My mother is there now, at least, with my father."

"This world, where we live, is the first, my mother said. And the world we go to when we die, that's the third." He paused and swallowed hard. "They meet, but just for a short hug, at twilight, and you can cross between them."

"Are you thinking of trying to cross between those worlds?" she asked, her voice quiet. "To find your mother?"

"She wouldn't be there," Bahdlahn said sadly. "She's in the second world, where the deamhan come from, and where we go if the deamhan kill us. There's no other way to get there, my mother said, and I shouldn't want to go there even if there were."

"Deamhain," Aoleyn repeated. "You mean the Usgar."

"There are other deamhan, but aye," Bahdlahn admitted. "There's also the lake monster, and the fossa. I think those are both deamhan, too."

Aoleyn wasn't about to argue at that time—how could she tell Bahdlahn that her people weren't demons after what they had done to his mother, to Aoleyn, to Bahdlahn for all of his life! She turned her thoughts to a calmer place, remembering that long-ago day when she had first glimpsed this ribbon of strange colored lights wafting in the southern sky. She was barely a woman, then, perhaps sixteen years old.

The view was not all that common, she had been told by Seonagh, and was almost always fleeting, and so it was this night, when the colors faded and the southern stars came clear.

"See," Bahdlahn cried out. "I wonder if anyone crossed . . . my ma."

"Someday, I'll take you up higher on the mountain, so you can see the colors better," Aoleyn promised.

"Not up this mountain," he replied. "I'm not climbing this mountain ever again."

She laughed, and pointed to another mountain, to the south. It was not quite as high as Fireach Speuer, but still towered. "That mountain," she said.

He looked at her, and he smiled, and she smiled back at him. He was quite striking even in the darkness, this young man who was her only friend.

She rested her head on his shoulder, and he wrapped his arm around her. The night wind was chilly, but Aoleyn felt as warm as she had ever been.

She stared into the fire in the little cave, but she was not seeing the flames. Her mind was full of images and memories and feelings too conflicted for her to make sense of them.

She felt Bahdlahn's strong arm against her, about her shoulders.

She felt Brayth's hands grasping her hips, his dirty fingers digging into her flesh, as he slammed against her from behind.

She remembered Bahdlahn's gasp of elation when they had floated down the mountain.

She heard Brayth's cry of ecstasy—no, of victory, it had seemed, for it was a growl of conquest and personal triumph, not of shared joy.

She was glad that Brayth was dead. She wished that she had killed him. So why was he still there, in her mind? Why was that awful moment still so clear, so nagging, bringing her into its grasp, echoing in her mind? Would it be there evermore, especially in those moments when it should not?

Aoleyn called upon her serpentine shield and poked her fingers into the fire, playing with the flaming sticks and angrily glowing embers, toying with that anger, denying it with her magical shield.

It would not burn her.

Her eyes reflected the flames, her crooked smile taunted them, as her fingers toyed with those embers that should hurt her, but could not.

She would not be a victim.

Not of the flames.

Not of Brayth.

"I am alive," she whispered, her voice hidden by the hiss of the fire, as if it was protecting her play. "And you are dead."

"Shh," Aoleyn whispered, her finger over pursed lips. Her magical diamond light glowed softly from her belly ring, casting upward across her face as she leaned over the furs of Bahdlahn's bed. She held her hand out to the young man.

Confused, Bahdlahn took the hand and rose, following her quietly out of the cave, in cadence with Aghmor's snores.

It was still quite dark, with dawn a long way off.

"What?" Bahdlahn asked, but Aoleyn just looked back at him with that crooked smile of hers, and put her finger over her lips once more.

She led him along a narrow trail around the side of the mountain, then to a steep shelf of stone and melting ice. She called upon her magic and grabbed Bahdlahn closer, and the young man held his breath as he felt his weight leave him, as he and the witch began floating up the steep and icy incline. Beyond that rise, Aoleyn picked up her pace and trotted along another trail, bringing them to a spot overlooking a place, a prow of stone, Bahdlahn knew well.

She had taken a different route to a ledge above his secret spur, the place from where he often viewed the mystical lights of the joining realms.

"What?" he said again, not sure of why she had brought him back to this place this same night, and noting that she had placed furs upon that stone spur. She turned back and smiled and winked, assuring him that it was all right.

She pulled him to the edge, then grabbed Bahdlahn about the waist. Again, he felt his weight diminish, and so he understood, but still he gasped with surprise when she stepped from the ledge, pulling him with her. Embracing, they floated down together from on high, through the chill night air.

Bahdlahn gasped again when they at last landed, and catching his breath, he began to laugh with excitement. He shook his head and looked back up the cliff, hardly believing that they had flown down. It was one thing to feel such magic going up an angled hill, but quite another to be high in the empty air and floating, where an end to the magic would mean an end to Bahdlahn!

When he looked back to his surprising companion, Aoleyn was already sitting on the spread furs. She patted the spot beside her, inviting him to join her.

He could hardly move, and no longer from fear. Nay, stepping out onto the outcropping had changed everything around him, it seemed. He felt the cool breeze more keenly, its soft whispers tickling and exciting his skin. He looked down to the left, to the wide lake far below, and in the glass of those waters he saw the reflection of the sky, though it seemed not a reflection. He looked far to the right, to the south, and there saw the wave of green and purple, the touching of the realms. Bahdlahn felt as if he was in the midst of the sky then, and not below it, as if the stars were below and about him, and not just above.

He eased down onto the fur, its softness only adding to the illusion that he was not upon firmament here, that he was floating somehow, joined with the vast eternity of the cloudless and moonless night.

He could hardly catch his breath; he felt somehow as if the wind was part of his own exhalations, as if he, and not just his perceptions, had been transformed, as if he had slipped free of his corporeal coil and into something more, something vast, something eternal and great and beautiful.

He noted a slight movement to his side, and out of the corner of his eye caught the flow of fabric on the wind, and when he turned he saw that Aoleyn had shed herself of her clothes. She reclined on her elbows, open to him, naked to him, and unashamed. The gemstones set upon her belly shined like the stars above. The curves and contours of her graceful form drew his eye all about her, basking in the beauty, the completeness of form—so overwhelmed was he that he couldn't seem to take it all in.

Then he saw her eyes, those wonderful eyes, and she looked up at him, those black eyes holding his gaze, holding his soul, and she lay back on the soft fur.

Bahdlahn didn't know what to do! He wanted to fall over her and leap off the mountainside all at the same time, as desire and terror both erupted within him, panic and wanting, desperate wanting.

But then, her eyes, those eyes and that impish crooked smile calmed him, telling him that it was all right, easing the fear and coaxing him. Hardly aware of his movements, Bahdlahn pulled off his smock and let it fall aside, his gaze never leaving Aoleyn.

Unsure, but unable to resist, he reached for her with one hand, lightly running his fingers down her face, across her lips, his middle finger just barely touching her chin.

So lightly. So teasingly, to both of them.

He ran his hand down her delicate neck, feeling the smooth curves and flow of her body, continuing down, lightly, so lightly, at times not even touching, as if catching the cool breeze between them. But even in those moments, he could feel her, surely, as if her body was reaching back to him. She closed her eyes and opened her mouth in a quiet moan.

Down he slid his hand, between her breasts, one finger brushing over her tumescent nipple, and Aoleyn inhaled deeply and arched her back to reach up to him.

But Bahdlahn instinctively kept his hand just beyond her, just lightly touching her, teasing her, teasing them both, as he slid it lower, across her belly, across her abdomen, and lower still, to the front of her hips and toward her most private place.

But then Aoleyn moved, suddenly, quickly, gracefully, and as she turned, she broke the support of Bahdlahn's planted left arm and so twisted him down to his back. He felt the fur beneath him, tickling him, and it seemed more the wind than anything solid.

And she climbed upon him, straddling him, guiding him into her, and there she sat upright, looking down at him, hardly moving. She began to sway more insistently, back and forth, side to side, and Aoleyn let her head lay back and began to moan once more with pleasure.

She was to him little more than a silhouette, then, but Bahdlahn saw her more clearly than ever before. Her back arched, her breasts swayed with her movement, and every shift beckoned him deeper, pulled from him. The heavenly stars framed her, their soft glow touching the edges of her small form. To Bahdlahn, they weren't on the mountain then, weren't even on the ground at all. No, they were among those stars, lifting toward something greater and eternal, a place of pure sensation. Aoleyn was taking him there, beckoning him to a place, a promise, he had never known and never imagined, but now so desperately needed.

Aoleyn shuddered and cried out, and Bahdlahn could contain himself no more, and he felt his life force being pulled right out of him, given to her, in a burst of pleasure he had never imagined possible, and he, and they, lifted up into night sky, seemed to be floating on the cool breeze.

Bahdlahn didn't know how long it lasted, all sense of time seemed to be lost to him, then, but gradually he opened his eyes again, to see Aoleyn's impish smile, and her starlit eyes soaking him in.

"I . . . don't . . ." he breathlessly tried to say, but she brought her finger upon his lips to silence him.

Still sitting upright atop him, she looked back over her shoulder up at the night sky, then lifted her arm and pointed.

"That light," she said. "That star."

That star? Bahdlahn saw millions of stars, and the great sky chasm of diffused heavenly light that hinted of millions more.

"Do you see it?" Aoleyn pressed, and she pointed more insistently. "The blue one, twinkling."

It was impossible, of course. There were too many for such a vague description and a pointing finger to distinguish . . .

But somehow, Bahdlahn did see it, did understand which speck of light Aoleyn was pointing at.

"That is the light of this moment," the woman said to him. "For it was not just a moment, nay, but now a memory for us both, a point of light, eternal in the sky. And it will be there for you whenever you need it, a light through the darkness, a light through the pain, a beacon through the fear."

And Bahdlahn understood, and realized fully then this great gift they had shared, out here, out from the mountain, out among the heavens.

Aoleyn lay down atop him then, and nuzzled her head against his shoulder, and he fell asleep inside of her and woke up in her arms, to a sunrise more glorious and full of promise than anything Bahdlahn had ever dared hope.

20

JILTED

In his mind's eye, he could still see Aoleyn's silhouette, swaying with pleasure under the starlight as she straddled the man. In fact, Aghmor could not purge that image from his thoughts, and it haunted him, every step.

How could she have done such a thing? How could this magnificent Usgar woman have so debased herself to swive with an uamhas, a nothing, an animal?

Aghmor stumbled along the snowy, muddy trails between the rocky spur and the secret cave, trying to make sense of what he had seen and heard, and of his own life. His leg supported him now, but it ached badly, particularly when his foot slipped a bit on the uneven and slippery trail.

"Should have known," he muttered under his breath, for indeed, he had suspected that there was more between Aoleyn and that slave. Deep in his mind, he had even suspected this, although he had not been able to bring the thought forward, so disgusting did he find the mere hint of it.

Sleeping with a slave! An Usgar woman giving her treasure to an animal. It was different for the Usgar men, he knew. The men needed the release, and so the uamhas women served, but for an Usgar woman?

Aghmor could only shake his head and spit in disgust.

Soon he was back in sight of the cave. He could see the slightest glow coming from within, from the embers of the fire.

He had thought to go right in, but he stopped now, and found that he could not. What might he say to her? Could he even look her in the eye again? And if he erupted in anger at her, if, in a fit of rage, he told her what he had seen, what then?

Aghmor had felt the power of Aoleyn keenly when she had healed his leg. Her magic had coursed through him, as powerful as anything he had ever known. If he angered her . . .

But how could he not? How could he look her in the eye, knowing what he knew, having seen what he had seen? At the very least, he wanted to kill Bahdlahn.

Before he even consciously considered the movement, Aghmor was past the secret cave, moving along the same trail where he had fallen and broken his leg. He sorted the details of his story, his alibi, in his mind, fearing that Tay Aillig would surely punish him, perhaps even murder him, for his desertion.

His fears faded with every step. He had been hurt and had forced the slave to support him, to find him food and kindling for the fire. Then Aoleyn had healed him.

A simple and believable tale.

Aghmor was nodding before he had put the cave out of sight behind him, confident that he would be welcomed back into the tribe, and that they, Tay Aillig and Mairen in particular, would take care of Bahdlahn, and would finish the ceremony they had started with Aoleyn up beside Craos'a'diad.

That last thought made him grimace, but the image of her swaying atop the uamhas turned any regret into deeper anger.

"Abandon your hopes for the Usgar," Bahdlahn bade Aoleyn as they made their way back to the cave. "Let us leave, now."

"Leave?" Aoleyn asked skeptically, but mostly because she didn't have an answer to the greater hints the young man was dropping here. She had made love to him, had given him that pleasure and had given herself that plea-sure, for many reasons. Bahdlahn's entire life was one of misery, so he de-served the moment. And Aoleyn had needed it, too, had needed to prove to herself all that she had proclaimed to Mairen, that it was her body and hers alone.

She also held great affection for Bahdlahn. The attraction was undeniable, and she felt a level of comfort with him that she had never known with another person. Did that mean that she loved him?

"To Fasach Crann and my people on the lake," he went on.

"They do'no even know you."

"Aye, but they'll know of me, and so accept me," he pressed. "And you. When I tell them . . ."

"No, Bahdlahn, I can'no. Not now."

"We can have children, a family," Bahdlahn said, rolling right through her denial. "There is food and water and all that we'll need about Loch Beag. Your people will'no come looking for you, and if they do, we'll be long out on the lake before e'er they arrive!"

Aoleyn wasn't even listening. His first sentence had shut her down. Perhaps she did love him, she thought, but still, she was a young woman only beginning to find her place in the world and her power in the magic of the gemstones. There was nothing about her current situation that made her want to set her life's course and raise a family at that time, either up on the mountain or down at the lake. When she looked out from Fireach Speuer, her gaze did not go to Loch Beag with longing, no! Her eyes scanned beyond, far beyond, across the low desert east of the mountains, or to the mystical lights in the night sky far to the south. The thought of becoming pregnant, of having children, of becoming someone's wife could not gain traction in her mind. Not then. Not hardly. She would never have made love to Bahdlahn if she had thought that a possibility, because she knew that with the gemstone magic, she could make sure that it was not.

Aoleyn had only begun to taste her freedom now, after the revelations of the deep caves beneath Craos'a'diad. She was growing in the magic of the gemstones and in the music of life itself, and that was a journey that would consume her for a long time to come, so she hoped.

Bahdlahn was still talking, but she hushed him with a reminder of the third of their little troupe as they moved into the foyer of the secret cave. Aoleyn put a finger over her pursed lips, bidding him to silence, then crept into the inner cave.

The embers burned low, so the woman enacted the power of her cat's eye, scanning.

She stood up straight, Bahdlahn bumping into her from behind as she brought up a brighter light from her diamond.

"What are you doing?" Bahdlahn whispered in her ear, but he bit the question short and moved about her, looking around. "Where is he?"

Aoleyn strengthened her diamond light, brightening the interior of the small cave more fully than any fire that had ever been lit in here.

Aghmor was not there. A sinking feeling came to Aoleyn's gut.

"Where is he?" Bahdlahn asked again. "Why would he go out? Was he attacked, do you think?"

Aoleyn put as much of her energy into her diamonds as she could, and filled the cave with a bright glow, as bright as the day.

"No bloodstains," she observed. "The fire still smolders."

Bahdlahn dug through Aghmor's sleeping furs, which were in the same pile Aghmor had always kept them in.

"His waterskin is still here," he said. "And his other supplies as well."

"But not his spear," Aoleyn said astutely.

A mask of concern grew over Bahdlahn's face. "Where could he have gone?" he asked breathlessly.

"His leg was not fully healed, so not far," Aoleyn replied, her voice grim.

Bahdlahn spun about, heading for the exit corridor, but Aoleyn grabbed him and stopped him as he moved past her.

"We have to go find him," Bahdlahn protested.

Aoleyn held up the wedstone pendant strung on her chain belt.

"I'll find him," she said. "You stay here and protect me."

Bahdlahn didn't seem to quite understand, but Aoleyn did not bother to fully explain. There wasn't enough time. She sat down cross-legged on a pile of furs.

"You stay and guard my body," she instructed. "Promise me. I'm sure to be helpless without you."

Bahdlahn still didn't seem to understand, but he nodded and moved to kneel beside her.

Aoleyn focused on the music of the powerful wedstone, heard the notes and fell into them, and stepped out of her body. She looked back as she headed for the exit, and felt a surge of comfort as she eyed Bahdlahn kneeling beside her so attentively, faithfully protecting her. He would give to her what she needed.

A pang of guilt stung her, for could she say the same? Could she give Bahdlahn what he wanted from her?

She knew the answer, but had to let it go. These were thoughts for a quieter time, a conversation for another day. For now, she needed to catch up to Aghmor, and quickly.

Talmadge belly-crept up the rocky slope, inching his way as stealthily as he could manage. He thought he was doing fairly well, until Aydrian came past him, moving swiftly and without a whisper of sound. Was there anything this self-proclaimed ranger could not do with amazing skill and competence?

Heavy clouds had settled overhead, making the night quite dark, which would have given Talmadge more confidence, except that they weren't sneaking up on humans, but on mountain goblins, and Aydrian had assured him that goblins could see as well as a hunting cat in the dark.

Talmadge crested the hill right next to Aydrian, to look down on the village of Carrachan Shoal, or what was left of it. The man ducked back immediately, shaking his head, for as Catriona and others had feared, the sidhe had not simply raided, collected their booty, and run off. No, they were still there in the village in large numbers. Few houses remained, and the occupiers had taken most apart, using the wood to fortify the place.

For now, a simple palisade encircled the main portion of the remaining village. No light came from within, nor were any torches upon the wall, but peering closer, Talmadge did note some movement up there, sidhe sentries walking parapets.

Talmadge grew uneasy. He wanted to get out of there, expecting a sidhe patrol to be about at any time. If they were this well-organized within the city, then they likely had sentries walking the perimeter without. He looked to Aydrian, and finally nudged the man, motioning back down the ridge to indicate that they should be gone.

But Aydrian shook his head and remained in place.

"You go," he whispered in Talmadge's ear. "Alert the camp and wait for me."

Talmadge hesitated. Aydrian nodded down the slope.

After a few moments considering the command, Talmadge decided that Catriona and the others really did need to know. He nodded at Aydrian the next time the man glanced his way, then began slowly backing down the ridge. At the base, he stood up and sprinted back into the trees, back to the small camp where Catriona and some others waited.

His expression told them as much as his ensuing words.

This would be no easy fight.

Aoleyn's spirit swept out of the cave, unbounded by the earth, the stone walls, even. She began a fast circuit of the area, soaring around, then widening her perimeter with each pass. Through the trees she flew, above the snow-pack, across the muddy trails and wind-cleared stones. She wanted to find Aghmor. She wanted him to be around.

She didn't particularly like spirit-walking, and after her recent tangles with the demon fossa, she couldn't help but feel vulnerable out of her corporeal form.

But she had to find Aghmor, and there was no faster or more thorough way to search for him.

Had he wandered off in search of Aoleyn and Bahdlahn? Had he gone out, perhaps simply to piss, and fallen victim to his still-injured leg?

Perhaps he needed her then, and that was her hope, a hope that was fast fading with every circuit of the area about the camp. In this spiritual form, Aoleyn could keenly sense any living people around her.

Aghmor was not near the cave. It quickly became apparent to her that he had gone out with purpose. Aoleyn was afraid what that might mean. Nor did she have any desire to go over to the west, to the Usgar encampment. Not in this form. She had no choice in the matter, though. She had to know. Off she sped, across the mountainside, very soon after cresting the ridge to the winter plateau. She expected to find the camp asleep, mostly, as it was very early in the morning, and when that was not the case, her fears escalated.

Even more so when she spotted Aghmor, and more still when she noted that he was speaking to Tay Aillig!

So many people around tempted her spirit—their bodies seemed like white lights to her, beckoning her back to a corporeal form, calling her to enter a new host and possess him or her.

No, she couldn't do that. She thought for a moment to try it with Aghmor—perhaps she could crash into his thoughts and prevent him from abandoning her and Bahdlahn to Tay Aillig, for that was certainly what she expected him to be doing.

Even the quick thought of that had her sliding into his mind, for the temptation proved simply too great. Aghmor recoiled at the intrusion, and Aoleyn caught herself quickly enough to slip right back out, flying high up above them, trying to put some distance between her spirit and those inviting hosts.

Even as she did, she considered Aghmor's thoughts, relayed in that instant, in that eyeblink, of their joining. An image of their secret cave. And now, above them, she heard the words.

"Close, yes," Aghmor said. "You could be there before they awaken."

The words seemed slurred and distant to Aoleyn in this spiritual realm, but she understood them enough to recognize the danger.

She thought to rush back into Aghmor then, to take over his body and attack Tay Aillig.

It would be a desperate and foolhardy ploy, though. Possessing another was a difficult task in the best of circumstances, and she had been out searching for a long while and was growing weary from this taxing use of magic.

She tried to tell herself that, but found herself drawing inexorably closer to the man.

"You will lead us," she heard Tay Aillig say, but he ended abruptly and snapped his gaze upward, staring right at Aoleyn.

How could that be?

His face took a vacant expression, a moment of confusion, but then he smiled, as if sorting out the riddle.

He knew that her invisible spirit was there, but how could that be?

Panicking, Aoleyn turned to flee. She had to get back to the cave, and quickly, to gather Bahdlahn and be on their way. She would fly him down the mountain, down to the town on the lake. What choice . . . ?

Her plotting fell away, for as she turned, Aoleyn noted another soul hovering about in the realm of spirit, staring at her, ready for her.

Mairen.

And with the dozen others of the Coven.

They had known she would be coming, and how she would be coming.

Down below, she heard Tay Aillig shout out, "Gather the warriors!"

"We should go at them straightaway," said Asba of Carrachan Shoal, the lone member of that village to accompany this scouting expedition back to surveil the sacked town.

"It would be costly," Aydrian replied after Talmadge had properly translated. With help from the magical gems and his work with Talmadge, Aydrian was becoming proficient in the language of the plateau already, but not enough to ensure that these critical conversations would be exact enough. "They are fortifying."

Asba, Catriona, and the others didn't seem pleased at the reply, which they understood well enough before Talmadge had offered a more polished translation. They discussed the matter back and forth, with Talmadge trying to offer snippets to Aydrian. The conversation, though, was fast and sharp, and heated.

"Well?" Aydrian asked when things finally settled.

"They want to attack," Talmadge replied.

"I got that much. Catriona seemed against it."

"She was," Talmadge confirmed. "At first. But she's come to see that the sidhe must be driven away and not allowed a foothold so near to Fasach Crann. The folk of Carrachan Shoal want their village, back, of course."

"These goblins, these sidhe, have you ever seen them behave such?" Aydrian asked.

"No," answered Talmadge.

"Aydrian turned to Catriona and asked the same question in the language of the plateau. Catriona turned and mumbled to her companions, and the young man named Asba offered some thoughts of his own. Aydrian tried to keep up, but they were talking too quickly for him to follow.

"She hasn't, no," Talmadge then said to Aydrian. "She's never seen them this near the lake, either. The sidhe mostly stay to the mountains, and on those rare times they've attacked a village, they strike quick and are quicker to leave."

"Much like the goblins in other parts of the world," Aydrian told him. "Usually, but not always."

"Have you ever seen sidhe do this?" Catriona said to him, speaking slowly.

"Aye," Aydrian replied directly to her. "Or I've heard of it, at least." He turned to Talmadge to better explain in the language of Honce. "During the wars of the demon dactyl, the goblins that you call sidhe became more organized. They conquered towns and held them. This is what I fear, and this is why I do not wish to attack blindly. This band in Carrachan Shoal did not come down the mountain singly. Three attacks, at least. We know not why the goblins are behaving as such, but if they are doing so on command from some greater power, some leader . . ."

"Then we should destroy this group now," Talmadge interrupted, "before that leader can reinforce them."

"And what if it already has?" Aydrian asked. "What if their strength is greater than we believe? Who knows how many may have come into Carrachan Shoal to crouch behind that palisade?"

Talmadge started to reply, but held his tongue and just stood there staring at Aydrian, trying to digest it all.

"Tell them," Aydrian bade him. "Tell them all of it."

"What would you counsel them to do?"

"Set scouts, all about Carrachan Shoal," Aydrian replied. "Every trail. And watch the town carefully, that we can better learn their numbers."

Talmadge nodded and turned to relay the counsel, but Aydrian stopped him by adding, "And tell them to have their boats loaded with supplies and ready to put out onto the lake."

All eyes fell over Aydrian as Talmadge offered the advice to the lakemen, and Aydrian noted that the young man, Asba, of Carrachan Shoal grimaced more than once. He was eager to get back at those who had sacked his home, Aydrian knew, and he surely understood.

"And send word to the other towns," Aydrian said to Talmadge. "All the folk of Loch Beag will want these goblins, these sidhe, destroyed, for who will be safe while they are about?"

Talmadge interpreted for Catriona, who stood there silent and stern for many heartbeats before finally nodding her agreement.

Behind her, Asba slapped his hands against his thighs and cursed in Aydrian's general direction.

They came at her from every angle, flashes of light, multicolored, elongated representations of the forms. Aoleyn felt as if they were dancing about her, these thirteen witches, darting at her suddenly, randomly, calling her name, calling her names, taunting her, threatening her. Fleeting shadows of the women who were indeed dancing, she knew, around the Crystal God in the sacred grove.

She was too near that place, she feared, too near their source of power, and one that they were now accessing.

She had not surprised them, as she had when she had intruded on the initiation ceremony on the solstice. Nay, quite the opposite.

They had been lying in wait for her.

She realized that. Aghmor had been here for a long time and had told them everything—it had to be.

Now what was she to do?

The witches' spirits encircled Aoleyn, dancing shadows of blue and red, yellow and green, their forms shifting through the colors of a rainbow as if to match their mood and charge. And they did charge, leaping in at her with curses and chants, their shadows mingling with hers as if to possess her.

Off balance, Aoleyn shifted from one to the other, snapping her thoughts shut to them with fury, denying them, ignoring them. In her mind, she pictured them as physical clouds of human form, some more substantial than others, clouds that stretched and warped and enwrapped bits of her, as if trying to pull her sensibilities apart.

With every distraction, she felt diminished, and felt unbound.

She thought of the fossa, of what it had done to her mother, of what it had done to Seonagh. Not so different from this, she recognized, and she tightened her thoughts in that moment of great fear, tried to become smaller, tighter wound, more substantial.

Mairen's face flashed to her, the woman's leering grin telling her of her doom, that she could not escape, that they knew.

Oh, they knew!

They knew of the cave, and of the slave.

They knew of Aoleyn's uamhas lover.

They knew and she was damned. By Usgar, she was damned.

Better you had died in the Mouth! rang Connebragh's voice in her thoughts. *Shame!*

Shame! another echoed.

Shame!

Shame! Shame!

Over and over, from every direction, a dozen voices, disparate yet united against her.

She couldn't think straight, she couldn't see straight. She wondered where she was more than once, and which direction was which, and how she could fly away. But no, she couldn't fly away, because if she did, she'd lead them straight to Bahdlahn.

I will have him, rang the loudest voice in her head, the voice of Mairen, who had been listening to Aoleyn's thoughts through the cacophony of the shrieking Coven, who had heard her reference to Bahdlahn.

Tay Aillig will have him, Mairen taunted.

We know the cave, Connebragh's spirit imparted. *He will have your head from your shoulders. Oh, but you've failed us, Aoleyn!*

Aoleyn's spirit managed to look out, then, to see torches moving along the trail to the east, toward the cave, where her physical form sat helpless, where Bahdlahn could not hope to protect her, but would surely die trying.

Tay Aillig would eat him, Aoleyn knew.

She thought of that, she focused on that. She pictured Bahdlahn beneath her as she swayed on the rocky spur. She heard his moans of pleasure and turned them into groans of pain. In her thoughts, she brought forth her memories of the fossa's cave, that pit of murder and despair. She let them all see it, and smell it, and feel the pervasive, evil coldness.

And while the witches of the Coven faltered beneath that weight of despair, Aoleyn stayed with Bahdlahn in her imagination. She thought of him now screaming in agony under the torture of Tay Aillig, and she grew angry, and her spirit began to brighten with the heat of that anger.

No longer a shadow, but a light, she burned with rage and glowed like the most powerful diamond. The wisps of witches reaching out at her dissipated under the brilliance of that angry light, unable to penetrate the cocoon Aoleyn had woven for herself, a shell of burning, denying rage.

It wouldn't be enough. She had to break the circles, had to escape.

She found the weakest link in their dancing chain and leaped for it, attacking now with all her fury.

Moragh.

It was Moragh, barely a woman. Aoleyn caught her and grabbed her. She found the link between this mere child and Moragh's physical body, a thin line of sensibility, a lifeline cord.

She could have snapped it, unbinding the woman, letting Moragh's disembodied spirit wander helplessly, unlikely to ever find her way back.

It would be so easy. The novice was no match for the power of Aoleyn!

She couldn't bring herself to do it, couldn't do to this poor girl what the fossa had done to Elara and to Seonagh.

She invaded Moragh with all her consciousness instead, and yelled into every corner of the witch's consciousness, *I am not what you believe!*

And Aoleyn was gone, passing through Moragh, flying fast across the encampment, chasing the torches.

She passed over them, over Tay Aillig and Egard and Aghmor—oh, Aghmor!—and a handful of other warriors, running fast and true for the secret cave.

Mairen's whispers nipped at her spirit, Connebragh beside her, others coming.

Aoleyn shot for the cave. She didn't go for the opening, to weave in through the foyer and the narrow passageway. No, she went right through the wall, finding cracks she could not have seen with her physical eyes in the brightest daylight.

She came into her body so forcefully that she tumbled over amidst the pile of rugs.

"Aoleyn!" Bahdlahn cried.

Her eyes snapped open and she stopped his approach with a striking stare.

"Run," she implored him. "Run!"

"Aoleyn," he said, hesitating, then stubbornly coming forward.

Aoleyn fell into her gemstone, into her moonstone, and created a burst of wind that sent the strong young man tumbling backward, into and down the narrow channel.

"They are coming!" she yelled.

I am here! Mairen said in her mind.

"Tay Aillig knows!" Aoleyn shouted. "Run! Flee!"

She felt them, then, in her mind, attacking her relentlessly. She tried to stand, but Sorcha took control of one leg and twisted it under her, pitching her face down to the side.

Aoleyn grabbed at the only thing she could find: the pendant on her hip. Hardly even considering the movement, she brought forth its power and lashed out at the natural hallway, turning stones to lava and dropping them to block the way before stubborn Bahdlahn could come back after her.

"Run!" she yelled with all her strength. "They're almost here! Just run!"

The witches swarmed her, then, her jaw clenching uncontrollably, so tightly that her teeth hurt. Her arms flailed, her vision failed, and she was there, but she was not, caught inside herself too deeply, as if in a sealed black room, a chamber of emptiness.

Rage, she told herself. *Rage!*

21

EXPLOSIONS

The heat was too intense, the falling stones glowing angrily under the strange enchantment Aoleyn had put upon them. Bahdlahn tried to get through, once, then again, yelling loudly to block out the terribly true words Aoleyn was shouting at him.

She convulsed. She told him to run. "They're almost here!"

She began to shake mightily, flopping about on the floor, and Bahdlahn couldn't get to her—and what might he do if he did get to her?

He wanted to die beside her, but he could not get through. He wanted to hold her and shield her and fight off their persecutors, but she was being persecuted in her mind, he understood, by spirits he could not punch. The damned Usgar witches had come for her and grabbed her, and now the warriors were coming, too.

For him.

He owed it to her to get away. She was imploring him, as he would implore her were the situation reversed. She would not want him to die in trying futilely to save her, as he would never want Aoleyn, his lovely, wonderful Aoleyn, to remain beside him at the price of her own life out of misguided loyalty.

Bahdlahn tried to get through one more time anyway, and was repelled.

He stumbled out of the cave and he ran. Bahdlahn ran. Tears in his eyes, sobs choking him, he ran.

He ran from the deamhans.

He ran for a home he had never known.

Aghmor slowed as he neared the area of the cave, even pretending to be unsure of the area, but right behind him, Tay Aillig shoved him and told him to move along.

What had he done? He wanted to rewind the last moments of his life!

But in the consideration of regret, Aghmor saw her again, straddling Bahdlahn, under the starlight, moaning with pleasure.

He charged away, past the spot where he had fallen and Bahdlahn had saved him. This was their fault, not his. He jabbed his finger ahead, pointing, when they came in sight of the cave, and started to lead the way in, spear in hand.

Tay Aillig grabbed him by the shoulder and yanked him back, rushing ahead. Into the alcove he went, easily discovering the narrow channel behind the half wall at the back of the shallow foyer. He went around, out of sight, fast, and came right back even faster, stumbling, rubbing at his eyes and face.

When Aghmor and Egard came in close behind, they understood, for behind that half wall, the heat shimmered in the air, the stones glowing angrily.

"She is powerful," Egard remarked. "Even now."

Tay Aillig and Aghmor moved to the entryway of the short natural passageway, squinting against the heat, which was only gradually diminishing. Peering through the smoking and steaming, they could see Aoleyn, squirming and thrashing on the ground, gurgling strange sounds, her arms and legs moving in a not at all coordinated manner.

"Mairen has her," Tay Aillig said, nodding and smiling.

"Bahdlahn is gone," Aghmor said, and it wasn't until both Tay Aillig and Egard regarded him curiously that he understood his mistake. "Thump," he explained. "Aoleyn calls him Bahdlahn."

"You seem to know much," said Egard.

"He kept me alive. They kept me alive. Throughout the winter, the slave served me."

"You would call for mercy?"

Aghmor stared hard at Egard. "I will throw him into Craos'a'diad myself, if Usgar-triath allows." He looked past the two men to those standing just outside the cave. "Gather snow," he ordered. "Bring it quickly."

They did, and threw it on the stones, Aoleyn's dying magic hissing and steaming in protest.

"When it cools enough, enter and hold her," Tay Aillig told three of them. "Bind her hands and feet and gag her, but nothing more."

He paused and looked to each of them intently, telling them with his eyes that they had better not fail him in this. "Nothing more," he restated.

He motioned for Aghmor, Egard, and the remaining two to follow, and started away.

Bahdlahn's trail was not hard to find in the muddy and sometimes snowy ground, a wide and deep path that showed him to be stumbling and slipping with every desperate step.

"She is more dangerous," Egard dared remind them as the five started out.

"Mairen has her," Tay Aillig replied. "And twelve others have her. I only hope there will be enough of the heretic's consciousness remaining that she will realize the pain I will inflict on her."

"When she goes into Craos'a'diad?" Egard asked.

"By the time she goes into the chasm, she will be begging for her death. If she makes it that far."

Aghmor swallowed hard and kept his eyes turned away. He understood what Tay Aillig was talking about. He remembered the uamhas women captured in the raids, taken halfway up the mountain and horribly abused before they were released and sent stumbling, blind with sorrow and terror and humiliation.

He knew what Aoleyn would soon face.

"Her fault," he whispered under his breath, because he had to, because to think anything else made him want to scream and leap into Craos'a'diad himself.

The five set off at a swift pace. Behind them, they heard one of the three left behind laughing, and Aghmor knew that they had breached the melted corridor, and were likely descended upon Aoleyn even then.

They came at her from every angle, with every thought, anticipating her moves and countering them before she could begin.

They had caught her by surprise, all thirteen. She should have known better than to fly so near the Usgar encampment. She should have gone up higher, to look back on them all, on the sacred lea and the Crystal God, where the witches danced.

Now they had her, and even her great rage couldn't expel them, for there were too many and they were too ever-present in her every thought as it formulated.

Aoleyn went away from plotting and away from rage, and went instead to a memory, distant. She saw a young mother with an elongated skull, a lakewoman, cradling her baby in her arms and telling him "You are stupid" over and over again.

There, Aoleyn remained, watching that scene, allowing her feelings to become a wall, a cocoon against the invading witches. They couldn't relate to her in that moment, couldn't begin to comprehend, even, what they were seeing as they chased Aoleyn's focused meditation.

She replayed the scene over and over again, basking in it, becoming wholly within that moment of her distant life, one of her earliest memories.

She didn't feel the warriors grabbing her and pulling her arms behind her back. No, she was not there, but was into her memory fully, in the cave with the uamhas, watching the mother.

"You are stupid."

Within the echoes of that simple sentence, Aoleyn began to reconstruct her feelings. As she had come to understand the implications, the truth of the uamhas and their inevitable fates, Aoleyn allowed her anger to grow, and her shame for her tribe, using those powerful emotions as further insulation in her cocoon. Inside, she curled, a speck of freedom within her spirit, hidden fully from Mairen and the others, who were out there, in the rest of her being, possessing her.

Even Aoleyn's anger came from a place of deep calm and acceptance then, and from, mostly, a sense of truth and simple right and wrong. She let it build and gather momentum—she pushed away any thoughts of urgency.

Her physical limbs began to twitch, to press against the bindings, though she felt nothing. Her eyelids fluttered, though she was seeing nothing.

She was just there, in her cocoon of a memory from long ago, in a spot of privacy and meditation, and letting that meditation lead to a singular truth, building, building.

Then exploding.

The spirit of Aoleyn came forth then with new heights of denial and anger. She couldn't speak aloud, for she hadn't control of her physical being yet (and had been gagged, anyway, though she didn't know it). But within her spirit and her mind, she came forth, roaring, pushing, rejecting the intrusions.

The minor witches flew away, easily and forcefully expelled.

She found the consciousness of Sorcha and hit the old woman with a wall of shame, one she knew Sorcha, who had been friend to Seonagh, could not deny.

Then there were but two, and Connebragh fast wilted under the weight of Aoleyn's truth—as Aoleyn had believed, Connebragh was one of a good heart, and having that memory bared to her, a tale of a mother so desperate to save her child that she told him he was stupid, that he had to be stupid or the Usgar would murder him horribly, was more than Connebragh could so nakedly face.

That left Mairen, just Mairen, who knew no shame with regards to the uamhas. Mairen alone within the mind of Aoleyn, vying with Aoleyn for control.

In the earlier fight, bolstered by her sisters, catching Aoleyn by surprise, Mairen had held the upper hand, but now they were evenly faced, these two women, and in the body of Aoleyn.

Get out! Aoleyn's every thought demanded.

Traitor! Heretic! Mairen's spirit countered, hitting Aoleyn with waves of accusations she believed would bring shame and defense.

What she didn't realize, however, is that her insults rang as compliments to Aoleyn, who knew the truth of Usgar, the god and the tribe, and knew that truth to be awful and wicked.

Mairen had no support here, and by the time she realized she had taken the wrong angle of attack, it was too late.

Aoleyn expelled her.

And Aoleyn took back her thoughts and her body fully, spasming and jolting about as she began to realize the physical world about her.

"Hold the witch!" she heard a warrior say, and a boot slammed down on her back, pressing her hard to the floor.

She was caught. She was tied. She was surrounded.

That realization came with the awful understanding that she could not use half-measures here, not if she had any hopes of surviving, or of protecting Bahdlahn, who was surely being pursued.

"Here now, why's the witch glowing white?" she heard an Usgar warrior ask.

Her spirit coming back into her body so unexpectedly and forcefully, Mairen stumbled away from the Crystal God, where she had been leaning, and fell to the grass of the sacred lea. She looked around at her twelve sisters, all shaking their heads, a couple in whispered conversations.

"That was powerful," Connebragh said, rushing over to offer the Usgarrighinn a hand back to her feet. "How did she come forth so . . ."

Before she finished the question, the whole of Fireach Speuer seemed to groan and shiver, and off to the west there came a flash, then a blast of flames, a tremendous fireball, rising up into the air and curling over like a gigantic flaming mushroom before flickering away.

"Aoleyn," Connebragh breathed as the others gasped.

"The Usgar-triath!" Sorcha cried, and others began to whisper and wail.

Mairen held up her hand to quiet them. "Hold faith," she ordered, and to Connebragh, she quietly added, "Go back out in spirit and see what you can learn."

The younger woman blanched, looking from Mairen to the east and back again repeatedly, clearly not thrilled about going anywhere near the dangerous Aoleyn, in body or in spirit.

As she turned back to the east again, though, Mairen grabbed her by the chin and yanked her head back, then fixed her with a stare to show her that Aoleyn was the least of the dangers before her.

Connebragh nodded and clutched the gray-flecked crystal to her breast, then closed her eyes and began to sing, falling into the magic, using the wedstone flecks to begin the journey of freeing her spirit from her corporeal form.

It all seemed so terribly familiar to Aghmor when Tay Aillig led the way onto an exposed ledge, looking down the northwestern slopes of Fireach Speuer to the lower trails and ridges where they expected the running uamhas to be.

"Your dagger," Tay Aillig said, and then again when Aghmor didn't register that the Usgar-triath was addressing him, calling for his crystal dagger, thickly flecked with flickering quartz. Aghmor peered through the translucent blade, trying to use the magic to grant him distant sight.

"I see . . . I don't . . ." he stammered.

Tay Aillig pulled the dagger from his hand. "You two," he said to Aghmor and Egard, and he motioned down to the right, where a ridgeline formed a trail down the mountainside. "Down to the pines," he explained, pointing to a large line of tall pines some few hundred strides below, "with all speed, and curl back in to the west. He had to go through there."

As those two started, Tay Aillig motioned to the other two to run down along a trail to the left, to the pines and then curling back to the east to meet up with Aghmor and Egard.

Off they ran and Tay Aillig brought the dagger up to his eyes and looked through the magical blade. "Mairen," he whispered, calling to his wife and hoping that she still held the spiritual connection to him. Even though the witches had blessed their weapons this morning as soon as Aghmor had alerted them of the traitor and the escaped slave, Tay Aillig knew that his power with the far-sight would be greatly enhanced if he could bring Mairen back into his thoughts.

She didn't answer his call.

But it didn't matter a moment later, and the Usgar-triath grinned, for he spotted the uamhas stumbling along an open expanse of slippery rock straight down from his perch. Just as he had expected, and he knew that his hunters, their feet lightened by the magic of the green flecks in their spear tips, would get to the pines before him.

Tay Aillig would have the slave, surely, but that thought did not excite him. Before, he had wanted to torment this uamhas mostly because of the obvious pain it caused to Aoleyn. But now he had Aoleyn, too, and that was the most delicious thing of all. She would die, and then who might challenge him?

Aoleyn would be forgotten before the snow had fully melted. Tay Aillig, Mairen beside him, would hold the Usgar in his grasp.

His smile became a mask of confusion then as the ground beneath him trembled, as Fireach Speuer itself, it seemed, roared. He looked back to see a massive fireball rolling up into the morning sky.

Mairen had done that, he told himself.

He hoped.

Egard led the way, eagerly running along the trail, his knuckles whitening with anticipation as he clutched his spear.

For Aghmor, it was quite the opposite. What had he done? His outrage had carried him from his cave to the Usgar encampment. Jealousy had driven him to betray Aoleyn and Bahdlahn—Aoleyn, whom he desperately desired, and Bahdlahn, who had kept him alive through the winter, selflessly. The slave could have killed him at any time, or could have simply refused to bring Aghmor any food and let him starve to death.

Now Bahdlahn was doomed, by Aghmor's witness. Horribly doomed, with Aoleyn condemned beside him.

"He deserved it," Aghmor muttered under his breath, and he conjured that horrible image yet again, that he might hide behind his shock and anger.

But he didn't believe his words. He would be long dead now except for the efforts of Bahdlahn.

"Keep up!" Egard said to him, circling back.

"My leg," Aghmor answered, and it wasn't completely a lie. Going downhill was much tougher on his injured leg than crossing the side of the mountain, or even climbing.

"I can'no kill him without incurring the wrath of Tay Aillig," Egard said. "You're to help in catching him."

Aghmor just waved him along.

"He's going to let you kill the uamhas," Egard said. "You have my envy."

"Who is?" Aghmor asked, genuinely caught off guard.

"Tay Aillig will let you murder the uamhas," Egard explained. "Might even let you be the first to torture Aoleyn before he finishes the witch. Might let us all have a turn with her."

Egard turned and started away again, and Aghmor, stunned, somehow paced him. He didn't doubt Egard's claims. Tay Aillig was the cruelest man Aghmor had ever known—he would let—nay, he would force—Aghmor to kill Bahdlahn precisely because he knew that doing so would bring great pain to Aghmor.

The warrior thought of the time his friend Brayth lay helpless after a fall, when Tay Aillig had ordered Aghmor to finish him. Aghmor had started to strike, but had been stopped, and mocked, by Tay Aillig, in front of all the others of the raiding party.

This time, Tay Aillig would make him push the spear tip through Bahdlahn's chest, surely.

And Aoleyn. Could he doubt Egard's claims? Tay Aillig would likely have all the Usgar men take turns humiliating and raping her, as he, as they did when catching uamhas women on their raids.

The image burned in Aghmor's mind.

He tried to cover it with the image of Aoleyn straddling Bahdlahn, but he could not.

He told himself that Bahdlahn deserved it, that Aoleyn deserved it, but he knew he was lying.

What had he done?

Aghmor's pace increased. He followed Egard around a shelf of boulders.

He called for Egard to wait, and when the young warrior paused and turned to regard him, Aghmor drove his spear into Egard's side.

The victim gasped and pulled away, the back edges of the crystalline spear tip tearing more of his flesh. He stumbled and Aghmor struck again, stabbing hard into Egard's hip, then retracted and slashed the spear across for the lurching Egard's face.

Egard somehow ducked the attack and even tried to counter, but his torn hip would not comply and he pitched forward, instinctively rolling to try to put some ground between him and his attacker.

Aghmor, caught in confusion by his own impulsive actions, didn't pursue, but he didn't have to, for Egard's roll put him right to the edge of the other side of the trail, where the rocky shelf dropped away. He tried to catch himself, but again, his leg gave out under him, and over he tumbled.

Aghmor ran to the ledge and saw the warrior crashing through the branches of some pines. He winced with the sound of every snapping branch, and fought hard to breathe when Egard came out the bottom of the trees, falling in a broken lump to the hard ground below.

Aghmor looked down the mountain trail, toward the pines where he was supposed to set the trap for Bahdlahn. He looked back up the other way, though Tay Aillig was not in sight.

What was he to do now?

Tay Aillig would still catch Bahdlahn, he knew without doubt, and Aoleyn was already caught up the hill in the cave . . .

Fireach Speuer trembled and Aghmor's eyes went wide as a massive fireball rose into the sky higher up on the mountain, up by the secret cave, he knew.

What was he to do now?

He moved back up the trail, ducking when he came in view of the rocky spur, Tay Aillig standing atop it and looking back up the mountain. He thought of going to Aoleyn. He thought of going to try to help Bahdlahn run free.

He thought of too much, and so, overwhelmed, Aghmor limped off to the southeast, trying to run from all of them.

22

HORROR

Clever woman.

When she had enacted her serpentine shield before her tremendous fireball, Aoleyn had managed to keep it under her wrist bindings, and so the fireball had incinerated them and Aoleyn freed her arms with an angry tug.

Before the flames had fully died within the cave, Aoleyn was already rolling to her back, sitting up and going for the bindings around her ankles. But there she froze, for right beside her was the Usgar warrior who had clamped his foot down on her back, lying there on the floor, burning, flames coming out of his eye sockets.

The young woman couldn't draw breath, and not for the acrid stench and smoke.

Three men were down about her, charred beyond recognition. Her fireball had melted their skin and boiled their blood, killing them before they hit the ground.

Aoleyn had killed three men, three men with families, with friends, with lives. Three men who were acting in the way of the tribe, in the way it had always been. Now they were dead, by Aoleyn's hand, by her magic.

She hadn't killed Mairen up at the sacred lea. She could have, after her initial burst of fiery wind it would have been no big feat for her to strike again with a blast of lightning and finish the Usgar-righinn. Certainly, if anyone was deserving of Aoleyn's wrath, it was Mairen, who had murdered Innevah and tried to murder Aoleyn.

But she hadn't done it, hadn't even thought of doing it.

Aoleyn didn't want to kill anyone—didn't even want to kill animals, except for the necessity of food. And even then, she hesitated.

Now here she sat, in a cave, with three mutilated, unrecognizable men dead around her, by her hand, by her magic.

She wanted to curl up and cry, but one thought had her moving, had her gathering the crystals she had collected from the witches and stumbling about the blasted cave: Bahdlahn.

He was out there, running for his life, with horrible Tay Aillig and the others in pursuit. He had no chance of getting off the mountain, not against the trained Usgar and their magic weapons, which would show them the way and lighten their feet that they could catch up to the fleeing slave.

The makeshift satchel Aoleyn had used for the crystals was gone, so she gathered what was left of the rug on which she had been laying and tied up her treasure, then stumbled out of the cave—and was there amazed to see that her fireball had extended beyond the rocky confines and melted the snow many strides from the cave entrance, and had burned the branches of the small trees up above the cave, as well. One tree was still burning.

She had barely gone two running steps before her legs became those of the leopard, propelling her along with tremendous leaps, her falls mitigated by the green gemstone in her belly ring.

She was a long way from the cave before she even took the moment to realize that Tay Aillig might be expecting her, for surely her blast had been seen all about this side of Fireach Speuer. Mairen almost certainly knew that Aoleyn had survived her magical blast, and Mairen was Tay Aillig's wife, joined with him spiritually. Even without that, even if Mairen had not been able to regain contact after her expulsion from Aoleyn's mind, Tay Aillig had certainly seen the fireball—how could he not?

She knew she should take care here, but she could not bring herself to slow her pace, not with Bahdlahn in such danger. She was not surprised, then, on one high leap from a ridgeline, to see movement below—a man, angling for the area near where she would land.

Aoleyn called upon her malachite and her moonstone, slowing her descent and turning it into a flight, moving to the side and easing herself down into a small copse of trees. As she landed, she saw that it was indeed Tay Aillig coming out from another tree line across the way.

The images of the three charred bodies flashed in her mind, but she fought them away, for even that horror could not dissuade Aoleyn from this fight. Not against this one, a man most deserving of her wrath.

He caught sight of her, roared, and charged.

Aoleyn called to the graphite of her anklet, stomped her foot powerfully, and loosed a mighty stroke of lightning, blinding in its flash. When her vision returned, she saw that she had stopped Tay Aillig—he stood in the clearing between the two groups of trees—but he didn't appear hurt at all.

Her bolt should have scorched him, should have, at least, taken control of his muscles and dropped him writhing to the ground.

But he just stood there, grinning at her.

Aoleyn stomped her foot again, sending a second, weaker, lightning stroke, and this time, not blinded, Aoleyn saw it reach for the man, then simply stop before it got to him, dissipating into a flash of nothingness.

How could that be?

Tay Aillig lifted his spear to throw, and Aoleyn felt something then, the slightest tug on her belly ring. She didn't know what that might mean, but it occurred to her suddenly that the spear and the belly ring had formed an attachment, calling to each other.

She ran to the side as Tay Aillig threw, and instinctively called upon her moonstone to put up a burst of wind against the missile to turn it aside.

But that spear then veered again, following her movement and flying for her belly!

Slowed only slightly by the burst of wind, the spear came on, and only Aoleyn's leopard legs saved her, a single twitch throwing her high in the air at the very last instant. Even so, the spear tried to turn again and come up at her, but the magic in that crystalline weapon was not strong enough and the energy of the throw had expired.

Dagger drawn, Tay Aillig charged in behind the throw and Aoleyn, descending from her leap, created a second burst of wind, this one full of flames, as she had done to Mairen. But the magic went past him on either side and did not touch him and did not slow him.

The desperate witch landed with an emphatic stomp of her foot, calling to the blue stone of her anklet, and the ground before her flash-froze into a field of ice, and this time, finally, Tay Aillig could not avoid the enchantment, his eyes going wide with surprise as he ran upon it. Skidding and sliding, he tumbled down hard, and Aoleyn sprang over him as he slid beneath her in a wide-limbed sprawl.

She looked down as he passed under, and noted that his hand went to something at his waist. Flying away, Aoleyn didn't understand, but she felt a sharp pain then in her legs, the cracking of bone, and the unexpected reversion to her full human form. She grabbed at the malachite to slow her descent, but so suddenly could not hear the song!

She crashed down and stumbled ahead on legs caught halfway between human and leopard. Her thoughts swirled, for she did not understand. Something was protecting this warrior from her spells, something he could throw at her to steal the song of Usgar.

She thought it must be Mairen and the Coven in a spiritual joining with Tay Aillig, for she could not know about the powerful sunstone he carried, a gem that could defeat magic.

Now she knew that she was in trouble, for she had no answers. She fell to the ground in the open area, and forced herself back to her feet as her legs finally completed the transformation. She glanced back over her shoulder to see Tay Aillig going for his spear—the spear that could somehow hone in on her belly ring.

Aoleyn was out of answers. Horrified, she just ran, trying to collect her wits and her breath.

With every step, she replayed the fight—what had worked, what had not.

With every step, she knew that she was running out of time.

Talmadge groggily opened his eyes, noting the morning light peeking in through the seams of the tent they had given him and his two friends. It wasn't the morning light that had awakened him, though, he knew immediately, for outside the village of Fasach Crann was stirring.

He sat up and shook the sleep from his mind, then glanced around to see Khotai fast asleep and Aydrian missing. Not disturbing his beloved, he slipped out of his bedroll, quietly grabbed his shirt, and put it on as he exited.

Half the town was out there, all milling about the central clearing and all looking up to the south, to the imposing mountain.

"I think you may wish to see this," Aydrian said as he approached.

Talmadge shielded his eyes from the glare of the rising sun limning the top snowy peaks of Fireach Speuer.

"A great fireball lifted into the morning sky," Aydrian explained. "Something is going on up there."

"Sidhe?" Talmadge asked. "Have they returned?"

He had barely finished the question when a bright white lightning bolt flashed, not much more than halfway up the mountainside.

"Usgar?" more than one of the villagers asked, for if it was indeed the magic-using Usgar, they were far down from their mountain perch.

A second bolt of lightning flashed. Talmadge winced, but instinctually understood. A flash of lightning, powerful and bright, without a cloud in the sky.

"It's her," he whispered.

"Perhaps," Aydrian replied with a shrug, and he held out his hand, palm up.

Talmadge fished in his pockets, then dashed back into the tent and fell to the floor to shuffle through his bag.

"What is wrong?" Khotai asked, waking. "Have the sidhe come?"

"No, no," Talmadge answered, holding up his crystal lens. "I just needed . . ."

He rushed out of the tent without another word. He could use the lens himself, and was sorely tempted to do so, but Aydrian was more proficient. And besides, if he was right, he wasn't sure he wanted to see what Aoleyn was doing, or why she might be throwing lightning about the mountainside.

He waited impatiently, tapping his foot and shifting constantly, as the ranger put the lens up to his eye.

Aoleyn stumbled, her fears putting her too far out ahead of her scrambling feet. She collected herself and dropped another patch of ice right behind her, hoping to slow the dangerous man.

With every step, she expected his spear to catch up to her and skewer her.

She crashed through some trees, grabbing the last of them to help her cut a fast turn to the side, then moved around one rock and down a narrow and bending trail between two others. She realized her mistake as soon as she rounded that bend, though, to find the trail spilling out to the top of a high rocky spur.

She had to collect herself and find the song of Usgar, to find the malachite or the moonstone to get her off that jutting ledge! She ran to the end, hoping to see a way to climb down it.

But no. It was a high prow of piled rocks, like so many others across

Fireach Speuer, like the one where she had made love to Bahdlahn. A peninsula in the air, it ended at, and was flanked on both sides by, a sheer drop.

"Find yourself," she whispered, closing her eyes. "Find your heart."

Aoleyn blinked open her dark eyes to see Tay Aillig rounding the bend back at the narrow trail. But now she heard the song. She could leap away.

"Or I can kill him and end this," she said, and instead of reaching for the malachite, she called upon two songs, those of the moonstone and the graphite.

Aoleyn wove their notes together and waved her hands in circles above her head, and in moments, the sky above the spur darkened suddenly under a dark and swirling cloud, one flickering with energy.

Tay Aillig skidded to a stop at the edge of the spur, looking up at her creation and grinning.

"Clever girl," he said.

Aoleyn brought down a bolt of lightning at him from the cloud above, and at the same time, stomped her foot and covered the front half of the spur with ice.

The lightning got right to Tay Aillig, and then stopped, just stopped, the thunder of it echoing all about.

Tay Aillig moved as if to throw his spear, but the cloud above was swirling, and it was obvious that no missile would get through that maelstrom.

"Nowhere to run, foul witch," he said, easing forward.

Aoleyn brought another lightning bolt down, and again, it was defeated before it reached him. A third stroke came down to strike the ground right before him, and that trick nearly worked, as the retort shook the spur and jolted Tay Aillig, who stumbled on the ice-slickened surface.

He laughed as he stood upright.

"You melted your own ice, fool," he taunted, stepping forward more confidently.

But his teeth chattered just a bit when he spoke, she noted. Her bolt had gotten through, at least a bit. Aoleyn understood the wear of magic, and so now believed that Tay Aillig's use of this strange anti-magic was also tiring him.

She had one trick left to play, and it would end this battle, she believed. She called to her malachite and ran toward Tay Aillig, then veered and leaped, calling down another lightning stroke to occupy his attention. She floated out wide of the spur, turning as she went to face him—and was surprised and hopeful to see that the lightning bolt, though again mostly defeated, had stung him this time. Whatever magic he was using was indeed beginning to fade!

She went to her moonstone with all her strength. Tay Aillig was on a slippery ledge—she meant to blow him off the other side.

A simple gust of wind to end the fight.

But her opponent reached his clenched fist out toward her and struck first, some wave of discordant notes, some unknown anti-magic, washing over Aoleyn, stealing her levitation as she focused on the moonstone.

Down she plummeted.

Talmadge hopped from foot to foot as Aydrian slowly swiveled his head, peering through the magical lens. The flashes on the mountain had lessened, but there remained one storm cloud—it seemed to be a storm cloud, at least, though it was tiny and roiling and flickering with lightning.

"I do not see the woman," Aydrian said to Talmadge in the language of Honce, and then, speaking so that all could understand, he added, "Only a man, atop a stony jag."

"It had to be her," Talmadge said. "It might be still. Why am I down here?"

"Halfway up the mountain," Aydrian replied. "A day's march! What might you have done?"

"I would have tried!"

"Tried to do what? This fight, if it was a fight . . ." He stopped and jumped back, startled, and lowered the lens.

"Lightning," Catriona said sharply, clearly annoyed that the two were speaking back and forth in a language only they could understand.

"A powerful bolt, from the cloud and at the man," Aydrian explained to her, and as he finished, the rumble reached them, the ground trembling under the angry growl.

"Not a day's march," said Khotai, rolling up beside Talmadge, then taking his hand. "Not for him," she added, indicating Aydrian.

"There is nothing we, or he, could've done," Talmadge admitted. "Too far."

"But you think it was her?" Khotai pressed. "This woman who saved you? Why?"

"I'm not for knowing," Talmadge admitted. "It's just a feeling."

"No matter now," Catriona said. "We've duty here, to our neighbors.

The sidhe await us at Carrachan Shoal, and so there we'll go to send them running."

Several about, particularly those from Carrachan Shoal, gave a cheer at that.

"Can you see that place, water walker?" she asked of Aydrian, who was once more intently staring up the mountain through the crystal. He didn't seem to be looking in the same area as the thundercloud, though, and yet seemed even more on edge.

Talmadge translated the question to his friend, but Aydrian nodded that he had understood and still didn't respond at all. Following Aydrian's gaze, he, Catriona, and the others peered up the mountainside, shielding their eyes once more. They saw more flashes then, far afield of the first, and far from where that small storm cloud still flickered.

Not lightning, though. These were flickers of light, like a mirror catching the rising sun, and tinged in gold.

All about the highest peaks of Fireach Speuer came those flickers. To the right, the west, and to the east, far to the left, and from that direction where the morning sun shone more directly, there came responding flashes much lower down the mountainside.

Without a word, Aydrian sprinted out from the town, over to the side and the ridge that separated Fasach Crann from Carrachan Shoal. The others followed, but the man, with his magic, went up the side of that ridge in long and sure strides, slowing not at all. At the top, he turned more to the east, and went to the crystal again, his expression obviously grim.

He only remained atop the rocks for a few heartbeats, then lowered the lens and leaped back down, floating the last few feet to land easily among the villagers.

Before he even began to explain, the look on his face, one of sheer, open dread, spoke loudly.

"What is it, my friend?" Talmadge asked as Catriona and the others crowded in.

"We cannot go after the Usgar woman," Aydrian replied.

"Carrachan Shoal!" the man named Asba insisted, seconded by the young woman named Tamilee.

But Aydrian stared him in the eye and shook his head. "We cannot. We must ready the boats, with all haste."

"The boats?" Talmadge and Khotai said together in surprise.

"What did you see?" Catriona demanded.

"They are coming."

"Who?"

"Demons."

"Demons?" Talmadge asked.

"Usgar?" Catriona pressed.

"No, not men. Demons."

"How many?"

Aydrian paused and stared. He turned back toward Carrachan Shoal, hidden behind the rocky ridge, then swept his gaze up the mountainside, all the way to the east, and now, all across Fireach Speuer came the flickers of mirrors, golden mirrors, signaling.

"How many?" Talmadge demanded.

"All of them."

Panic gripped her, for she was too low to get her malachite or moonstone working in time to break her fall, and too high to accept the fall.

She gripped the pendant on her hip, grabbing for the wedstone, thinking to heal as she landed. But in her desperation, the songs jumbled, and she gathered the power of the orange stone set atop the wedstone instead.

It didn't matter, she knew.

It didn't matter in her conscious thoughts that her hand on the pendant was no longer a hand, but was instead, a leopard's paw.

Aoleyn hardly took any of it in, hardly realized that her panic alone had elicited the power of her tattoo, and more fully than she had ever known. Not just her arms had transformed, but her legs, as well, and on those hind legs, the legs of a cloud leopard, the drop was not so high.

She landed hard, but not too hard, and dismissed her luck from her mind immediately, going with the energy of the gemstone cupped in her feline paw, bringing forth its power fully.

High above her, she saw Tay Aillig hoist a rock over his head and heave it down at her.

"Demon fossa!" he yelled. "What beast are you?"

Aoleyn easily dodged and didn't allow the attack to distract her as she fell more fully into the orange stone.

She saw Tay Aillig gather up another rock to throw, and she was glad.

He should have been moving from the high outcropping of piled boulders, but then again, from his angle, he couldn't see the side of the spur glowing an angry red as the orange gemstone's power ate into them, exciting them, heating them.

Tay Aillig's next missile barely missed, clipping off the ground near to Aoleyn, and nearly cracking her shins as it rebounded weirdly.

She called another lightning stroke from her conjured storm down upon him, and he jolted and clenched, and seemed to be barely holding his stance.

"I'll have you, demon," Tay Aillig promised through chattering teeth.

"No," Aoleyn whispered, shaking her head, noting her handiwork with the orange stone, eyeing the piled boulders and those areas where the edges of the stones solidified the pile—edges now softening, even dripping in small bits where the stones had become molten.

She looked back at Tay Aillig, who began picking his way down, spear in hand. He had barely gone below the ledge, though, when he stopped and stared, mouth agape, at the angry orange glow of Aoleyn's magic.

"What?" he asked, and turned to see Aoleyn below, looking up, her face locked in determination.

She stamped her hind leg and threw a lightning bolt—not at him, no, but at what she believed to be a critical joint in the outcropping pile.

Immediately, the stones shifted.

Immediately, they began to tumble.

Again, luck alone saved Aoleyn, for she had not reverted her limbs to their human form, and the power of her leopard legs alone allowed her to leap away as the entire outcropping tumbled down, boulders bouncing, magma splashing, huge rocks twisting and settling right where Aoleyn had been standing.

Lost in the thunder of the rockslide were the screams of Tay Aillig. Aoleyn heard them, though, in her mind if not in her ears.

She leaped back in after the stones and dust had settled to find the Usgar-triath wedged between two massive slabs of rock, only his upper body visible.

Amazingly, he was still alive, still conscious.

"Demon," he spat at her approach, blood flying with his spittle.

She stared at him. In her mind, she saw, too, the charred bodies in the cave. Was this to be her fourth kill of the day?

"Save me, witch," Tay Aillig pleaded then, surprisingly, his entire aspect changing—likely, he had come to understand that he was dying here, and horribly. "The stones . . . they are crushing . . . bleeding."

"Save you?" Aoleyn said, but weakly, for she was certainly not enjoying this horrid moment. "As you would save me? Or spare me? Or spare Bahdlahn?"

"I will," Tay Aillig promised, his words trailing off into a groan of sheer pain, then followed with a violent cough that spewed blood.

Aoleyn's hand—and it was a hand once more, as she dismissed the magic of the tattoo—went to her wedstone. She thought of the malachite and whether she'd be able to alleviate the weight enough to slip the broken man out of there.

"Save me, witch," Tay Aillig repeated, every word forced through teeth gritted by agony. "My wife."

My wife.

Like Brayth's wife.

Aoleyn let go of the wedstone, called upon her tattoo, and raised her arm, her leopard arm, her leopard paw, claws protracted.

She showed mercy to this man, her tormentor.

She took out his throat cleanly, one swipe, ending his pain forever.

23

OTONTOTOMI

Aghmor stumbled aimlessly, not knowing where he should turn. From afar, he heard the lightning, then the thunder of an avalanche, though he had moved too far to the west, down along a stone-filled dell, to see the incidents.

He couldn't go back to the Usgar. He had killed Egard.

He wanted to be with Aoleyn, to beg her forgiveness, but was she even still alive? Again, he wished that he could replay this terrible morning, wished that he had been less impulsive.

Even the image of Bahdlahn beneath Aoleyn couldn't change his mind now.

He had murdered Egard.

Aoleyn was caught and likely dead.

Bahdlahn was doomed.

The man stumbled and continued along the trail, not even knowing where it might lead.

His surprise was complete when she stepped onto the trail before him. His first thought was that she was an older woman, perhaps Mairen's age, and that she was beautiful, whoever she was, whatever she was.

For he had never seen such a being.

He thought of Bahdlahn's story of the fight on th'Way—was this the same creature?

She said something he could not understand and took a step toward him.

Aghmor lifted his spear, noting that she carried a bat-like weapon, a flattened club of some dark green wood, with edges serrated by lines of what appeared to be actual teeth.

She said something again, and motioned to the ground before Aghmor.

She was asking him to kneel, he realized, to surrender.

Aghmor was in no mood for that. He laughed, and leaped at her, stabbing his spear.

How easily she dodged, the slightest of movements, but just enough so that the thrust went wide, and with her bat coming across to ensure that Aghmor couldn't sweep the weapon back in at her.

The man retracted and leaped back.

His opponent easily rolled her weapon hand to hand, spinning it over and over.

A skilled warrior, Aghmor was not dazzled by the movements, nor even impressed. No, he was instead looking for patterns, waiting for an opening.

He saw it and he struck, a thrust for her gut that could not miss.

But it did miss, and badly, and from the side—how had she moved to the side?—came the bat, swinging across, striking Aghmor's spear mid-shaft and cleanly breaking it.

Before Aghmor could even react, before he could bring the remaining half of his spear in close to defend, the woman turned a sudden and perfect circuit, and suddenly her bat was up high, slashing down diagonally at the left side of his head.

He fell back desperately, but felt the bite as the bat grazed him. Still, he thought he had avoided any serious injury.

Until his blood began to spray up from the severed artery in his neck.

Aghmor gasped and grabbed at the wound. He turned and started to run, but got whacked across the back of his legs and found himself on the ground.

"No, no, no," he said, he begged, as he got up on all fours and began to crawl for all his life.

He heard her walking calmly behind him.

"No, no, no."

He felt a burst of hot pain across his back, and could hardly believe the weight of the blow.

Now his legs wouldn't answer his call, but he grabbed ahead with his hands, clawing, crawling, begging.

"Egard!" he cried, for he saw the Usgar warrior, hanging limply, but alive, and in the grasp of two more strange-looking humanoids with painted faces.

Aghmor didn't understand, was beyond comprehension, was too overwhelmed by this morning—Aoleyn making love with a slave, his betrayal, the fireball and lightning bolts, the avalanche he had heard, his murder of Egard, and now this! All of it, all of his life's choices, seemed to speed past him then in this moment that was simply too terrifying to allow him to make sense of anything. Was this all a dream?

The bat came down hard on Aghmor's head, a final explosion, an instant of bright white, burning light before eternal darkness.

They came over the mountain ridges like a plague, a thousand riders, tall and terrible on their lizard mounts, and behind them the dark lines of huddled infantry, more numerous than could be counted. The whole mountain shook, and Loch Beag rippled with the impact of their march.

Over at the boats of Fasach Crann, the villagers and the refugees of Carrachan Shoal looked back in shock, with many, led by Catriona, then reflexively grabbing for their weapons.

"No!" Aydrian shouted as soon as the would-be defenders began to form. "No, run! Sail out!"

But off many ran, calling for a defensive line akin to the one that had earlier defeated the mountain goblins.

Beside Aydrian, Talmadge kissed Khotai, drew his sword, and started off, but before he had gone two strides, Aydrian grabbed him by the shoulder and, with frightening strength, yanked him back, then kept pushing until he had pushed the man over the side and into the boat beside Khotai.

"We can'no leave them!" Talmadge implored, but Aydrian, strength enhanced by the magic of his armor, lifted the prow of that large boat, which was filled with more than a dozen villagers, and began driving his legs, pushing it out onto the lake. Aydrian leaped over that prow as the boat floated free of the sands, hoisting yet another villager, a refugee from the neighboring town, over with him.

"We can't leave them," Talmadge protested, moving for the rail.

Again, Aydrian grabbed him.

"They have come to trust me and you," he said. "If we go back, many others will follow, and will die. For nothing! We cannot win."

As if in answer to his prediction, both men gasped then, for the approaching lizard riders hoisted spears on strange Y-shaped handles. As one, they threw, snapping their arms forward, launching the missiles from the atlatls with frightening speed and accuracy.

More than half of the two-score villagers rushing back to defend went down under that barrage, many hit by more than one, more than two, long spears, and with such force that they were thrown down hard to the ground.

On came the strange-looking humanoids astride their green, golden-headed lizards, and those villagers who had not been hurt, or not hurt badly, turned back for the beach and ran for all their lives.

"Row, row!" Aydrian implored those in his and nearby boats. "Sails up!"

Sounds echoed across the water west and east, screams of fear and pain, and it quickly became clear that the other villages, too, were under attack.

Aydrian jumped out of the boat, calling upon his amber gem, running across the lake surface back toward shore, toward a boat that Catriona and some others were trying to launch. They got off the shore as another rain of missiles descended upon them, spearing several more.

"A line!" Aydrian yelled to them, and Catriona herself, a spear stabbing through her side, stumbled to the prow and threw a rope out toward the man. It didn't reach him, falling into the water, but Aydrian was fast to the spot, grabbing it up.

He turned and hunched it over his shoulder, then ran on, towing the craft.

Back at the shore, more villagers died.

On Catriona's boat, several offered their thanks, relief evident, but looking back, Aydrian's expression could not return any consolation.

For the front ranks of the invading cavalry hit the beach and hardly slowed, the sleek lizards rushing into the water and gliding out with great speed.

They were doomed, all of them, and Aydrian knew it.

Cold and wet, Bahdlahn ran out of room. In a small clearing in the copse of pines, he saw the shadow of an Usgar warrior rushing before him, and when he turned, a second man came out from behind a tree, crystal-tipped spear leveled his way.

"Where will you run, uamhas?" the warrior taunted.

From the trees to the right of the speaker came a living missile then, so suddenly, a feline form flying fast into the Usgar warrior, slamming against him before he could turn and bring his spear to bear, and tumbling with him into the trees the other way.

Bahdlahn heard the growls, the roar, the screams of shock and terror. He wasn't about to wait around to learn the outcome, though, not with a second Usgar behind him. Off he ran, right past the tree where the first warrior had been, crashing through the limbs and stumbling on, out of the copse and then again down the mountainside.

He heard that second Usgar shout out behind him, a call of anger and surprise. How quickly those shouts, too, turned to screams of terror, accompanied by the leopard's growls.

Down Bahdlahn ran, certain that he was being pursued once more, by Usgar or by the great cat. He cut a sharp turn around a boulder, veering to his left along the descending trail, then skidded to a stop as something flew down in front of him, landing on the trail. For a moment, he was sure it was the leopard, but then it was not, not fully, at least.

Aoleyn! She stood before him on shaky legs, trembling as they turned from those of a great cat to those of the young woman. Her face glowed with tattoos of a cat's face, mingling with her features, but then fading.

And it was Aoleyn, just Aoleyn, standing on the trail, her clothing torn and ragged, barely covering her, her hands red with blood.

Bahdlahn ran to her and hugged her, and checked those hands, only to realize that it wasn't her blood caked about her fingers and under her nails. He stepped back, staring at her wide-eyed.

She held her arms up and he pulled her in to hug her once more, crushing her close.

"Tay Aillig is dead," she whispered in his ear. "I can'no go back. They'll not hear my words."

"Where then?" Bahdlahn asked. "To Fasach Crann?"

Aoleyn nodded. "And fast. We must be fast away. Mairen hunts me."

Bahdlahn took her by the hand and started to move off, but Aoleyn tugged, resisting, and shook her head when he glanced back to regard her.

"Too slow," she said, pulling him in close to her side. She moved to a high point, then began to sing softly, words—if they were words—that Bahdlahn could not decipher. The couple rose up from the ground, as if on a pillow of air, and down the mountainside they floated, gaining speed.

It was not long before they both realized that something was wrong across the mountainside, though. From their lofty vantage, the lake was spread before them, and its shores appeared . . . wrong. The entire eastern and southern parts of the shore—those closest to their position—looked like a writhing mass of insects. Out on the water, Bahdlahn saw the ships, heading away from shore from several of the lakeman villages, and he noted the odd wakes trailing after them.

Suddenly the truth dawned on Bahdlahn—and on Aoleyn, too, he knew from her gasp. His eyes widened in shock.

"Hold on more tightly," Aoleyn told him, and a burst of wind came up from nowhere, it seemed, speeding them down the mountain.

A pair of mundunugu led the way, one helping Pixquicauh, who was not skilled on a lizard mount, the other bearing the mirror, as Scathmizzane had insisted. They clambered over the high ridge, scouts to either side guiding them, and down to the highest small plateau on the mountain, one that held a deep chasm.

The High Priest dismounted unsteadily and collected himself carefully before daring to approach the gorge. He waved to his escorts, who carried the mirror to him.

Pixquicauh closed his eyes. This was his most important task, his most sacred duty. He heard the whispers of Scathmizzane. He positioned the mundunugu accordingly and had them angle the mirror to the east, to catch the reflection of the rising sun. Barely had the polished gold flashed with a brilliant and blinding catch of those beams than the mirror suddenly sparked and seemed to leap from the grasp of the two warriors, who helplessly flailed in trying to catch it as it pitched into the chasm.

Panicked, one fell to the ground grabbing, grabbing, and the other seemed about to leap in after the sacred item.

"At ease, you fools," Pixquicauh said to them. Both turned back to regard him as he stood there, nodding, and though his skull face couldn't smile, the pair surely noted the lightness of the augur behind that permanent mask.

"This is as Scathmizzane desired," he explained. He motioned to the lizards. "You may go."

"You will ride with us, High Priest," said one.

Pixquicauh shook his head, then walked around the chasm and climbed the northwestern ridge, the top of which afforded a grand view of the human tribe's mountain encampment. When he peered over those stones, Pixquicauh found that he could barely breathe, for in looking down, he saw the pines, the patch of eternal summer, and the nearly translucent, giant orange crystal.

"My Glorious Gold," he whispered, he prayed.

And he watched.

Climbing magically was one thing, floating down to the ground on malachite magic was one thing, but speeding down the mountainside, the trees whirring past below, was something else altogether!

Fortunately, Aoleyn had expected this, so when Bahdlahn held on for all his life, crushing himself against Aoleyn's back as she worked the magic, she was able to maintain her concentration.

She had to.

As they neared the lower slopes, the couple saw clearly the swarm of enemies that had come against the lake towns, thousands of strange-looking humanoids, tall and thin and with faces streaked red and blue, forehead to lips. Many rode lizards. Others lifted spears on throwing sticks and launched them at the flying witch.

Aoleyn called upon her moonstone to create gusts of wind to deter those missiles, and then she climbed higher. At first, she figured to land outside one of the towns, hopefully the one named Fasach Crann, that she and Bahdlahn could go in to introduce themselves and possibly gain acceptance. Now, though, such a course was clearly impossible. These strange monsters held the towns, held all the land about the northwestern base of Fireach Speuer, as far as Aoleyn could tell.

The boats were their only hope, and to get to those boats, Aoleyn had to fly out over the water, and so over the lizards and their riders, which were swimming out after the flotilla.

Aoleyn was desperately tired. Flying was a difficult and draining magic, going down the mountainside even more so, but with Bahdlahn on her back . . . she might as well have been physically piggy-backing the man as she ran across a field.

She dismissed the negative thoughts and found her focus, sweeping down above Fasach Crann, too fast for the spear-throwers to react and let fly, then right out over the beach and above Loch Beag. It took the woman little time to recognize that the lizards would catch the boats, and so she eased her moonstone flight just a bit and sent her energies into the gray bar on her anklet.

A bolt of lightning shot down from the witch to the water, there dispersing into a stunning ball of energy that crackled about the lead lizards. They faltered and slowed.

"I'm sorry, Bahdlahn," Aoleyn said, weighing the good of the many in the boats over that of herself and Bahdlahn. She understood what it would take to drive back the chasing swimmers, and knew that such magic would not allow her to find the strength to get the couple out to those fleeing craft.

Another lightning bolt shot down, then a third.

Aoleyn and Bahdlahn dipped toward the lake, the witch catching them only at the last moment.

Up she flew, up and away, her last burst of energy thrown into her moonstone and malachite. And as she rose, she threw another lightning bolt, and the leading lizards all faltered, and those behind began turning for the shore.

"Hold me close," she bade the young man, and he did as the magic expired, that last burst of flight carrying them further out over the water, to splash down hard into the cold lake.

The song wouldn't come to them. Their dance became a jumbled mayhem of uncomplimentary movements and stumbles.

"Aoleyn!" Mairen cursed, wrongly believing that the apostate was somehow still defeating them. Aoleyn had thrown them from her mind, unbelievably, and now was somehow interfering with the harmony of Usgar.

From the sacred lea, the witches could hear the rumbles of thunder down the mountain, the lightning explosions, and then, finally, the tremendous grumble of the avalanche as the rocky spur collapsed. Down Fireach Speuer below the Usgar encampment, smoke and dust rose into the air.

"She can'no be this powerful," Sorcha said to Mairen. Sorcha held up her hands in surrender, giving up her dance altogether. "There is something else."

Cries from the encampment just north of them interrupted the old witch. Several moved as if meaning to go investigate, but Mairen held them back.

"Connebragh," she called, waving for that one alone to go investigate. Just returned from her fruitless spiritual searching, the younger witch held up her arms helplessly, her stare incredulous.

"Just run," Mairen yelled at her, and the flustered woman sped off, disappearing into the jumble of small pines.

To the rest of them, Mairen ordered, "Dance! Dance! Find the song of

Usgar in your hearts. Sing the song of Usgar with your lips. Deny the apostate!"

They tried, forming their circle near the perimeter of Dail Usgar, and beginning again their slow-turning dance, beginning again their singing, which sounded horribly off-key.

"Damn her, Usgar," Mairen cursed Aoleyn again and she moved right beside the crystal god and even reached out to place her hand upon the physical manifestation of their divinity.

As soon as her fingers touched the warm—very warm!—obelisk, Mairen understood her mistake. It was not Aoleyn. It could not be Aoleyn, no!

For she felt a presence within that giant crystal such as she had ever known before, something mightier than she had ever imagined, something foreign, some new song so beautiful that it stole her breath and froze her thoughts upon its melody alone.

"Usgar-righinn?" Sorcha called, but Mairen didn't hear.

The witches stopped dancing and cautiously approached, but Mairen didn't know it.

All she knew was the power within the crystal, within the mountain. Something bright and glorious, something bubbling up from inside the heart of Fireach Speuer.

The ground beneath her feet began to shift and liquefy, but Mairen didn't know it. All of Dail Usgar churned and melted, the twelve witches standing in the lea sinking suddenly to their waists in mud, but it wasn't until her fingers slipped from the side of the crystal that Mairen even realized it.

She came from her trance, hearing the cries of shock from her fellow witches, glancing about to see them all struggling to get to the edge, to the still-solid ground near the pines. Mairen, too, tried to wade through, but she felt the ground already hardening about her.

Hardening about them all.

"What is this, Usgar-righinn?" Annagh pleaded.

"Aoleyn!" Mairen answered, for she had no other name to put to it.

They were caught, then, all of them, the ground firming about them, as solidly as if it had never been disturbed, except that instead of thick grass carpeting the place, there were only twelve sprouts, the witches themselves, as if they were trees planted about the crystal.

"Pray to Usgar," Sorcha implored them. "Sing!"

But there was no music.

They floundered in the water, for neither really knew how to swim. Aoleyn tried to use her malachite to lift them, but Bahdlahn was terribly heavy and the magic had worn too greatly on her. She needed time to simply rest and recover her thoughts and breath.

But they had no time.

On impulse, she called to the blue stone of her anklet, creating a sheet of ice, but under them, directly below. It shot up fast, colliding hard and causing more than a few bruises, but when it surfaced, the small ice floe had Aoleyn and her companion's heads above the water, at least.

Not that it would do them any good unless she could find more magical strength, she realized, for the lead lizards and riders, too far back now, perhaps, to catch the boats, could surely catch these two!

"Do something," Bahdlahn implored her. "I can'no . . ."

He didn't even know a word for "swim."

Aoleyn listened for the song, then looked about desperately for an answer. Turning to gauge the distance to the boats, she saw a man, stocky and muscled, and wearing a gleaming silver breastplate, running at her.

"Who?" she gasped.

"I do'no know," Bahdlahn said, his voice just as breathless.

Running with long strides, obviously magically enhanced, the man cut the distance quickly and soon pulled up right beside the couple. He reached down and took Aoleyn's hand, and as soon as she grasped his fingers she felt the magic that was keeping him atop the water, now gripping her and lifting her up as well.

Aoleyn caught that magic, which was nowhere near as exhausting as her malachite or moonstone, and reached back to Bahdlahn, sharing it down the line.

The three turned and ran. The nearest lizard riders tried to launch spears at them, but the attempts flew wildly and splashed down harmlessly.

Soon after, the trio neared a boat, and they heard arguing there, lakemen pointing and cursing, and Aoleyn heard the name "Usgar" spoken more than once.

Another man came up between a pair of angry lakemen, and his head was not elongated from wrapping, and Aoleyn took heart, for this man, she recognized.

"Talmadge," she called.

"Aoleyn!"

"No, she is Usgar!" the man beside Talmadge said, shoving him.

"She is a friend. She saved me."

More arguing ensued, and the trio cautiously slowed their approach.

"Not him!" Aoleyn heard a lakeman demand, and she knew he was speaking of Bahdlahn. "No Usgar!"

Talmadge seemed to be making little progress in this fight, with the dozen lakemen and women on the boat arguing against him, his only support, a woman's voice from someone Aoleyn could not see.

"He's not an Usgar," Aoleyn called. "Talmadge, this is Bahdlahn of Fasach Crann, son of Innevah, who was with child when the Usgar captured her."

The yelling on the boat stopped immediately, all of them crowding near the stern, trying to get a look.

"Innevah," more than one said. "Innevah."

The older ones had known her. The younger ones knew her name.

Aoleyn and her two companions were soon on the boat, the woman sitting against the back rail, trying to gather her strength, physical and magical, once more, while Bahdlahn was pulled away by the lakemen, questions coming at him from every direction.

A couple of others, along with Aydrian and Talmadge, managed the small, square sail.

Apart from the conversations with Bahdlahn, which quickly ebbed, many arguments broke out about where they should go. Most argued for a turn to the east, the nearest bank, which could be reached in a couple of hours, despite the unfavorable winds. But a few kept pointing to the north and west, straight across the long lake.

"Ask her," Talmadge said finally, pointing to Aoleyn, and all eyes turned her way.

"What?" She didn't know the question, and didn't know what to think about any of this, still stunned by the sheer magnitude of life-changing events that had happened this day—and the sun wasn't even up above the top of Fireach Speuer yet!

"You have seen the attackers," Talmadge told her. "The argument across the boats is to flee fully, across the lake, or take to shore and counterattack."

"Run," Aoleyn said before even thinking about it. "They are thousands, many thousands. You can'no beat them. Even the Usgar . . ."

Her voice trailed away, and the arguing continued, with shouting from boat to boat in the large and growing refugee flotilla. Square sails catching the southern wind, whatever choice they might eventually make, at this point the goal was simply to put the lizard-riding attackers far behind.

Cries of terror and pain echoed across the waters sporadically, most from the south, from those who had tried to hide instead of fleeing, no doubt, then a larger communal shout went up somewhere along the lake's western shore.

"Car Seileach," Talmadge said and sighed.

No sooner had Connebragh arrived at the northern edge of the winter platform to better see the mounting turmoil down the mountainside than cries rang up from both the east and the west. The witch ran about, trying to get a measure of the situation that she could report to Mairen, but she stopped dead in her tracks, her eyes going wide, for never had she seen such creatures as these riding in on lizards to meet the line of Usgar warriors.

She thought them beautiful and hideous all at once, with their red and blue faces and golden skin. Mesmerized, Connebragh hardly noted the swarm of spears flying at the warriors from every ridge, it seemed, and it wasn't until half the defending line went down hard, writhing and spurting blood, that she came to truly appreciate the situation.

Only the Coven could stop the Usgar camp from being quickly overrun.

She rushed for the trees, hearing calls for Tay Aillig, who had not returned, and for Ahn'Namay, who had taken the lead in the Usgar-triath's absence.

Connebragh passed him near the center of the compound, barking orders, waving warriors all about. The witch had barely cleared him, though, when his calls became sudden grunts and groans, and the stones about him clattered with falling missiles. She glanced over her shoulder to see him lying on his back, a dozen spears sticking from his body.

On she ran, into the grove, pushing through branches toward Dail Usgar.

The crystal obelisk flared brilliantly, its light so blinding that it stopped her where she stood among the second rank of pines. As the initial brilliance wore away and her eyes readjusted, Connebragh saw her sisters, all of them, buried to their waists in dirt—and where was the soft grass of the beautiful lea?

She focused on Mairen, struggling near the crystal god, reaching for the obelisk, her fingers barely touching it.

The crystal flared and Connebragh gasped, for it seemed as if something, some humanoid, was inside!

"Usgar?" she breathed, and she dared hope.

The ground before the crystal began to churn, rolling over, and then a gigantic head rose from the ground before her, showing the distinctive markings of the invaders, the red nose and bright blue streaks. He, for it was a male form, continued to rise, up, up, standing thrice the height of the tallest Usgar.

He reached down with one hand, giant but slender, and cupped Mairen's chin, tilting her head back so that she had to look up at him.

Connebragh nearly fainted. A million questions darted through her thoughts. Was this Usgar? But how could it be Usgar, looking like these strange monsters now slaughtering the tribe?

She did well to stop herself from screaming.

She did better by rushing away, out of the grove and to the highest point on the plateau's northwestern edge. There, she clutched the green-flecked crystalline tip of a spear she had collected in her run—Ahn'Namay's spear. She called to the song within, and leaped, fast-floating down the mountainside.

You hear my voice inside of you, the godlike giant imparted to Mairen. *Echo it. Sing.*

Mairen couldn't possibly refuse. She had never seen anything so beautiful as this creature in all of her life, had never heard anything so beautiful as his voice in all her life.

This was Usgar, she believed, come to her in her time of need.

She found the notes, the harmony of light, of beauty, of life itself, and so she sang, and the ground did roil beneath her, the churning soil lifting her up, releasing her from the earth's grasp.

She stood by the crystal god and she sang, and the great giant moved to each of the sisters in turn and showed them his light, and they, too, sang, and they, too, were lifted from their earthen traps.

Dance! the giant compelled them, and so the Coven danced once more and sang in harmony, and even Moragh, so new to this music, so tentative before, twirled and sang at the top of her voice.

The crystal flared with power, its tip glowing as brilliantly as the sun above.

Beneath the northeastern section of the grove, directly ahead of the crystal's tip, the ground began to glow angrily, and smoke began to rise.

One of the pines in that area flared with fire, then others joined, a sudden and ferocious conflagration.

Sap exploded and cinders flew, small fireballs launched into the air to be caught on southern winds.

But the witches didn't shy and didn't stop their dance and song.

A great gust of wind came up, a hurricane to mock the blast Aoleyn had used to topple Mairen and the others, and so aimed was it that not a branch shook on any tree that was not within the conflagration. But those burning trees, their roots incinerated, the ground beneath them more molten than solid, flew away like great flaming spears.

Through that opening in the grove, the view opened wide, down to Loch Beag's eastern banks.

Sing! the giant godlike creature told them, and how could they not? For none of them had ever heard a sweeter music, a song promising peace and eternal joy.

Gliding on the southern winds, the boat holding Aoleyn was more than halfway across Loch Beag as the sun neared its zenith that day. Many of the other boats of refugees moved beside them, most ahead. Dozens of other boats had broken off, most going for the eastern shore, but some turning west, intending to land north of Car Seileach.

"The Carrachan Shoal survivors are not pleased by our choice," Talmadge said to Khotai, Aydrian, Aoleyn, and Bahdlahn.

"I should be with them," Khotai answered. "I would be, except that I'd be only a burden."

Aoleyn stared at the woman, awkwardly sitting, her one leg tucked under her, its girth tilting her to the side.

A call from another boat had them all turning, looking back to the south, to Fireach Speuer. There, high on the mountain—at the winter plateau, Aoleyn believed—a host of trees went up in a sudden burst of angry flames.

"Mairen," Aoleyn reasoned, but she was wrong.

Smoke billowed into the sky and moments later the fiery line blew out, exploding forward and scattering on the mountain winds.

Aoleyn was standing then, staring hard. "Mairen?" she repeated, this time questioning. She couldn't tell from this distance, of course, but she feared that the fire was up by her tribe, was, perhaps, at the sacred grove about Dail Usgar, trees she had climbed as a child.

All of them, on all the boats, stood and stared—some of the lakemen on Aoleyn's boat quietly cheering at the apparent demise of the Usgar. From that spot high on the mountain, there came a bright light, brighter than the midday sun, and Aoleyn shielded her eyes and could not stand to look at it directly for more than a brief moment at a time.

White light, searing light, light so brilliant that it mocked the noon sun on this clear day.

A beam shot out from it, from that spot, down the mountainside, hitting a high outcropping and melting the stone, then bursting through on its path of obliteration. It shot through a stand of tall trees, which immediately burst into flames, then continued down the mountainside, crossing east of Fasach Crann, high above the sacked village of Carrachan Shoal.

A great hissing sound to the east broke the trance and all the refugees on all the boats swiveled their heads to regard the source, and all gasped as a spray of steam arose from the lake, the water superheating under the power of that strange beam of white light.

Then came an explosion, huge and terrible, and a gout of molten stone leaped into the air, breaking the waves, and then a second line of fiery stone, fountaining from the rocky ground along that eastern shoreline.

"By the gods, what . . ." Talmadge started to say.

Another explosion shook the whole of the plateau, and another geyser of lava leaped forth.

"Sail, row," Aoleyn whispered. As with anyone who had ever looked down upon Loch Beag from the higher perches of Fireach Speuer, Aoleyn had often wondered what might happen if the mountains forming the eastern banks of that huge lake had ever broken and split. Beyond that narrow bank of mountains, the land fell away for nearly half a mile, way down to the lifeless lands of Fasail Dubh'clach, the Desert of Black Stones.

Another explosion, and another after that rocked the Ayamharas plateau, more gouts of liquefied stone spewing into the midday sky.

And deeper grumbles followed, as if reaching far below the lake.

"What is that?" asked Talmadge and many others across the water.

"Sail, row," Aoleyn said again.

"What are they doing?" Talmadge demanded of her.

"I do'no know," Aoleyn answered.

"Breaching?" Aydrian asked his friend, but he did not know the word for that in the language of the plateau. Khotai gasped and translated.

"Sail!" Talmadge yelled, to those on his own boat and all the others. "Get off the lake! Get off the lake!"

Many of the boats were already trying to do so—many of those already on the way to the east fast tacked and tried to turn about.

Unseen explosions could be heard beyond the mountains, and screams came from unseen folk—the folk of Sellad Tulach, no doubt, as it was the only village along that shore—and more fountains of lava reached up among the eastern mountain range.

Fiery boulders flew high, some arcing out over the lake to splash down angrily. A rain of them dropped near to the bank, among the leading boats that had turned that way, pummeling them, igniting them, sending men, women, and children leaping helplessly into the sizzling waters.

"We have to go to them," Khotai cried.

"No!" came an emphatic denial, from Aoleyn, which surprised all others listening.

"Deamhan," one man said.

"The boat is drifting," Aoleyn told them. "All the boats are drifting. The lake, the lake!"

"The lake?" Bahdlahn and Khotai asked together.

"It is draining," Talmadge explained before Aoleyn could, as he, too, noticed the new current. "The eastern wall of the plateau is breached."

He ran to the side of the boat, grabbed one of the simple rigging lines, and leaped up on the rail, shouting for all the boats to row hard and sail hard to the north or the west.

A huge explosion shook the lake and nearly sent Talmadge overboard.

Then came another answer, this time from the lake itself, as the water broke not so far away and a huge, serpentine head appeared, rising up above one of the other boats, all teeth and horns and primal fury, as angry as the spews of lava, as unstoppable as a volcano.

Down it crashed, splintering the boat into a thousand pieces, crushing the poor sailors or sending them flying.

Aoleyn stood and lifted her arms, facing the sail. She called upon her moonstone and brought forth a tremendous rush of wind and the boat leaped away, speeding to the north.

The man in the silver breastplate protested, she knew, though she couldn't understand his words. Using his own magic, the man took the end of a rope

in hand and leaped out from their boat, running across the water to tie off a second boat, the one carrying Catriona of Fasach Crann.

Aoleyn paused in her magic, but listened not at all to the shouts coming at her.

"We go or we die" was all she would answer, and given the growing catastrophe all about them, it was hard to dispute the notion.

Everyone on that boat, on all the boats, wanted to help their fellow lake dwellers.

Everyone on that boat, on all the boats, realized to their horror that there was nothing that could be done.

Aydrian came back to the rail then, looking miserable, but with Catriona's boat somewhat in tow, and now tied to their own. He said something to Talmadge, who turned grimly to Aoleyn and nodded.

"Bring the wind," the man named Aydrian agreed.

What else could they do?

Aoleyn brought forth the power of her moonstone, the sails bending, the boat racing away to the north. As they passed other craft, Aoleyn bade the man at the rudder to move them near, and she offered as much wind as she could to the other boats, as well, though the focus remained on her own. Soon they were far in the lead, speeding toward the northern shore.

To the east, the explosions and gouts of lava continued. Out of sight, along the sheer mountain wall dropping to the desert far below, huge boulders shifted and blew out, the pressure of the lake sending great waterfalls spraying forth, falling, falling.

Far behind, boats were swept away on the rolling tide. The great monster of the loch came forth again and took a second boat, then a third.

Up atop Fireach Speuer the beam continued, reaching down to eat at the eastern wall, to crack the mountain bowl that held Loch Beag.

Aoleyn collapsed with exhaustion when her boat at last slid ashore the northern beach—a shoreline that was noticeably lower than it had been earlier that same afternoon. She let Bahdlahn help her out of the boat and fell down on the wet sands, her magic gone.

The second boat, towed by the line Aydrian had given them, came in right after, but the next in line was still far away, oars splashing, sails trying to catch those southern winds.

Aoleyn watched the strange man in the silver breastplate run out from the beach, rope in hand. He was a good man, she decided. He would try to help.

Aoleyn wanted to, as well, but she had no strength left, had nothing left at all. She doubted she could stand on her own at that time, and the song of her magical gemstones was naught but a distant buzz, inaccessible.

When the sun went down and twilight fell, the beam continued and bright lava leaped high, and the crackles of explosions intertwined with the continual thunderous roar of gigantic waterfalls.

And the waters of Loch Beag lowered, waterfalls raining on the desert far below, sweeping boats and refugees away to the east.

EPILOGUE

She had only two magics in the spear tip she held: the green-flecks of malachite to lighten her step or allow her to float down the mountain, and the small bits of diamond that allowed her to brighten or darken the area around her.

Connebragh used the second of those magical powers most of all now, down off the mountain and along the western bank of the fast-diminishing Loch Beag. Surrounded by enemies, human and nonhuman alike, the terrified witch crouched in the shadows, and enhanced those shadows around her.

She didn't know where she could possibly go, so she kept moving away from the mountain. Her people were all dead, she believed—how could any of them have survived the hordes of attacks and that giant, godlike creature she had seen rising from the ground of the sacred lea?

What could she do?

Where could she go?

She had passed by a town of lakemen only moments before a horde of those painted-faced humanoids had sacked it. So many had fled, the same way Connebragh had been running. Over and over again, she had heard the screams as the invaders caught them and cut them down.

The sun was setting now before her. Terribly afraid, Connebragh found a cubby under the exposed roots of a leaning willow tree, and there she huddled.

She closed her eyes tight and kept them shut, but she did not sleep. She could not sleep because the night was full of screams and thunderous explosions, and earthquakes that shook the ground about her so violently that she feared the tree under which she huddled would topple over at any moment.

She didn't know what to do.

Aoleyn awakened the next morning to find herself alone in the shallow cave she had shared with Bahdlahn and some others. She came out, bleary-eyed, still exhausted from the events of the previous day. She had slept more than most because of her sheer exhaustion, for she had used the magical gemstones of her jewelry more extensively the previous day than ever before—even counting her battle with the fossa. Still, hers had not been a solid sleep, for the ground had shaken and rolled so many times, as if entire mountains had fallen.

She crawled out and looked about the lower trails to the north and west, but saw little activity, though she did note that many of the huge stones of this boulder-strewn region seemed as if they had moved in the earthquakes. She couldn't be certain because she did not really know this area, and had only glimpsed it in the twilight briefly, and while exhausted. Still, it looked different to her.

Everything looked different to Aoleyn.

Making her way around the rock that formed this shelter, she found her companions, many of them standing along the higher ridge up above, all looking back toward Loch Beag.

Aoleyn crawled up the slope, noting Bahdlahn, Talmadge, the strange man in the silver breastplate, and the crippled, dark-skinned woman named Khotai. When she got up beside them, she had no voice with which to greet them.

For there before her, Loch Beag was gone, and in its stead lay a vast and huge valley. To the east, a large section of the mountains had indeed fallen away, leaving a wide opening, and just below the lower edge of a massive crack in the bowl of the Ayamharas plateau, as far as Aoleyn could see, the Desert of Black Stones was no more, replaced by a seemingly endless lake.

She turned her attention to the uncovered valley, and it seemed strange to her, unnatural, as if some giant hands and not simple nature had shaped it. She noted worked stones all along its steep sides. Steps? Structures built among the dark holes that appeared to be caves?

Her gaze traveled to the valley floor, half a mile below, and to a large mound, it seemed, down there in the center.

No, not just a mound, she realized, but a strange four-sided, mountain-like structure, too constant and homogeneous, its sides symmetrical.

"It's a pyramid," Talmadge said.

Aoleyn stared at him blankly.

Aydrian stepped over and held something out to her. As soon as she took the item, a lens, she felt its magic. She brought it to her eyes and called upon the song, and gasped as the "mountain" at the bottom of the valley came clear to her.

The sides were all stepped, evenly and beautifully, though mounds of silt covered many of the stairs.

She moved her gaze about, seeing many structures, hundreds of structures, thousands of structures, and came to understand that she was looking down upon what once had been a massive settlement, a village a thousand times larger than all the lakemen villages and the Usgar encampments combined. It lay in disrepair, of course, with mounds of mud and waste, vast puddles, even small ponds, of water, and fields of dead fish, all about.

But it was there, without doubt. A city, once a glorious and massive settlement.

How could it be?

Aoleyn's magically enhanced gaze roamed far to the south wall, to the stairs there, carved along the wall, climbing out of the vale to the shadows of Fireach Speuer. She saw the invaders, swarming like hungry ants, working their way down those stairs, cleaning them.

Reclaiming them.

Aoleyn brought the lens down from her eyes and stared openmouthed at Talmadge and the others, completely at a loss.

"'Tis not possible," she whispered, and none of them had an answer.

On a sudden impulse, the young woman brought the lens back up to her eyes and gazed far across the valley-that-had-been-a-lake, to Fireach Speuer, up, up, to see what had become of her people. From a still-distant vantage, she found the sacred grove, and saw that a part of it had been blown out, as she had suspected the previous day. She started to magnify that image, wanting to peer inside, and she did see a shining point that she believed to be the obelisk of the crystal god.

But then she screamed and dropped the lens, and fell away in shock and fear.

Aydrian gathered up the lens and took her place, quickly looking back to the mountain. He, too, gasped and backpedaled, and waved for all the others to get down.

They all understood a few heartbeats later when a gigantic snake came into view, swimming in the air the way a normal snake might have swum the waters of Loch Beag.

No, not a snake, they realized as it came closer, for this creature had a more lizard-like head and jaw, and great horns, and behind that head, perhaps a quarter of the way down its serpentine body, were wings, small wings and nothing that should have held it aloft.

"The lake monster," many about whispered, and then many began to gasp yet again.

For as the lake monster moved down below them, into the vast mountain valley before them, they saw that it had a rider, one who looked very much like the invaders who had come against them.

Except that this one was huge, a true giant, large enough to ride a serpent that seemed a hundred strides long and as wide as a house.

"'Tis not possible," Aoleyn said again and again, a sentiment echoed all throughout the hundred refugees who had managed to get to this northern bank, a hundred survivors who had left thirty times their number behind.

Everything looked different to Aoleyn.

THE END

MORE

TOR

THE

EDUCATION

OF BROTHER

THADDIUS

This is madness! Master De'Unnero St.-Mere-Abelle at the head of a great army, beside the son of Elbryan and Jilseponie, the boy who declared himself king, the boy who should be king!

Does lineage not matter? And is there a more worthy heir to the throne of Honce-the-Bear than the son of the heroes of the Demon War? Particularly when one of those heroes is the Lady Jilseponie, the Disciple of Avelyn. By all accounts there is no one in the world more powerful with the sacred Ring Stones. Surely she is blessed by God.

And therein lies my madness, my confusion, and my pain. The measure of holiness rests in affinity to the gemstones—of this, I am sure. I have been ordained as an Abellican monk for only two years, but before that I trained in the nunneries, or more precisely, I was tested there, repeatedly. I did not understand my training at that time, for I was not allowed to handle the sacred Ring Stones, of course. None of us were. But the stones were being handled, quietly, all about us, as those who would decide which lucky few could enter the class of God's Year 845 at St.-Mere-Abelle determined which held affinity to the stones.

Not everyone can use them. Fewer still can use them well. I am one of those few; there is no doubt in the mind of the Masters and Father Abbot Fio Bou-raiy as to my proficiency. I am the youngest student ever to be allowed to light the diamond sconces of many of the lower halls of St.-Mere-Abelle, and I can do so with the intensity one would normally see from a Tenth-Year Immaculate, or a Master, even!

Brother Avelyn was blessed in the stones, and was declared a heretic and murderer, and hunted by the Church.

The new powers of St.-Mere-Abelle have reversed that edict wholeheartedly, and there are whispers that Brother Avelyn will soon be beatified, and almost certainly sainted soon after that.

Brother De'Unnero now approaches to battle this reversal, to battle the brothers who have declared this intent, and yet Marcalo De'Unnero, too, is possessed of great affinity with the sacred stones. None have ever called upon the tiger's paw more powerfully than he! Nor were any of recent memory as dedicated in the physical training—is there anyone in the world who can defeat the man in martial combat?—though that means little to me. The physical training is a distraction. The Ring Stones are the power *of God, and holding that, who needs to throw a punch? Still, though, Brother De'Unnero's willingness and expertise in the training surely speaks to loyalty.*

And yet, here we are, a Church torn against itself, with the sacred Ring Stones surely to be used by both sides in the coming conflagration.

This is madness!

For only godly men can use the stones, and proficiency should be the highest test of worth! Are they, or are they not, the direct gifts from God?

So many seek to obfuscate that question, it seems, to weave in shades of gray about that which is black or white. And always they do it for their own convenience and personal gain!

Human failing has no place before Godly magic.

I must fight in the next few days for St.-Mere-Abelle, for the Church, which I hold above all else. But is that the Church of Fio Bou-raiy or the Church of Marcalo De'Unnero? Is that the Church which is generous with the sacred stones and their powers, granting them to all in need, based on sophistry, even, on justifications other than the word of God? Or is it the Church, as Brother De'Unnero has always claimed, which holds the gemstones close, which bestows the power upon the deserving alone and which teaches the undeserving the error of their ways through lack of mercy?

Is not such a lack of mercy truly merciful if the result is to enlighten the undeserving?

And that is my madness, roiling within me these last years and now forced to the head by the storm that approaches. I serve the Abellican Church and so I must fight for St.-Mere-Abelle, but I see the truth of Brother De'Unnero's vision, and wish my current brethren, Father Abbot Bou-raiy, Bishop Braumin, Master Viscenti, and all the rest, would see the error of their ways, would see that their generous and liberal sharing of that which is sacred diminishes the value of the Church itself, diminishes the mystery of God, and diminishes the glory of those of us who, through God's good grace, understand the power of the stones and can channel it through our imperfect mortal coils.

Oh, but how I wish that diplomacy would win the day and that brother De'Unnero would return to his rightful place as a Master of St.-Mere-Abelle! A Master and soon enough to be elected as Father Abbot, for that is a vote that I would surely cast!

By the Pen of Brother Thaddius Roncourt

This troubled midsummer day, God's Year 847

PART 1

THE

POWER

VOID

The great hall of St.-Mere-Abelle had remained untouched in the hours since the battle. Even the bodies remained, exactly where they fell. Braumin Herde and the other masters had ordered this—they wanted every monk at the monastery to see the harsh reality of this most awful day.

Father Abbot Fio Bou-raiy lay crumpled on the floor just before the throne, a hole blown through his head. The result of a hurtling lodestone, certainly, and the reality of a gem propelled so powerfully by someone considered an enemy of the Church stung Brother Thaddius profoundly, a poignant reminder to him of the madness.

Before the throne, the gigantic circular stained-glass window was no more than twisted metal and shattered shards. A dragon had flown through that window, so the story went.

A dragon! Never in his life had Brother Thaddius expected to see such a beast, never had he even believed that such beasts existed.

Most of the other brothers who were now filtering through the great hall on their way to the front doors of the monastery focused on that window, of course. It was a recent construction, a beautiful depiction of the petrified arm of Brother Avelyn, standing defiantly in the midst of the carnage of the Barbican volcanic explosion. Now it was gone, so suddenly, so violently, so . . . amazingly.

For one of the other brothers, however, the window seemed to hold little interest. Brother Thaddius smiled as he watched the stocky monk, a bruiser named Mars, standing before the sweeping stairway that led up to the balcony encircling the room. On those stairs lay two bodies: a woman Thaddius did not know and Marcalo De'Unnero.

Thaddius moved over to stand beside Brother Mars, measuring the intensity on the monk's face. Thaddius knew him well, for though Mars was several years older than Thaddius, they had come into the mother abbey in the same month, Thaddius as a newly ordained monk and Mars transferring in from St. Gwendolyn. Because of that circumstance, Mars had made more acquaintances among Thaddius's peers than among those of his age.

It hadn't taken Brother Thaddius long to figure out that he didn't much like the man. For Mars was everything Thaddius was not. He was handsome and powerful, as solid as stone and as good a fighter as any brother of the class.

But he could barely light an oil-soaked rag with a ruby, and anyone needing magical healing from Brother Mars's soul stone would surely perish. By Thaddius's estimation, brothers like Mars were the reason the Abellican Church was in such disarray and dire straits. The man was not worthy to be a brother.

A situation that might soon be remedied, Thaddius understood as he noted the moisture gather in Brother Mars's eyes as he stared at the facedown body of Marcalo De'Unnero.

"They know the truth of your loyalties," Thaddius remarked quietly, and Brother Mars turned to him with a start.

"I . . . of what do you speak, brother?" the man replied.

"Your loyalty to De'Unnero. To the heretic. It is obvious. It has been obvious for a long while. The masters know, and so does everyone in the room who sees you now, your hero dead before you."

"You presume much, brother," Mars answered.

"I think not," Thaddius was quick to reply. "There were many here at St.-Mere-Abelle, serving under Father Abbot Bou-raiy, who were intrigued with the vision of Marcalo De'Unnero. I can name myself among those. It is no secret, nor does it need to be, for we brothers are expected to question and explore. But some, it would clearly seem, moved beyond simple intrigue. Some brothers here were loyal not to the Father Abbot, but to the man they thought should hold the title. This man, De'Unnero."

Brother Mars did not reply, and stared stoically straight ahead, all signs of his grief gone.

"They know, brother," Thaddius said. "You are my classmate, perhaps a friend, and so I tell you this with confidence that you will pretend this conversation never happened. Surely you are smart enough to realize that Bishop Braumin has spent many weeks studying the remaining brothers of the Order, and that he will claim the position as Father Abbot—who else could it be?—and among his first duties will be a purge. Bishop Braumin hated Marcalo De'Unnero above all, of course, and he will surely root out any followers of the heretic."

Brother Mars chewed his lip for a bit, trying to find some response to that reasonable claim. He turned back to Thaddius to find that the small man had simply walked away.

Bishop Braumin Herde stood as if in a daze in the blasted and bloodied courtyard of St.-Mere-Abelle. All about him, his fellow monks worked frantically with magical hematite, the soul stones, to bring healing to scores, hundreds, of injured warriors who had done battle this dark day within the abbey and on the fields beyond her shattered gates. Those brothers didn't ask the allegiance of those they healed; the battle had been settled in no uncertain terms when Prince Midalis and his closest allies had defeated King Aydrian.

Still, so many had died, and would die, and Braumin could only shake his head at the horrors of war and all the misery that had plagued Honce-the-Bear in the last decades.

But in that darkness, Bishop Braumin had found, too, hope.

Now Midalis would be King of Honce-the-Bear—he already was in the eyes of those huddled about St.-Mere-Abelle. Indeed, even by Aydrian, who had laid claim to the throne!

Many times in the course of that morning had those healing brothers turned to Bishop Braumin with their gemstones, and truly it appeared as if Braumin could use more of the soul stone magic. He was a muscular man, not tall and no longer young, having passed his fortieth year. Usually he seemed as solid as any, strong of frame and with determined features, but now his jaw hung crooked, and Bishop Braumin stood crooked, favoring ribs that had been pulverized by the heavy kick of Marcalo De'Unnero. He was missing a few teeth from the right side of his mouth, too, from a punch that had knocked him nearly senseless.

De'Unnero had almost killed him with that strike; indeed, that apostate monk could hit with the force of a fomorian giant!

What a day it had been! Four armies joined in furious combat on the fields about the ancient and huge monastery.

What a day it had been! A dragon—a true dragon!—had crashed through the huge circular stained-glass window of the great foyer of St.-Mere-Abelle, only to be thrown back out by the demonic power Aydrian possessed, a bolt of searing white lightning that seemed as if it was still resonating within the deep stones of the high seaside cliff wall that held St.-Mere-Abelle.

What a day it had been! The great warrior, the ranger Nightbird, had been pulled from the grave and summoned halfway across Honce by the dark power of Aydrian, to fight by Aydrian's side as a horrid zombie.

But love had conquered the darkness of demonic powers, and Elbryan Wyndon, the ranger the elves had named Nightbird, had been coaxed from his state of undeath by Jilseponie, the wonderful Pony, the woman who had loved him for so many years, the woman who had been his wife, and who had given birth to his child soon after his death those two decades before.

And that child, tainted by the demon dactyl, had taken the throne of Honce-the-Bear. By sheer force and unrivaled power, that child had become King Aydrian.

Bishop Braumin Herde had watched the conclusion of the titanic battle within the monastery this day. Laid low by Aydrian's second, the apostate De'Unnero, the Bishop had managed to hold on to consciousness just enough to witness the glory, the beauty, of Elbryan and Pony expelling the demon from their son's heart and soul.

And so the battle had ended, so abruptly. De'Unnero was dead, killed by Pony, as was the woman, the bard, who had come in beside De'Unnero and Aydrian. Indeed, for some reason Bishop Braumin had not yet discerned, De'Unnero himself had killed the woman in the last fleeting moments of his own life.

And the demon was gone, expelled from this young man it had taken as host. The light had returned to the shining eyes of young Aydrian Wyndon, but with it, too, had come the sorrow of great regret. Bishop Braumin glanced over at the broken young man, sitting in the shadow of the wall with the centaur, Bradwarden, and Belli'mar Juraviel of the Touel'alfar.

"A centaur," Braumin whispered. "And an elf, with wings, fighting for St.-Mere-Abelle." He shook his head.

What a day it had been!

What might brothers reading the accounts of this battle a century hence think of the tale, he wondered? Would the reclusive elves, the Touel'alfar and the Doc'alfar, certain to return to their hidden lands and magical shadows, be forgotten again in the lands of men by that time? Would the rare centaurs be no more, again, than fireside tales?

And would the lessons of the travesty of Aydrian Boudabras be forgotten, only to be painfully realized once more in the land of Honce?

With that dark thought in mind, Bishop Braumin moved a bit closer to eavesdrop on the two most important people in Honce, Prince Midalis, who would soon be King, and Pony, perhaps the most powerful person in the world (and if not her, then surely her son Aydrian, who was under her control once more, it seemed).

"I have so much to do, so much to repair," he heard Midalis admit to Pony, and it was hard to dispute the remark, for not far from where they stood, many of Midalis's soldiers piled the dead beside a hole that would become a common grave.

So many dead.

"You have pardoned Duke Kalas?" Pony asked him.

"It will be done," the soon-to-be King replied. "In time. I want him to consider long and hard all that he has done. But yes, I will pardon him. I will invite him into my Court, to serve me as he served my brother. He was deceived by Aydrian . . ."

Braumin held his breath as Pony's eyes flashed, but Midalis calmed her with a warm smile.

"He was deceived by the same demon that stole from you your son," he corrected, and Pony nodded.

"A wise choice," Pony replied. "Vengeance breeds resentment."

How true, Bishop Braumin silently noted, for that lesson would be something that he would need to keep in mind in the coming days, he knew, and he feared. He would have to rise above his very human emotions.

"Jilseponie would serve me well," he heard Midalis say, drawing him from his contemplation.

Pony smiled and managed a little laugh. Braumin held his breath, knowing what was coming. "Jilseponie is dead," she said, and though it was a joke, Braumin couldn't miss the fact that her expression became more serious suddenly, as if she noted some definite truth in her own words, an epiphany she would not escape.

And how it pained the gentle monk to hear such talk from this woman!

"Twice I have personally cheated death," Pony went on. "In the Moorlands and on the beach of Pireth Dancard. I should have died, but Elbryan would not let me."

"Then credit Elbryan with saving the kingdom," Midalis was quick to say.

"But that was not his purpose," Pony explained. "He saved me to save my son, and so I shall. And then I will join him. As I rightfully should have already joined him."

Midalis stammered for a response, and Braumin surely understood that shock, given the woman's startling remarks. This woman, Pony, the most powerful gemstone user in the world, trained and skilled in the elven sword dance, a woman who was younger by perhaps a decade than Braumin Herde, had just claimed that she would not live much longer!

"You will leave us now?" Braumin heard Midalis ask when he turned his focus back to the conversation, and the monk held his breath. He did not want her to go.

"My time here is ended," Pony replied. She hugged Midalis. "Rule well—I know you shall! For me, I will spend my time in Dundalis, back home again. How long ago, it seems, when Elbryan and I would run carelessly about the caribou moss, awaiting the hunters' return or hoping for a glimpse of the Halo."

Pony stepped back and motioned to the side, to her son and his two companions sitting in the shade of the wall.

Braumin's gaze went that way. The centaur stood up—Pony had healed his broken leg so completely that he barely limped now, only hours later. Yet another reminder of the power of this woman, Braumin thought.

He couldn't help himself. "Wait!" he called, and he ran over to Pony and Midalis. "Wait, I beg!"

Pony greeted him with a great hug.

"I cannot believe you are leaving us," the monk said, and he wouldn't let her go. He wanted to say so much more! He wanted to tell her that he and his brothers had discussed the prospect of handing her the Abellican Church, to serve as the first Mother Abbess! It would be a monumental action. It would change the world! Surely she could not refuse such an opportunity . . .

Before Bishop Braumin could begin to spout out the many thoughts

swirling in his mind, though, Pony replied, "You have your Church to restore, and I have my son to save."

It wasn't just what she said, but how she had expressed it, and that included a bit of magic, Braumin realized, as the woman used her soul stone
to speak within his heart and mind.

You have your Church to restore.

You. Bishop Braumin. Pony wasn't simply making an offhanded and
obvious remark about the state of the world, she was charging Braumin
with this most important duty. She was giving him her blessing—nay, her
demand—that repairing the broken Abellican Church, the institution that
had suffered so greatly under the De'Unneran Heresy, fell squarely upon
the shoulders of Bishop Braumin Herde.

And indeed, this would prove a heavy burden, the monk knew. The
Abellican Church lay in ruins. So many brothers had been killed or driven
out by De'Unnero's minions, and many of those minions, fanatically loyal
to the vile man, remained in positions of power at various chapels and even
abbeys! Other chapels were empty and in disrepair, and even one of the great
abbeys, St. Gwendolyn-by-the-Sea, was now by all reports a deserted and
haunted place.

Braumin Herde gave a great sigh. A sniffle from behind turned him to
regard his dearest friend, Master Marlboro Viscenti, standing there with
his head bowed.

"What better place to save him than St.-Mere-Abelle?" Braumin slyly
remarked, more for Viscenti's sensibilities than his own.

For Braumin already knew the answer, and he was already nodding as
Pony replied, "Dundalis."

True to her word, Pony left later that same day, with Bradwarden, Juraviel, and her son Aydrian, bound for the Timberlands and the town of
Dundalis.

From a high window in the monastery, Bishop Braumin and Master Viscenti watched them go, and knew the truth: Pony would never return to
Honce-the-Bear.

"We have a lot of work to do, my friend," Braumin remarked, trying to
sound as optimistic as he could manage—and surely he thought the attempt
pitiful. "I fear that our struggle has only just begun."

"No," Viscenti said, draping an arm about his friend's broad shoulders.
When Braumin turned to regard him, he found Viscenti staring at him intently, and nodding.

"No," the skinny man said again. "The demon is expelled and King Midalis will help us as we help him. A lot to do, yes, but we go with honest hearts and a desire to do good things. We will prevail."

It wasn't often that Viscenti served as the calming and optimistic voice.

Braumin was glad that this was one of those rare occasions. He dropped his hand over Viscenti's and looked back out at the distant procession, hearing again the words of Pony, the charge that he must fix the Abellican Church.

He straightened his shoulders and steeled his broken jaw.

He knew what must first be done.

Brother Mars hunched low and tried to remain inconspicuous as he went about his work in tending the wounded soldiers, and traveled the battlefield perimeter as far as possible from St.-Mere-Abelle's wall. Normally, he was an imposing man, solid as a monastery wall, so it was said, and never one to shy from confrontation. But now, at this time, after the whispers of Brother Thaddius in the great hall of the monastery, after this disastrous battle, the man believed that a low profile alone could save him.

They knew.

It all made sense now. The masters of St.-Mere-Abelle had placed him in the background of the great battle, out of the way manning one of the high catapults. By all rights, Mars should have been on the front lines, for despite his young age and short training, few at the monastery, few in all the Church, could outfight him.

But no, they knew the truth of his loyalties, as Brother Thaddius had warned.

And it was the truth, the man admitted to himself out there on the bloodstained field. Mars had thrown his loyalty to Marcalo De'Unnero. He had remained under the command of Father Abbot Fio Bou-raiy as a spy, mostly, for his heart lay with the vision of De'Unnero, even if some of the man's tactics seemed a bit extreme.

De'Unnero did not believe that the sacred gemstones should be out of Church control, or that their blessing should be offered so liberally to the common folk of Honce-the-Bear.

De'Unnero did not believe that the peasants should be coddled. No, loyalty to God was a difficult and demanding task, one requiring vigilance and sacrifice.

To Brother Mars, Father Abbot Fio Bou-raiy and those others, Bishop Braumin and his allies, were weak and soft.

But they had won the day, and so, Brother Mars lamented, the Abellican Church might never recover.

More immediate concerns weighed on Brother Mars this day, however, concerns for his own future, or lack thereof. The masters suspected his turn from their way and toward De'Unnero. They surely would not tolerate him now with De'Unnero dead and the cause so badly disrupted.

He thought of his coming fate—and he was certain things would fall this way, with him in the dungeons of St.-Mere-Abelle, chained to the wall and fed food not fit for the rats. Even though he was outside of the monastery at that time, hoisting another wounded soldier over his shoulder to carry to the brothers with the soul stones, Mars felt as if the walls were closing in around him, suffocating him, damning him.

He knew what he must do. He kept at his work until the call for Vespers, the sunlight fast fading. Off in a far corner of the battlefield, he stripped off his bloody robes and threw on the shirt of a man killed in the battle. He crawled to the farthest point where he could remain undercover, and as soon as darkness fell, he put his feet under him and ran off into the night.

He didn't stop running until he came upon the town of St.-Mere-Abelle, some three miles inland.

The place was overfilled with soldiers, men from every corner of Honce, and more than a few from Alpinador, even. Mars understood the nature of war, and knew enough to realize that many of these people would remain in St.-Mere-Abelle, would make of it their home.

So would he.

Doors of the common rooms, taverns, and inns of the town were thrown wide by order of Prince Midalis, who was surely soon to be crowned King of Honce-the-Bear.

From one of those rooms, where songs of lament, of loss, of victory, and of hope all blended together in the many toasts and laments offered by the men, Brother Mars stared up the long hill toward the silhouette of the dark monastery beneath the starry skies.

Not so long ago, his heart had leaped with joy at the whispers that Marcalo De'Unnero approached St.-Mere-Abelle and would claim the Church as his own. How thrilled was Mars to believe that he could throw off his facade, discard this lie his life had become, and proclaim openly his support for De'Unnero! How he had hoped that he would stand beside that man, the greatest warrior the Abellican Order had ever known, to reshape the Order into one of sacrifice and valor and utter devotion!

Guilt brought many pained squints to Mars's eyes that night as he replayed the disastrous battle. He should have been stronger. He should have gone to Marcalo De'Unnero in the great hall and fought beside the man.

He conjured the image, burned forever into his memory, of De'Unnero lying dead on the stairs beside the woman called Sadye. Brother Mars should have been there, fighting with his idol, dying beside De'Unnero if that, too, was God's will.

He should have.

But he had failed.

At first glance, the brown-skinned man seemed quite out of place in this monastery, the mother abbey of the Abellican Church, but Pagonel walked with a quiet confidence and ease, and if he was out of place, no one had bothered to tell him.

He was a small man, well into middle age, thin and wiry, though not a nervous and excitable type like Brother Viscenti. He walked in sandals, or barefoot, as he was now, and in either case, a shadow made no less noise than he. He wore a tan tunic and loose-fitting pants, tied at the waist with a red sash, the Sash of Life, the highest rank of the Jhesta Tu mystics of Behren.

He stood in a grand hallway now, the Court of Saints, lined on one side by windows looking out over All Saints Bay, and on the opposite wall by grand paintings of the heroes of the Abellican Order, amazing works of art that each stood twice the height of Pagonel. Few who were not of the Abellican Order had ever seen this place, but Bishop Braumin had offered Pagonel free rein of St.-Mere-Abelle, naming the mystic as one of the true heroes of the battle that had, in Braumin's words, "defined the world."

Pagonel hadn't even really fought in that battle, not conventionally at least, although if he had, then surely many would have fallen before him. He was Jhesta Tu, and a grandmaster of that martial art. An Allheart Knight's shining armor would not protect him from the lethal hands of Pagonel, for the mystic could strike with the speed of a viper and the strength of a tiger. A warrior's sword would never get close to striking him, for Pagonel could move like the mongoose, faster than the sword hand, faster than the eye.

But no, he hadn't fought in the battle, other than to fight against the battle. When Midalis and Aydrian and their closest cohorts had engaged in their duel in the great hall of the monastery, Pagonel, riding the dragon Agradeleous, had flown low about the larger battlefield, calling for peace, insisting that the victor would emerge from within St.-Mere-Abelle, no matter the outcome on the field. He had saved many men and women that day outside of St.-Mere-Abelle, and in the aftermath, many indeed had come to him with their thanks and praise.

None of that had been lost on Bishop Braumin. On Braumin's word, Pagonel could go where he pleased in St.-Mere-Abelle, and could stay as guest of the Church for as long as he desired.

Truly the mystic had been pleasantly surprised by what he had found in the quieter corners of the great monastery, whose walls ran a mile long atop the cliff wall, and where secret stairways led to quiet rooms full of wondrous treasures—of sculpture, painting, glassworks, tapestries, and jewelry design.

As in this hall, lined with huge paintings meticulously and lovingly crafted.

Lovingly.

Pagonel could see that truth in every delicate stroke, in the favorable and painstaking use of light, in the frames, even, wrought of gold and as artistic as the paintings themselves.

One in particular caught the mystic's eye and held him, and not only because of the subject—the only woman depicted in any of the hall's masterpieces—but because of the sheer grace in the form, her form. She was dressed in a long white gown, her heavy crimson cape flying about her shoulders as she moved and played a beautiful morin khuur of burnished, shining wood, her fingers gracefully working the bow across the four strings.

The light in the hallway, dying as the sun set in the west, was not favorable at that time of day, but Pagonel remained, transfixed, until darkness filled the hall, and then some more.

A young brother entered the far end of the hall, a small man and exceptionally thin, given the way his robe seemed to flop about him with every step. Pagonel watched him closely as he lifted his hand and placed a tiny, glowing diamond upon a platter lined with crystal. He chanted quietly and moved along, placing a second enchanted diamond near to the middle of the room.

Again he moved down the hall, chanting, but his prayer was surely interrupted when he noted Pagonel standing before the one of the paintings.

"Master Pagonel," he said with a seemingly polite bow, though the perceptive mystic caught a bit of unease accompanying the dip, for it was not offered sincerely and more out of necessity. "I am sorry if I have disturbed you."

"Far from it," the mystic replied. "I welcome the light, that I might continue to stare at this most lovely figure."

The young brother, his narrow features seeming sharper in the diamond light, stared at the image before the man. "St. Gwendolyn," he explained.

"I have heard this name."

"A great warrior, so the legend claims," the brother explained, moving near to the mystic.

"Legend? Is she not sainted, and does such an action not declare the legend as fact?"

The small man shrugged as if it did not matter.

"She has an interesting choice of weapon," Pagonel said, motioning back to the picture and the woman. "One might expect a bow of a different sort on a battlefield."

"St. Gwendolyn was known as a fine musician," the monk explained.

"The morin khuur," Pagonel replied. "A most difficult instrument to master."

"Morin khuur?"

Pagonel pointed to the instrument, then turned his fingers to match the pose of Gwendolyn as she handled the bow.

"It is a violin," the young monk explained.

"Ah," said the mystic. "In To-gai, they have such an instrument and name it morin khuur."

The monk nodded, and again, to perceptive Pagonel, he seemed as annoyed as enlightened by the news. The furrow in this one's brow came quite easily, Pagonel noted, as if he was not a contented man, by any means. He was young, quite young, perhaps in his early twenties and surely no aged master of the abbey, and yet he was handling the magical gemstones with ease and proficiency, as the lighted diamonds clearly reminded.

"Tell me of St. Gwendolyn," Pagonel bade him. "A warrior, you say."

"With her violin," the monk explained. "So says the legend that when a band of powries gained the beach along the Mantis Arm and came at the brothers and sisters of her chapel, Gwendolyn took up her instrument and boldly ran to the front of the line. And so she played, and so she danced."

"Danced?" There was more intrigue than surprise in Pagonel's voice, as if he suspected where this might be going.

"Danced all about her line, all about the powrie line," the monk went on. "They could not turn their attention from her, mesmerized by her movements and the beauty of her song, so it is said. But neither could they catch up to her with their knives and spiked clubs, no matter how furiously they turned in pursuit."

"And thus they were not prepared when Gwendolyn's allies struck them dead," Pagonel finished, smiling and nodding at the monk.

"The powries were chased back to their boats," said the monk. "The town was saved. It is considered a miracle in the Church, indeed, the miracle which allowed for the canonization of St. Gwendolyn."

"You do not agree."

The monk shrugged. "It is a fine tale, and one tailored to admit a woman among the saints—a necessary action, I expect. Perhaps St. Gwendolyn was clever, and her ruse helped save the day from the powries. More likely, she bought the defenders enough space to launch some lightning or fire at the dwarves, driving them from the beach."

"Ah," the mystic said, nodding in understanding. "And there is the true miracle, of course, the barrage of magical energy from the sacred Ring Stones."

The young monk didn't reply, and stood impassively, as if the truth should be self-evident.

Pagonel nodded and turned his full attention to the painting once more, enchanted by the beautiful face, the thick black hair, and the graceful twist of this exquisite woman. The movement was so extreme and in balance, the cloak flying wildly, and yet obviously she remained in complete control. The artist had done his work well, the mystic knew, for he felt as if he understood St. Gwendolyn, and felt, too, that she would have made a wonderful Jhesta Tu.

Might Gwendolyn still have a lesson for the Abellican Order, Pagonel wondered?

He turned to the young monk. "What is your name?"

"Brother Thaddius," the man answered.

Pagonel smiled and nodded. "These are the Saints of the Abellican Church?"

He nodded.

"Tell me of them," the mystic asked.

"I have my duties . . ."

"Bishop Braumin and the others will forgive you for indulging in my demands. I expect that this is important. So please, young Brother Thaddius, indulge me."

"What am I to do?" Braumin asked Viscenti a few nights later in the private quarters of Fio Bou-raiy, where the two were separating dead Bou-raiy's private items from the robes and gemstones reserved for the office of the Father Abbot.

"It falls to you," Viscenti replied. "Of that, there is no doubt."

"It?"

"Everything," said Viscenti. "I do not envy you, but know that I will be there standing behind you, whatever course you chart."

"A bold claim!"

"If not Braumin Herde—Bishop Braumin Herde—then who?" Viscenti asked. "Is there an abbot left alive after the De'Unneran Heresy?"

"Haney in St. Belfour."

Viscenti snorted and shook his head. "A fine man, but one who was not even ready for that position, let alone this great responsibility we see before us. Besides, he is a Vanguardsman, as is Midalis who will be King."

"Perhaps an important relationship, then."

Again, the skinny, nervous man snickered. "Midalis would not have it," he declared, and Braumin couldn't disagree. "Our new King is no fool and having a Vanguardsman as King and as Father Abbot would surely reek of invasion to the folk of Honce proper! Duke Kalas would not stand for it, nor would the other nobles.

"Abbot Haney would be the wrong choice, in any case," Brother Viscenti went on. "He has no firsthand understanding of De'Unnero or his potential followers. He does not understand what drove the heretic, or even, I fear, the true beauty of Avelyn. He is no disciple of Master Jojonah!"

That last statement, spoken so powerfully, jolted Braumin upright. Just hearing the name of Jojonah bolstered him and reminded him of the whole point of . . . everything. Master Jojonah had trained Brother Avelyn, and had shown a young Brother Braumin and some other even younger brothers the truth of the Abellican Church, as opposed to the course Father Abbot Dalebert Markwart and his protégé De'Unnero had charted for the Order.

Master Jojonah had been burned at the stake clinging to his beliefs, had gone willingly into the arms of God—and had charged Brother Braumin with carrying on his bold course. So many others, too, had died for those beliefs. Braumin thought of brave brother Romeo Mullahy, who had leaped from the cliff at the Barbacan, the ultimate defiance of Marcalo De'Unnero, an action that had shaken De'Unnero's followers and resonated within those who had opposed him.

And Brother Castinagis, one of Braumin's dearest friends. The excitable fellow had never wavered, even in the face of certain death.

De'Unnero had burned him in his chapel in Caer Tinella.

"He is a good man," Braumin at last replied. "He witnessed the miracle of Aida . . ."

"He is not even as worldly as Master Dellman, who serves him!" Viscenti interrupted. "Were he to ascend, then to those outside the Church, it would seem a power play by King Midalis, forcing his hand over the Abellican Church even as he strengthens his hold on Honce. We have walked that dark road already, my friend."

Braumin Herde kept his gaze low, chewing his lips, and he nodded in agreement.

"Nay," said Viscenti, "it falls to you. Only you. St.-Mere-Abelle is yours, surely. The Order is yours to chart."

Braumin Herde shrugged, and it seemed more a shudder. "I want her back," he said quietly.

Viscenti nodded and wore a wistful expression suddenly, clearly recognizing that his friend was speaking of Jilseponie.

"I feel as if I best serve the Church by enlisting our southern friends to fly me on their dragon to the Timberlands, that I might drag Pony back to St.-Mere-Abelle to save us all."

"That we will not do," came another voice, wholly unexpected, and both monks jumped and spun about to see Pagonel standing quietly in the shadows of the room.

"How did you get in here?" Viscenti shouted as much as asked.

"Have I upset you, brother?" the mystic asked. "I was offered free travel through the monastery, so I was told . . ."

"No, no," Braumin put in, and he dropped his hand on Viscenti's shoulder to calm the man. "Of course, you are welcome wherever you will go. You merely startled us, that is all."

The mystic bowed.

"And heard us, no doubt," said Viscenti.

"I took great comfort in your advice to Bishop Braumin," Pagonel admitted. He stepped up before Braumin Herde. "I take less comfort in your expressed fears."

The monk stared at him hard.

"I will not take you to Jilseponie, nor to her should you go," Pagonel insisted. "She has done enough. Her tale is written, for the wider world at least. Besides, I have witnessed the power of Aydrian and believe that Jilseponie would best serve the world if she can instill in her son a sense of morality and duty akin to that she and her dead Elbryan once knew. You wish to go to her, to beg her to return and assume the lead in your wounded Order. This is understandable, but not practical."

Clearly overwhelmed, Bishop Braumin fell back and into a chair, nearly tumbling off the side of it as he landed hard and off balance. "What am I to do?"

"Summon a College of Abbots," said Master Viscenti. "I will nominate you as Father Abbot—none will oppose!"

"Abbots?" Braumin asked incredulously. "Myself and Abbot Haney are all that remain, I fear!"

"Then bring them all in, all together," said Pagonel. "Summon every brother from every chapel and every abbey." He lifted a fist up before him, fingers clutched. "This is the strongest position for the hand," he explained. "Bring your Church in close and move outward one piece at a time."

Braumin didn't respond, but hardly seemed convinced.

"Brynn Dharielle and the dragon will fly south in the morning, going home," the mystic explained. "I was to go with them, but I have quite enjoyed my journey through the catacombs of this wondrous place. With your permission, I will remain longer."

Braumin Herde looked at the man curiously.

"Call them in," Pagonel bade him. "I will stand beside you, if you so desire."

"You have a plan," said Viscenti, and it seemed as much an accusation as a question.

The mystic glanced over at him and smiled. "Our Orders are not so different, my friend. This I have come to understand. Perhaps there are lessons the Jhesta Tu have learned which will now be of use to Father Abbot Braumin Herde."

He looked to Braumin.

The man who would rule the Abellican Church nodded. He summoned again the memories of Jojonah, and Mullahy, Castinagis, and the others, and silently vowed to find the courage to lead. If Midalis would rebuild the kingdom, then Braumin Herde would rebuild the Abellican Church.

PART 2

THE

COLLEGE OF

ABBOTS

Master Arri couldn't help but smile as he looked down on the young couple dancing in the evergreen grove. The sun, high above in the east, stretched shadows from the pines about them so that they twirled and spun in light and then shadow, repeatedly, the woman's white robes flashing, the man's light green robes somewhat muting the effect, serving almost as a transition from light to darkness. Their smiles shone even in the shadows, though.

She was such a pretty thing, her light hair dancing in the breeze, her bright eyes shining back at the sun, her slender frame carrying her gracefully through the twirling dance. Her partner was heavier set, stocky and strong, with long and curly black hair and a beard that could house a flock of birds! His robe was open at the chest, and there, too, he was a shaggy one. Unlike the fair-skinned woman, his skin was olive, speaking of ancestry in the south, likely.

Master Arri should not be smiling, he knew. Indeed, he should be horrified by the scene before him, for though it was obvious that they were in love, they could not be. The wider world would not have it.

For Arri knew this woman, Sister Mary Ann of St. Gwendolyn-by-the-Sea, the same monastery where Arri had been ordained as a brother and as a master of the Abellican Church. And while he didn't know the man, he knew the truth of this one, Elliot, and had been watching him from afar since he had returned to the region from his wandering, to learn of the disaster that had befallen his beloved abbey. According to the folk of the nearby towns, Elliot was a Samhaist, that most ancient religion of Honce, a practice deemed heretical and driven out by the Church in the earliest days. The Samhaists and the Abellicans had battled long and hard for the soul of the people of the lands, the former with warnings of brimstone and divine retribution, the latter with softer promises of peace after death and a loving God.

Few Samhaists could be found in Honce-the-Bear in God's Year 847, even counting the wild lands of Vanguard. Indeed, as far as Arri, who had recently come south across the gulf from Vanguard, knew, there were no Samhaists south of Alpinador.

Except now he knew better, for there was no doubt as to the religious leaning of this man, Elliot.

To see young and bright Sister Mary Ann dancing with him did pain Master Arri, but at the same time, his heart could not deny the joy on her face or the lightness of her step.

And in truth, Arri was glad to see one of his brethren from St. Gwendolyn alive! The heresy of De'Unnero had brutalized this abbey more than any of the others. De'Unnero had publicly executed the Abbot and had cleansed the place as a barn cat might seek the mice. The monastery up on the hill overlooking the dark Mirianic was, by all accounts, deserted.

And haunted.

Marcalo De'Unnero had left demons in his wake, so it was whispered.

But Sister Mary Ann had escaped (in no small part because of this Samhaist, so the whispers in the town had claimed), so perhaps there were others.

Master Arri moved down to a stretch of underbrush near the south road and waited. And not for long, as it turned out, for the sun had barely passed its zenith when Mary Ann came skipping down the road. Her face was all smiles, her young heart surely lifted.

Arri stepped out into the road before her.

She skidded to a stop and half turned as if to flee, her expression one of surprise and fear—but that latter emotion fast faded when recognition came to her.

"Master Arri!" she cried, and she ran to him and wrapped him in a great hug.

Arri responded in kind, crushing her in his long and skinny arms. He had always liked this young woman, who had come into St. Gwendolyn only months before he had begun his wandering. He moved her back to arm's length.

"You look well," he said. "I feared that I would find . . ."

"They're all dead," she interrupted. "The Abbot, the Masters, the brothers, the sisters. All dead, I fear, or turned to . . ." She hesitated there and took a longer and suspicious look at Arri.

"I am no follower of Marcalo De'Unnero," he assured her. "You have nothing to fear." He paused and considered the Samhaist, and added, "in that regard."

"There is word that he advances upon St.-Mere-Abelle with King Aydrian and . . ."

"Old news," Arri assured her. "Word spreads across the lands that the battle was fought, and won by our Father Abbot and Bishop Braumin. Marcalo De'Unnero is dead, and King Aydrian removed."

Sister Mary Ann wrapped him in another great hug, seeming genuinely elated.

Again, Arri pushed her back to arm's length. "Perhaps not such good news for you, though," he said.

A dark cloud passed over the young woman's face.

"I saw you," Arri explained. "In the grove. With him."

She swallowed hard.

"Do you know who he is? Do you know what he is?"

"We are not so different," she said quietly.

"You denounce the Abellican Church?"

"No . . . no, I mean," she stammered and sighed as if she could not find the right words. "He is a good man. He saved me from De'Unnero's followers. He fought for me . . ."

"You were lovers!"

"No!" she cried. "I did not even know him. I knew nothing of him. De'Unnero's men were chasing me, and then they were not! The trees came alive and swatted them! The grass grabbed their boots and held them . . ."

"This is Earth magic!" Arri cried, and that was all he had to say, for all in the Church knew the official position on such enchantments, that they were of the demon dactyls!

"But he saved me! Did I not deserve to be away from the followers of the heretic?"

"The enemy of your enemy is not necessarily your friend, sister."

"But Elliot is," she said, and she seemed to grow stronger then, firming her jaw. "He rescued me from the heretic mob. They came for him later. I found him grievously wounded." She reached into a pouch and brought forth a soul stone.

"You used godly Abellican magic on a Samhaist?"

She didn't respond, but neither did she blink or back down.

"You would do it again," Arri said, and his tone was that of a statement and not an accusation.

"Yes."

"Have you given over any of the stones to this man, Elliot?"

"No, of course not. I have just a few," she fumbled in her pouch again and produced a few minor gemstones. "He has no interest in them anyway."

Arri put his hands on Mary Ann's shoulders, squaring himself up to her and looking her right in the eye as he asked, "Are you a Samhaist, sister?"

She hesitated, tellingly, before quietly replying, "No."

"But you are thinking it a possibility!" Now Arri was accusing her, clearly so.

"I am thinking that the world is a wider place than I knew, and that my Church, the brothers of my own faith, tried to do great harm to me and murdered my friends!" she replied. "And that a man stepped forth, despite the danger, and told them no, and fought them. You think him a demon for his beliefs, which you likely understand less than I, and yet who were the demons, Master, when Marcalo De'Unnero fell over St. Gwendolyn?"

"Are you a Samhaist?" he asked again.

"No," she replied immediately, and more forcefully. "But I will learn of Elliot's ways, if he will tell me. Perhaps they will ring of truth to me, perhaps not. That is for me to decide."

"Do you think the Father Abbot will agree with that?"

She shrugged.

"I am going to St.-Mere-Abelle," Arri explained. "I leave at week's turn. The Order of St. Gwendolyn must be rebuilt. You will accompany me."

Sister Mary Ann's lip quivered. Just a bit, but Arri caught it.

"I cannot guarantee your safety. I know not what judgment the Father Abbot will put upon you for . . . for being with this man."

Sister Mary Ann made no movement at all, just stared at him, and with an expression he could not decipher.

"I will speak for you," he promised. "Surely these are extraordinary circumstances. I will beg for leniency."

"I have done nothing wrong."

"Then have you the courage to come and tell that to the Father Abbot?"

The young woman nodded. "I am not ashamed," she said. "I survived, and have done nothing wrong."

Master Arri offered her a comforting return smile and nod, but in his thoughts he wasn't so confident at that moment. Abellicans, in recent history, had been burned at the stake for less than the crime of loving a Samhaist.

"You are familiar with this game?" Bishop Braumin asked Pagonel. The two and Master Viscenti were in Braumin's private chambers when Pagonel had wandered away from the hearth to a chessboard set up at the side of the room, the game half completed.

"Vaguely," Pagonel replied.

The two monks joined Pagonel over by the board.

"You were playing against the Father Abbot," Viscenti remarked, and Braumin nodded.

"A fine opponent was Fio Bou-raiy," said Braumin. "He had me beaten, I fear."

"He was playing black, then," said Pagonel, and Braumin looked at the board, then back at Pagonel curiously. A casual glance at the board revealed little advantage for either side—indeed, black had lost more pieces—and given the mystic's response that he "vaguely" knew the game, how could he have known the truth of the situation on the board?

"This piece," Pagonel asked, tapping one of the white bishops, "it runs along the white diagonal squares, yes?"

"Yes," Braumin answered.

Pagonel nodded. "We have a similar game in Behren, at the Walk of Clouds. More pieces, but the concepts align, I believe. Sit." He motioned to the chair behind the base for the black side, and he slipped into the chair behind the white king.

"Pray show me how each of these pieces move and attack," the mystic bade.

Braumin and Viscenti exchanged a curious glance, and proceeded. When they were done, Pagonel wore a sly grin. "I will replace your opponent, if you allow," he said. "And yes, if my objective is to defeat your king, then you are defeated."

"Then why play?" Viscenti asked.

"We could play anew," Pagonel started to offer, but Braumin waved that thought away.

"It is your move," Braumin told the mystic.

A short while later, Bishop Braumin conceded, and accepted the mystic's offer to begin anew.

"If he offers you a bet, do not take it," Master Viscenti said with a laugh just a few moves into the new game. "I do believe that our friend here has been less than forthcoming regarding his experience with chess!"

"Not so," said Pagonel.

"Then how do you play so well? This is no simple game!"

"Your monks fight well," Pagonel answered. "The best of your fighters would match up favorable in single combat against a Jhesta Tu of equal experience."

"We pride ourselves . . ." Braumin started to reply, but Pagonel kept going.

"But were a group of four brothers to line up in battle across from four Jhesta Tu, they would lose, and badly, and not a single of my acolytes would be badly harmed."

"Quite a claim," said Viscenti.

"You will see, my friend," Pagonel said.

A few moves later, the game was clearly and decisively turning in Pagonel's favor, so much so that Braumin, one of the best chess players remaining at St.-Mere-Abelle, suspected that he would soon resign.

"How?" Viscenti asked when Braumin soon groaned and moved his king away from Pagonel's check, the outcome becoming clearer.

"This is not a battle of individual pieces," Pagonel explained.

"It is a game of strategy," Braumin remarked.

"It is a game of coordination, and within the boundaries of this board lie your answers, Bishop Braumin."

The monks stared at him hard. "Answers?" Braumin asked.

"How will your Church survive, and thrive, after the punishment the heretic De'Unnero inflicted upon it? That is your fear, yes? How will you lead them out of the darkness and rebuild from the ashes of De'Unnero's deadly wake?"

"It will take time," Viscenti said.

"Given the way you select—or should I say, deselect?—your brethren and the way you train them, I would agree," said Pagonel. "But it does not have to be like that."

He turned to the board and lifted the castle-like piece, the rook. "This piece is straightforward in attack, and thus easily detected as a threat," he explained. "But that is not its purpose. This piece shortens the board, and creates a defensive wall that limits your opponent's movements."

Braumin nodded. He hadn't thought of a rook in those terms before, but it made sense.

"This piece," Pagonel said, lifting a bishop, "is more clever. The eye of your opponent will not see the angled attack lines so easily, and so the bishop strikes hard and fast and with devastating effects."

"That is true of the knight," Viscenti remarked.

"Ah, the knight, the battlefield dancer," said Pagonel. "St. Gwendolyn."

That last remark had the monks leaning forward with surprise and intrigue.

"It is true that the knight is deadly, but the piece better serves to turn your opponent's eye. The knight is a feint and a fear. You cannot block her from moving . . ."

As he spoke, he lifted one of his knights over Braumin's pawn and set it down in a position to threaten the king.

"And as you watch her," Pagonel went on slowly as Braumin shifted his king aside, further from the threat.

Pagonel moved his bishop down the line across the board, taking Braumin's rook, which was no longer protected by his king. "As you watch her," he said again, "the bishop strikes."

Viscenti blew a low whistle of admiration. Braumin Herde shook his head and knocked over his king, defeated.

"She is St. Gwendolyn, dancing about the battlefield with her violin," Pagonel explained, lifting the knight. "Her job is not to defeat you, but to enable her allies to defeat you."

"We are talking of how St.-Mere-Abelle trains her monks," Braumin remarked.

"There is your answer, Bishop Braumin Herde," said Pagonel.

"Arri?"

The name struck the monk profoundly, not just because it was uttered without "brother" or "master" before it, but because the speaker emphasized the second syllable and because the voice was known to Arri.

He stopped short and turned his head to the side, to the porch of the small tavern, to the man standing there, a man he had known as a companion before he had even been born.

"Mars?" he whispered, somewhat confused, for his brother was not wearing the brown robes of an Abellican monk. Arri and Sister Mary Ann had learned much in the days of their journey from the Mantis Arm. All the land buzzed with rumors of the great battle at St.-Mere-Abelle, of the dragon, of the death of Father Abbot Fio Bou-raiy, of the defeat of King Aydrian and the death of Marcalo De'Unnero.

They had heard, too, that disciples of De'Unnero had fled the Order, including some who had been at St.-Mere-Abelle at the time of the battle.

That last rumor resonated in Master Arri's ear now as he looked at his twin brother.

The man came forward from the shadows of the porch, rushing up to Arri and wrapping him in a great hug. "Oh, Arri," he whispered. "I thought you dead. I have heard of the troubles of St. Gwendolyn . . ."

Arri pushed him back to arm's length even as Sister Mary Ann spat, "Troubles? You mean murder by the heretic De'Unnero. Troubles?"

"No," Mars said, shaking his head as he regarded the woman. "There is no simple . . ."

"It is that simple, brother," Master Arri interrupted. He turned to his traveling companion. "Sister Mary Ann, this is Brother Mars—my twin brother."

Mary Ann looked from Arri to Mars skeptically, for at first glance, they surely did not appear to be twins, each of very different body types, Arri tall and lean and Mars short and stocky. She noted the resemblance in their facial features, however, and surely could have guessed them as brothers, if not twins.

"Where are your robes, brother?" Arri asked.

Mars swallowed hard and stepped back. His mouth began to move as if he meant to say something, but he wound up offering only a slight shake of his head and a helpless shrug.

"De'Unnero is dead," Arri said a few moments later.

"On the stairs of the great hall, beneath the shattered window of Brother Avelyn," Mars explained. "Perhaps there is some significance there."

Arri stiffened at that remark, for this was an old wound between himself and his brother. Arri favored the gemstones and was quite adept with them, and, not coincidentally, he also agreed with the premise of the promise of Brother Avelyn, that the stones could be used to benefit the world.

Quite the opposite, his brother had never shown much interest in, or ability with, the Ring Stones. Mars was a brawler, and often spoke of Marcalo De'Unnero as the epitome of dedication within the Abellican Order. Often had the brothers argued over the respective, and colliding, philosophies of Avelyn and De'Unnero. Those arguments had become so heated that Arri had supported his brother's decision to leave St. Gwendolyn those five years before.

"The window of Brother Avelyn will be rebuilt," Arri replied, and he saw that his remark had stung his brother. "Perhaps it will be dedicated to St. Avelyn when it is finished anew."

He studied his brother hard as he made that statement, and he saw no resistance there, no surprise, even. Was it resignation, he wondered? Or an honest epiphany?

"Why have you left St.-Mere-Abelle?" Arri asked. "Did you fight beside Marcalo De'Unnero?"

Beside him, Sister Mary Ann sucked in her breath in shock, and more than a little budding anger.

"No, of course not!" Mars replied. "I served on a catapult crew, throwing stones and pitch at the approaching army of King Aydrian."

"Then why are you here, without your robes?"

"They know," Mars admitted, lowering his gaze. "Or think they know."

"Know?" Sister Mary Ann asked.

"They believe me loyal to De'Unnero and I fear Bishop Braumin's retribution," Mars admitted. "He is an angry man. There has been much tragedy and will be more, I fear."

"And are you?" Mary Ann pressed, her jaw tight as if she meant to lash out at the man at any moment. "Loyal?"

Mars shot her an equally hostile stare.

"Denounce De'Unnero," Master Arri insisted, stepping between them. "Here and now, to me, your brother."

Mars looked at him incredulously.

"Can you?" Arri asked.

"Of course."

"Then do it," said Mary Ann. "Renounce the man who led to the murder of many of my friends at St. Gwendolyn. Renounce the man who murdered many who had been friends to Brother Mars—or did you leave any friends behind, brother?"

"Enough, sister," Master Arri demanded.

"I renounce Marcalo De'Unnero," Brother Mars said simply, never blinking and never turning his gaze from Sister Mary Ann as he spoke. "I was not part of his heresy, nor is there any evidence contrary to that claim."

"Yet you ran from St.-Mere-Abelle," Sister Mary Ann pressed.

"Sister, you have your own . . . situation to consider," Arri reminded, silencing her. He stepped more fully between the two and turned to face his brother directly. "You accompany me to the mother abbey. I will speak for you."

Mars stared at him doubtfully.

"I intend to return to St. Gwendolyn. I will ask Bishop Braumin and the others to grant me the abbey as my own. I would like my brother by my side in that endeavor."

Mars leaned to the side to stare at Sister Mary Ann one last time, then met his brother's gaze and nodded.

"Dancing?" Master Viscenti said skeptically, shaking his head as he stared at the chessboard and Bishop Braumin's toppled king. He looked up at Pagonel. "Our answer is dancing?"

"Your answer lies in harmony," the Jhesta Tu explained. "I have studied your martial training techniques, and they are quite good, though quite limited."

Viscenti stiffened uncomfortably at that slight, and Braumin Herde turned his gaze over the mystic.

"Your monks train to fight, and fight very well," Pagonel went on. "Matched up singly, they would prove formidable opponents to any of the other warriors I have known throughout the lands. I have no doubt that the best of your warrior monks could ably battle the average Jhesta Tu in single combat, even without the gemstones."

The two monks glanced at each other then back at Pagonel, neither appearing certain if they were being insulted or not.

"But a group of Abellicans would fall quickly before a similar group of Jhesta Tu," Pagonel explained. "We train in harmonious combat." He pointed to the chessboard. "We train to assume different roles in the battle, working in unison to uncover our opponents' weaknesses. You do not, and that is a major flaw in your techniques."

"There are examples of groups of brothers working in unison to bring forth great power from the Ring Stones," Viscenti argued.

"Such would do little for a group of monks engaged in close combat against a band of powries," Pagonel said. "A fine defense behind your high walls, I agree. Has your Church that luxury now?"

Viscenti started to counter, but Braumin Herde held him back. "What do you suggest?" he asked the southerner.

"Train teams of monks to work in unison, like a singular weapon possessed of deadly options."

"Our methods date back centuries," Viscenti argued.

"Have you the luxury of adhering to tradition in this time?" Pagonel asked. "Are there not, even now, disciples of Marcalo De'Unnero roaming the countryside or claiming chapels as their own? Do you doubt that they will come against you, and in short time? New King Midalis's kingdom is no less in disarray than your Church, good monks. Fix that which is near to home and the King will be forever grateful."

"You speak of altering our training," Braumin said, shaking his head doubtfully. "Yet, regarding your last statement—and I do not disagree—if you are correct, it would seem that we have weeks, not years!"

"The sooner you begin to change, the sooner you will arrive at your goal."

"We haven't the time!" said Viscenti. He held up his hands helplessly. "We do not even know how many brothers remain after the purge of De'Unnero. We haven't the time and we haven't the bodies!"

"Look to the future as you battle the present," the Jhesta Tu advised. "You must bring many into the Church, and quickly."

Bishop Braumin sighed profoundly. He looked to Viscenti, both reminded of their long years of preparation and testing before they were even allowed within St.-Mere-Abelle. "It takes years to determine which young hopefuls have affinity to the stones," he explained to the foreigner. "Even with all that the land has endured in the last years, there are hundreds of young men, some barely more than boys, gathered in academies—convents— and being tested."

"Convents? I do not know this word."

"It is like a chapel, but for women who wish to serve the Church," Viscenti explained.

"I thought the women of your Church served at St. Gwendolyn, mostly, as Sovereign Sisters."

"Some," Braumin replied. "But only a very few, and even that practice is not without strong opposition in the Church. Now that St. Gwendolyn-by-the-Sea is, by all reports, vacated, I doubt the practice will continue."

Pagonel smiled and nodded as if he understood something here the others did not. "So these sisters . . ."

"They are not sisters," Braumin interrupted, and adamantly. "They are missionaries. Their role is to serve the towns and to teach the young hopefuls who would be brothers in the Church."

"And to judge this affinity you speak of?"

"Yes."

"So these missionaries in the convents understand the Ring Stones?"

"Yes."

"Possess some stones and can use them?"

"Soul stones, mostly," Braumin confirmed. "It is not uncommon for the women of the convent to offer some minor healing to the community about them in times of illness."

The Jhesta Tu flashed that grin again and nodded knowingly.

"And many cannot use the stones?" the mystic pressed. "Even many of those attempting to join the Church? And this is disqualifying?"

"The Ring Stones are the gifts of God, given to the Order of Abelle," Viscenti said, his tone showing that he was growing somewhat annoyed with Pagonel's prodding, and seemingly superior attitude. "A man who cannot use the Ring Stones . . ."

"Or a woman who can," Pagonel added, and Viscenti narrowed his eyes.

"A man who cannot use the Ring Stones . . ." the monk began anew, and again was interrupted.

"Cannot properly serve your god?" the mystic remarked. "It would seem that you serve a narrow-minded god, my friend."

Master Viscenti started to argue, but this time Braumin Herde cut him short. "Tradition," Braumin said with a derisive chortle. "Who can know the truth? We thought we followed tradition when we sent the Windrunner to the island Pimaninicuit."

"Bishop Braumin!" Viscenti scolded, for such matters were not to be openly discussed with those who were not masters, let alone in front of non-Abellicans.

Braumin laughed at him. "Tradition," he scoffed again. "So we were taught, and yet, through the actions of Master Jojonah, we found that so much we thought traditional was the furthest thing from it!"

Viscenti stammered and could not respond.

"It is all too confusing," said Viscenti, and he threw up his hands in surrender.

"Then follow your heart," Pagonel advised. "Always. Look to the spirit of morality to find those best traditions you should seek, but be not dogmatic. Seek the spirit that rings true in your heart, but fit that spirit to the needs of the time. And the time, Bishop Braumin, calls for . . ."

"Reformation," Braumin Herde said, nodding.

"A bold move," Viscenti remarked, his voice barely a whisper.

"Did Master Jojonah truly ask of us anything less?" Braumin asked. "In those days when we hid in the bowels of St.-Mere-Abelle, we five with Master Jojonah, hoping Father Abbot Markwart would not discover us, was he calling upon us to do anything less? Is the sacrifice of Brother Mullahy worth less?" he said, referring to one of their conspirators who had leaped from the high walls of the blasted Mount Aida, a public suicide rather than renouncing the teachings of Jojonah. "Or the murder of Brother Anders Castinagis by De'Unnero?"

"We do not even have a Father Abbot at present," Viscenti reminded him. "Yet you would seek a rewriting of Church Doctrine?"

He turned to Pagonel. "Reformation is a formal council of the leaders of the Church, to rethink practices and make great and enduring decisions," he explained. "In the first Reformation, it was determined that gemstones could not be used to make magical items. In the third and last Reformation, it was decided that some few stones could be sold to lords of the land—a tradition that is formally denied to this day and known by only a few."

"It was not a decision with which Marcalo De'Unnero agreed," Viscenti said dryly, for indeed, as Bishop of Palmaris, De'Unnero had begun a purge of privately owned gemstones and magical items, usually accompanied by great punishment to the merchant or lord caught with them in his possession.

"That last Reformation was almost six hundred years ago," Viscenti reminded them.

"Then the answer is clear before you," Pagonel insisted.

"To allow entry to all of the brothers currently in training," Braumin said, "regardless of their affinity with the Ring Stones."

"You are half correct," the mystic replied with that grin. "As your Church is half of what it could be."

The two monks looked to each other, then back at him curiously, and skeptically.

"When I return to the Walk of Clouds, I will train Brynn Dharielle further in the ways of the Jhesta Tu," he explained. "Half of those at her rank will be women."

"A monumental proposition," Viscenti said. "We should begin training women in the ways . . ."

"You already have them, so you have just told me," said Pagonel. "Need I remind you of your own St. Gwendolyn? If Jilseponie had agreed to remain at St.-Mere-Abelle, as you begged her, would you have not nominated her to serve as Mother Abbess of your Church?"

"Jilseponie is a remarkable exception," Braumin replied.

"Perhaps only because you prevent any others from proving the same of themselves!" the mystic countered. "Bring them in, brothers and sisters equally. Indeed, empty your convents and fill your chapels and monasteries! These are proven Abellicans, are they not?

"And you take them in at too old an age!" he went on, passionately. "Twenty? Find your disciples among those just becoming adults. The clay is softer and easier to mold."

"Men and women, cloistered together," Viscenti said, shaking his head doubtfully. "The temptation."

Pagonel, who had lived most of his life in the mountainous retreat of the Walk of Clouds, surrounded by the men and women of the Jhesta Tu, laughed aloud at that absurd notion.

"If we are cloistered, then perhaps we have already lost," Braumin said to Viscenti. "Is not the word of Avelyn that we should go out and serve? Do we not consider Brother Francis redeemed because he went out among the sick and died administering to them?"

"Perhaps Brother Avelyn has shown us the way, then," Viscenti agreed.

Braumin patted his friend on the shoulder and moved to stand directly before the mystic, looking him in the eye. "Stay and help us," he begged.

Pagonel nodded. "Where is the nearest convent?"

"In the village of St.-Mere-Abelle, an hour's walk."

"Take me."

"We cannot formalize the changes you desire until the College of Abbots is held, and that will not be for months, perhaps a year."

"And on that occasion, we will show your brethren the error of their ways."

PART 3

THE

BATTLEFIELD

PHILOSOPHER

"Pagonel returns," Master Viscenti announced one dreary Decambria morning in God's'Year 847, nearly four months after the Jhesta Tu mystic had left the monastery for the town of the same name some three miles away.

Bishop Braumin had expected the news; the winter weather had broken for a bit in that last month of the year, and for the previous week, young brothers and sisters from the convent of St.-Mere-Abelle, and even from some other convents of nearby towns, had begun pouring into the monastery, bearing word from Pagonel that they should be considered for immediate ordainment into the Order.

"We are well ahead of the College of Abbots," Viscenti ominously warned, for the formal meeting of the remaining Masters and Abbots of the Abellican Order wasn't set until the fourth month of 848, or perhaps even later if the Gulf of Corona was still impassable and the brothers from Vanguard could not safely make the trip south. "These dramatic changes you are instituting are hardly approved."

"Necessity drives our decisions," Braumin replied.

"You rely wholly on the counsel of one who is not of the Church."

"Brother, who is left among the Church to counsel us?" Braumin countered. "Brother Dellman and Abbot Haney? Dellman is with us—we know that much. He has been an ally since the days of Jojonah and our quiet revolt against the edicts of Dalebert Markwart. And he has been young Abbot Haney's invaluable advisor and confidant these last years up in Vanguard at St. Belfour. King Midalis will support us, as well. There are leaders of the other abbeys, and indeed other brothers, who will no doubt bristle at these changes, and some perhaps who will openly argue. But I will be elected as the next Father Abbot, and with you, and Dellman, and Abbot Haney by my side, and following the guidance of Pagonel, we will rebuild the Abellican Order."

"With women open to ascend to any rank? And with these dramatic changes in a training regimen that has stood for centuries?"

"Do you see another choice?"

"No," Viscenti admitted, and he gave a self-deprecating chuckle. Ever was Viscenti the worrywart, they both knew all too well.

"Dangerous times," Braumin admitted, and he patted his friend on the shoulder. "But not as terrifying as those which we faced last midsummer, yes?"

Viscenti could only laugh at that, for it seemed a trivial matter when measured against the recent events at St.-Mere-Abelle, when De'Unnero and Aydrian had come to kill them all—and with an army behind them that had made De'Unnero's victory seem almost a foregone conclusion!

A knock on the door signaled the arrival of the Jhesta Tu, and Braumin greeted Pagonel with a warm hug. "So many have come in," the Bishop said. "You think them all worthy?"

"I think you need many dedicated disciples to fill your Church and to undo the damage of the last years," Pagonel replied. "Fortunately, I found many willing and able to serve in such a role. Eager, indeed. Your Order excluded half of your possibilities, my friend, and now they are ready to take their rightful place."

"The women, you mean," said Viscenti.

"Of course, and many, I found, were quiet adept with the Ring Stones, though their practice and variation with the gems is limited," the mystic replied. "But they will learn, and are eager for this opportunity, and more eager to help the Church they love. You are very fortunate, Bishop Braumin, in that you have a congregation at your call to replace the many your Church has lost."

"So all that you have sent to our gates have affinity with the sacred Ring Stones?" Braumin asked hopefully.

"No," Pagonel replied. "Not half. Affinity with the stones is a rarer thing than you believe."

Crestfallen, Braumin looked to Viscenti. He had hoped for an opening here, where only one great alteration of tradition would be needed, that of allowing women in large numbers to join the Order.

"All the women, at least?" Viscenti asked.

"Not half, I believe," said the mystic. "Affinity is no more common in women than in men, it seems. But those who have come to your gates are able, all of them, and they will serve you well."

"How do we proceed from here?" asked Braumin.

"I will train your brothers to train the newcomers, and themselves as they go forward. The martial techniques will be precise and broken into three distinct disciplines of fighting. And I will select from among your ranks a team of four to train privately by my tutelage."

"The College of Abbots is in just a few months," Viscenti remarked. "It would be good if we had something worthwhile to show them."

"You will," Pagonel promised, and with a bow, he left the room.

The very next day, the newcomers, nearly a hundred women and half that number of men younger than would normally enter St.-Mere-Abelle, were gathered in a large room to begin their journey under the watchful eyes of Pagonel and a score of older brothers.

So it went as the year turned to 848, and through the first month of the new year. By the second week of the second month, Pagonel had made his choices.

"Three women," Viscenti lamented to Braumin, who sat with Master Arri of St. Gwendolyn-by-the-Sea.

"Who is the fourth?" asked Arri, but Viscenti could only shrug.

Arri turned to Braumin. "This is the band you will send to reclaim St. Gwendolyn?"

Viscenti's eyes widened when Braumin nodded, for he had heard nothing of any such journey.

"I should accompany them," Arri remarked.

"You must stand for your brother at the College of Abbots, as we agreed," Braumin reminded him. "I will do all that I can for Brother Mars, but the accusations against him are strong."

"And I will speak for your ascension to the role of Father Abbot," a resigned Arri replied with a nod.

"And hopefully, when the college is adjourned, Abbot Arri, Brother Mars, and Sister Mary Ann can return to a reclaimed St. Gwendolyn."

"It would seem as if I have missed much of your plotting," Viscenti remarked, and he didn't sound happy about it.

"Everything is moving quickly," Braumin replied with a grin.

No sooner had he spoken when a courier rushed to the still-opened door with news that the mystic would see them in the private training area he had been given for his personal recruits. The three hustled down to the secluded chamber and found Pagonel alone in the place, seeming quite at ease. He motioned to some chairs he had set out, inviting them to sit and be at ease.

"One of your younger brothers has taught me of your saints," the mystic explained. "As with those heralded in my own order, many came to their place of historical importance through their actions in desperate battle, and so, with your permission, good Bishop, I have modeled the roles of your newest students after the legends of your Church."

Viscenti's eyes widened with surprise, but Braumin seemed unfazed, and motioned for Pagonel to continue.

"Sister Elysant," Pagonel called, holding his arm out toward an open door at the side of the room. A small woman with long light brown hair, barely five feet tall and barely more than a girl, entered the room. Her frame was slender but solid. She was quite pretty, the brothers noted, with eyes that seemed to smile, even though her face was set determinedly. She strode confidently to the mystic, carrying a quarterstaff that seemed far too large for her. She moved up to Pagonel and dipped a low bow, then turned to the three monks and bowed once again.

Pagonel barked out a sharp command, and Elysant leaped into a fighting stance, legs wide and strongly planted, staff slowly turning like a windmill before her.

"Elysant fights in the tradition of St. Belfour, the Rock of Vanguard," Pagonel explained. "She will invite the enemy to attack her in close combat, but they will not easily dispatch her, or move her. Sister Elysant is the tower, turning the blows."

"Saint Belfour was a bear of a man," Braumin said with skepticism. "Elysant is a wisp of a creature."

"Her center is low, her balance perfect," Pagonel replied. "You could not move her, Bishop Braumin, though you are twice her weight."

"Quite a claim," Braumin replied. "Do you agree, sister?"

Elysant smiled confidently and twirled her quarterstaff.

"Sister Diamanda," Pagonel called, and a second woman came rushing through the door. Her hair was short and flaxen, her jaw a bit square, and her face somewhat flat, showing her to have northern heritage—Vanguard, likely, or perhaps even a bit of Alpinadoran blood. She was much taller than Elysant, and broad-shouldered. Every movement she made spoke of strength. Like her predecessor, she bowed to Pagonel and to the monks, then added a third, matched, to Elysant. Unlike Elysant, however, Diamanda carried no weapon.

Pagonel barked out his command again, and Diamanda leaped to Elysant's side, her hands coming up like viper heads before her, while the smaller woman altered her stance and sent her staff into position to protect Diamanda.

"St. Bruce the Striker," Pagonel explained, referring to an Abellican warrior of the fifth century, from the region of Entel, deadly with his hands and credited with turning back a boat of Jacintha warriors single-handedly.

"And Sister Victoria!" the mystic called, and in came the third, as tall as Diamanda but much thinner. Her hair was red, long and loose, her eyes shining green, and her movements graceful, making her approach seem as much a dance as a walk. She carried a long and slender sword tucked into the rope belt of her robe. She offered her respectful bows to Pagonel, the monks, and her sisters, then drew her sword on Pagonel's command.

"St. Gwendolyn," Master Arri remarked, his smile shining brightly.

"Indeed," Pagonel confirmed. "The Battlefield Dancer."

"The rook, the bishop, and the knight," Bishop Braumin added, remembering the chess matches and Pagonel's description of the knight.

"Three women," Viscenti said, and he didn't sound impressed or confident.

"Is there to be a fourth?" Braumin asked. "You indicated four. The queen, perhaps?"

"Not from among the newcomers, for none of them have enough proficiency with the Ring Stones to properly complement the martial training I will provide. But yes, with your permission. I would like the young brother who taught me of your saints, Thaddius by name."

"So your queen is to be the only man among the four," Braumin said with a snort.

"In the tradition of St. Avelyn," Pagonel replied.

"Brother Thaddius is strong in the Ring Stones," Viscenti remarked.

Braumin nodded, and kept staring at Pagonel. Thaddius was strong in the Ring Stones, and from what Braumin knew of him, he was strong on tradition, as well. Braumin had been watching the promising young brother closely, for he had heard rumors that Brother Thaddius had spoken in admiring tones of Marcalo De'Unnero and the man's distorted vision of godliness. Surely one such as young Brother Thaddius would not be pleased with these dramatic changes, or with having so many women brought into the Church!

And perhaps that was part of Pagonel's ploy, Braumin realized, for he had learned not to underestimate this wise and exotic man, who always seemed to be thinking two layers beneath the surface.

"There may be a problem with Brother Thaddius," Viscenti whispered into Braumin's ear, apparently considering the same rumors.

But Braumin waved Viscenti back, and said to Pagonel, "Granted."

"I will have them every day, all the day," Pagonel insisted.

"They are yours to teach."

The mystic bowed, and motioned to his team to begin their work. As the three women launched into all manner of stretching and focused breathing, Pagonel accompanied the others out of the room.

"The College of Abbots convenes in the fourth month," Braumin reminded him as they parted at the doorway. "Will they be ready?"

"I have much work to do, but much substance with which to work," Pagonel assured the man. "Pray tell Brother Thaddius of his new lot in life. I am sure he will be overjoyed."

Braumin smiled at the sarcastic tone, which he took as confirmation of his silent guess regarding the mystic's choice. "I will send him to your side immediately."

"Grant him a soul stone," Pagonel said, and he glanced back into the room at the three women. "There will be many wounds and much blood spilled."

The smile left Braumin's face and he looked past Pagonel to the young sisters, second-guessing his decisions.

And not for the first time.

And surely not for the last time.

"Are they ready?" Braumin asked Pagonel as the season began to turn. The third month of Bafway was in full swing and winter was letting go of the land. There was still some snow, but the roads were open, though muddy. Still, a band traveling light could cross the tamed lands of Honce-the-Bear. Word had come from other abbeys that many brothers were on their way.

"I would like years more with them, particularly with Elysant," Pagonel admitted. "Her movements are solid, her work with the staff commendable, but her skin is not yet properly toughened. There is no way to accelerate that."

"Dolomite," Braumin said immediately.

Pagonel looked at him curiously. "One of your gemstones?"

"A mineral, a rock—dolostone, actually, but yes. It can be used to cast an enchantment to toughen the skin and strengthen the constitution."

"Elysant has little affinity with the Ring Stones," Pagonel said. "If any."

"But Brother Thaddius does, and used in conjunction with a soul stone, he could impart the enchantment . . ."

"Brother Thaddius has enough to do already, should trouble arise," Pagonel interrupted. "The other sisters can use the stones, though they are not nearly as proficient or powerful as Thaddius."

"The other sisters? Victoria? She is not old enough. My friend, we do not even allow brothers of less than four years in St.-Mere-Abelle to handle the stones. Brother Thaddius is one of very few exceptions!"

"My band is exceptional. By design."

Braumin started to reply, but paused and grinned. "Dolomite. There is a way," he said, and then grew somber. "But are they ready?"

"As I said, I would prefer more time. But yes, they move in wonderful coordination and have learned enough of the basics of their disciplines to complete our task. None of them were novices to fighting when I discovered them, and they have been willing students to alter their techniques. They will make the journey to St. Gwendolyn and scout the road and the monastery. If they are challenged, they will acquit themselves well."

"You have watched the training of the others from afar. Are there any brothers you would wish to see in the challenge?"

"Do you ask me to seek unfair advantage before the exhibition?"

"It has to work," Braumin said bluntly.

"It will. A band of third-year brothers, if you would, Bishop Braumin."

"Third year? Not those of the new class? And all men? That hardly seems fair."

"There is nothing fair about it," Pagonel assured him with a sly look. "I have trained my beautiful sisters in the harmony of the Jhesta Tu. Pray have many soul stones about to heal the bruises of your brothers, and if you have a stone to mend their feelings . . ."

The mystic turned and walked away.

"This is highly unusual, Bishop," Abbot Haney said to Braumin when he met up with the man in St.-Mere-Abelle near the end of the fourth month of 848, the last of the invitees to arrive for the College of Abbots. "A serious breach of protocol."

Beside Haney, Master Dellman shuffled nervously from foot to foot.

Braumin looked around the wide room, to see many accusing stares coming back at him. They had all been thrown off balance by what they had found at the mother abbey. So many youngsters—too young, by Church edict! And so many women! It was not without precedent that women could be brought into the Order, but not here in St.-Mere-Abelle, and surely not in such numbers! The Sovereign Sisters of St. Gwendolyn-by-the-Sea were not subject to the training of the brothers who entered the Church, and were not expected to assume the tasks and roles of the young brothers.

Until now.

Braumin matched stares with Viscenti, and could see the man squirming where he stood. Their unannounced changes had left the visiting brothers mystified and uneasy, and for many, unhappy.

Braumin continued his scan of the room. It struck him how young this gathering was! Indeed, the Church had been decapitated, with most of the older masters and abbots killed in the Heresy. How many of these men standing about him were abbots, he wondered? How many of the Abellican abbeys were without abbots? And how few masters remained? Most of the brothers here did not look old enough to have formally attained that rank. Normally, the College of Abbots was reserved for abbots and their highest ranking masters alone, but Braumin had specifically tailored the invitation to all and any who would come. And many had, and this was perhaps the largest gathering the Abellican Church had ever known.

But they were so young!

Braumin's scan finally brought him back to his dear friend Dellman and Abbot Haney. Dellman offered him a nod of encouragement, though he could see the fear in the man's eyes.

He focused on Haney, the young Vanguardsman who was perhaps his greatest rival for the ascent to the rank of Father Abbot. They were not enemies, though, and Braumin thought highly of the man, and he saw in Haney's eyes more sympathy than anger; the man was clearly made uncomfortable by the grim tone of the gathering.

"Welcome, brothers!" Bishop Braumin suddenly shouted, formally opening the College of Abbots. He looked across the room to the contingent representing St. Gwendolyn, and pointedly added, "And sister!"

All eyes turned to Sister Mary Ann, who stood resolute and unbending.

As she had since Master Arri had brought her in to St.-Mere-Abelle months before. The accusations against her were tremendous, and she would not deny them! In her heart, she had done nothing wrong, and Braumin found it very hard to find fault with such an attitude. She would have fit right in with his band of conspirators in the bowels of St.-Mere-Abelle in the days of Markwart, he believed.

He doubted if that would save her, though, given the frightened mood of the gathering.

They were in no humor to hear of any Samhaist.

"Tonight we feast, tomorrow we argue," Bishop Braumin announced. He paused, and put on a sly smile. "Though perhaps we will argue tonight, as well, yes? The age of the new brothers! And sisters, so many sisters! Too many sisters! And yes, my brothers, the whispers you have heard are true. There are many within this abbey, in the robes of an Abellican, who have no affinity with the stones."

Many calls came back at him, none supportive, and more than a few gasps could be heard among the brothers. Braumin had expected as much, and certainly understood. Every brother in here, and Sister Mary Ann, too, had spent years proving an affinity with the sacred Ring Stones as part of the selection process for ordainment. Many had known friends through their years of training who had been denied entry into the Order because they could not feel the power of the gemstones.

And now, without consultation, Bishop Braumin had thrown that rule aside.

Braumin let the commotion die down, and tossed a wink at the nervous Viscenti.

"It is, or will be, all up to debate and argument, of course, brethren," he said.

"But you have already brought them in," one brother of about Braumin's age remarked loudly.

"Temporarily, perhaps, though I hope that is not the case," Braumin replied. "You have seen the scars of the battle that was waged here at St.-Mere-Abelle—on your way into our repaired gates, you passed a grave holding scores of bodies. In this very hall, there is wood holding back the wind where once there was a grand window of colored glass. The window of the Covenant of Avelyn, shattered by the entrance of a true dragon! I say none of this to diminish the losses that many of you have suffered at your own abbeys and chapels. Witness Master Arri here, and Sister Mary Ann, perhaps all that remain of the brothers and sisters of St. Gwendolyn-by-the-Sea.

"But know that new King Midalis required of St.-Mere-Abelle a measure of strength that we simply no longer possessed," Braumin went on. "I could have recalled many of you to my side—such an edict would have been well within my power as the steward of the position with the death of Father Abbot Bou-raiy! I could have emptied many of your chapels, abbeys even, to solidify this, the Mother Church of Saint Abelle."

He paused and let that sink in, and was glad to see the nods of agreement from many of the monks, even some he recognized as masters, and one or two he assumed were now serving as abbots.

"But a man from Behren, a hero of the battle, has shown me a different way," Braumin explained. "If you have heard the tales of the battle of St.-Mere-Abelle, then you have heard the name of Pagonel, a mystic of the Jhesta Tu. A hero of the day, I say! There are hundreds now alive who would have perished had not Pagonel flown about them on the dragon Agradeleous, calling for them to stand down as the fate of the lands, state, and Church were determined in this very hall.

"This very hall where Marcalo De'Unnero was defeated. This very hall where the shadow of the demon dactyl was cleansed from the soul of Aydrian Wyndon! At my bidding, Pagonel of the Jhesta Tu remains at St.-Mere-Abelle to this day, and his generosity cannot be overstated. He has revealed to us secrets of his Order."

Unsure of how much he should tell rather than show, Braumin paused there and measured the gathering. Every eye was intently upon him, many doubting, some horrified, others intrigued.

"Come, brothers, and Sister Mary Ann. Before we feast, let us go and witness the work of our guest, who has offered me this path back to the security of the Church we all cherish."

He waved his arm to the side, where a pair of his monk attendants threw wide double doors, leading to a long and wide corridor and a flight of stairs that would take them down to where the exhibition waited, where three strong brothers, among the finest fighters of their class, waited to engage the trio of young new sisters tutored by Pagonel.

Braumin tried to show confidence as he was swept in by others on their way to the viewing, but in truth, his guts churned and twisted. Pagonel had assured him that the trio of Diamanda, Elysant, and Victoria would acquit themselves wonderfully, but everything the Bishop knew about fighting, about strength, about size, and about the simple advantage a man might hold over a woman in combat told him that the mystic's optimism might well be sadly misplaced.

Failure here would hold great consequence in the discourse of the next day, and likely in the election of the next Father Abbot.

Because of the dearth of masters and abbots, even tenth-year immaculate brothers were allowed a vote the next day when the Father Abbot was to be chosen.

The process moved along smoothly, but Braumin Herde watched it with a strangely detached feeling, his thoughts continually returning to the events of the previous night. He could see again the doubts, even the mocking expressions, on the faces of the gathered when Pagonel's team of three young sisters stepped into the arena. Most pointedly, many chuckled at the sight of small Elysant, carrying a quarterstaff taller than she.

And when the brothers opposing the trio had come out, those expressions had grown more sour, and more than one, Haney and Dellman included, had spoken to Braumin in whispers of great concern that the women would be injured, and badly so!

The voting went on around him, but Bishop Braumin wasn't watching. In his mind's eye, he was viewing again the beauty of the battle, the movements of graceful Victoria weaving about the opposing lines, the agility and balance of Elysant as she used her staff left and right to block nearly as many attacks aimed at her sisters-in-arms as they themselves blocked, at the sheer speed and power of Diamanda's strikes.

He closed his eyes and winced, recalling the first opponent felled, a large young man who had to weigh near to three hundred pounds. Elysant had deftly turned his bull rush, and Victoria swept past him, turning him, bending him into her wake in inevitable pursuit.

And leaning right into the driving fist of Diamanda.

The man had fallen like a cut tree, just straight down, facedown, to the hard floor. He was awake this morning, at least.

After that, Pagonel's three tigresses had cleverly and neatly caged, worn down, and clobbered the remaining two brothers.

Had any of the sisters even been hit?

The one sour note of the evening, though, had come when Braumin had torn his gaze from the spectacle in the arena to note the expression of Brother Thaddius. The man's sour look spoke volumes, and again Braumin had to wonder if the mystic hadn't erred in choosing this man as the fourth in his legionem in primo.

Master Viscenti's call brought him from his private thoughts and concerns. As the highest-ranking member of St.-Mere-Abelle whose name was not on the ballot, it was Viscenti's place to count the votes.

He called in the stragglers now, offering any a count of ten to come forward and place their colored chip into the box.

None did. The ballots were all in.

Viscenti produced a key and unlocked the metal box, carefully lifting back its hood. The thin man licked his lips and glanced over at Braumin, offering a slight nod.

So began the count.

Abbot Haney received a few votes, but the yellow chips assigned to his cause were dwarfed by the two piles beside them, one for Master Dusibol of St. Bondabruce of Entel, who had spoken passionately against the changes Braumin had made in St.-Mere-Abelle even after the display of Pagonel's team. Dusibol was a traditionalist, and judging from the pile of red chips on the table, he was far from alone in his ways!

But the largest pile was blue, blue for Bishop Braumin, and by enough of a margin, with his pile larger than those of Dusibol and Haney, the only other to receive any votes, combined. There would be no second ballot. The victory was Braumin's, and on the first ballot.

The cheers came forth, some excited, some polite, when Master Viscenti counted it out and declared Braumin Herde as Father Abbot, and spoke, too, of the rarity that their leader would be chosen in a single ballot!

Yes, it was quite an accomplishment, so Braumin heard from his friend and the supporters in the crowd, but he could not really believe it.

Dusibol was not even an abbot, and still had challenged him reputably. In normal times, Master Dusibol would not even have been on the ballot!

Braumin Herde had been an Abbot, and was a Bishop even, and had led to the great victory that had saved the Church at St.-Mere-Abelle.

And yet, his victory was not overwhelming.

He looked around at the gathering as he moved to stand beside Viscenti. He understood their hesitance, their fear. Perhaps it would have been better if they had gone through several ballots, with speeches and debates between each!

"I move that Master Dusibol be elevated to the rank of Abbot of St. Bondabruce immediately," Braumin opened, and now the cheers grew louder. The new Father Abbot looked over at the contingent from St. Honce in Ursal as he spoke, and noted some disconcerting expressions coming back his way. They had wanted Master Ohwan on the ballot, but Dusibol had beaten him out for the third spot, in no small part because of the whispers of Viscenti and Dellman, both noted followers of Braumin Herde.

St. Honce was being punished, they believed, and not without reason. For that abbey had supported King Aydrian and Marcalo De'Unnero—it was rumored that Aydrian had meant to elevate Ohwan to the rank of Abbot of St. Honce, some whispered that the King had actually done so.

Dusibol was a traditionalist, and clearly not enamored of Braumin's changes, clearly, but Ohwan . . .

Ohwan could be real trouble, Braumin Herde feared. Particularly now, where Master Dusibol had garnered far more votes than Abbot Haney, who supported Braumin (and probably voted for Braumin, the new Father Abbot understood) and the emergency measures he had taken to secure St.-Mere-Abelle.

Braumin looked at the pile of red chips again, and understood that the early years of his reign would not be without great challenges.

And honest ones, he had to admit.

He was asking a lot of an Order that prided itself on rituals and ways nearly a millennium old.

"So be it," he thought, and he said, loudly, and he slammed his fist down on the table.

"I am a devout follower of Avelyn," he decreed. "I make no secret of that. Do not believe that his canonization will be slowed by the tragic events of the last year. The Chapel of Avelyn will be rebuilt in Caer Tinella in short order, and fully staffed, and I will see Avelyn Desbris declared as a Saint of our Order."

He saw a lot of nods. He noted no overt looks of discontent.

"You have seen the changes I have made in bringing in new brothers—and sisters."

He paused there and let the murmurs roll through the hall, and surely they were lessened because of the amazing exhibition the brothers had witnessed in the arena. Still, though, they remained, a buzz of anger just below the surface in many of the gathered brothers.

"My first act as Father Abbot, though, will be to declare a full inventory of the Ring Stones. We have thousands in our possession—Avelyn, who will be sainted, brought back nearly two thousand alone!"

A few scattered claps echoed about the hall.

"It was said to be the greatest haul of sacred stones ever returned," Braumin went on, careful not to overstep too greatly by naming the process. "And indeed, for one man, the feat was beyond impressive—yet more proof that Avelyn walked with God. But there was a time, brothers . . ."

He paused and shook his head and sighed for effect, then said cryptically, "We will discuss this at length in the coming days. You will come to see, as I have learned, that much of what we have been taught is not the full, not the only, truth of our sacred heritage."

He had to pause again and hold up his hands to quiet the uneasy rumblings that began to echo, more loudly now.

"You will see," he promised. "And this, too, we shall debate long into the nights, I promise. And in those nights, I will show to you why another will ascend behind Avelyn, why Master Jojonah will find his sainthood in the flames foul Markwart set beneath him!"

Even Viscenti looked at him in shock, stunned, horrified even, that Braumin had moved so boldly, so quickly! He hadn't even put on the robes of the Father Abbot yet!

"What admission of failure and complicity is this?" demanded one of the Masters of St. Honce—speaking for Ohwan, of course.

"Our failures are already known, and now better admitted," the Father Abbot insisted.

"He was your friend, but that is not an impetus for canonization!" the man shouted back.

Braumin smiled as warmly as he could manage. "He was my teacher. He was the guidepost for all of us who defied the demon Markwart, and Marcalo De'Unnero after him. I nominate him—indeed, I do so right now! And I will champion him, as I champion Avelyn, these two men who, by

God's wisdom and grace, guided us through our darkest hours. It was the spirit of Jojonah, I say, that led Brother Francis out onto the fields to minister to those afflicted with the Rosy Plague, an action that cost him his life, as he expected and as he accepted! It was the spirit of Jojonah surging within the body of Brother Romeo Mullahy, who threw himself from the Barbacan Shrine of Avelyn to let his persecutors see the foul truth of their journey!"

He paused again, expecting a retort, but none came forth. Bolstered, and really with nothing to lose, Father Abbot Braumin pressed on.

"The gemstones will be used to alleviate the suffering of the people, brethren or not—indeed, Abellican or not! A brother possessing a soul stone who ignores the pain of a man of Behren or Alpinador, does so by turning his back on God.

"And yes, there are now many sisters among us, most young, some who have served in convents for decades. They will train, we will train, and we will go forth and reclaim every abbey, every chapel, and every heart for St. Abelle!"

He slammed his fist on the table once more, indicating that his speech, and this gathering, was at its end, and he turned and left through the back door of the room, the one leading to the private quarters of the Father Abbot, Masters Viscenti, Dellman, and Abbot Haney at his side.

They left to rousing cheers.

"A fine beginning, Father Abbot," Haney congratulated him.

"But a long way to go," Braumin replied, and he was glad when Haney put a hand on his shoulder, in full support.

And bringing with him, Braumin believed and prayed, the full support of new King Midalis.

"The community is greater than the individual," Father Abbot Braumin said to an agitated Brother Thaddius. "Is that not what Pagonel preaches? And is it not true?"

"This is not the Order I joined, Father Abbot," Thaddius insisted.

"But it is indeed."

Thaddius stared at him incredulously. "For years, I studied the ways of St.-Mere-Abelle. None were more prepared than I when first I entered these gates!"

"Beware your pride, young brother. Perhaps I will tell you the tale of

Avelyn Desbris, that you might find humility. Perhaps I will tell you of Avelyn's first great demonstration of Ring Stone power, one that shocked the Masters and Father Abbot. He was no older than you are now, and yet none in the Church, not even Marcalo De'Unnero, could have matched the fireball he created over the bay, and that after leaping from the roof and walking across the water!"

Brother Thaddius seemed to labor for his breath. The inclusion of De'Unnero in the lesson (particularly since De'Unnero did not stand as the pinnacle of Ring Stone affinity in the days of Avelyn) had stolen the young man's bluster, as it had surely been added as a subtle warning from the Father Abbot.

"I knew the ways of the Abellican Order. I cherished the ritual, the solemnity, the . . ."

"A dragon flew through our great window," Father Abbot Braumin reminded him. "A great battle was fought about our gates and within the monastery. You witnessed the carnage and destruction. We cannot go back. Not now."

"I know," Brother Thaddius said quietly, "but . . ." He ended with a profound sigh.

"You do not value your training with the Jhesta Tu? My understanding is that his techniques have strengthened you in your use of the sacred Ring Stones."

"Women," Thaddius spat. "St.-Mere-Abelle is thick with them!"

"I would expect that a young man would not object so strenuously."

"Father Abbot!"

"Forgive me, young brother," Braumin said, and he tried not to laugh.

"Tradition," Thaddius said, shaking his head. "The continuity of ritual and rite through the passing centuries . . . without it, I am ungrounded. I am lost and floating free of that which brought to me spiritual joy and eternal hope. We have brothers, and sisters, among us who cannot coax a flicker of light from a diamond. And never will they, yet we name them as Abellican monks!"

"I do not disagree," Braumin replied in all seriousness. "My crude attempt at humor notwithstanding. Brother Thaddius, do you understand how profoundly the De'Unneran Heresy wounded our Order, and the kingdom? There is a void of power in both, with King Midalis trying to tame the local lords to fealty, and with half of our chapels and abbeys empty! We are without many options. The Samhaists have been seen about Vanguard, and indeed even within Honce-the-Bear. You have heard the tale of Sister Mary Ann, no doubt.

"And the misery of the common folk cannot be overstated. They need us. They need us to keep clear the way to the Barbacan and the Covenant of Avelyn. They need us to heal their wounds and cure their sicknesses. They need us, and King Midalis, to keep Entel and the Mantis Arm secure from Behrenese pirates and powrie raiders.

"And we are not secure enough in our own institutions to offer that aid. Goblins still roam the land. Powries roam the land. De'Unnerans roam the land! There is fear of the Rosy Plague! Without those basic securities, our words to the common folk ring hollow. They need us, young brother, to coax their spirits to a place of blessed divinity, and they will not hear our sermons when all we can offer to them are words."

"Pagonel is not of our Order, yet he dictates . . ."

"He offers advice, at my bidding," Braumin said, more forcefully, demanding Thaddius's full attention. "And I am Father Abbot. Do you dispute that?"

"No, Father Abbot, of course not," the young man said and lowered his eyes.

"The community is greater than the individual, and you are called upon to be an important member of our community, Brother Thaddius. I know not why Pagonel selected you as the Disciple of Avelyn for his adventuring legionem in primo. But it is a great honor."

"One I share with three women," Thaddius replied rather sharply. "With one who cannot use the Ring Stones at all, and another too young to even enter the Order, even if she were a man!"

"You are among the most important Brothers of Blessed Abelle," Braumin insisted. "More than most of the remaining Masters, yet you are only a few years into your training. If you are successful, if your mission is successful, it will help me to chart a strong course . . ."

"One apart from tradition!" the distressed young man dared to interrupt.

"No!" Father Abbot Braumin yelled in his face. He grabbed Thaddius by his skinny shoulders and forced him to square up and look him in the eye. "No," he repeated, more softly. "Much of what we have come to believe as tradition does not date to the earliest days of the Church. I do not blaspheme the message of St. Abelle. Never that! You must trust me, young brother. Everything I do, I do with purpose to save the Church from what it had become under the perversion of Dalebert Markwart and the Heresy of Marcalo De'Unnero."

That elicited a wince.

"He killed people," Father Abbot Braumin said quietly. "He murdered innocent people, thinking it for the greater good. You said you were prepared to enter our Order, but have you not studied the last two decades of our history? Do you not know the story of Brother Francis, who gave his life administering to the sick? Or of Brother Mullahy, who killed himself rather than renounce his faith? Or of Master Jojonah!"

Brother Thaddius wore a curious expression as tears began to flow down the Father Abbot's face. "Oh, Jojonah, my teacher," the Father Abbot went on. "He showed me the truth of our traditions, and that many of our practices were not traditions at all!"

"I do not know of any time when women were allowed into the Order in great numbers," Thaddius dared to say.

"True," the Father Abbot admitted. "But have you ever known of any person more deserving than Jilseponie Wyndon? She would be your Mother Abbess now if she had accepted our offer. Not a brother in the Church would have questioned it, and none, not one, would have voted for anyone other than Jilseponie if her name had been on the ballot."

Thaddius wore a horrified look.

"Do you doubt me? Do you doubt that Jilseponie brought down Marcalo De'Unnero and Father Abbot Markwart? Do you doubt that Jilseponie served as the shining light to our Order in the time of the plague?"

Thaddius shrugged, but it seemed as if he had no more arguments to offer.

"And so we honor her by allowing women into the Order. Perhaps it will work out for the betterment of us all. Perhaps not—in that case, it will be a temporary thing, out of necessity. Pagonel's order is not unlike our own, and he insists that half of it is comprised of women, equally so, and at all ranks of achievement and honor.

"I need you, young brother," Father Abbot Braumin said earnestly, and he gave the thin man a slight shake. "And I trust in you."

He turned about and went to his desk, and returned a moment later bearing a small pouch. He moved to a table off to the side and carefully upended the contents.

The sparkling gems took Brother Thaddius's breath away. They were all there, it seemed, garnet and malachite, bloodstone, moonstone, serpentine, and a large ruby, and a larger soul stone!

"These I entrust to you, young brother," Father Abbot Braumin explained. "You will take them to St. Gwendolyn-by-the-Sea, and use them at your discretion. You, young brother, are the leader of this legionem in primo, and this band, your band, is critical to the rebuilding of the Abellican Order."

He wasn't sure if Thaddius was even listening, for the man's eyes were surely glowing as he looked upon the precious cache.

"Go ahead," Braumin bade him, and he slid the ruby Thaddius's way. The young man lifted the gemstone in trembling fingers and clutched it tight to his chest, closing his eyes.

Sometime later, Thaddius looked at the Father Abbot, and now he was crying, overwhelmed.

"Never have I felt such . . . purity," he admitted. "The depths of this ruby . . ."

"Be sure that your serpentine shield is full and strong, and encompassing your allies, if ever you choose to use it," Braumin warned. "Your power is considerable, and that stone will hold all that you can impart to it. Take care or you will curl the skin from your own bones!"

"Yes, Father Abbot," Thaddius said, though it seemed as if he could hardly speak.

"Have you anything more to say to me, young brother?"

"The community is greater than the individual," Thaddius replied, and the Father Abbot nodded, contented.

Braumin looked up as the door opened and Viscenti entered. "To the roof with Master Viscenti," the Father Abbot explained to Brother Thaddius. "There you may properly measure these sacred stones and your own power."

The Father Abbot nodded when the pair were gone, then went to his desk, collected a large backpack, and set off for Pagonel's training room. He found the mystic with the three young sisters, preparing packs for the road. They stood as one when he entered, dipping a bow of respect.

"Are they Abellican sisters or Jhesta Tu?" Father Abbot Braumin said with a lighthearted laugh.

"The bow is a sign of respect," said Pagonel.

"Then I should return it," Braumin said, and he did, to Pagonel and then to each of the startled young women in turn.

"Your exhibition has bought me time and great political capital," he explained to them. "Had you failed in your fight, then all of this, your admission into the Order, the acceptance of those who show no affinity to the stones, the alteration of training traditions—all of it—would have been erased. We would limp along, vulnerable, for decades, as those who would weaken the Order of Abelle eagerly watched.

"I believe in these changes," Braumin went on. "I believe in you, and your worthiness as sisters of my Order. If I did not, I would never allow this journey to St. Gwendolyn to commence."

He looked to the tall Diamanda, the Disciple of St. Bruce. "Why did you join in the convent of St.-Mere-Abelle?"

"I was an orphan, Father Abbot. The nuns took me in and raised me as if I had been born to them."

"Is it habit, then, or belief?"

"It is both," Diamanda admitted. "I was raised an Abellican, and have come to see the truth of the word. I am no child—nearer to thirty than twenty—and even had I not been raised in the convent of St.-Mere-Abelle, I would have sought entry."

"As a nun?"

"I always wished for more. To serve at St. Gwendolyn as a full sister. Pagonel's offer rang as sweet music to me."

"And you have danced well in that song," Braumin replied. He held forth a small pouch for Diamanda, then emptied it into her hand, revealing a small cat's eye set in a circlet, a soul stone, and a tiger's paw. "I expect you will find good use for the first, I hope you will not need the second, and I trust that you will use the third only when necessary," he said with a warm smile. He glanced around at the others in reflection, then turned back and offered a fourth stone, a malachite. "Dance to make St. Gwendolyn smile," he whispered.

The woman seemed as if she could hardly draw breath as she stood staring at the stones.

Braumin stepped up to her and hugged her tightly. "Be well," he whispered, and he moved along to the next in line.

"Your grace in that exhibition brought hushed whispers to every Abbot and Master watching," he said to Victoria, the Disciple of St. Gwendolyn, the battlefield dancer. "'St. Gwendolyn reborn,' Master Arri said to me."

"Too kind, Father Abbot," Victoria replied, lowering her eyes respectfully and humbly, though humility surely did not come easily to this one.

And why should it, Braumin thought? She was powerful and full of grace, and strikingly beautiful with her fiery hair and shining eyes. Her every movement spoke of confidence. By Braumin's estimation, Victoria could dominate the Court of King Midalis—every eye would be upon her, the ladies with contempt, no doubt, and the men with lust.

"How does one such as Victoria come into a convent?" he asked her.

"Is there a better place to be, other than an abbey?" she replied. "And now I am here."

"A nobleman's court?"

Victoria snorted as if the thought was absurd.

"Her beauty distracts you, my friend," Pagonel said to Braumin, and the Father Abbot turned on him in surprise. "And indeed, it will serve her well in her role in battle. You will find few among your Church more dedicated than Sister Victoria Dellacourt."

Braumin conceded the point with an apologetic nod, but halfway through it, his eyes widened with recognition. "Dellacourt?" he asked.

"Master Francis was my uncle, though I never knew him," Victoria answered. "Through his actions in the end, he became the pride of my family. His name is spoken of reverently."

The Father Abbot smiled warmly. "We will speak at length of him when you return," he promised. "I knew him well."

"And hated him profoundly," Victoria said, and Braumin stepped back as if slapped. "I know the story, Father Abbot."

Braumin nodded, for he could not deny the truth of her words. Certainly Brother Francis Dellacourt was no friend to Braumin Herde in their days together at St.-Mere-Abelle. Francis served Markwart, dutifully, and was allied with Marcalo De'Unnero. Francis had played no small role in damning Master Jojonah to the flames.

"Do you believe in redemption?" the Father Abbot asked Sister Victoria.

"Yes," she said without hesitation. "If I did not, I would not wear my surname openly."

"So do I," Braumin agreed. "When you return, we will speak at length. I will tell you some things about your uncle you do not know, I am sure. He was led astray by Markwart, but he was not an evil man, and I can prove it."

Braumin smiled again as he remembered one particular encounter with Francis, when the meddlesome young monk had barged in on one of the secret sessions Master Jojonah held for Braumin and the others. Francis had not turned them in to the hateful Markwart!

Braumin brought forth another small pouch from his pack, and from it pulled a small lodestone and another cat's eye circlet. "Brother Thaddius will instruct you in the use of the lodestone," he explained. "It is more than a bullet, and will aid you in bringing your sword to bear, and in turning aside the sword of your enemy."

"Thank you, Father Abbot," she said reverently, taking the stones and setting the circlet about her head.

"And this," Braumin added. He drew a slender sword from his sack and pulled it free of its sheepskin sheath. It was not a broadsword, surely, but long and thin, with an open groove running half its length up the center of the blade. The pommel and crosspiece were thin and graceful, dull steel used sparingly, the hilt wrapped in blue leather, and seemingly nothing remarkable. But how the blade gleamed, even in the meager candlelight of the room!

Victoria's eyes lit up when she took the weapon, no doubt in surprise at the lightness of the blade. Even with the open blood channel, it weighed no more than a long dagger.

"Silverel," the Father Abbot explained. "A gift from the Touel'alfar many centuries past, so say our records, and after meeting Belli'mar Juraviel, I know those old records to be true."

"It seems so . . . light," Victoria remarked.

"It is stronger than our finest steel," Braumin assured her. "You'll not break that blade."

Victoria looked to Pagonel, who seemed as surprised as she.

Braumin gave her a great hug, one she returned tenfold, and then moved to stand before the last of the sisters.

"Saint Belfour laughed from the grave to see the look on Brother Markus's face when he slammed into you and was repelled as surely as if he had run into a stone wall," he said with a grin. "I know that I laughed, and with delight. It defies logic and reason!"

"She is connected to her line of life energy," Pagonel interjected. "Greatly so. And she has trained hard and well."

"Indeed," Braumin agreed. "And so for you . . ."

"I am not skilled with the stones, Father Abbot," she said. "Less so than Sister Victoria, even!"

"So Brother Thaddius has complained to me," the Father Abbot admitted.

Victoria and Elysant rolled their eyes and looked at each other, and Braumin could only imagine the grief Thaddius had given to these two!

Braumin pulled a cloak from his sack, which then seemed empty as he set it down on the floor at his feet. He shook the cloak out and turned it to show Elysant a pair of small diamonds set about the collar.

"Put it on," he instructed.

She swung it about her shoulders.

"This was fashioned for the bodyguard of a long-dead King of Honce-the-Bear," he explained, "and only returned to the Church when Marcalo De'Unnero, then Bishop of Palmaris, began confiscating those magical items circulating among the nobles and merchants. Feel its power, young sister, and bring it forth."

Elysant closed her eyes and concentrated, and a moment later, her image seemed to blur a bit, as if shadows had gathered about her.

Braumin looked to Pagonel. "A more difficult target," he explained, and the mystic nodded.

"But I cannot call forth the power of the sacred stones," a confused Elysant remarked.

"You need not with such an item," the Father Abbot explained. "Which is why the Church frowned upon creating them for those not of the Order. And this," he said, bending low and retrieving one last item from the sack, which was not empty after all, "is among the most precious ever made in this abbey."

He brought forth a small coffer, and opened it reverently before the woman, who gasped, as did the others. For within the coffer, on black silk, sat a leather bracer, set with a large and beautiful dolomite, and surrounded by five others.

"It was made for a queen in the fifth century, because she was beloved and ever sickly. But alas, she died before it was finished, and so it has remained locked away in the lower chambers of St.-Mere-Abelle these four hundred years."

He glanced again at the mystic. "Pagonel feared that for all of your hard work, he simply did not have enough time to properly toughen you against the blows you will surely face."

He picked up the bracer and dropped the coffer, then took Elysant's right arm and tied the item about her wrist.

The small woman's jaw dropped open. She felt the magic, apparently, and to the others, she seemed sturdier somehow.

"Saint Belfour had such sacred dolomite sewn into his robes," he explained.

"It is a precious gift," Sister Elysant said, her voice barely a whisper, so overwhelmed was she. "I cannot . . ."

"Keep it well," said Braumin. He hugged her tightly, then stepped back. "All of you," he said. "These gifts I entrust to you. Let them remind you of the importance of this journey you are soon to take. I do not give them lightly!"

The three women nodded solemnly, and Braumin knew that they understood the weight of the responsibility he had put upon them, and the trust he had shown in them.

He was taking a great chance here, he knew. If this group, this legionem in primo, was waylaid and defeated on the road, then his doubters and enemies in the Church would be bolstered greatly, and so his hopes for Reformation could fast dissipate.

But he believed in Pagonel.

And, he knew in looking at these disciples of the saints, he believed in these extraordinary young sisters.

The meetings the next day among the members of the Church leadership had begun quietly, but as those who opposed Father Abbot Braumin came to believe that they were under no threat of retribution, the discussions became more and more contentious.

Braumin listened more than he spoke, and realized as the arguments raged that his proposed changes would only hold if they brought very positive results in short order.

He nodded through every point raised by those supporting him, and opposing him. He was no dictator here, and given the disruption to every abbey and chapel, now was the time for the brothers to air their every concern and let their opinions be known.

In the back of his mind, through every shout and growling response, Father Abbot Braumin reminded himself that the pile of red chips, for a man who had not even attained the rank of Abbot, was substantial, and that he was the Father Abbot of all the Abellican Church, not just those who had supported his ascension.

He grew concerned, however, when he looked over at Master Arri and Sister Mary Ann. He had thought to take care of that messy business initially, before the two sides had dug in their respective heels, but then had reconsidered. He glanced over at Arri then, and offered a reassuring nod, for he understood that now the animosity was palpable, and that many of his allies would support him regarding the two monks from St. Gwendolyn-by-the-Sea even if they disagreed.

"My brethren," Braumin called, and he banged the heavy gavel down upon the wood, demanding the attention of all. When the room quieted, he continued, "Particularly since we are considering the matter of so many sisters entering the Order, perhaps we should now discuss the disposition of the one abbey where such was not uncommon. To begin the matter, and since St. Gwendolyn is emptied of her brothers and sisters, I nominate Master Arri to the rank of Abbot."

"Perhaps we should adjudicate the matter of Sister Mary Ann first," Dusibol remarked—Abbot Dusibol, who had been promoted that very morning.

"Arri is the obvious choice," Braumin countered. "He has never held any mark against him, is well known among the supporters of Avelyn, and would seem to be the only remaining Master, if not the only remaining monk, other than Sister Mary Ann, of the abbey! Do you intend to oppose the nomination, Abbot?"

Abbot Dusibol held up his hands in surrender and gave a slight shake of his head. He would not oppose the nomination, were it now or the next day, Braumin knew. None would. But to promote Arri before the decisions were brought regarding the wayward sister would afford the man tremendous influence in that trial.

And so a fourth Abbot joined the ranks of Braumin Herde, Haney, and Dusibol soon after, and a fifth followed closely when, to Braumin's dismay, the contingent from St. Honce selected Ohwan, a man who had been the choice of Marcalo De'Unnero! Father Abbot Braumin would have fought that choice, except that the large contingent from St. Honce had been united on the choice, and were not without allies from the other abbeys and chapels, particularly the myriad chapels from southern Honce-the-Bear, all closely connected to the great city of Ursal.

Braumin Herde wasn't surprised, but the easy ascent of Ohwan served as a poignant reminder to the Father Abbot that those who believed in the vision of De'Unnero had not all died that fateful day in the fight at St.-Mere-Abelle. Now the Father Abbot would have a man who had been loyal to De'Unnero serving as Abbot of the second most important abbey of the Church, just down the lane from the palace of King Midalis in the largest and most important city, Ursal.

"So what of my abbey, Father Abbot?" Abbot Arri asked a short while later. "Will you grant me a force to go and reclaim it?"

"The group is on the way," Braumin replied. "The three sisters you witnessed in battle last night, along with one of our most promising brothers. They will return to us the information we need to properly reclaim St. Gwendolyn."

"I would begin rebuilding my abbey now, from this place, if I may," said Arri, and Braumin nodded.

He looked to Mars, who held his breath. He had renounced De'Unnero to the Father Abbot, though Braumin wasn't convinced. Still, considering what had just happened regarding St. Honce . . .

"I would bring my brother back to St. Gwendolyn," Arri suggested. "Master Mars."

Father Abbot Braumin looked around, and the most disconcerted look he saw coming back at him was from his dear friend Viscenti (who, like Braumin, was far from convinced of Mars's loyalty to this current incarnation of the Church).

"I ask, too, that we four Abbots retire to private quarters to determine the disposition of Sister Mary Ann," said Arri.

"No!" someone called from the back. "It is a matter for all of us!"

Many arguments erupted immediately at that, but above them came the demand of Abbot Arri. "This would be a matter for my abbey alone, were it properly staffed. As it is not, I would ask for a quiet place of reason and justice, among the Abbots alone. It is my right."

More shouts came back, but Father Abbot Braumin slammed his gavel to silence them. "It is Abbot Arri's right."

He adjourned the meeting immediately and the five retired to a smaller room, where Braumin bade Sister Mary Ann to speak on her own behalf.

He loved the fire the woman showed! She would not back down and would not deny the truth: that she was in love with a Samhaist priest.

"And where does this love place your loyalties with regard to our Church?" asked Abbot Dusibol pointedly. "Surely you are demanding excommunication!"

"Or perhaps she is choosing the man, and not his ways," Abbot Arri offered to soften that blow.

"Are they not one and the same?" Dusibol pressed.

"Sister?" Father Abbot Braumin prompted.

"It is hard to know what I believe," Mary Ann admitted. "I believed in my Church and my brethren, and yet they came against me, to kill me. This man, who I am told I must despise, saved my life, and almost at the price of his own." She reached into her belt pouch and produced a soul stone. "I called upon God, my God, our God, and he granted me the powers of the Ring Stone, and through it, I returned the act and saved Elliot's life. Does that matter not at all?"

"He is a Samhaist," Ohwan said with open disgust. "Need I list to you the atrocities of that foul religion?"

"Need I recount for you the image of the skin curling from the bones of goodly and godly Master Jojonah?" Father Abbot Braumin countered.

The hateful look Abbot Ohwan flashed him at that served as a warning of things to come, Braumin knew.

"What would you have, Abbot Arri?" Braumin asked.

"I would take Sister Mary Ann back to St. Gwendolyn with me, if she will," he answered. "Her reputation is without blemish."

"Until this," Abbot Ohwan said with a sneer.

"I will not denounce Elliot," Mary Ann insisted. "Nor will I pretend that my love for him is no more."

"But you wish to remain an Abellican?" Braumin asked.

Mary Ann hesitated and looked to Arri. "Yes," she then answered.

"Are you sure?"

"I am sure of nothing anymore, Father Abbot," she answered honestly. "I thought my life settled and complete, but Marcalo De'Unnero and his followers showed me differently."

Braumin nodded, and bade her to go into the anteroom that they might discuss their decision, and when it came to that moment of truth, Father Abbot Braumin was greatly surprised and greatly relieved to discover that he would not have to exercise his greater rank to break the tie, for Abbot Dusibol voted Sister Mary Ann innocent along with Arri and Braumin, and Abbot Ohwan, frustrated as he was, had no recourse and so agreed to accept the decision.

"All that we ask of you," Braumin explained to Mary Ann later on, "is that if ever you learn something of the Samhaists that is important to our Church, to your Church, that you not be silent."

"You would have me be your spy?"

"I would have you be honest," Braumin replied immediately. "To us and to your love. Should you come to see the Samhaist way as suited to your heart, then you must renounce your position in the Abellican Church. Until you have done so, you must never forget your responsibilities to St. Gwendolyn-by-the-Sea and to the other abbeys and chapels. If the Samhaists plan to return in large numbers and vie with us for the hearts of Honce, then we will know of it, Sister Mary Ann."

She started to argue, but Braumin cut her short in no uncertain terms.

"When we go back out among the others, there will be calls for you to be executed, sister," he said harshly, and Mary Ann stiffened her jaw and did not blink. "Do you understand what Abbot Arri and I, and even Abbot Dusibol, have offered to you? In any normal time, you would be found guilty of heresy and burned alive. Or even if mercy were to be shown, you would have your head shaven and would be stripped of your robes, outcast from the Order of St. Abelle forever. Do you understand that?"

"Yes, Father Abbot," she said quietly, and humbly.

"But these are not normal times," Braumin went on. "Abbot Arri trusts you, and needs you, as do I. You accept our offer to remain in the Church, so you cannot dismiss the responsibilities that come with the white robe you wear."

"Yes, Father Abbot," she said.

"Good then, it is settled. Be true to your heart, sister, in all matters."

When they went back out among the others, and Sister Mary Ann took her place beside Arri and Mars, Braumin's prediction came true, and indeed calls of "Burn her!" erupted in the hall, and so began another great argument, like all the others before it.

Except this time Father Abbot Braumin would not hear it. He slammed down the gavel repeatedly, demanding quiet, and when finally it came, he spoke with the voice of Avelyn, and Jojonah, and Jilseponie, and Mullahy, and Francis even. He spoke with the voice of all who had stood up against the abomination that had festered in his beloved Abellican Church.

"We are Avelyn!" he shouted. "We are not Markwart! We are Jojonah—Saint Jojonah, I say, and so I will prove! We are Jilseponie, who battled the demon dactyl beside Avelyn, and who should now be sitting as Mother Abbess of our Order—would any have dared vote against her?"

The Father Abbot paused there again, but not a sound was to be heard in the hall.

Pointedly, staring at the contingent from St. Honce, he finished, "We are not Marcalo De'Unnero."

And so the debate of Sister Mary Ann ended, but had Father Abbot Braumin glanced her way with his final proclamation, he might have noticed the scowl that crossed the face of Master Mars, standing right beside her.

"I've rarely seen a man pout for so long without reprieve," Diamanda teased Thaddius as they gathered about the fire on their third night out of St.-Mere-Abelle. The weather was cold and miserable, with cold rain, sleet, and even snow taking turns falling on the adventuring foursome.

Still, the other three knew well that Diamanda wasn't talking about the dreary weather. The three sisters, so thrilled at being able to fully realize their dreams in joining the Abellican Church, so excited about the possibilities Pagonel had shown to them and their remarkable progress in just a few weeks of intense training, could not be muted by clouds and cold rain. Their steps could not be slowed by the mud.

And they had embraced Brother Thaddius fully, their every discussion in the days before their departure pertaining to how they could properly incorporate him into their defensive formation for maximum effect, or of how they had to protect him, so proficient with the Ring Stones, at all costs. When they had left St.-Mere-Abelle, Father Abbot Braumin had told them all that Thaddius was considered the leader of the band, and not one of the sisters had protested publicly or privately.

But Thaddius wouldn't engage them, wouldn't answer their talk with anything more than a noncommittal grunt, and wouldn't even look any of them in the eye. His every expression exuded disgust.

And he was disgusted, and thoroughly, and not only by the inclusion of so many sisters, which before had been a matter of tokenism and nothing substantial, but by the inclusion of unworthy individuals, like Elysant, who could not use the Ring Stones, or even Diamanda, who could barely bring forth their powers. Thaddius had left friends who could not enter the Church with him those few years ago, and most of them, in his mind, were far more worthy than these three.

He had complained about that very thing to Father Abbot Braumin on the day of their departure, and Braumin had promised that he would go back and call upon many of the brothers who had not come to St.-Mere-Abelle beside Thaddius.

Thaddius didn't believe him, but even if he had, those friends he had left behind did not deserve this honor of ordainment in any case!

But this, these three and the others Braumin had pushed into St.-Mere-Abelle . . . this was an abomination!

And Mars, Master Mars! Thaddius had gone to great lengths to chase the man out of the Church, and now he was back and as a Master? The man couldn't light an oil-soaked rag with a ruby on a sunny day!

"Have you ever before seen a man whose entire life had been proven a lie?" Thaddius shot back at the tall and powerful Disciple of St. Bruce.

"Are you a follower of De'Unnero, then?" a smiling Elysant teased, and it was just a lighthearted remark, they all knew, for smiling Elysant seemed incapable of harboring a malicious thought.

The look Brother Thaddius threw back at her, however, was full of just such a sentiment.

"Your home was attacked by De'Unnero!" Diamanda exclaimed.

"He did not say that he followed the man," Elysant cut in.

"Need it be one or the other?" Thaddius said. "Perhaps there is good in what Father Abbot Braumin is trying to do . . ."

"But perhaps there was truth in De'Unnero, too, yes? And in Markwart before him?"

Thaddius stared at her but didn't respond.

"It galls you that we are in the Church now," Diamanda asserted.

Brother Thaddius didn't reply, but did glare at her.

Elysant hopped over to sit on the fallen log beside the man, and put her arm about him. He looked at her with a shocked expression, and she kissed him on the cheek. "You will come to love us, brother," she said with a grin.

Thaddius didn't reply, but this time because anything he tried to say would have been stammered gibberish. He was quite relieved when Elysant moved away again, to the laughter of the other two.

"We will prove ourselves," Victoria said then, and in all seriousness. "That is all we ever asked for, brother, a chance to prove worthy of the Church we all love."

"And does loving the Church count for nothing with you?" Diamanda added.

Thaddius looked down into the bowl of stew, and lifted another steaming bite to his lips.

Diamanda started to speak again, but she was overruled then by a gruff, unexpected voice.

"Yach, but there ye are, ye blasted monks," came a call from the side, through the trees, and the four looked over to see a group of squat and square figures coming their way. Short and powerful warriors wearing distinctive red berets.

"Powries," Diamanda whispered.

Elysant moved as if to reply, but she really couldn't get any words past the lump in her throat. She looked to Thaddius, as if expecting, hoping, praying that he would launch some lightning of fire, or some other enchantment to blow these monsters away! But he sat as wide-eyed and dumbstruck as she.

"Be ready," Victoria whispered harshly from the side. "We have prepared for this!"

"Ye said ye'd be meeting us in the morn, and so ye was nowheres to be found!" the powrie grumbled.

"Yach, but never could depend on weakling humans," said another, and he spat upon the ground.

There were five of the dwarves at least, moving in a tight but disorganized bunch straight through the trees toward the camp. They all carried weapons: an axe, a spiked club, a couple of long and serrated knives, and the one in the middle, the primary speaker, held something that looked like the bastard offspring of a double-bladed axe and a handful of throwing daggers, all wrapped together into a long-handled weapon that seemed like it could do damage from about ten different angles all at once!

To the side, Victoria slowly picked up her short bow.

"They think us allies," Thaddius whispered.

"Well, see, then, what your words might do," said Victoria, who appeared very calm through it all, more than ready to fight. Her hand held steady the bow, her other eased an arrow from the quiver she had set upon the ground against the log she used for her seat. When she got that one out, she stuck it in the ground beside her foot in easy grasp and began subtly reaching for the next one.

That movement, so calm, so practiced, so mindful of the lessons of Pagonel, proved infectious for the other two sisters. Elysant moved off the log, but stayed in a crouch, quietly bringing her quarterstaff up before her, while Diamanda slowly shifted around the back of Elysant, putting the defensive Disciple of St. Belfour in the middle, between herself and Victoria.

"Quite far enough," Thaddius said, standing up. "What do you want?"

"Eh?" the powrie asked, and he stopped, as did the four flanking him.

"We said we would meet you in the morning, at the appointed spot," Thaddius bluffed. "Tomorrow morning!"

"Not what was said," the dwarf replied. "And not said be yerself, either."

"Yach, who's this one, then?" asked another of the powries.

"Ain't seen him before," said yet another.

The one in the middle, clearly the leader, patted his thick hands in the air to quiet them. "In the morning, meaning tomorrow morning, eh?" he asked, his voice conciliatory and reasonable.

"Yes, when we join with the others," Thaddius replied.

"Where might they be?" asked the dwarf. "Over in the farmhouses, then?"

Thaddius looked around at his allies, searching for some answer. "Aye," he blurted. "That's where we were to meet them, and with important news from the west. And in the morning, tomorrow morning, we'll all gather and talk."

The dwarves looked around at each other. A couple mumbled under their breath, too low for the monks to hear.

"Ah, but I'm losing me patience," said the leader. "Right at dawn then, and don't ye be late!" He spun about and slapped the dwarf near him on the shoulder, and the group started away.

"By God," Elysant breathed a moment later. "Bloody cap dwarves!"

"We should move, and quickly," Thaddius advised, and the two women nearest him nodded.

"No," said Victoria, surprisingly, and when the three looked at her, they noted that she had set an arrow to her bowstring, two others stuck into the ground in easy reach. "They will be back," she quietly and calmly whispered. "Ready your gemstones, Brother Thaddius. Diamanda, slip off to the side and put that cat's eye circlet to use."

"How can you know?" Elysant asked, but Victoria held up her hand to silence the woman.

On Victoria's lead, the three slipped back a bit, to the edge of the low glow of the campfire.

And waited. Their hearts thrummed, but every passing moment seemed an eternity.

"You will stay close, but behind Elysant, Brother Thaddius," Victoria reminded him.

"I am the leader," Thaddius replied.

"Elysant, dear sister, fall back on your training," Victoria quietly encouraged her, ignoring Thaddius. "Remember the arena. Those brothers were formidable, yet not one got a strike past the swift movements of your quarterstaff. We are ready, sister."

"We are ready, sister," Elysant echoed.

"Right, southeast!" came Diamanda's call from the side, just as the dwarves appeared again before them, four this time, weapons high and charging through the trees.

Victoria stepped forward, right before Elysant, and leveled her bow, pointing out in the general direction Diamanda had indicated.

"Two fingers left," Diamanda corrected, and Victoria shifted and let fly.

"They come!" Thaddius warned, but Diamanda noted movement in the woods and knew that her arrow had not missed the mark by much. She reached back and grabbed a second, and that too flew off, and this time, they heard a grunt as it struck home!

"They are here!" Thaddius cried. "Swords! Swords!"

Victoria ignored him altogether, reaching for the third arrow, trusting in her sisters.

Elysant leaped past her, back by the fire, and smashed her quarterstaff across it, launching a spray of embers into the faces of the charging dwarves. The two to the left fell back in surprise, the next in line to the right stumbled and grabbed at his stung eyes, and the one furthest right lifted an ugly knife and leaped in at the woman.

But coming behind him, beside him, and past him, with a great malachite-aided leap, came Diamanda, and she swept her hand across the side of the powrie's face as she went, only her hand wasn't a hand, but a great tiger's paw. The dwarf howled, grabbed at his torn face, and stumbled right into his nearest companion, who was also off balance.

Diamanda landed and sidestepped fast as Elysant cut before her, sliding down to her knees and thrusting her staff into the midst of the tangled legs of the two dwarves. Up she came immediately, the tip of her quarterstaff planted, and she used the leverage to pitch both the dwarves to the side.

Into the fire.

At the same time, Victoria saw her target clearly, the powrie racing in at them, an arrow sticking from one shoulder, his axe up high over his head. She shot him in the face and he fell away.

And away went the bow, too, the Disciple of St. Gwendolyn drawing the fine sword Braumin had given her, and rushing around Diamanda and Elysant to anchor the far right of the line. She warned Thaddius to keep up as she went.

"Behind Elysant!" she clarified as the brother hustled in her wake.

In mere moments, the three sisters had flanked the confused powries, shifting their entire defensive posture to the right side of the dwarf four-some.

The two in the embers scrambled up, but one took a wicked crack in the face from Elysant's staff, the other got his arm ripped by Victoria's sword.

The other two, though, recovered and swept around their fellows, rushing in at Diamanda, who met them with a scream and quick rush, only to feint and roll away, turning a complete circuit as Elysant swept before her, the quarterstaff banging against that strange multiheaded weapon and driving it to the side so that the further dwarf couldn't get in close enough to score a hit on the retreating Diamanda.

Elysant seemed a blur of motion, then, and indeed a blur, as she called upon the shadows offered by the diamonds in her cloak.

Victoria quickly followed her, cutting in front of the second powrie on that end and stabbing at his face, but not to score a hit, for she could not. No, she simply drove him back a step, so that she could skid to a stop, reverse her footing, and throw a backhand with her sword at the furthest to the right, batting down his dagger arm.

Just then Diamanda came around, her tiger's paw raking at the dwarf's face, the stiffened fingers of her other hand shooting forward to jab the dwarf hard in the throat.

The dwarf staggered back, and then fell back more as starbursts erupted in his face, a series of tiny explosions from the hurled celestite crystals of Brother Thaddius. They burned and stung, smoked the dwarf's dung-dipped beard, and poked little holes in his face.

Diamanda glanced back as she moved to keep up with Victoria, to see Thaddius fumbling with several stones, seemingly at a loss. One hand went back to his pouch where he kept the little firebombs of celestite, while in the other he rolled several stones, in no apparent coordination.

"Brother!" she said sharply to shock him into the moment.

But she couldn't say more than that or do more than that. Victoria rolled behind Elysant, flanking her to the left, and Diamanda had to move in tight to the right of the centering defensive warrior. She hoped Thaddius would have the good sense to get behind Elysant, but if not, there was nothing she could do for him.

The three dwarves came on, more angry than hurt. The fourth moved to join them, but got hit by another celestite barrage and fell back once more.

Victoria flipped her sword to her left hand and sent it out across in front of Elysant, inviting the dwarf before her to bear in, which he, predictably, did. The agile woman rolled backward, bending her knees to keep just ahead of the dagger, and as the dwarf bore in, Elysant's staff stabbed across before him, right under the thrusting arm, and drove upward, lifting the blow harmlessly.

And under the upraised staff, to the left, went Victoria, between Elysant and the dwarf she had driven back with her sword thrust, moving into the dwarf battling Diamanda, commanding his attention with a sudden flurry and rush.

She stopped again, retreating quickly between her sisters, but the distraction was all that Diamanda needed, and out lashed the tiger's paw, tearing skin from the dwarf's face and shoulder.

"Ah, ye ugly runts!" the dwarf gasped, falling back.

Diamanda pursued, thinking she had a kill, but Elysant's cry stopped her, and turned them all, to see another dwarf, an arrow in his shoulder, another in his face, rushing in at Thaddius. Elsyant dove back to intercept, but the dwarf she had blocked recognized the movement and his knife chased her and caught her, sliding into her lower back.

Still, the small woman did not turn, but continued forward and drove the newcomer aside before he could get to Thaddius.

Victoria intercepted the knife-wielder so he couldn't do more harm. Diamanda closed tight to her, both moving with Victoria to re-form the defensive line.

By all rights, they were winning the fight. They had hit their enemies many times harder than they had been hit.

And yet they were losing. They all knew it. The powries, stuck with arrows, faces clawed, throats jabbed, hair burned, seemed hardly hurt!

"Victoria, flee and tell St.-Mere-Abelle of our fate," Diamanda said, and she slugged a dwarf hard across the face.

But he laughed and swatted at her with his spiked club—which Elysant blocked with her staff.

The cunning bloody cap rolled the club over that block, though, and clipped Elysant across the arm, tearing the sleeve from her white robe and gashing her shoulder-to-elbow.

The tough Disciple of St. Belfour just growled through it, though, and spun her club like a spear and jabbed out, once, twice, thrice, into the dwarf's face and throat.

Pain burned in Elysant. Blood ran liberally down the back of her leg and from her arm, but she growled through it and worked furiously to keep the ferocious dwarves from her beloved sisters.

But they were overmatched and outnumbered, and for all of the beauty in movement and precise strikes, the dwarves would not fall down.

"Go, Victoria, the Church must know," Diamanda cried, and the end was garbled as she took a glancing, but painful, blow from that many-headed weapon. She barely managed to straighten and fall back as the axe of another swept in at her, and still would have been hit had not Elysant's quarterstaff flashed across yet again.

"No!" Victoria cried.

"The Church is greater than any of us! Go!" Elysant yelled at her.

A dwarf leaped up high, descending upon Elysant, but Victoria sprang between them, her sword longer than the dwarf's knife, the blade catching the descending powrie just under the ribs, driving up as his weight carried him down, down.

Blood erupted from the wound and the dwarf tried to scream, but all that came forth was a shower of red mist and spurting liquid.

Victoria couldn't possibly disengage in time to bring her sword into a defensive posture, so she simply let the blade fall with the powrie—their first kill, and one, at least, would not be dipping its beret in the spilled blood of the sisters!

Up and around came Victoria, seemingly unarmed, and that proved an advantage, as the powrie she had been facing thought her an easy kill and came in with abandon.

She slugged him square in the face, sending him staggering backward, and how she wanted to leap upon him and choke the life from him!

But she could not, and she followed her training and fell back in line beside Elysant.

"Go," Elysant pleaded with her yet again, and she meant it, for while one dwarf was down, the others pressed them hard from every angle. They couldn't hold on against the fierce bloody caps—Elysant's left leg was going numb and the fingers on her left hand tingled so that she could hardly hold her quarterstaff.

A powrie blade flashed out at Diamanda to Elysant's right. She sent the staff out to block.

But too late, and Diamanda staggered, her belly stabbed.

"Tell them, sister," Elysant pleaded with Victoria. "Tell them we fought well."

And Victoria almost fled, and intended to, but a hand fell upon her shoulder, and before she could react, a blue-white glow encompassed her.

"Sister!" she cried to Elysant, and she moved a step closer and grabbed Elysant's wounded upper arm.

How Elysant howled, and started to pull away.

But she too saw the blue-white ghostly glow flowing over her form, and instead she reached her staff out toward Diamanda, calling to her to grab it.

And as the woman did, inviting the glow to encapsulate her as well, Elysant managed to glance back at Brother Thaddius.

He, too, was glowing, for he had initiated the enchantment, after all, from the serpentine he held in his upraised palm, its texture blurred by the blue-white shield.

The other gem he held, though, the mighty ruby, was not so dulled, for it was outside the shield.

It glowed fiercely—Father Abbot Braumin had promised Thaddius that this stone would hold all that he could put into it and more.

And so it had.

And so Brother Thaddius lived up to his reputation with the Ring Stones, for from that ruby came a tremendous burst of fire, a blast that rolled about the four monks and the five powries, that rushed out to the trees and into the boughs, and despite the dreary rain and sleet, set them ablaze.

And set the powries ablaze!

But not the sisters and Thaddius, no, for the serpentine shield held strong.

Elysant felt the warmth in her face, but the biting fires could not get through the shield and could not curl her skin.

The fireball lasted only an instant, and when the immediate flames rolled to nothingness, the three sisters went at the dwarves with fury, for the stubborn beasts had not fallen.

But the fight had turned, and the dwarves, wounded, horribly burned and dazed, could not get their bearings, could not mount any defense against the staff of Elysant, the pounding fists of Victoria, and the deadly tiger's paw of Diamanda.

One of the dwarves did get out of the immediate area, fleeing through the trees.

"Sister, your bow!" Elysant cried to Victoria.

They both realized that wouldn't work when they glanced at the bow on the ground behind them, its string melted by the fireball, its wood smoking.

"Catch him!" Diamanda cried.

"Hold!" said Thaddius, stepping toward Victoria with an outstretched hand.

All three women looked at him curiously for a moment, but then Victoria grinned and brought forth a gemstone, pressing it in Thaddius's palm. He took it and clenched his fist up before his eyes, sending his power into the gem.

Clever Diamanda removed her cat's eye circlet and placed it over Thaddius's head, and his vision shifted with the magic, turning night into day, showing him the fleeing powrie clearly.

He didn't even need to see the dwarf, though, for he could feel him. He could feel the metal rivets in the dwarf's leather armor, and could feel keenly the long metal knife he held tight against his chest.

Ah, that knife!

Brother Thaddius thrust his hand forward and opened his fingers and the lodestone shot forth, speeding until it clanged against that blade.

Of course, to reach the blade, it had to first drive right through the dwarf.

The powrie fell to his knees, then toppled to his face.

The arguments raged day and night, one issue after another.

"The Church has been through terrible times, Father Abbot," Haney kept reminding Braumin Herde.

Braumin nodded each time, and tried to offer a smile, truly appreciating Abbot Haney's attempts to keep perspective on this trying College of Abbots.

This late afternoon, the argument centered on the southern city of Entel, the only city in Honce-the-Bear serving as home to two separate abbeys. With Dusibol ascending to the rank of Abbot of St. Bondabruce and St. Rontlemore in chaos, the idea had been floated to give the man the lead of both abbeys until the situation could be better sorted.

Of the seven major abbeys of Honce-the-Bear, St.-Mere-Abelle, St. Gwendolyn-by-the-Sea, St. Honce, St. Belfour, St. Precious, and the pair in Entel, no two were more ferocious rivals than Bondabruce and Rontlemore! St. Bondabruce was the larger, and had prospered greatly because of the Duke of Entel's affinity toward the southern Kingdom of Behren. Many of Bondabruce's monks claimed Behrenese heritage—Blessed

St. Bruce himself was dark-skinned, and claimed ancestry in the fierce Chezhou-Lei warrior class of the Behrenese city of Jacintha.

St. Rontlemore, on the other hand, had ever stayed faithful to the line of Ursal, and indeed had been built by one of the former kings who was angered by the Abbot of St. Bondabruce and the man's overt love and loyalty to Jacintha. In the De'Unneran Heresy, Bondabruce had sided with the powers of Ursal, with De'Unnero and King Aydrian.

St. Rontlemore had been routed.

And now, with the smell of blood still lingering in the heavy air about the mother abbey, the upstart new Abbot of St. Bondabruce was trying to spread his covetous wing over St. Rontlemore!

The volume in the great hall reached new heights that day, a volume not seen since the battle in that very room. A weary Father Abbot Braumin hadn't even lifted the gavel, and could only shake his head, knowing that this had to play out, however it might.

"Dusibol will challenge you if all of Entel falls under his domain," Viscenti warned Braumin and Haney at one point. "Entel is strong, very strong."

Braumin Herde merely nodded and rubbed his weary face, with so many trials hovering about him. Given his bold moves, all controversial even among his supporters, he knew that he was not strong here, certainly not strong enough to determine the situation in Entel, which, with its proximity and strong ties to Jacintha, had always been a trouble spot for the Abellican Church.

And so the arguing continued.

"Vespers cannot be called soon enough," Braumin lamented to Haney and Viscenti. He perked up even as he spoke, seeing the room's outer door swinging open and a young brother rushing in, perhaps to call that very hour.

Braumin's excitement turned to curiosity when he noted that the clearly agitated young monk was rushing his way and holding a very wet sack.

The man dared approach the Father Abbot directly, ignoring the stares of many in the room who were beginning to catch on that something must be amiss.

"From legionem in primo, Father Abbot," the young brother explained, handing him the sack, along with a rolled parchment. "It was brought in by a peasant rider. The man was nearly dead from starvation, as was his horse, for he had not stopped for many hours."

Braumin stared at him, unsure of what to make of the curious turn of the phrase describing the band sent to St. Gwendolyn, a playful name that had been no more than a private joke among Braumin's inner circle, Brother Thaddius, and the three sisters who had gone off to St. Gwendolyn-by-the-Sea.

Braumin unrolled the parchment, his eyes widening with every word.

"Brothers," he cried, rising from his seat. "Brothers! Sisters!"

Now he did reach for the gavel, but he didn't need it, for his tone had demanded and received the attention of all.

"What news, Father Abbot?" Abbot Dusibol called—for no better reason than to inject himself into what seemed an important moment, Braumin recognized.

Braumin could hardly read, for his hands began to tremble, and as he digested the text scrawled before him, he realized that he might have erred in calling attention to it before he fully understood its contents.

He looked up, the blood drained from his face, and he knew it was too late.

"Our dear sisters and brother bound for St. Gwendolyn were waylaid on the road by bloody cap dwarves," he stated.

A collective gasp was followed by more than a little grumbling and smug proclamations of some variation of "I told you so."

Father Abbot Braumin handed the parchment to Viscenti and grabbed up the sack, pulling it open.

His eyes lit up as he stared into the bag. He looked up at the crowd, leaning forward as one in anticipation.

With a knowing smile—knowing that Pagonel's band had, for the second time, bolstered his position, Father Abbot Braumin reached into the sack, and very deliberately began removing the contents.

One powrie beret at a time.

The cheers grew and grew and grew.

Father Abbot Braumin knew then that he would indeed have a great voice over the events in Entel.

"There they are," Sister Diamanda announced. She lay atop a bluff, under drooping pines with branches pulled down by heavy, melting snow. Down the slope before her sat a collection of farmhouses, and in the lane between them stood a man in Abellican robes.

Elysant, Victoria, and Brother Thaddius crawled up beside her. They had been hunting for these monks since their encounter with the powries several days earlier—the powries had hinted pretty clearly that they were in contact with some monks, after all.

"They deal with powries," Diamanda went on. "They must be De'Unnerans."

"We do not know that," Thaddius replied, rather sharply. He stared down at the houses and the brother in the square. A second brother joined the man, and Thaddius's eyes flashed with recognition. He knew this man, Glorious, and knew, too, that Diamanda's claims of allegiance were quite true.

"Are you ready for a fight, sister?" Diamanda asked Elysant, who smiled and nodded.

"She was ready before Thaddius used his soul stone on her wounds after the battle," Victoria put in.

"Truly," Diamanda agreed, tapping Elysant's forearm. "I cannot believe how powerfully you shook off the pain and continued the fight."

Elysant shrugged.

"The dolostones," Diamanda said with a shrug, indicating the stone-set bracer Elysant wore.

Elysant shrugged and smiled. "I will thank the Father Abbot when we return," she said, and meant it.

"It was not the bracer," Thaddius remarked as he moved around Elysant. "It was you."

Surprised by the apparent compliment, all three women turned back to regard Thaddius, who was moving around Victoria then, at the end of the line.

"I know these brothers," he explained, continuing off to the side, down the side slope of the bluff, and motioning for the women to stay put. "I will determine their purpose and intent."

"If they are De'Unnerans, they will kill you," Diamanda warned.

Thaddius stopped, not because she had given him pause or reason for concern, but because of the simple unintentional irony in the naive woman's remark. They were De'Unnerans—at least, Glorious was—and as far as Glorious knew, so was Thaddius.

And Thaddius still wasn't sure that Glorious was incorrect.

"If they seek to attack me, I know you will be there," Thaddius said to keep the three in place. "Be ready, I beg."

Once he was away from the women, Thaddius stood up and brushed off his brown robes as thoroughly as he could. He rubbed his face, too, but out of concern and confusion. More than once, he looked back up the bluff, where lay these three women who had fought the powries beside him. He thought of the demands of Elysant and Diamanda that Victoria run off, for she could outdistance the dwarves, no doubt, and the Church needed to know.

Above all else, the Church needed to know.

But Victoria would not run away, because she would not admit defeat, no matter the price. Above all else for her, loyalty.

Brother Thaddius stared long and hard at the top of the bluff, unable to see the women, but knowing they were there. He couldn't reconcile their admission to the Church, particularly Elysant who had no affinity with the sacred Ring Stones.

And yet, there was so much about them Brother Thaddius could not deny . . .

The young monk bolstered himself and started toward the houses, determinedly erasing all fear from his face.

The two monks turned sharply on him when he crossed into the lane, making no attempt to hide himself, both assuming fighting stances.

From a porch to the side, a third monk leveled a crossbow his way.

"Brother Glorious!" Thaddius called excitedly. "After all that has happened, it is good to see you alive!"

"Thaddius?" the young man called back, and his face lit up. "Ah, brother, have you heard the terrible news?"

"I was there when Father Abbot De'Unnero fell," he said, never slowing as he joined the two.

The third heretic came down from the porch, crossbow lowered. "You are alone?" the older man, whom Thaddius did not know, asked suspiciously.

"Can we trust him?" Diamanda quietly asked as the three watched the gathering in the lane below. "They are De'Unnerans, certainly."

"Yes," Elysant replied confidently.

"There is a chapel not far from here," Diamanda said. "If they are loyal to Father Abbot Braumin, then why are they out here? And surely this is the band the powries thought us!"

Victoria nodded, not disagreeing, but she added her own affirmation to Elysant's claim regarding Thaddius.

"Pagonel would not have chosen him," Elysant reasoned. "He could have escaped the powries with his gems, but he did not use his malachite and fly away."

"They seem quite friendly," Diamanda warned. "How do we know that Thaddius was unaware of this band when we left St.-Mere-Abelle?"

The others wanted to argue, but really couldn't. Together, the three lifted up in a crouch and eased to the edge of the bluff, ready to leap away to Thaddius's aid.

Or perhaps to run off if their hopes were dashed.

On and on went Brother Glorious and the other two, and then a fourth of their band came in happily.

"My prayers are answered!" the newcomer exclaimed. "More will join our cause. More will recognize the truth of Marcalo De'Unnero."

"Avelyn was a fraud," another insisted.

"Demon possessed," Brother Glorious agreed.

"Bishop Braumin has been elected Father Abbot, so say the rumors filtering out of St.-Mere-Abelle," Thaddius remarked, and that brought disgusted gasps from all about.

"Jojonah's lapdog!" the newcomer cried. "Oh, but we have much fighting ahead, brothers."

"They will reinstate us, brothers," Thaddius said.

The looks that flashed his way sent chills down his spine.

"They seek healing, I am told," Thaddius went on, a bit less assuredly. "Truce and compromise."

"They demand fealty, you mean," the one with the crossbow growled, and Thaddius wondered if the man was about to shoot him.

"Ohwan has been elected as Abbot of St. Honce," Thaddius argued. "Ohwan was no enemy to Marcalo De'Unnero, and was his choice for that position."

"Then let us go to Ursal," Brother Glorious said to all. "Ohwan will have us. We will bolster his cause when he marches on St.-Mere-Abelle."

"No, he will summon the Father Abbot to Ursal, to the Court of the King," said the newcomer. "And there we will end the reign of foul Braumin."

They all began talking excitedly about their fantasies of murder, and of keeping true the cause of De'Unnero. For a long while, they lost all interest in Thaddius, too consumed by their hopes. Brother Glorious himself spoke of a sister of St. Gwendolyn they had hunted down and killed, and what a godly deed that had been!

"We will find our sunrise, Brother Thaddius!" Glorious finished, at last turning back to the thin young monk.

Glorious's expression changed indeed when he looked upon his old acquaintance from the shadows of the monastery where Marcalo De'Unnero's name had been spoken with quiet reverence, to see Brother Thaddius encased in the holy blue-white glow of magical serpentine, his hand uplifted, a ruby teeming with fiery energy, begging catastrophic release.